CONFESSION OF SIN

NOT ALL SECRETS SHOULD BE KEPT

Victoria M. Patton

Dark Force Press – www.darkforcepress.com

Dark Force Press
www.darkforcepress.com

Publisher's Note: This is a work of fiction. Names, characters, places, and incidents are a product of the author's imagination. Locales and public names are sometimes used for atmospheric purposes. Any resemblance to actual people, living or dead, or to businesses, companies, events, institutions, or locales is completely coincidental.

Book Layout © 2016 BookDesignTemplates.com

Confession Of Sin/ Victoria M. Patton. -- 1st ed.
ISBN 10: 1-946934-04-6
ISBN 13: 978-1-946934-04-8

Library of Congress Control Number 2017941444

Cover Photo: Credit/Copyright Attribution: Credit/Copyright Attribution: Paul Mathews Photography /Shutterstock
Editor: Mari Farthing, Oklahoma City, OK www.marifarthing.com

Author's Note:

I had the concept for this story already outlined, when my mother shot herself. I didn't write for sixty days. When I did finally start writing again, I used this story as my release.

All the feelings of hurt and anger came out through the killer's character. My mother lived with a lot of pain. And although part of me understands how miserable she was, part of me can't understand why she did it.

This story was hard to write. I broke down several times getting these words out. But in the end, it helped me through one of the worst moments of my life.

I used my mother's suicide note as part of the opening chapter. Not everyone will agree with that, but for me, it was the right thing to do.

If you feel like you are at that point in your life where you think suicide is the answer, please reconsider. I know life can get so hard. Please seek help. Reach out to a family member or a friend or call the National Suicide Prevention Lifeline: 1-800-273-8255. There is someone there 24 hours a day 365 days a year.

DEDICATION

I must thank my husband. He put up with a lot of crazy days and nights while I wrote this. I am most grateful that he still sleeps with me, in the dark, even though he knows what's in my head.

To my kids Ariel and Zachary, I love you both.

To Mari Farthing, my editor. She teaches me so much with each book she edits. My writing is so much better because of her.
www.marifarthing.com

CONTENTS

CHAPTER ONE

Mackenzie's hands shook as she gripped the tattered piece of paper. Her mother's handwriting was smudged from her tears. Her lungs constricted, and the painful tightness in her throat made it hard to breathe.

My dearest daughter;

My body aches, and I have found no relief. My sorrow strangles me. Please don't blame yourself. Your love and devotion after your father's death kept me going. Without you, I would not have made it as long as I did. I watched you grow from a child into a beautiful woman. Now you must live your life for you and your purpose. Not care for a withering old lady.

My heart pounds against my chest, and I am breathless as I wait to see Him and stand in the presence of Christ. Please understand much thought and prayer has gone into this decision. I know my death will wound you. Your strength with the wisdom and guidance of the Lord will help you get through this. Trust in His written Word and listen to Him. He will guide you and show you what you need to do.

I love you, my sweet child.

Mother

Mack wiped her face with the back of her hand. "Mother, oh Mother, why didn't you say anything? Why? You let me believe you were fine. You lied!" The note fluttered to the floor as Mackenzie paced the length of her living room, clenched fists banging against her thighs with each step.

Her nostrils flared as her lips pulled back, baring her teeth. She picked up a heavy paperweight and threw it across the room. The glass shattered on impact like a car bomb exploding, sending glass shards everywhere.

A guttural roar bellowed out of her. "You had no right! You were selfish. You cared about yourself with no regard for me. You've left me behind with no one!" She yanked on her hair, pulling long strands from her head. Mackenzie fell to her knees and wept.

Her hand brushed against the note. She pressed it against her leg and smoothed the edges down. She clutched the paper against her chest. Mack stood and gazed at her mother's picture. She always loved Mother's long hair and the way it cascaded down her back. Mack laid the note next to the frame.

Moving back from the mantel, her gaze became unfocused. Her eyebrows squished together as she rubbed her forehead. "I miss you, Mother." Mackenzie clenched her teeth together. "The priest was mad at me, Mother. I forgot to tell you. After your service, he voiced his disappointment that I chose not to bury you in the cemetery. I explained it was my decision—my decision! Not his!"

She paced and fisted the air. She screamed, "What about their decisions? What about that? They didn't care for you. They turned their backs on you when you needed them the most. Why would I leave you in the cold dark earth? You need to be here with me." Mack's long skinny fingers reached out and touched the urn. "I don't blame you, Mother. None of this is your fault."

She turned, and her eye caught a crucifix hanging on the wall. Mack's breathing labored. She cocked her head to the side. "I blame You. You have let this happen." She stepped closer to the crucifix. "You have left men in charge that no longer do Your will. They don't care about Your flock. The priests care more about the gratification of their flesh than anything else. I've seen the reports. I've seen what they've done."

Mack crumpled to the floor. "Forgive me, Father. The blame lies not at Your feet. You gave these men charge to do Your will. The priests chose not to follow Your commandments. They put other gods before You. They gave in to their desires. Desires of the flesh and mind. The priests no longer keep themselves pure to carry out Your teachings. They can't lead Your flock if they serve more than one god.

"I will make them pay. I will hold each of them accountable for their lack of judgment." Mack laughed. "I didn't understand at first; now I do. You have used the last few months to bring clarity to the task at hand. Now I understand they must answer for their sins. Their deaths will bear witness."

Mack grabbed the rosary beads dangling from the crucifix. Her fingers tightened around them. "Their sins led them to choose their will over Yours. They need to be struck down. They need to beg at the gates of Heaven for entrance into Your Kingdom. Your grace no longer covers them. Your house must be cleansed."

CHAPTER TWO

November 28th
Early Monday morning

Damien admired the woman beside him. Her long, honey blonde hair fanned out around her. His heart pounded against his chest. He reached out and caressed her cheek. A tingling jolt shot through his fingers.

Between their schedules, they had few consecutive days off together. This weekend was one of those rare ones. They had spent the entire weekend in bed, stopping long enough to eat and shower.

Dillon's eyes fluttered open. A soft sigh escaped her lips. "Why are you gawking at me?" She reached out and touched Damien's chest.

"I can't help myself." Damien scooted closer, closing the gap between them. He dragged his hand along her slender silky thigh.

"Hmm, you're going to tell me it's Monday, aren't you?"

"Unfortunately, yes. We still have two hours before we have to get out of bed." Damien's hand slid from Dillon's hip to her breast. He rubbed his thumb across her nipple.

Dillon sucked in air as her whole body tingled. She reached down and wrapped her fingers around his length. "Well, seeing as how I'm awake, maybe I should take care of this for you." She moved to him. Her body slid down his, her tongue blazing a trail across his skin as she licked her way down his body. Dillon took him in her mouth.

Damien's fingers threaded through her hair. "Dillon." Her name came out as a whisper.

Dillon's tongue slid back up his torso. Her lips crushed down on his.

Damien lifted her hips as she guided him into her. Wet slick heat sucked him inside. He dug his fingers into her flesh. Her back arched. Damien watched her as she came closer to her climax. Her body tensed and trembled as an orgasm overtook her. Dillon's muscles clenched around him.

In one quick movement, Damien flipped her onto her back. He thrust into her. Dillon wrapped her legs around his waist, allowing him deeper access. Grasping his hips, she met each thrust. She called out his name as another orgasm ripped through her body. His own orgasm exploded, and he emptied himself into her.

"Oh my God, you're going kill me," Dillon said. "I don't even know if I can walk." Her fingers trailed up and down Damien's back while his head rested on her chest.

"I'll move as soon as my brain can tell my body." He stayed there another minute before he rolled off her. "Every man should be so lucky to wake up this way."

Dillon snorted. "I don't think I could do this for every man, every morning." She raised up off the bed and headed toward the bathroom. She glanced over her shoulder, "You need to join me in the shower. Help me wash my back." She winked at him and disappeared through the doorway.

Damien jumped up from the bed and headed after her. "Well, I wouldn't want you to go around with a dirty back all day."

***

An hour later, Dillon watched Coach try to sneak a piece of bacon off Damien's plate. He pointed his finger at the fat cat causing Coach to retreat to his chair. His head raised above the table so he could monitor and wait for leftovers. Dillon's phone chirped, interrupting the idyllic scene.

"McGrath."

Damien watched her give Coach a piece of ham while she listened to the caller on the other end.

"Yes Sir, I can be there in about an hour. I can have the video conference ready to go by—say nine-thirty?" Dillon nodded. "I'll round everyone else up. Talk with you soon. Wait, what? You're kidding me? Okay. Yes, Sir."

"What's up?" Damien asked. He gathered up the dishes and rinsed as Dillon filled Coach's bowl with leftover bacon and eggs. "You know; Coach will weigh fifty pounds if you keep giving him leftovers."

Dillon laughed. "I guess I feel sorry for him. He gives me that look, and I can't help myself. Anyway, that was Deputy Director Sherman. A video conference scheduled for later today has been moved to this morning. I'm responsible for letting everyone know and getting together the files needed. I can't get into it, but it concerns Jason Freestone."

Damien stopped loading the dishwasher. "What do you mean it concerns Jason and why can't you get into it? I worked that case too."

"I can't tell you anything because I know nothing. As soon as I do, I will let you know. I promise." She checked her watch. "Damn, I better get going." At the entryway table, she picked up a slim wallet holding her credentials, and then placed it in her back pocket.

Damien eyeballed her. She pulled her hair back and wrapped it in a loose bun above her collar. He strolled to her, grabbed her by the waist, pulling her close. "Did you decide on what I asked you at the start of the weekend?" Damien's lips grazed her neck.

"Yes, yes I did." She stepped back and locked on to those intense blue eyes. Dillon felt as if she could drown in the unbridled emotion that swirled there. She ran her fingers through his wavy black hair, tugging slightly on the ends. "Are you sure you're ready for it?"

"It's somewhat stupid to keep two places. Mine is bigger, you can have your own office space, and I like having you in the morning." He wiggled his eyebrows at her. Three months ago, he had met Dillon on one of the worst cases of his career. Jason Freestone had abducted, raped, and murdered over fifteen girls. Some he buried on his farm and some he dumped across Illinois. As one of the FBI's top profilers, Dillon had been called in to assist on the case.

Dillon sighed. "I am pretty tired of bringing a bag every time I come here." She felt the weight of his stare as he waited for her answer. A move like this terrified her. "Yeah, I'll move in here."

Damien leaned in to kiss her. His phone signaled an incoming call from Dispatch. "Lieutenant Kaine." He nuzzled her neck as he listened to the drone of the operator. His back straightened. "Okay, send the address to my phone. I'll notify Detective Hagan." He tapped on his phone with one hand while holding on tight to Dillon with the other. "Joe, we got a DB. I'll pick you up. See you in thirty."

"What do you have?" She asked him.

"Dead body at St. Florentine Cathedral, no other details. The witness who found the body couldn't give any information over the phone. Officers are securing the scene as we speak." He pulled out a little box and handed it to her. "I got this for you."

Damien watched her turn the box over and inspect it. She lifted the lid and sniggered.

"A key," Dillon said.

Damien took the key from the box and took her key ring from her hand. He placed the key on the ring and handed it back to her.

"Thank you." She wrapped her arms around his waist. "You're sure?" She asked him.

"Yes. Quit asking me." He kissed her. "You belong here with me. Always." He kissed her again. "I'll text you later and let you know when I'll be home."

They both walked out into the large two car garage. "We need to get a Christmas tree. We'll go sometime this week and get one."

She beamed at him. "I haven't decorated a Christmas tree in years. You, me, and a bottle of wine beside the tree. It sounds perfect." She kissed him. "Keep your ass safe."

CHAPTER THREE

Police tape surrounded the front of St. Florentine Cathedral. Several officers kept out the unauthorized.

"What the hell is going on?" Joe asked. "Who the hell is dead inside?"

Damien peered around. His stomach twisted in a knot. An officer sat on the front steps. His face had no color and sweat covered his brow despite the chill in the air. "I think we're about to walk into a shit storm."

The metallic smell hit them the moment they opened the church doors. Out of habit, Damien and Joe dabbed their fingers in the Holy Water, crossing themselves and genuflecting like good Catholic boys. At the end of the central aisle, dressed in white coveralls, two men from the ME's office stood off to the side. A third man stood dead center, about five feet from the police tape. He turned and focused on the detectives making their way down the aisle.

"Good morning, Lieutenant Kaine, Detective Hagan." Head CST Roger Newberry held out boxes of gloves and booties. "You're not going to want to walk any farther without putting these on."

"Have you touched anything yet?" Damien asked.

"No, Sir. The captain informed me to sit tight and not touch anything. The captain also wants the ME techs to wait for Dr. Forsythe. He should be here in about ten or fifteen minutes."

"How about a name? You guys got that?" Joe asked.

"Yeah, the cop on scene said the victim is Father Shri Mandahari. Came to this parish five years ago from India." The tech fixed his stare on Joe. "You still seeing that girl Taylor from Springfield? The one with you at Mulligan's a few weeks back?" He raised an eyebrow at him. "I haven't seen you hanging around with her these last few weeks. She dump your ass already huh?"

Damien smirked at Roger and ogled Joe with a humorous gleam. "Yeah Joe, has she dumped you yet?"

"Ha, hilarious." He glanced between Damien and Roger, "she didn't dump me. We're having a casual relationship. I see her when she can come up and stay for a weekend."

Roger snickered and shook his head. "Hey Johnson," he yelled to the other tech. "You owe me a beer." Roger turned back to Damien. "I bet

Johnson that Joe would deny having a girlfriend."

Damien chuckled at the exchange. Joe met Taylor during the same case he met Dillon. Joe just couldn't bring himself to commit to one woman. Damien and Joe walked past Roger and stepped under the police tape. Their jovial attitude disappeared. Joe cursed under his breath. Damien grabbed the St. Michael medal from around his neck and said a quick prayer in Italian.

A priest lay on the steps of the altar, posed as Christ on the cross. That's where the similarities to that iconic picture ended. He wore an open cassock and his collar. The killer had cut the garment and fanned it out around his bloody naked body. A cross had been gouged into the man's chest, each line close to three inches wide.

Damien walked around the massive pool of congealed blood. "*Madre Maria di Dio*," Damien whispered. The priest's entrails had been arranged in a macabre design outside his body. Coins spilled out of the cross-shaped cut and floated in the semi-dried blood. Damien crouched down taking a closer look at the coins. "I see half-dollars, pennies, and quarters."

Joe moved to the top of the steps. He gave a cursory visual exam of the head using his penlight. "I don't see any kind of obvious head wound. This isn't a small guy. Our killer subdued him somehow."

Damien stepped up next to Joe. "The ME will run a toxicology panel. I bet the killer drugged him." He noticed something sticking out from the corner of the dead man's mouth. "Hang on, Joe. Hey Roger, hand me a pair of forceps."

Roger moved to stand next to Damien. "Whatcha got?"

"I'm not sure. I think something is in his mouth." Damien pried open the priest's jaw. He took the forceps and pulled out a folded piece of paper.

Joe held the corners as Damien unfolded it. He read the hand-written message.

No one can serve two masters.
For you will hate
one and love the other;
you will be devoted to one and

despise the other.
You cannot serve both
God and money.

Damien turned toward Roger. "Hand me an evidence bag. Please."

Joe studied the verse. "What verse is that?"

"Didn't you pay attention during Sunday school, Hagan?" A tight smile tugged at Damien's mouth. "It's Matthew 6:24."

"Mr. Know-it-all." Joe teased as he left the altar area and walked toward the confessionals. He gave each one a once-over. Nothing seemed out of order. "When was the body discovered?" Joe called out across the chancel.

"The officer first on the scene reported the witness called it in about eight this morning." Another CST answered.

The church doors opened as Joe spoke. "Hey, Doc." He nodded in the ME's direction.

Damien glanced up from reading the note. The soft haze of sunlight cast shadows throughout the atrium. Dr. Forsythe's rail-thin frame seemed to float down the aisle. "Good morning, Dr. Forsythe. If you can give me an estimated time of death, I would appreciate it."

"Ahh Damien, for you anything. Just give me a few minutes." The doctor smirked as he stepped under the police tape. The case he carried crashed to the floor. "Oh, holy saints and angels." He staggered back and caught himself on the edge of the pew. Dr. Forsythe had difficulty swallowing as a searing pain filled the back of his throat. He crossed himself and bowed his head. "I know this man." His body shuddered as he focused on the face of his friend.

Damien moved toward the Doctor handing the note off to Roger, as he placed his hand on the Doc's shoulder. "Sit down, Bernard. We can get another ME in here."

"No. He's my friend." Dr. Forsythe bent over and took an instrument out of his bag. "There's so much damage done to his abdomen area. Getting an accurate reading will be hard to do here on scene." He fumbled with the thermometer.

Roger removed the instrument from his shaking hands. "Let me do this, Dr. Forsythe." Using care, Roger stuck the thermometer into the liver. He moved one of Father Mandahari's arms to check for rigor. "I'm leaning toward sometime between nine pm and two am. Dr. Marshall will narrow down a more precise time of death."

Dr. Forsythe clenched his jaw to stop the vomit from escaping. Tears flooded his eyes. "He didn't deserve this. No one deserves to die like this."

Damien studied the doctor. The loss of color from his face and his salt and pepper hair made him look as if he had just stepped out of a black-and-white photo. Even at the sight of his friend, Dr. Forsythe's breathing remained slowed and controlled. Damien considered his past as an avid long-distance runner, could explain his reaction. "Bernard," Damien said, "tell me about Father Mandahari. What do the coins represent? And why would the killer leave a note behind? A note referencing money? What's the significance to Father Mandahari?"

Dr. Forsythe glanced up at Damien. He closed his eyes, and his shoulders sagged.

Damien witnessed Dr. Forsythe struggle with an internal battle. "Please. Doc. Tell me everything you know about him."

Dr. Forsythe sat in the first row of benches. His head hung low; his elbows rested on his knees. Damien noticed a few tears splattered onto the floor. Dr. Forsythe inhaled a deep breath through his nose, exhaling through his mouth. He lifted his head; the corners of his mouth drooped as he watched the techs prepare his friend for transport.

His gaze fixed on Damien and Joe. Tears spilled down his cheeks. "Shri—Father Mandahari—had a gambling problem. He blew off some of his responsibilities. When he hit rock bottom, he reached out. I helped him get into an outpatient treatment facility. He dealt with it head on, and he gave up gambling."

"How long ago did he quit gambling?" Damien asked.

"Mandahari gave it up, stopped cold-turkey, almost a year ago. That's why this doesn't make any sense."

Joe sat next to the ME. "How many people do you think knew of his addiction?"

Dr. Forsythe frowned. "A Few. Outside of Bishop Cantor and the workers here at the church. I'm sure none of the parishioners knew of it. If any of them were aware of it, they never talked about it. Shri never stole from the church to gamble. He just didn't show up for certain meetings or jobs he was supposed to do. Gambling had become more important than his service to God." Dr. Forsythe glanced between Damien and Joe. "He changed, though. This last year he had fallen back in love with his role as a priest, with serving God."

Damien pinched the bridge of his nose. A heaviness settled in his stomach. "Dr. Forsythe, did Father Mandahari have any other vices that may make him a target?"

"No." Dr. Forsythe wiped his brow with his arm. The Doc stared at his gloved hands. His friend's blood coated his fingers. "No. Shri had no other vices. He didn't watch porn, or lust for women, men, or children. He was a good man and great priest. Shri controlled his gambling habit. He rededicated his life to following and teaching the ways of Christ."

A knot forming in Damien's stomach tightened. "Bernard, you know how this works. Can you tell me when you last saw Father Mandahari?"

Bernard's voice stammered as he glared at Damien. "Are you fucking serious right now?"

"C'mon, you know anyone connected with this man must be questioned. The sooner I can eliminate you from the equation the sooner we can move on," Damien said.

Dr. Forsythe leered at Damien. "Maybe I should contact my lawyer?" He noticed the slight flinch in Damien's expression. Bernard interlaced his bloody fingers and placed his hands on his lap. "The last time I saw Father Mandahari was roughly three or four days ago. We met for a late lunch at Hutch American Bistro. Given a few hours I could hunt down my credit card receipt, or manufacture one if nothing else."

Damien raised his hands. "Listen, I'm not trying to make you angry or hurt you. I need your help. Your friend," he pointed to Shri Mandahari lying dead on the floor, "he needs your help, Doc. I have a job to do. You of all people should understand that."

Dr. Forsythe's arms fell to his side. His chest deflated as the tears resurfaced. "I know, Damien. I know. This is a fucking nightmare." The ME glowered at Damien. "Find the bastard who did this to my friend."

CHAPTER FOUR

Damien leaned back in his office chair. He studied the murder board he'd started. They'd left the church interviewing no one. Father Jessup had asked them to return in a few hours. Sister Mary Francis, the woman who found Father Mandahari, had been too distraught to answer questions. Father Jessup promised he would have everyone available for questioning upon their return.

A picture of Father Shri Mandahari sat in the center of the board. Father Mandahari had a warm and inviting smile. Damien closed his eyes. The horrific scene at the church told him someone wanted to humiliate the priest, not just kill him. That's what made what had happened to him seem even more heinous.

Per Dr. Forsythe, Father Mandahari had rededicated himself to his vocation, and everyone liked him. Damien considered the possibility he owed someone money from his past, but the more Damien examined the crime scene photos, the more it didn't hold for him. His computer beeped with an incoming report. The ME narrowed down time of death. Mandahari's murder had occurred between nine p.m. and midnight.

Hagan walked into Damien's office with two sandwiches. "Figured we needed to eat." He handed one to Damien and a bottle of diet soda.

"You mean you had to eat. You always have to eat."

"I'm a growing boy, what can I say?"

"The only thing on you still growing is your fat ass." Damien took the sandwich and opened the soda. "Carlitto's," he said. He threw a ten-dollar bill across the desk. "Thanks, man. I was getting hungry. Now, all we need is candlelight." Damien winked at Joe.

"Ha, I'm already involved with someone, and she has better knockers than you. You'll have to be content with lusting after my ass. You get anything back from the ME yet?" Joe asked through a mouthful of food.

"I did. The time of death is between nine and midnight." Damien took a long drink of his soda. "We need to head back to St. Florentine and talk to Sister Mary Francis. She found Father Mandahari this morning. She should be able to speak with us now." Damien nodded toward the murder board. "This crime doesn't involve gambling. I know we need to eliminate all lines of possibility, but my gut says this goes deeper."

Joe wiped his mouth with his napkin. "If it involved an old debt he hadn't paid, they wouldn't have killed him. Rough him up or threaten with exposure—whatever it took to get the money. I bet the Diocese would have paid for the whole thing to go away."

"That's where my line of thinking was heading. I'll let the captain know I want to talk to Bishop Cantor. However, I'm thinking I'll need something more to make that happen. I can't imagine Bishop Cantor will be too keen on answering questions about his gambling priest." Damien studied the small digital case board on his wall. Identical to the larger one that hung in the pen. All his detectives had open cases.

Joe finished up his last bite of his sandwich and turned toward the pen. "I see Cooper and Harris closed that case of theirs. I watched them interview that puss bucket excuse for a human being."

"I'm glad they got him to confess. They had no results from the lab yet. They did a good job tricking him into giving up the goods. Had it not been for the confession, we would've had to cut him loose." Damien said.

Joe gulped down half his soda. "Hey, that case Hall and Alvarez are working on, you got anything on that yet?"

Damien shook his head. "They're waiting on some results. Not a lot to go on, why?"

"Nothing really. Something seems familiar about it, but I'm not sure what it is," Joe said.

Damien finished up his sandwich. "If you come up with anything let me know. I don't like having to sit around and wait on the lab." He rose from his desk and leaned out his doorway. "Hey Ivanski, come here."

Officer Ivanski came to the doorway. "What do you need, Lieutenant?" He walked in and took a handful of jellybeans out of Damien's candy jar.

Damien tried to scowl at the officer and managed a smirk catching the gleam in Joe's eyes. "You started this, you're filling up the jar next time."

Joe chuckled. "You got the pay raise."

Damien turned back to Ivanski. "I need you to find out everything you can on Father Shri Mandahari. Everything about him. Get Travis from Electronics and Cyber Division to run down his financials. Tell him to get everything he can going back five years."

"You got it, Lieutenant." Ivanski headed to ECD.

Damien wadded up his trash. "You done?" He asked Joe.

"Yup. I suppose you want to go to the church?" Joe stood up heading for the door.

Damien grabbed his jacket. "Yeah, let's see what we can get from everyone at St. Florentine. Somebody knows something. We need to get in to see Bishop Cantor. The captain will go to bat for us if we can get something substantial."

Joe shrugged, "Funny, you would think a dead, mutilated priest on the predella would warrant a conversation with the Almighty Bishop."

"Yeah, you would think."

CHAPTER FIVE

The sign outside St. Florentine stated Mass would resume the following Sunday. The scene had yet to be released, and two uniformed officers stood guard outside the doors. Damien walked past the dried pool of blood on the floor, he couldn't see Mass ever being the same again.

Sister Mary Francis waited in Father Jessup's office. The Father sat behind a beautiful mahogany desk while Sister Mary Francis sat on a small sofa. As Damien and Joe entered both rose to greet them.

"Lieutenant Kaine, Detective Hagan." Father Jessup came around his desk, hand extended. His large stomach made it almost impossible for him to see his feet. His hand, the size of a baseball glove, reached out to shake Damien's. "Thank you for coming here to speak with Sister Mary Francis. Her quarters are here in the church and doing this interview here helps her."

Damien smiled at the nun. "Sister, thank you for taking the time to speak with us. I can't imagine the horror and shock of finding Father Mandahari this morning."

Sister Mary Francis gripped tight to a handkerchief. At the mere mention of Father Mandahari's name, her eyes filled with tears. She nodded to both Damien and Joe. "I'll answer your questions as best I can."

Father Jessup sat next to Sister Mary Francis. He took one of her hands in his own and patted it. "I'd like to stay while you question her. I may know answers to things she doesn't."

"That's not a problem, Father. We appreciate your cooperation," Damien said. "Sister Mary Francis, walk me through your Sunday evening. Let's start with when did you last see Father Mandahari?"

Sister Mary Francis glanced between Joe and Damien. Her hands trembled as she spoke. "On Sundays, we all have dinner together after the five-thirty Mass. There aren't any meetings or clubs on Sundays. Every week we plan a different meal. Last night we had Indian fare. Father Mandahari, we call him Father Shri, he planned the whole dinner." She wiped a tear from her cheek.

Damien touched her hands. "Take your time, Sister."

"Yes, well, Father Shri had everything premade. A simple reheating and everything would be ready in a short amount of time. Umm—we sat down for dinner around seven-thirty." Sister Francis eyed Father Jessup for confirmation.

"Yes," Father Jessup said. "We were all sitting down by that time. That included Father Shri, Sister Mary Francis, Deacon Fry, and George Sanders, he's our janitor. He lives on the premises as well. Lola Ferguson, our secretary. She doesn't live here, but she has no family, so she eats here every Sunday. That's who brought you into the office."

Damien nodded to Joe. "We will need to speak with each of them. Besides Lola, are the others here?"

"Yes," Father Jessup said. "I can have them come right down." He rose to go to his phone and called for them to come to his office.

"Joe can speak with each of them in the outer office. Please have them come in one at a time," Damien said.

"Deacon Fry will come down first, then he'll call for each of the others." Father Jessup nodded to Joe as he left the room.

Damien turned his attention back to Sister Mary Francis. "After dinner, what did everyone do?"

Sister Mary Francis' forehead wrinkled. "I know Lola went home. Deacon Fry had an appointment early Monday, so he left early. I helped Father Shri clean up and then I retired to my quarters." Sister Mary Francis again sought assurances from Father Jessup.

"Father Shri and I stayed up talking for a few more minutes. I guess it was nine-thirty, maybe nine-forty-five when I left him. He liked to go through the church one last time before he locked the doors at ten."

Damien's brow furrowed. "Are there people in the church that time of night on Sunday?" He asked.

"Not too often. A few individuals will come in seeking the comfort of Christ that late. Some like to sit in the quiet and stillness praying in front of the altar. I walked to the side door of the church; we keep it locked. It allows access to this area of the church from the sanctuary. I noticed no one in the first few rows, but I couldn't see past that area from where I stood. I went upstairs to my quarters. That's the only way to get to the quarter's area."

Damien tilted his head. "Can you hear anything from downstairs when you're in your rooms?"

"No." Both answered at the same time.

Sister Mary Francis wiped her damp cheeks. Father Jessup patted her hand. He sighed, "No, Lieutenant Kaine. Once you're upstairs, you can't hear anything going on down here. Sometimes that's a blessing; last night was not one of those times."

"How long did it take Father Shri to lock up and close everything down?" Damien asked.

Father Jessup closed his eyes. His head bobbed while he added up the minutes. "When I've done it, I take about an hour. I lock the doors, then I begin the other tasks—putting out the candles on the altar, checking the pews and confessionals. If I find any personal articles left behind, I gather those up and place them in our lost and found bin. I check the Tabernacle and make sure it's locked, and the vestibules. Sometimes items need returning to their proper places. It takes no more than an hour if that."

"Was Father Mandahari's routine for locking up the church widely known?"

Father Jessup frowned. "I don't know. I guess it wouldn't be hard to find out. If someone is sitting in the sanctuary, we continue with our routine and then ask them to leave at the last moment before locking up. They could easily witness our procedures."

Damien paused, "Father Jessup, were you aware of Father Mandahari's gambling problem?"

Sister Mary Francis gasped as her hand flew to her chest. She glanced from Damien to Father Jessup and back to Damien. Fury raged below the tears. "Father Shri was a good man and a good priest. How dare you ask if he had such a filthy habit!"

Father Jessup squeezed Sister Mary Francis's hand. "It's okay, Sister. Yes, I knew of his problem, and I knew he received help last year. Dr. Forsythe and Father Shri had become good friends. Bernard helped him get into recovery." Father Jessup sighed. "It was disappointing that Father Shri had to deal with such a vice, but he was human. He got past it and dedicated his life to serving the Lord."

"Did anyone else know about his addiction?"

"I know the bishop, myself and Dr. Forsythe. Now if he shared it with somebody else that I don't know."

Damien smiled at them both. "I know these are difficult questions. I don't ask to be disrespectful or insensitive. My sole purpose is to find who killed Father Mandahari. Can you think of anything? Anyone, hanging around after Mass, that seemed out of place?" Damien asked.

Sister Mary Francis shook her head. "No, I didn't go to Mass Sunday night. I attended Mass that morning. I didn't come down from my quarters until after the evening Mass had finished. I didn't venture into the church at all last night." Sister Mary Francis wept again.

Father Jessup handed the sister a box of tissue. "I was in the foyer right after Mass. I like to greet the parishioners as they exit the church. There are always a few who like to corner me and ask me questions. I love spending time with them, but Sunday I wanted to get to dinner. Father Shri had outdone himself this time."

Damien was about to rise when Father Jessup's eyes widened. "Wait a second," he said. "After everyone had gone, a young man sat on the far-right side of the church about half way from the front. He remained behind and seemed to be in prayer." Father Jessup sighed. "We don't ever rush anyone out."

Damien sat on the edge of his seat and leaned toward Father Jessup. "Tell me what you remember about the young man?"

"Unfortunately, not too much. The young man sat in the pew so I couldn't give you any height guesses. Medium length hair, brown. I couldn't tell you what he wore. I didn't see his face either."

"Do you have any idea when he left the church?" Damien scribbled on his notepad.

Father Jessup frowned. "No, Lieutenant Kaine. I don't. I locked the doors on either side of the vestibule. When I walked past the altar area to secure the far doors, the young man had his head down."

Damien rose. "Thank you so much for your time. Sister Mary Francis, if you think of anything, please call me and let me know. Even if you think it isn't relevant." Damien held his hand out to Father Jessup. "You too, Father. Here is my card. Thank you again."

CHAPTER SIX

Damien walked around the altar using his penlight. He held back a scream when he raised up from behind the altar to find Joe standing there looking at him. His heart nearly exploded in his chest. "For Christ's sake, quit sneaking up on me." Damien believed Joe could sneak up on the devil himself.

"Dude, you a little jumpy or what? You *sicín*?" Joe asked with a grin on his face.

"I'm not a chicken. How do you move so damn quietly with a butt as big as yours anyway?" Damien asked stepping around the altar.

"Panther-like qualities. What can I say? So, what did you learn from the sister and Father Jessup?"

Damien continued moving around the altar and the steps leading up to it. "Sister Mary Francis didn't know about Mandahari's gambling problem." He cocked an eyebrow at Joe. "She got upset at me for implying he had such a filthy habit, too. Father Jessup mentioned a young man sitting in the church after the Mass. He had a vague description that's about it. What about you, did you get anything useful?"

Joe wandered around the outer area of the altar. "No. Lola came for dinner then left. The deacon came back for dinner after Mass. The other deacon doesn't come to Sunday dinners. He's married and spends Sundays with his family. As for the janitor, he came in after Father Mandahari had almost finished closing the church. He watched Jessup go up to his quarters, but he saw no one in the pews. Father Mandahari likes to spend a few minutes in the quiet of the church when he locks up. The janitor left before ten-thirty. That was the last time he saw Mandahari."

Damien sat in the first row of pews. He crossed his arms and sighed. "Father Jessup stated that the bishop knew of Mandahari's gambling. I'd like to ask the bishop some questions. The timeline makes sense. The ME puts death between nine and midnight. According to the janitor, he left Mandahari before ten-thirty, so that narrows the time of death window even further. His attacker had to have been hiding somewhere in the church, waiting for his opportunity to ambush Mandahari from behind."

Damien stood glancing around. "Father Jessup mentioned that he saw Shri briefly. Then he left, and in came the janitor. He spends a few minutes with Shri, then he leaves." Damien cocked an eyebrow at Joe. "Where would you hide?"

"The confessionals."

"Father Jessup checked those, said they were empty. Where else?" He moved to the outer aisles of the church. "There aren't any areas along the walls. No doorways, except to the cry rooms, and they have glass fronts." Damien peered through the glass. "If you pressed yourself against the wall, you might not be seen. Someone would have to walk-in or stand right next to the glass."

Joe moved to the back of the church. "If someone waited and hid, they had to know Mandahari's routine. They would've known he likes to spend time in the church after he closed up." Joe moved to the back area. "Hey come here."

"What you got?"

"Over there." Joe pointed to a door leading to a small staircase.

At the top, they found themselves in a medium sized room. It had a few cubbies, a place to hang clothes, and a small bathroom off to the side.

"I bet brides or bridal parties do last minute touch-ups here. This would be a perfect place to hide. This reinforces my theory that the killer was familiar with Mandahari's habits and this church," Joe said.

They both headed back down the narrow staircase and examined the door. They heard a noise behind them. Damien and Joe spun around with their hands on their weapons.

George Sanders held his hands in the air. "Whoa boys, don't shoot me. I was just checking on the doors. The Father wants them to remain locked."

Damien smirked. He was jumpy and didn't understand why. "Sorry George. Hey, listen, is this door locked at all times?"

George's eyebrows furrowed. He scratched his head. "Uhh—yeah, that door remains locked all the time unless there's a wedding here. Was it unlocked?" He stared at Damien.

"Yes, it was. We opened it up and went upstairs. Why?" Damien asked.

"I locked this room Sunday after the Mass ended. When I left Father

Shri here for his meditation time, I double checked it. That was about ten-fifteen last night."

Joe moved behind Damien and opened the door. "Son of a—uh—gun." He pointed to the little lock button on the doorknob. "This locks from the inside."

Damien examined the lock. Tiny scratches were visible around the keyhole area. "It wouldn't take much to pick this lock. This is where our killer hid out." Damien turned to George. "Thank you, George. We're done here today. We'll have someone go over the room upstairs." He handed him a card. "Listen, if you think of anything or see anything unusual, please let me know. You can call me anytime."

"You don't think the killer will come back, do you?" George's eyes darted between the detectives and the front doors of the church.

"No. The killer has no need to come back here. He got what he wanted." Damien smiled and patted George on the back as he and Joe walked out into the cold November Chicago air.

CHAPTER SEVEN

Damien sat in the chair across from Captain Mackey. He left Joe behind for this. No reason for Joe's ass to lose a patch of skin for his call.

"Damien, have you lost your fucking mind? What in God's name were you thinking calling Bishop Cantor's office?" Captain Mackey glared at Damien.

"No, Sir. Last I knew I still possessed my mind." Damien smiled at the captain.

"Son, your humor is sorely timed. Why in fuck's name did you call Cantor's office without contacting me first on this? Did I make a mistake putting you as Lieutenant of the VCU?"

"No, Sir. You did not make a mistake." Damien pursed his lips together. "Listen, Captain, I should've gone through you. I didn't mean to overstep. Joe and I had just left the church. Father Jessup had informed us that Bishop Cantor knew of Mandahari's gambling. Bishop Cantor could shed light on this case."

The captain's lips pursed together. "You're a damn fool if you think this would get you an interview with the bishop. You might as well try asking God himself at this point." The captain sighed. A slight smile tugged at the corners of his mouth. "Damien, you know I like you. I wouldn't have put you where you are if I didn't, and you are the best qualified. But you can't pull a stunt like this again.

"First, I know you know how the Catholic Church works, but let me explain something to you. Archbishop Jacobs is over the Archdiocese. He has several Auxiliary Bishops under him. Each Bishop handles several parishes and everything that goes on in those parish jurisdictions.

"Bishop Cantor is one of those auxiliary bishops, but he is pretty much up the archbishop's ass. His responsibilities include the daily activities of the Diocese. Think of him as the CEO of the company."

The captain leaned across his desk. "If you want to request a meeting with the bishop, you'll come to me. If after I see all your evidence, and it warrants a sit down with Bishop Cantor, I will facilitate that. Do you understand?"

"Yes, Sir. I understand." Damien rose. "You would think one dead priest would be enough evidence for Bishop Cantor to want to help find his killer." Damien stood still while he waited for the captain to excuse him.

The captain smiled. "Damien, you'll learn soon enough the politics involved in your position. Archbishop Jacobs won't touch this until he has to. Everything goes through Cantor. Cantor won't get involved until Archbishop Jacobs tells him to. Ask your dad sometime about the politics of the Catholic Church and how to play the game. It isn't fun, and your hands are often tied behind your back. If the time comes to question the bishop, I'll get you in, but not with what little you have. Now go."

Damien turned to leave, his hand reached for the door, then fell to his side. "No disrespect to you or your chair—more priest will be killed. I'm sure of it. This isn't a one-time revenge hit. I'm curious to see how many priests have to die before the bishop thinks it's important."

CHAPTER EIGHT

Damien walked back into the pen. "Davidson, are you trying to make us all blind?" Damien covered his eyes as if to shield them from the sun.

Detective Hall reared back in his seat and laughed. "A present from his wife. See why I'm not married?"

"No, you're not married because you have a small dick," Detective Alvarez said. Jenkins high-fived her across their desks.

"That's not what your sister said last night. You're just jealous cause you're a girl, and you want a dick." Hall threw a wadded-up piece of paper at Alvarez.

"Crap, what is this, kindergarten class?" Damien scanned the room for Officer Ivanski. "Has anyone seen Ski?"

"He's in ECD," Davidson said.

Joe twirled his finger in the air. "Spin around Kaine."

"What? Why?" Damien asked.

"I want to see how much of your ass you have left. What did Mackey say?" Joe's eyes twinkled, while a smile pushed his cheeks up high.

"I still have most of my ass. The captain said there was no way in hell I would get a meet with the bishop. And not to call Cantor again before going through him." Damien turned toward Alvarez and Hall. "Where are you two on the floaters? Anything from the lab yet?"

Hall dragged his hand across his face. "No, not anything substantial. So far it looks like the killer used a standard rope from any home improvement store to tie up the men. They were secured to each other, so when the weight holding them down came loose, they all came up. Lucky for us. Otherwise, we never would have found them."

"Have you been able to identify them?" Damien asked as he leaned against Alvarez's desk.

"Yeah. They were all crew members on the boat Shenandoah. It's a fishing and salvage vessel. The Coast Guard found the ship floating outside the harbor. Jefferson from Autopsy gave us a preliminary report. It states the men were alive when they entered Lake Michigan." Sheila said.

Damien closed his eyes. Drowning was not a way he wanted to die. "Let's get an idea of what this company has been doing lately. Check out where and what they usually fished for. When I think of fishing, I think of day trips out on the lake. I'm betting this company didn't do that kind of fishing. Trolling or net fishing is what I'm thinking. Have you found out anything about their salvage company?"

Hall thumbed through a file on his desk. "Their licensing paperwork shows they only recently became a salvage company. We're trying to hunt down the lawyer listed on the paperwork and their families to try to get some information. Can't seem to get a hold of anyone yet."

"Keep me informed. Let me know if I need to help you with anything," Damien said.

"How about a muzzle for Hall? You got one of those?" Sheila asked.

"Fuck you, Sheila," Hall said.

"With whose dick? You ain't got one," she said.

Joe let out a whistle, and a smile spread across his face. "Wow. You are looking fantastic Agent."

All heads turned toward the hallway. Damien's head spun around, and his eyes drank her in. "Hey Agent McGrath, what are you up to?"

"Not a lot. I'm meeting with the brass upstairs and wanted to check in on you and your merry band of ruffians." She smiled and winked at Hall. "Damn, Davidson that's some kind of shirt. Gift from the wife, huh?"

"You know it, Agent," Davidson responded with a gigantic smile.

Damien lifted an eyebrow. "Hmm, what's the meeting about? Anything in particular?"

Dillon cocked her head to one side raising an eyebrow. "Should it be about anything in particular?" She eyed Damien.

"No. Not really. How much time do you have?" Damien asked.

"About twenty minutes, why?"

Hall smiled. "His office has a lock on the door." He wiggled his eyebrows at her.

Damien smacked him on the back of his head. "I need more than twenty minutes." He turned back to Dillon. "It's in regards to that case I got this morning. Can you spare a minute?"

"Sure." She followed him into his office.

Damien glanced over his shoulder, "Joe, come on in here for this too."

Hall's smile grew wider. "A threesome."

Dillon smiled at Hall, "they're the appetizers." She blew him a kiss and followed Damien into his office.

"Seriously, you shouldn't tease him. He's like a pubescent boy around you," Damien said. He gave her a soft kiss on the lips.

"Hey, what about me?" Joe asked. He puckered out his lips waiting for Damien to kiss him.

Damien ignored him. "Our priest died a violent death. The killer left a note." He handed her a copy. Damien watched her as she read it.

Joe sat on the corner of Damien's desk. "Damien is convinced this is the first of many." He popped a bunch of jellybeans into his mouth.

"This is from the book of Mathew. It has to do with money and putting it ahead of God. Did the killer leave money behind?" Dillon asked.

"He did. I haven't gotten much back from the lab, but they did get a count on the money. The killer left thirty dollars in coins."

Dillon's forehead wrinkled. "In the days of Jesus, thirty pieces of silver were paid to a master if his slave was gored by an ox." Dillon shook her head. "You don't have to be Catholic to see what that represents. I can't see this killer not having an agenda. The note and that exact amount of money would seem out of place if it were just one killing. I'd like to see the scene." Dillon checked the time. "Listen I can't come back afterward. I have to get back to my office and speak with my director. Bring home the file. I'd like to see what you have so far."

Damien watched Dillon rush from his office. He turned to Joe, "go get Ski, and see what he has so far. I'll call the lab and see if they have anything else."

Damien glanced over the evidence he and Joe had gathered so far. It wasn't much. He picked up his phone and punched the number for the lab. "Hey gorgeous, what's up?"

Rachel knew his voice. She'd had a few conversations with Lieutenant Kaine before. His voice had a silky-smooth tone that just made her pulse beat a little faster. "Hi, Lieutenant Kaine."

Damien's eyebrow wrinkled as he quickly glanced at his phone making sure he had dialed the right number. "Uhh hey there, I was looking for Marsha. Did I dial the right office?"

Rachel giggled. "Yes silly, Marsha just stepped away from her desk. She should be coming—oh hang on she just walked back in."

Damien heard a muffled conversation, and then Marsha's voice filled his ear.

"Sorry about that Kaine. I didn't realize it was you on the phone."

"That's okay. Who was that? I don't remember there being another girl in your section at the lab."

"Oh, you have met her a couple of times in passing. She is one of the interns we have working here. She should be coming on as full-time when the next spot opens." A Marsha giggled softly, "she definitely knows who you are. She's mentioned you a couple of times when you have picked up some lab results in person. I think the girl has a crush on you."

"Well, no one can ever take your spot in my heart Marsha. You are still my favorite person in the lab."

"Don't try to schmooze me. You aren't the only one wanting results. I know what you're up to." Marsha chomped on a piece of gum.

"Oh, how do you know I'm not calling to see how you're doing? Maybe I was hoping to steal you away from your fiancé. By the way, how are the plans for your wedding going?" Damien asked.

"Kaine, you are so full of shit. You don't give one rats ass about my wedding." Marsha chuckled on the other end of the phone. "Listen, babe, I'm still going through your stuff." She sighed, "Okay, this is what I've got so far. No fingerprints anywhere. He gloved up. No hair, no fibers, nothing left behind on the body. Also, all the coins—not one fingerprint. We did find traces of bleach on the coins, so your guy was extra thorough covering his tracks."

"Well shit, gorgeous you're not helping me any," Damien said. He tugged on the ends of his hair.

"Well, I do know Steven has something for you, let me transfer you."

"Thanks, Marsha."

"Anything for you, Kaine."

Horrible music played while Damien waited for Steve to pick up. *No wonder people were so pissed by the time they spoke to someone.*

"Yo, this is Steven."

"Hey, Steve-O it's Kaine. What do you have for me?"

"Hey Kaine, how is that sexy Agent you bagged?"

Damien's cheeks pushed up with a smile. "Steve, she would whip your ass if she heard you say that. Now, tell me you have something for me?"

"I'm sure she would. You're a lucky man. Okay, as for the evidence, I got something. Ran the blood through regular toxicology screens and

I got nothing. So, I ran several samples through the GC-MS. Dr. Forsythe wants all the stops pulled out for this one, you know. He's taking this hard. Anyway, your killer used a homemade version of Trichloromethane."

"You're shitting me, Chloroform? The killer made his own chloroform. *Madre di Cristo.*"

"Yeah. See, regular chloroform is made with chloride and chloromethane or methane, your killer used acetone and six percent bleach. That's all I got for now."

"Alright. Let me know if you guys get anything else. Thanks, man." Damien hung up as Joe and Officer Ivanski walked in.

Joe grabbed a handful of jellybeans. "Hey did you get anything from the lab?"

"Mhm. The killer used homemade chloroform to subdue Father Mandahari. The killer could've soaked a rag in the chloroform and stored it in a baggie. We're going off the assumption the killer hid out in the church and waited for Mandahari. The killer somehow knew Mandahari would sit and meditate. He could've come up behind him and covered his mouth and nose with the rag. Using homemade chloroform, the killer could've made it incredibly potent. It wouldn't have taken more than a few minutes to knock him out. Damn fucking smart."

Damien nodded at Ivanski. "Did you get anything from ECD?" Damien watched as Officer Ivanski removed a small piece of lint from his immaculate uniform. When Damien needed an intimidating uniformed officer, he used him.

"Well, not a lot. Father Mandahari had nothing hinky in his financials. Before last year, he spent every penny he had. He racked up a large credit card balance. Made a lot of cash withdrawals. However, about a year or so ago, he changed. He started keeping a balance in his account, and he made monthly payments on the card. No complaints against him regarding inappropriate behavior of any kind. Except for his gambling, he was a squeaky-clean guy."

"Is ECD still working on his computer?" Damien asked.

"Yeah, so far they don't see any unusual correspondence or threats."

Damien leaned back. "Joe, finish up any reports you have open and give me some time to get my report sent up to Mackey. I'll take you home since I picked you up this morning. Ivanski, keep digging."

Ivanski rose, "you got it, Lieutenant." He and Joe left the office, both with another handful of jellybeans.

CHAPTER NINE

By the time Damien made it out to get Joe, only a few detectives had remained in the pen. Damien sent home those on call. Davidson and Jenkins headed out to chase down a witness they had a bead on. Joe sat at his desk, engrossed in something. Damien smacked him on his shoulder. "You almost ready?"

"Hey. Almost. Remember earlier I told you there was something nagging me about that case you gave Hall and Alvarez?" Joe asked.

"Yeah, what about it?"

"Do you remember anything about a ship that sank a while back?"

Damien scowled at Joe. "No, fill me in." He sat in Hall's chair and put his feet on his desk.

Joe leaned back and opened a file he had. He held it out to Damien. "About a year ago this huge ass yacht sunk between here and Michigan. I think the depth of water was around two hundred feet. A cooperation tied to the Metacruze Cartel owned the ship. The rumor around town had the vessel loaded with weapons, drugs, and a shit load of gold and silver."

Damien read the file as Joe spoke. "Go on."

Joe took a swig of his diet soda. "What if the captain of the Shenandoah found the wreck and claimed it? Maritime salvage law allows for him to receive a percentage of the total value of the cargo."

Damien raised an eyebrow. "If they did find the ship, it could be the reason the for the crew being murdered."

"I doubt the Salvage Laws take into consideration the value of recovered illegal drugs and weapons. However, the gold and silver are covered."

"The recovery of the cargo would be a damn good reason for the Cartel to go after these guys." Damien rubbed his eyes. "Is everything in this folder?" Damien picked it up off the desk.

Joe nodded. "Everything I have gathered so far is in there."

"Okay, tomorrow I'll go over this with Hall and Alvarez. Let's get the hell out of here."

Joe put on his jacket. "Fucking A on that. I'm meeting Jesse for dinner." He wiggled his eyebrows at Damien. "I intend to have her for dessert."

***

Damien stewed all the way to his vehicle. Joe whistled as he followed Damien through the garage. Once in the vehicle, Damien put his keys in the ignition, but he didn't start it. "What the fuck are you doing?"

Joe shrugged. "What the hell are you talking about?"

"I thought you were dating Taylor?" Damien glared at Joe. "You're going to fuck up any chance you have with her."

Joe's nostrils flared. He hissed out a breath. "Listen, Taylor is seeing other people. She hasn't come up for a few weeks. Although we talk on the phone, we aren't exclusive. Taylor said she wouldn't put her life on hold while I screw around with other chicks. If it works out that we can see each other, she told me she's happy with that. She said she wouldn't sit around and wait for me. I'm not dating just one fucking woman. Why is that so hard for you to get through your thick skull?"

"Fine. I won't mention anything again. If Taylor is okay with what you have going on, then fine. That's all that matters." Damien sat in silence for a few moments before he spoke again. "I think you're making a mistake. If you continue to screw around with all these other chicks, you're going to miss out on the perfect woman for you. You'll lose her. That's it. That's all I'm saying."

Joe glared at Damien. "You just said you weren't going to say anything else. Are you done now?"

"Yeah, yeah fine. I'm done." Damien sighed. "Crap I forgot to text Dillon." He pulled his phone out and texted her he was on his way home after he dropped off Joe. As Damien started up the SUV and headed into traffic, they rode in silence for several minutes. Damien looked at Joe with a huge smile plastered on his face.

Joe stared at Damien. "What is so freaking *gas*, huh? What's with the smile? You go from ragging my ass to smiling. Do you need medication?"

"Shut up asshole. I don't need medication." Damien's smile grew wider. "I asked Dillon to move in with me this past weekend."

Joe's face lit up with a grin. "Get the heck out." Joe squinted his eyes. "What do you think will happen when Camilla finds out?"

Damien's eyebrow furrowed as he pursed his lips together. "Who the fuck cares what Camilla will think?" A wicked smile spread across Damien's face. "Although I would love to be there when she gets the news.

The expression on her face would be priceless." He parked in front of Joe's apartment.

Joe laughed. "Look at you. A year ago, you swore off women. Now you can't sleep, eat, or breathe without Dillon." Joe jumped from the vehicle. "I'll see you in the morning."

CHAPTER TEN

Coach greeted Damien at the front door. He rubbed and weaved his way between his legs. Damien picked him up scratching his head and chin. "Hey buddy, how was your day? Did you miss me?" He put him down, and Coach ran ahead and disappeared into the kitchen.

Damien leaned against the door frame and watched as Dillon set dishes and cups on the table for dinner. She had changed into snug shorts and a t-shirt. Her hair hung loosely down her back. He couldn't stop the smile as it spread across his face. Damien couldn't explain the sheer joy he had knowing he had her to come home to every night.

Dillon sensed him, and her stomach fluttered at the awareness of his presence. She spun around to find him staring at her. Damien's eyes roamed over her. Dillon's body responded instantly to those dark sapphire blue eyes. They made you want to strip naked and beg to be ravaged. They held way too much power over her. The man was undeniably sexy. Tall and lean with a mess of gorgeous black wavy hair, and he was hers. "Hey there. You're staring at me again."

"I can't help myself. You are the most beautiful creature I've ever seen." Damien took two steps toward her. She wrapped her arms around his waist and snuggled into his chest.

Dillon leaned back and smiled. "Well, you aren't hard on the eyes either." She kissed him gently at first. Then passion took control. Tongues collided, and her grip tightened around him.

When they broke for air, Damien's pulse raced. "Hmm, if I weren't so hungry, I would carry you to the bedroom."

Dillon stepped back and laughed. "I'm pretty hungry too. Sit down. Let's eat." She winked at him. "There's always dessert."

Coach took his spot on an empty chair. They ate in a comfortable silence for a few minutes. Dillon lifted her eyes to find Damien staring at her. "What gives? You seem like you have something spinning around your brain. Spit it out."

Damien filled his plate with more of everything. "This Chinese food is great. Thanks for getting it." He took a drink of water. "I want to beat the shit out of Joe."

Dillon's jaw dropped open. "What happened?"

Damien's shoulders sagged. "He mentioned tonight he had plans with this other chick. We discussed his relationship with Taylor. Evidently, she's okay with his philandering ways." Damien set his fork down. "I know he's in love with her. He's just too damn scared to act on it. Something is holding him back, but he hasn't told me what it is. The stupid fuck is going to lose her." Damien pinched the bridge of his nose. "Why the hell do I care so much about his damn love life?"

Dillon didn't like keeping secrets from Damien. Although Taylor asked her not to say anything, she couldn't let Damien fester. "I'm not supposed to say anything, but I think you need to know this. I'm telling this to you in confidence, and you'll not say anything to Joe. No matter how much it kills you."

Damien's eyebrows crinkled together. "What is it?"

Dillon swallowed her bite of food. "Taylor called me two weeks ago. She told me all about that conversation with Joe. Taylor was in tears. She figured she had to say it. She'll take what she can get from him, for now, because she's in love with him, but she won't wait forever.

"She also told me she received a promotion. She's the new head administrator at the DC Chicago crime lab. She's coming up this Wednesday to finalize some paperwork and find a place. Then she'll move up in the next two weeks." Damien's stoic face stared at her. "She hasn't told Joe yet. She's planning on calling him tonight to let him know she's coming up, and that she needs to speak with him."

Damien's lips pursed together. "Why would she want to take a job, knowing she'll be this close to Joe, and he doesn't want a relationship with her?"

Dillon's expression softened. She fed Coach, a little piece of chicken while she spoke. "This is her dream job. The opportunity came up, and she wasn't about to let Joe or any other man ruin something she worked hard for. She also hopes that if he sees her dating other men, it will drive him crazy. Then he'll want to be in a serious relationship with her. If he doesn't, then she'll accept it can't go any further than what it is now. She'll either move on or continue the current relationship."

"Joe's going to freak out for sure. I think if he sees her out with someone else, he'll go ballistic. I just don't know if it will be enough for him to quit fucking up his life."

"Listen, babe, you got to let Joe do what he needs to do. He and Taylor have to work this out themselves." Dillon took a bite of her egg roll. "Now tell me the second thing that has gotten your hackles up."

Damien smiled at her. "You know me so well, don't you? It's this case we're working. I got nothing. We think this killer sat through the Mass, then waited in hiding for Father Mandahari. This asshole left nothing behind. I have no idea how to find him."

Dillon gave a piece of beef to Coach as she listened. Damien scowled at her. "What? I can't help it," she said. "He gives me a pouty face, and I am compelled to give him a treat."

Damien hung his head to hide a smile that pushed the corners of his mouth up.

Dillon filled their drinks. "Now back to your case. Did you bring the file home?"

"I did. I'm hoping you can give some kind of direction."

Dillon stood. "Let's get this cleaned up and go to the office and see what we have."

***

Damien had converted a spare room into an office after he first moved in. This weekend they would bring Dillon's items from her apartment, including her desk which would soon sit next to his.

Dillon planned on making the other spare room into a bedroom. Her grandparents were coming for Christmas, and she wanted them to stay here. They were all she had left of her family. After the murder of her parents and three brothers, her grandparents raised her.

Damien moved to the desk and pulled out all the photos. Dillon sat next to him. "Wow, it's a good thing I don't have a queasy stomach. This is horrible." She gasped at the photo.

"These photos don't do the scene justice."

Dillon grabbed all the pictures and placed them on the magnetic board. She arranged them into a rough layout of the crime scene. She stepped back. "Tell me what you see." She walked over and took two glasses and a bottle of Sauvignon Blanc from the built-in bar. Dillon filled their glasses and sat on the edge of the desk. She handed him a drink and waited.

Damien sipped his wine. "As brutal as this looks, this wasn't a personal attack on Father Mandahari. I think you could take him out and put any other priest in his place if he had a sinful habit or vice. Although, I'm not sure why." Damien moved closer to the pictures. He pointed to the one with the dead priest front and center. "The killer did this to make a statement. He had a gambling habit. He put his addiction ahead of his work as a priest. However, he had straightened up more than a year ago. Either the killer didn't know, or he didn't care. The killer also had to have first-hand knowledge of Mandahari's habit, or he found out somehow. Both Father Jessup and Dr. Forsythe think only a handful knew about his addiction."

Dillon set her glass on the desk. "I think you're correct about it not being personal against Mandahari. I do believe this is personal against the Church. This guy is pissed off because someone didn't do their job, or the Church didn't do its job."

Damien spun around and faced her. "I think that's it. If it's someone the killer is angry with, why not go after him? Why Father Mandahari?"

Dillon took a sip of wine. "Various reasons. Maybe he hasn't gotten to the guy yet, or Mandahari was a substitute. Or it isn't one person at all. It's the whole."

Damien paced back and forth. "No. I don't think so. I mean I think it's a combination. I believe there is someone this guy is angry at. I also believe he holds the Church responsible as well." Damien stopped. "This is going to sound crazy. I don't think he blames God. The way the scene had been set, it specifically pointed to the priest and the Church. Not God. Do you understand what I mean?"

Dillon's brow furrowed. "I'm not Catholic. I don't know about all the traditions of the Catholic faith. I think I understand. The Catholic Church performs certain rites, based on tradition. The crime scene is heavy on symbolism. The coins, the Bible verse, and the way he laid out the priest seem to mock his position in the Church. As I look at it, I don't see a mockery of God, but what the Church represents *for God.*"

"Yes! It's almost as if—they aren't doing the job God gave them or they signed up to do." Damien sat next to Dillon on the desk.

Dillon watched him. This case already gnawed at him. "Joe mentioned earlier you think there will be more."

Damien turned toward her. "Yes. And I have no idea who to protect. I'm confident another priest will die. I hate feeling helpless. Knowing something is going to happen and I can do nothing to stop it."

Dillon stood there silent for a moment. She needed to tell Damien something, but she hated adding to his stress. "So, I have to go somewhere this week. Not sure which day, the details are still being worked out."

Damien cocked his head. "Okay—where?"

"I have to go interview Jason."

"You're fucking with me, right?"

"No, I wish I was." Dillon took a sip of her wine. "He's willing to make a deal."

Damien crossed his arms. "Something tells me this isn't just any old deal. What's up Dillon? Quit stalling."

She sighed. "Jason is willing to give the locations of the still missing dead girls, and all their details for a transfer to the Federal Facility in Marion. But he will only speak to me."

Damien's nostrils flared. "He just wants to screw with you. You threatened him in that basement, and he wants to screw with you, and your boss is going to feed you to the wolves."

She shrugged her shoulders. "It's what I signed up for. What we all sign up for. It won't be too bad. I only have to meet with him once. Then it will be over. I'm not sure of all the details. That's all I know right now."

Dillon finished her glass of wine. She took Damien by the hand and led him up the stairs. "I need a break from this conversation, and you need a break from this case. Your mind is thinking too much about clues you don't have. Let it rest." She led him to the bathroom. "I have a pretty good idea on how to distract you." Dillon undressed him. "Let me help you. Tomorrow you can pick it back up."

CHAPTER ELEVEN

November 29th
Early Tuesday morning

Damien stood next to Dillon's little sports car. He wrapped his arms around her and inhaled her luscious scent. "I have no idea when I'll be home tonight. I have so much crap to handle, I'll text you later. If I find I'm gonna be late, don't wait for me to eat."

Dillon had her arms wrapped around his waist. "Don't worry about me. I'll be getting some of the small stuff from my apartment between meetings today. I have a late afternoon conference with the group out of Springfield regarding Freestone. That will give me a better idea of when I need to drive down there this week. This weekend we can get the larger stuff."

Damien kissed her. "Joe mentioned he would use his truck to help us. Won't take us more than a couple of hours." He kissed her again, this one long and slow. "I love you, Dillon."

Her eyes smiled at him. "I know." Dillon stepped back from him and opened her door. Damien started toward his SUV. She called out to him, "keep your ass safe. I like it the way it is."

***

Damien left the meeting with his Captain. The one thing he didn't like about being a Lieutenant was the endless meetings. His entire morning wasted, listening to discussions about budget cuts and when this class of cadets would be entering the force. Damien rubbed his temples as he entered his office. "How the hell does this shit just appear?" He said as he shuffled the large stack of mail and messages. Damien squeezed his eyes shut hoping the headache would retreat just a bit.

Lieutenant Diego from Vice stuck his head in the door. "Hey Damien, got a minute?"

"Hey, Diego. What can I do for you?"

"Can you tell me what you guys have so far on your floater case?"

Damien smiled. "Are you trying to take credit for our homicides? Don't you have enough in Vice to keep you guys busy?"

"Ha ha," Diego said as he and a couple of his detectives walked into Damien's office. "You know we class up this randy bunch of hoodlums," Diego smiled.

Damien started to sit back down. "You know what, you guys go to the conference room, we're going to need a little more space." Damien stepped out into the pen. "Hall, Alvarez, and Hagan—you guys gather your stuff on the Shenandoah and meet up in the conference room."

Detective Ross was showing off pictures of his new baby when Damien walked into the conference room. Lieutenant Diego ran a clean squad. He was a good Lieutenant and a damn good cop. "Joe, what did you find out about the Shenandoah?" Damien asked as he opened a can of soda.

"Hall, Alvarez, and I have been hunting down as much information as we could get on the captain's business. He and his crew did find the shipwreck. He spent most of the money his company had made this past year on the salvage," Joe said.

Hall pulled a piece of paper from the folder. "They found the weapons and turned those in and received a percentage of their value. However, he claimed he never found the drugs or the silver and gold." Hall nodded toward Lieutenant Diego. "We think he turned in the weapons because the risk associated with trying to sell them on the black market was just too high."

Diego nodded in agreement. "Yeah, it is much harder to get rid of those weapons than the rest. Especially if you are trying to not bring attention to yourself."

"I think it's a damn good indication that they wanted the cash and not the contraband," Joe said. He leaned forward placing his elbows on his knees. "I believe they sold the gold and silver, on the black market, and they've stashed the drugs somewhere. I think the families had an emergency plan in place, and when the murdered crew turned up, they vanished. They've probably prepared for this kind of scenario."

"You mentioned the lawyer the other day, have you found him yet?" Damien asked Hall and Alvarez.

Alvarez shook her head. "We can't find him anywhere. His office said he hasn't been in for a few days. They didn't think much about it because he travels a lot." Alvarez glanced at Hall nodding. "We believe the Cartel got to him. We don't have a body or a crime scene; it's just a feeling."

Hall glanced between the two Lieutenants. "We haven't been able to find the families anywhere."

"It's like they just vanished. We haven't found a credit card trail or any other trail," Alvarez said.

Lieutenant Diego scrutinized Damien. "I'm assuming Mackey is going to want to bring in your girlfriend?"

Damien smirked. Amusement and a hint of jealousy danced in Diego's eyes. "Yes, Agent McGrath will be brought in. Mackey will want us to get everything we can first. Once we ring the Fed bell, we can't unring it. However, the Feds will be able to do a lot of stuff we can't." Damien paused, "Okay. Hall and Alvarez, you track the families. These people went somewhere, and they must have access to money.

"Diego, you guys follow the drugs. We'll monitor the gold and silver. We'll get ECD on that and see if they can track anything on it. I bet our paths will cross. Let's set up a tentative meeting for Monday, Captain Mackey will want to pull in the Feds for that meeting and inform them of all our information. Your Captain, Captain Mackey, the Feds; all of us will discuss everything. I'll push for us to stay on this case. If an op is going to go down, we need to all be part of it. I think there is a good possibility they'll try to take it from us and lock us out. I know Dillon will work to keep us in the loop. How about Monday at nine?"

Lieutenant Diego stood up. "Those damn idiots, if they had gone through the proper channels they would still be alive." He reached out and shook Damien's hand. "I hope we get to these families before anyone else."

Damien nodded. "You're preaching to the choir."

Diego smiled at Damien. "If Agent McGrath gets tired of your ass, you need to send her my way."

Damien chuckled. "You couldn't handle her even with a set of instructions. She would eat you up and leave your lifeless carcass on the side of the road."

Diego laughed. "But it would be a hell of a ride." Diego caught the fire in Damien's eyes. "Whoa cowboy. You know I'm just giving you shit. She's a beautiful woman. We're all jealous as hell and long for the day when you piss her off. Hey, thanks for the help on this. Like I said, I hope to God we can get these families before the Cartel does."

Damien watched Diego and his men as they left. He pointed at Hall and Alvarez, "I want you two on this. If you need extra help, pull in one of the uniforms assigned to our unit. Take everything Joe has, he will assist as he can."

Hall gave Damien a cheeky grin.

"Hall, what the hell are you grinning at?" Damien asked.

"You know if you do piss off Dillon, I call dibs." He winked at Damien and ran out of the room before he could pound him into the floor.

As they left the room, Damien grabbed Joe by the shoulder. "I called St. Florentine, Father Jessup is expecting us. Something's nagging me, I feel like we missed something at the church."

Joe scowled at him. "What could we have missed?"

"I don't know, just humor me, okay?"

"I live to humor you. Let me get my jacket, and I'm ready to go." Joe went to his desk.

"I'll meet you in my office." As Damien entered, his phone rang. "Kaine."

"How's the sexiest cop in Chicago doing?"

Damien cursed. If he had paid attention to caller ID, he wouldn't have answered the phone. "What the hell do you want?" Damien waved to Joe to sit and wait for him.

Joe raised an eyebrow at him.

"Oh, come on Damien. I wanted to see if we could get together to-night. I'll bring some wine and dessert, or I could be the dessert." Camilla swooned on the other end of the phone.

"Camilla, I've moved on. You should too."

"Damien, you and I both know you haven't moved on. You might be dating, but you won't find anyone to take my spot. The sooner you real-ize that, the quicker we can get back to the way things were."

"The way things were? What way was that Camilla? When you lied to me or when you were fucking that guy from your office. Who knows how many other men you were banging behind my back." The other end of the line was silent. Damien smiled at Joe. "Listen, Camilla, I told you I'm involved with someone else. She's moving in with me. There's no chance of you and I rekindling anything."

"Who is she?" Camilla barked at him.

"You don't know her; she's new to the area." Damien tried not to laugh as he watched Joe make funny faces across the desk from him.

"Damien, you know it's not going to last. I'll wait, and when you come to your senses, you can call me."

"Well, you'll be waiting a lifetime. She's more of a woman than you'll ever be. Go back to your office jockey. You liked him so much when we were together."

"You know I'm the best..."

Damien hung up on her. "Shit. She chaps my ass."

Joe laughed. "I do wish I could've seen her face. You know she always assumed you two would get back together. Knowing you're moving in with someone will drive her crazy. You may want to keep an eye out for her. You better let Dillon know what Camilla is capable of."

Damien grabbed his jacket. "Dillon carries a gun. I'm more worried about what Dillon will do to Camilla. Don't let her beautiful exterior fool you. Dillon could kick both our asses."

CHAPTER TWELVE

The front doors of St. Florentine remained locked. The scene had been released but had yet to be cleaned. All foot traffic still entered through the church offices. Damien and Joe entered the building to a loud crash echoing off the walls. Both took off running and found the source of the noise, flat on his back in the hallway.

Damien and Joe ran up to Father Jessup. Broken teacups and spilled tea surrounded him. Damien caught the slight smile on Joe's face. "Father Jessup, are you alright?" Damien reached down to help him up.

A deep laugh escaped the prone Father. "Oh, good Lord, yes. Other than looking like a fat beached whale, I'm all right." He reached for Damien and Joe's hands as they helped him off the floor. "Evidently, I'm not good at carrying a tray and walking at the same time. Thank you." Father Jessup brushed off his clothes.

Damien picked up the broken dishware while Joe placed a mop marker on the floor. "Father Jessup, have you called the clean-up crew to come out and get the sanctuary ready for Mass?"

Father Jessup straightened his shirt and clerical collar. "Yes. They're scheduled to come tomorrow. Why?"

"I know we released the scene, but we need to go over it one more time. I wanted to make sure it hadn't been touched."

"Nothing has been touched. Go on and do what you need to do. I'll be in my office if you need me." Father Jessup waddled his way down the hallway.

***

Damien and Joe entered the sanctuary to the fetid scent of dried blood. Damien flipped a switch on the wall, turning on a series of lights. Another switch turned on the lights above the altar. The dried blood on the floor had a glossy shine under the glare of the bright lights. It looked like nothing more than a sheet of plastic that could be peeled off the floor.

"What are we searching for?" Joe asked as he made his way around the congealed blood, taking great care not to step on it.

Damien stood behind the altar looking at the empty pews. He never wanted to be a priest. He couldn't imagine the responsibility that came with leading a congregation. "I'm not sure, but something keeps nagging at me."

For a few minutes, neither spoke. Damien spun around and stared at Joe. "Did the CSTs take the clothes?"

Joe frowned at Damien. "What clothes?"

"Father Mandahari's clothes. I'm sure he didn't run around naked under his cassock. So, where the heck are his clothes?"

Joe's shoulders sagged. "Ah hell." He crossed himself as he pulled out his phone. "I'll call Roger. See if the lab has them."

Damien didn't wait for Joe to get an answer. The lab wouldn't have the clothes. *Why the hell did the killer take his clothes?* That made little sense.

"Nope. They didn't take any clothes." Joe stood in the middle of the aisle.

Damien pulled a pair of gloves from his back pocket. "Out in the truck, I have some evidence bags. Will you go grab a large one? I know the clothes are here."

Joe nodded. "No problem." He grabbed a hymnal from a pew to prop open the church door.

Damien continued to search as Joe came down the aisle. "Start searching. Those clothes must be somewhere. There is no reason for the killer to take the clothes with him. I'm venturing he cut them off; that would've been faster than undressing him."

Both Damien and Joe searched everywhere. They stood on opposite sides of the altar. Joe scanned the area. "Damien, where else could this douche bag hide the clothes? We've looked everywhere."

"If the killer didn't take the clothes, they have to be here somewhere." Damien surveyed the area, his eyes rested on the one place they hadn't checked. He caught Joe's eye. "I think I know where the killer put them." Damien made his way to the back of the altar. "If the killer wanted to make a statement against the Church, the Tabernacle would accomplish that."

Joe's eyes widened. "Ooh no. No way. That goes against everything the Church stands for. You don't mess with that. That is the most sacred symbol of the Church. We aren't even allowed to touch it."

"We're the police we can touch it," Damien said. He had never been this close to a Tabernacle. It held the Eucharist and wine used in Communion. Even as an altar boy he was not allowed to get the Host out of it.

Damien stepped closer to the box. Made from a solid block of marble, about one foot by one and a half feet in size. It had a scalloped edge etched into the marble, and a tall gold cross sat at on the top. The gold door had been scratched and bent slightly out of place. Damien glanced back at Joe and noticed he stood a few feet away. "Joe, what are you so afraid of?"

"Man, I don't want to be anywhere near you when the lightning strikes. We shouldn't be breaking into the Tabernacle."

"I'm not going to get struck by lightning, and we don't have to break in. The lock is already broken. Open the evidence bag." Damien opened the little door. Stuffed between the Eucharist and the wine chalice were Mandahari's clothes. Damien removed the clothes carefully and placed them into the large paper bag. He had Joe call Roger and ask him to send a CST to the church to dust the Tabernacle and the surrounding area for prints.

"Roger is on his way. He's near here for another case. Said to sit tight. He promised while he was here he would give everything one more look before the cleaning crew showed up." Joe rolled the top of the evidence bag and sealed it.

Damien finished a cursory examination of the box, not finding anything. "Let's go let Father Jessup know what's going on. He may have a heart attack when we tell him what the killer did. Be ready to give CPR."

"Why me? Why do I have to give CPR?" Joe scowled at him.

"That's easy, I'm the lieutenant."

CHAPTER THIRTEEN

November 30th
Wednesday morning

Damien and Joe walked through the doorway of Autopsy room two. Soft jazz music played while Dr. Forsythe closed the wound on his friend. He lifted his head when Damien and Joe entered the room. Dr. Forsythe blinked trying to stop the tears that hovered near the surface.

"Don't worry. I didn't do the autopsy. I asked Dr. Marshall if I could close him up. I made sure to keep my distance. Especially after I received a phone call from the restaurant's manager." Dr. Forsythe raised an eyebrow at Damien. "He wanted to make sure I was okay and not in any trouble."

Damien's shoulders sagged. "C'mon Dr. Forsythe, you know I had to check out everything you told me."

Dr. Forsythe sighed heavily as he nodded toward a file on the counter. "I get it. I made you copies of everything we have so far. The lab is still working on some stuff. If anything new comes up, I'll make sure you're made aware of it." Dr. Forsythe continued to work on Father Mandahari.

Joe picked up the folder.

Damien noticed the care Dr. Forsythe took with his friend. The skin bunched around the Doc's eyes, and he had a pained stare as he worked. "Thank you. I appreciate it. This saves us a trip to the lab. Can you tell me if anything unexpected was found?"

Dr. Forsythe's lips twitched. "Interesting question, Damien. Yes, something unexpected was found. When we removed the coins, we found a St. Dymphna medal on his sternum."

Damien turned to speak to Joe.

"Don't look at me," Joe said raising his hands. "We already established I didn't pay attention in Religious Education. I have no idea who St. Dymphna is."

Damien frowned. "Do you know who St. Dymphna is?" He asked the doctor.

Dr. Forsythe smiled. "I do now. She's the Patron Saint of Mental Illness or Sickness. However, I can't tell you her importance in this case. I'm not sure if the killer is referring to Shri and his gambling, or to someone else."

The doctor finished the last suture and placed his tools to the side. Bernard Forsythe caressed his friend's head. He pulled the sheet up to cover Mandahari's chest and folded the priest's arms across his body.

Damien watched the intimate act. "Thank you, Dr. Forsythe. I'm so sorry for the loss of your friend. If you need anything from me, please call me."

Dr. Forsythe nodded. The tears made their escape and flowed down his cheek. "Thank you, son."

As Damien left the autopsy room, he glanced over his shoulder. Dr. Forsythe held his friend's hand and wept. Damien silently promised Bernard he would find Shri Mandahari's killer.

***

Damien sniffed his clothes. "Man, that place smells like someone dumped a gallon of Pine Sol. I'm going to smell that the rest of the damn day."

"Well, I bet it's better than smelling decomposing flesh all day." Joe's stomach growled. "I'm hungry, you?"

Damien chuckled as he nodded. "Only you can go from decomposing flesh to food. You want to go to Henry's?"

Joe's face lit up. "Sounds good."

Damien's phone rang. "Kaine."

"Hey, baby. What's up?" Dillon's sexy voice carried over the auto's Bluetooth system.

"Joe and I were heading to Henry's for something to eat. Can you meet us?" Damien asked.

"You're the only other woman I can have a meal with that Damien won't give me shit over," Joe said.

"Oh hey, Joe. As much as I'd love to eat lunch with the two most handsome men I know, I can't. I'm getting ready to get on the road to Springfield. I'll be back tonight. I may be late."

Joe tilted his head to the side. "Don't let this fucker get in your head."

Dillon snickered on the other end of the phone. "Jason Freestone is the last person I'm worried about getting into my head."

"Have you been given any of the details yet?" Damien asked.

"Nope. Director Sherman said the DA could fill me in when I get there. Evidently, the agreement just now got finalized. I'll text you when I'm heading home. I love you, Damien."

"Hey, what about me?" Joe asked.

"Oh, I love you too Joe. As a matter of fact, give Damien a sloppy wet kiss for me. Talk to you later."

"Love you, babe." Damien peered at Joe as he disconnected the call. His partner puckered his lips waiting to kiss him. "If those lips touch me, and it's not to give me CPR, I will kill you."

"Ahh come on, you know you want a wet one."

"From Dillon. Hell, I'll take it from Coach before you."

Joe laughed. "Fine. I'll save my kisses for Taylor. She's coming up late tonight. Said she had some business in the city and needs to talk to me."

Damien cringed inside. He wanted to say something, but he had promised Dillon. He needed to let Taylor tell Joe everything. Damien pulled into Henry's parking lot when his phone signaled a call from Dispatch. "Kaine," Damien frowned at Joe.

The operator's voice came through the Bluetooth. "Lieutenant Kaine, DB located at St. Constantine's Catholic Church. Officers on scene. CST has been notified."

"Kaine and Hagan in transit now." Damien grabbed the steering wheel and turned the SUV around. He hit the lights and siren and flew across town. Neither he nor Joe said a word.

CHAPTER FOURTEEN

Damien pulled into the parking lot of St. Constantine's Church. He and Joe sat there for a few minutes. An uncomfortable silence filled the SUV. Damien removed his phone from the Bluetooth cradle. "Damn, why didn't you and I ever open that sports bar we always talked about?"

Joe chuckled. "It's still a possibility. An excellent possibility. Hey, do you think all this time we're spending in church will give us credit for all the Masses we've missed?"

Damien laughed. "Crap, I hope so. Lord knows I keep missing enough of them." Damien nodded to the officers who stood at the front of the church. The last of the sunlight cast an eerie shadow down the aisle. He followed Joe as he dipped his finger in the vessel containing holy water. For a split second, he considered maybe it wasn't such a good idea, crime scene and all. Yet the fear of a lightning strike outweighed crime scene contamination.

Joe and Damien advanced down the aisle, seeing no blood and no body. Both scanned the foyer of the church. "Are we being punked?" Joe asked.

"No. We aren't being punked." Damien pointed toward the opposite hall. In a slightly recessed area stood three confessionals. "There's the party."

Beautiful massive wooden structures, each one ornate, decorated with different colored wood inlays. Benches lined each wall, offering those waiting to confess, a place to sit.

Roger leaned against the wall. "I'm tired of running into you guys like this, but it's about damn time you two showed up." He winced at the curse and made the sign of the cross. "I didn't touch anything. Dr. Forsythe is on his way."

Damien and Joe both ducked under the police tape. They stood at the door of the confessional for what seemed like an eternity. Joe turned toward Damien, who prayed in whispered Italian, then opened the door. Neither of them moved.

The priest stared at them with vacant eyes. A deep slit turned his throat into a macabre smile. The killer had stuffed the cut with Hosts, causing the throat to bulge out. The communion wafers fell from his mouth and throat, spilling onto his chest. He still wore his clothes, sort of. His pants had been pulled down, and his hand held his severed dick. A nail pinned a piece of paper to his chest.

"Oh, *Madre beata Maria di Cristo*," Damien gasped. He kissed the St. Michael medal he wore around his neck.

Joe turned to the officers who stood on the other side of the tape. "Who is he?"

One officer stood like a sentry. "Father John Belgosa. He's been at this parish for the last four years."

Damien stepped closer to the priest. "Roger, grab two evidence envelopes for me. One for the note and one for this nail." Damien stepped into the confessional. He had to tug on the nail, and it made a slurping sound as it pulled free from the priest's chest. Damien dropped the nail in one of the envelopes Roger held open. Holding the note by its corner, Damien stepped back out of the confessional so he and Joe could read it. It appeared to be the same lettering as the note found at St. Florentine's. This note contained two verses.

If a man is found sleeping
with another man's wife,
both the man who
slept with her
and the woman must die.
You must purge the evil from Israel.

Elders who direct the affairs of the
Church will, are worthy
of double honor especially
those whose work
is preaching and teaching.
But those elders who are sinning
you are to reprove before
everyone so that others
may take warning.
I charge you in the sight of God,

and Christ Jesus and the elect angels
to keep these instructions.
Keep yourself pure.

Joe exhaled the breath he held. "Bloody hell. I know the first verse. I think it's Deuteronomy. I don't have a clue about the second one."

Damien studied the note before he placed it in the evidence envelope. "The second comes from 1st Timothy. The killer has combined a few verses to make it say what he wants. It's out of chapter five. I can gather from the first verse this guy was having sex with women. I don't think our killer plans to go after the women. He's using the verse to let us know what sin he committed." Damien turned to Dr. Forsythe as he came toward them. "Hey, Doc. Umm—are you familiar with Father John Belgosa?" Damien wanted to avoid a repeat of Monday morning.

A smile pushed the corners of Dr. Forsythe's mouth up. "Now Damien, are you looking out for my well-being? No, I'm not familiar with a Father Belgosa. I guess it's that disturbing huh?"

"You could say that," Damien said. He and Joe stepped aside to let the ME through.

"Wow. I have to give this guy credit for creativity." Dr. Forsythe hung his head. "I'm sorry—that was uncalled for. Sick humor makes this easier to stomach. Please forgive me if I have offended any you." He turned back to the grisly task at hand.

"Doc, you don't have to worry about us," Joe said.

Dr. Forsythe stepped back. He motioned to his two helpers. "Let's get him out of there and on a stretcher. The two techs opened a body bag and laid it out on the ground. The confessional proved hinky. One tech wedged himself into it while the other grabbed the priest's feet. Between the two of them, they managed to get Father Belgosa out and place him on the opened body bag. Dr. Forsythe knelt next to the body and jabbed the temperature gauge into his liver. "This guy is still warm. You're looking at death within the last two hours."

Damien stepped to the wall where a cork board hung. "That makes sense. This bulletin says the church holds confession from eight until ten every Wednesday morning. That puts his death right around ten or ten-thirty. Making our killer probably the last one in confession."

Joe made a growl-like sound. "Great. Let's run an ad and ask who came to confession on Wednesday morning at St. Constantine's. No bloody problem." He kicked the side of the confessional.

Damien stared at the dead man on the floor. In the glare of the lights, Father Belgosa's skin was waxy like one of Madame Tussauds' Museum figures from her chamber of torture. "Dr. Forsythe, let me know when you get results."

"You got it, Lieutenant. Okay, boys let's take him and all his goodies back to the Morgue." Dr. Forsythe took the body, leaving the CSTs to gather all the remaining evidence from the crime scene.

"Joe, let's go talk to Ricin. He has the guy who found Belgosa." Damien turned toward the church offices. He stopped to see Joe had a pained look on his face, and his steps were hesitant. "You coming, pokey butt?"

Joe's eyebrows squeezed together. "Yeah, but I don't want to."

"C'mon big boy, after the interviews I'll buy you an ice cream." Damien laughed as he pushed the door open.

Joe shook his head. "Man, it's looking like priests are an endangered species."

CHAPTER FIFTEEN

Dillon walked into the Springfield Detention Center. The officer on-duty glanced up, and a smile lit up his face. "Hey Agent McGrath, how have you been?"

Dillon smiled as she approached the window. "Good Officer Todd, how's your wife?"

"Oh, she's doing great. The baby is due in a month. She can't wait for the day. Said she's tired of being fat."

Dillon raised her eyebrow at him. "And I know you told her she's the most beautiful woman ever, and that she's not fat?"

He laughed at her. "You know it. First, she is. Second, she can still whip my ass." He buzzed the door for her to enter the facility. "The Director and the DA are in the conference room waiting for you."

As Dillon walked through the door, several other deputies glanced up. A few nodded in her direction. She made her way through the maze of hallways to the conference room.

Director Fitz glanced up and smiled. "Hey, Agent McGrath, thanks for coming."

Dillon sat at the table. Her lips flattened in a tight smile. "Sure. Alright. Fill me in."

Director Fitz glanced at the DA. "Jason had his lawyer contact me a few days ago with a proposition. I informed the DA, and here we are. I'll let DA Peppers explain the rest." Director Fitz nodded to DA Peppers.

The DA pulled a piece of paper from his briefcase. "He wanted a deal. He said he has information that the FBI didn't find during their searches." He held up a sealed manila envelope. "His lawyer gave me this with the instructions it wasn't supposed to be opened except by you in front of Jason. I don't know what's in it. You'll find out in just a little bit. The deal was to include a transfer to the Marion facility and a cell to himself."

Dillon felt the warmth of heat flushing through her body. Her heart pounded against her chest. Her director gave no indication about this when he called her earlier that morning. *Damn him.* "Did you inform Director Sherman of this when you spoke with him?"

"Of course. We weren't sure if we should give into this or not. I called

Sherman to ask him before we contacted you, and he said he'd take care of it." DA Peppers' eyes squinted as he gave a slight head shake. "Did he not tell you why you were coming down here?" DA Peppers asked in an uncertain tone.

Dillon's chest tightened. She drew a breath and released it before speaking. "He didn't go into all the details." She nodded toward the paper in the DA's hands. "He'll give details concerning all the girls he abducted and the ones that are currently still missing? As well as their locations? And he'll waive his right to trial and plead guilty, for those two conditions, nothing else?"

"That's correct." DA Peppers put the envelope in front of Dillon.

Dillon didn't touch it. "Are you guys able to give him what he wants?" Dillon asked.

"In regard to placement. Yes. We're willing to let Jason have that facility and the condition of a cell to himself. He wouldn't be put in general population. However, for him to receive these conditions, he must divulge everything. Supposedly everything is in that envelope," DA Peppers said.

Dillon stared at the envelope. "What if I say no?"

The men glanced at each other. DA Peppers squared his shoulders. "I guess you have the right to say no. I could try and force the situation, but I don't want to. To be honest, Agent, I don't think you'll say no. I've heard about you. Your ability to work across all barriers of law enforcement.

"Your background has given you a great insight into how victims of violent crimes feel. You have a reputation for your ability to get into someone's head. It gives you the best chance to manipulate this situation. You're what he wants in the end. He's willing to give everything up, but only to you."

The same system Dillon believed in and dedicated her life to was about to screw her royally. Losing her family so violently did give her an edge, but she didn't want to be victimized by Jason. Dillon pinched the bridge of her nose. "What about Amy Custer and her parents, they agreed to this? The Hautes? All the parents. They're ok with this?"

"They are," DA Peppers said.

Dillon paced. *Crap, crap, crap.* She turned to the two men. "Bring him up. Make sure he's in cuffs and secured to the table. Don't offer him anything to drink. Instruct the officers who bring him up to not say a word to him. If he asks them a question, they need to ignore it. I want him to sit in there for a few minutes before I go in." Her focus shifted between the two men. "I need a notepad and a cup of coffee or soda pop. I don't care which."

The men shared a glimpse with each other. "Sure," Director Finch said. "We'll meet you at Interrogation room three."

The DA rocked back in his chair. "What's up with the requests?"

Dillon sat on the corner of the table. "Did you ask Jason why he asked for me?"

The DA's brow furrowed. "No. I assumed he asked for you because you were there during his arrest and you have a lot of authority as an FBI Agent."

"That's not why he asked for me. I threatened him with the worst possible cell and prison I could get him into. I didn't interview him. Right after the news conference, I had another case in Charleston. I had to leave all the interviews to one of my colleagues. I'm sure Jason thinks I snubbed him. As the Agent in charge of the investigation, I would've interviewed him. Jason set up this deal, asking for something specific and you guys handed him everything he wanted. He's feeling superior, in control. He has the Feds and the local boys eating out of his hand.

"Jason has no respect for women. I would say he has a deep-seated hatred for us. He needs us for his sexual perversions, but he thinks we are beneath him. I need to impress upon Jason that I'm the one in control of this meeting."

Dillon noticed the DA's reaction. His eyes narrowed as he tapped his finger on the table. "Listen, I won't do anything to jeopardize your arrangement. However, if I'm going to do it, I'm going to do it my way. Jason wants to make sure I'm nothing more than a pawn. That I have no importance. He's setting the scene, the men have decided what to do, and I'm supposed to follow your leads and commands. Because that's what women do."

The DA's eyes widened. "That's not what's happening at all. You know that, right Agent?"

Dillon smiled at him. "Right. I need a minute before I go in there. I'm not removing my weapon. That's why he needs to be secured to the table."

The DA stood in a huff. "That goes against this facility's interview protocol."

She smiled at him as she headed for the door. "Do I look like I give a rat's ass about this facility's protocols?" Dillon walked into the restroom. She locked the door and leaned against it. After a few minutes, she splashed cool water on her face. She pulled her hair into a loose bun at the nape of her neck. She took a few deep cleansing breaths. Dillon pushed her emotions to the side and prepared to sit in the same room with a monster.

CHAPTER SIXTEEN

Damien knocked on the door of Father Ricin's office as he opened it. "I'm Lieutenant Kaine, and this is my partner Detective Joe Hagan. We need to ask you a few questions."

Damien estimated Father Ricin's age around sixty. Tall and skinny as a broom. He reached out long, bony fingers to shake Damien's hand. "Welcome. I'm devastated by what has happened to Father Belgosa. I can't understand why anyone would do this." Father Ricin motioned to two empty chairs.

Damien nodded at him and the two others who sat on the long sofa, a man and a middle-aged woman. "Can you tell me who found Father Belgosa?"

The man raised his hand. "Me, I'm Jeff Blake. I came to speak with Father Belgosa. I knew he would be in the confessionals, so I went there to look for him." He paused for a moment. The woman sitting next to him took his hand in hers. A weak smile graced his lips.

Damien nodded slightly. "Can you tell me why you were here to see Father Belgosa?"

"I wanted to ask him about the marriage classes. I plan on asking a girl to marry me, but she isn't Catholic." Jeff glanced quickly at Father Ricin. "I knew when confession time ended and I thought I would catch him just at the end."

Father Ricin spoke to Damien. "Jeff came to me, and we began a search for Father Belgosa. I checked in the back where we live," Father Ricin said.

"Your residence is here on the premises?" Damien asked.

Ricin nodded. "Belgosa and I live here, just beyond the garden. We have a little house behind the church. It's a duplex."

"We'll need to have the CSTs go through it." Damien turned his attention back to Jeff. "Go ahead and finish. You didn't find him in his office or home. What did you do next?"

Jeff glanced at his trembling hands. "I went through one part of the church while Father Ricin went through the other. I came back into the main atrium area and went down the hallway where the confessionals stand. I guess Father Ricin tried calling him because I heard a faint hum as I opened the confessional door, that's when I found him." Tears streamed down the man's cheek.

Damien turned his attention to the woman. She introduced herself as Myra Sampson, the church secretary. Myra didn't arrive until after Jeff called for help.

Joe listened as each person described where and when they'd last seen Father Belgosa. The vision of the note nailed to his chest popped into Joe's mind. He winced. He hoped Belgosa was dead when the killer pounded that nail into his chest. As he continued to listen, he was surprised each person described Belgosa as a saint. The note the killer had left behind alluded he'd been a womanizer, a man of the cloth who banged women in the church. Joe leaned in toward the sofa. "Are any of you aware of Father Belgosa's affairs with the ladies in the church?"

Myra and Father Ricin lowered or averted their gaze.

Jeff gasped slightly. He looked to Father Ricin then back to the detectives.

Joe faced Father Ricin who slumped and bit his bottom lip. "Father, can you tell us how many people may have been aware of Father Belgosa's affairs? We need to explore the possibility that his behavior may have contributed to his murder. Please understand, we aren't trying to nor do we want to disparage his memory. We need all the information we can get to catch his killer."

Father Ricin sank into his chair. He didn't make eye contact. "Several were aware of his... penchant for women. He'd been a good and faithful man of God. However, Father Belgosa battled inner demons. He went to Bishop Cantor and asked for a sabbatical. The bishop denied his request." Father Ricin winced with a pained expression.

Myra's face softened as she stared at Father Ricin. She glared at Damien and Joe. "I will not sit here any longer and listen to you harass Father Ricin."

"Myra, it's okay," Father Ricin said.

"No, it isn't. Father Belgosa lost his faith. He searched out sins of the flesh to fill a void left behind. He was a good man, but he lost his way. He slept with women for the last year. He wanted to go away. Take a break from the church and Cantor wouldn't allow it."

Myra squared her shoulders and stared Joe in the eye. "That arrogant man told him to seek counseling. It wasn't enough. Father Belgosa needed time away from the rigors of parish life. He needed a change. However, he couldn't walk away. If Cantor had given him the time away, he would've made the right decision." She crumpled under Joe's scrutiny. She turned her face into Jeff's chest and wept.

Father Ricin motioned for Damien and Joe to go out into the hallway. His shoulders drooped and his eyes filled with tears. "I'm sorry for his death. No matter Father Belgosa's sins, he didn't deserve such a cruel death. He'd been a good priest until the sins of the flesh took over. I know Myra harbors a lot of animosity toward Bishop Cantor. She feels he should've done more to help Belgosa.

"I'm disappointed Bishop Cantor didn't give him the time away. I had several phone calls with the bishop asking him for a special waiver for Father Belgosa. He denied every single one. I personally think Belgosa should've left. Taken the time he needed. For all his faults, though, Belgosa couldn't do that."

Damien glanced around the hallway. "Father Ricin, are there any surveillance cameras?"

Father Ricin shook his head. "Not really. Cameras monitor the doors to the offices. We don't have any inside the church itself."

"Did you or your staff see someone waiting for confession today that you recognize? I'm hoping someone waiting their turn may have seen the last person to go into the confessional. Or may have seen someone lingering around."

The Father's lips pinched together. "Let me think a minute. Margarete Sanchez came before ten. She stopped in the office and then headed to confession. I can call her and ask her."

Damien smiled. "Actually, we'd need to speak with her. If you think she'd be more comfortable coming here to meet us, we can do that. Could you arrange that for us?"

"I can call her later today and see when she can meet with you. I will phone you as soon as I know. I'm assuming you'd like it to happen ASAP?"

Damien nodded. "Yes, if not today, no later than tomorrow. She may have seen something which can help us find Father Belgosa's killer." Damien took the man's hand in his own. "We will find his killer. I promise you, Father." He pulled his card from his pocket. "Here's my number, please call me as soon as you have a time for us to meet with Margarete.

Also, I'd like for you to consider giving us a name of one of the women Father Belgosa slept with. She may be able to give us something to go on."

Father Ricin's jaw clenched. He rubbed the back of his neck. "I'll see what I can do," he said.

Damien believed Father Ricin wanted to help. He just had a few demons of his own to wrestle with first.

CHAPTER SEVENTEEN

Dillon approached the Interrogation room. Several deputies had joined the DA and the Director of the facility in observation. She rolled her shoulders and readied herself. She opened the door carrying the envelope, notepad, and soda. Jason sat facing her. His hands and feet were cuffed and chained to the table. He had enough slack to allow minimal movement.

She watched as Jason glanced up and smiled at her. He had a handsome face and piercing steel gray-blue eyes. His hair had grown out, the natural wave adding to his youthful good looks. His physical appearance was what had drawn those young teenage girls to him, making it easy for him to abduct, rape, and murder them.

"Jason, I'd say it's good to see you, but then I'd be lying," Dillon spoke in a flat voice. She didn't smile or reach out to shake his hand. She sat in the seat across the table from him. She glanced at her watch and opened her soda. After a long sip, she scribbled on the notepad. She yawned as she put the pen down. "So, what would you like to talk about Jason?"

A slow easy smile tugged at the corners of his mouth. "Well, Agent McGrath. You're looking prettier than the first day I met you."

Dillon picked lint off her shirt as he leered at her. The silence draped thick between them. "Alright Jason, you made your deal with the DA. I'm here." She pushed the envelope between them. "What's in the envelope, Jason?"

Jason shifted in his chair. He interlocked his fingers and rested his elbows on the table.

Dillon could see how much he was enjoying this.

"How's Amy? Has she healed yet?" Jason closed his eyes and inhaled deeply. "She was so tight, I had to work extra hard at pushing my dick into her pussy." He leaned back opening his eyes. "I can still hear her screams as I thrust into her. I loved it when the girls screamed. It does something to you, makes you feel alive and in power. Do you scream when you're having your wet pussy pounded, Agent McGrath?"

Dillon's insides twisted. The vision of Amy's assault in that basement made Jason's description all too vivid. "Jason if you don't want to talk, I can just go. She glanced up from her notepad. She could see the vein in his neck throbbing.

"You can open it," Jason said as he nodded in the direction of the envelope. "Would you like to know where it came from?"

She raised an eyebrow at him as she scribbled on her pad, but she didn't respond.

"I had it in a safe deposit box." A broad grin filled Jason's face. "Surprised, huh?"

Dillon breathed slowly. The coil in her belly tightened. "I guess you outsmarted us there. Too bad you weren't smart enough to not get caught." She stared into those beady eyes, now almost black with rage.

"Well, it's here now. A gift to you." A cheerful giggle escaped. "A bonanza for me." He nodded toward it as his fingertips pushed it closer to her. "Go ahead, open it." He sat back like a cat waiting to pounce on a mouse.

Dillon slowed her breathing. Under the table, her knee bounced feverishly, but her hands remained steady. She opened the envelope, dumping its contents on the table. Dillon couldn't control the involuntary reaction. She sucked in air through gritted teeth. The top photo was of Beth Haute—Jason's first victim. It looked as if it had been taken toward the end of her captivity in Jason's basement. At least Dillon prayed it had been.

Not one patch of unbruised skin could be seen. The bruises were all different colors, indicating they had occurred over an extended period. Her face was swollen and bloodied.

Dillon's heart raced. Her pulse pounded in her chest and ears. She swallowed what little spit she had in her mouth. The second picture was all she could stomach. Beth hung upside down from a chain. At some point her throat had been slit so deeply that her head was nearly decapitated; but not before Jason had tortured her. Dillon's heart sank. The journals that had been found when Jason's house was searched had indicated Beth had been tortured. The burn marks and cuts to her body showed the depths of Jason's depravity.

There were several more photos and several pieces of paper. Dillon quickly put it back in the envelope. She should walk now. She had the envelope, he had his deal. But Dillon stayed in the seat. If she left, he would win.

Jason leaned into her. "Beth was a bitch. She had led me on at that summer party. Acting like she wanted me to kiss her. Flirting with me, stealing a glance here or there. Then when I made a move to kiss her, she fucking cries about it. Acting like she was some innocent sweet girl. That bitch's whining made my life hell after that party. Her parents bitched to my father, and he kept me on lockdown at the farm for months. Said I was a disgrace."

Jason's cheeks pushed up by the grin that spread across his face. "That's when I began planning the last part of my takeover of the farm. My father was going to have to go."

"So, you pushed him into the combine? Made it look like he'd been drinking?"

"Yeah, that was easy. I gave him some sleep medicine. Just enough to make him off balance. He had mentioned earlier he needed to change out one of the blades. I snuck up on him while he was in the barn. I slammed into him knocking him onto the blade." Jason smiled broadly. "He was alive for about ten minutes. I stood over him and watched him die."

"Everyone in Waverly thought your parents were good people. Kind and caring. Never turned away someone in need." Dillon smiled faintly at him. "As a matter of fact, most everyone has said your parents aren't to blame for the way you turned out. Everyone seems to think you must be a bad seed."

Jason clenched his hands into fists pulling against his handcuffs. "They don't know anything about my parents."

Dillon made a note on her pad before she lifted her gaze to him. "Tell me about your mother."

Jason's lips pulled tight with tension. "Listen, my mother was a fucking idiot. She believed that since she provided sex to my father, she had power. Like most of you women." His lip curled. "You think because you spread your legs and allow men to fuck you, that gives you the authority to tell everyone what the hell to do. My father was weak. He let his heart and his dick give her permission to make major decisions. She walked around the house like she owned it. My father put in all the hard work. He milked the cows, kept the farm running. She fucked him, fed him, and cleaned up after him. That didn't give her any power."

"When your mother became pregnant, how did you feel? It must have made you jealous?" Dillon scribbled on her pad.

Jason frowned at her. "Jealous? Jealous of what? An embryo? No, I wasn't jealous. When I heard Dad and her talking about it after we moved into the new house—I knew what I needed to do. We didn't need a baby in the house. They had me, which should've been enough for them. They were selfish and thought only of themselves—I was going to have to take matters into my own hands."

Jason shifted his weight. "I had to wait to do it. Mother needed to be farther along in the pregnancy for my plan to work." He scooted his chair back. His arms stretched out against his restraints. "See, my dear, sweet Mother pranced around every day. Singing and humming. Always rubbing her stomach. Her and my father spent endless hours thinking of names. They would ask me what name I wanted to call my little sister or brother. I played along. Offering suggestions, never intending to let the pregnancy get that far."

"How old were you?" Dillon asked.

"I turned twelve when my mother was three months pregnant. We had a small get together with a few other family members. Some of my aunts and uncles and their kids. They all lived an hour away. Everyone was so thrilled about the baby. *The baby* this, *the fucking baby* that. Jesus; I was so sick of hearing about the baby. It was my birthday party, and everyone cared about a child that would never be born.

"I waited until my mother was six months along. My father was out in the field. I'd just come home from school. Mother told me to clean my room if I wanted to go to my friend's house the next day. I'm in my room cleaning when she comes in yelling about something I had forgotten to do."

Jason leaned on his elbows. "She should've been cleaning my room. Cleaning was her job. Cook, clean, fuck my father and leave me the hell alone. That woman always had something to bitch about. She couldn't be satisfied. Like most fucking women."

Jason sat back with a sneer on his face. "A piece of the rug at the top of the stairs had come loose. She tripped on it several times in the past. I loosened it and re-tacked it creating a bigger bump. For weeks, I waited for her to trip on the damn thing. I hoped she wouldn't be able to catch herself before she went head first down the stairs. That day, as she left my room, I called out to her just as she got to the landing at the top of the stairs.

"I wanted to distract her. She turned back to look at me and caught her foot on that part of the carpet. I ran to help her," Jason paused. A feral smile crossed his face. "I pretended to trip and bumped into her, causing her to go right over the edge of the stairs. I watched her tumble down hoping she would break her neck."

Dillon's skin crawled. Excessive amounts of saliva filled her mouth. He spoke as if he were recounting a movie he had just seen. Her throat tightened making it hard for her to swallow. "Her fall caused her to lose the baby. Chief Winsley said she was never the same after that."

Jason had a satisfied smile. "Nope. Poor old Mother never got over the loss of her unborn child. Of course, I ran to the bottom of the stairs." Jason mocked Dillon with a frown. "I was so upset. I cried and screamed for my mother. I called the office at the dairy farm and told the secretary to call Dad. Not too long after, Dad busted through the door with a few ranch hands. An ambulance came and off she went. She spent the week in the hospital."

Jason's eyebrows crinkled together. "They had to do some kind of operation on her to get the baby out. She was a mess. Of course, I played up the whole troubled and frightful son and cried a lot. For a while, my dad and I became closer. That didn't last long."

Dillon tapped her pen on the table. "When did you start poisoning her?"

His lips formed an evil grin. "When she came home from the hospital, she was a different woman. She didn't bitch at me like she used to. She never wanted to be alone with me." Jason sighed. "She still managed to fuck my father. They grew closer together.

"When I turned sixteen, I realized that if I was going to gain control of the farm, I had to get rid of my parents." Jason scooted his chair closer to the table. "I added antifreeze to her drinks and food. Occasionally I mixed in a minimal amount of rat poison. Only enough to make her violently ill.

"She became sicker and sicker. I thought she would never die. She lingered on and on. Even in death, that woman was a pain in my ass. No one suspected anything, so no tests were done. I think, deep down Dad knew—but he didn't want to face it. He couldn't prove anything. After she had died, my father and I grew apart."

The soda Dillon had been drinking now churned in her stomach. She couldn't take it any longer. She didn't care if he won. She had to get out of there. They had what they needed to find the other missing girls. The local police and Feds would recover all the bodies. Dillon stood and gathered all her belongings. She didn't look at Jason even after he slammed the table with his hands.

"Where the fuck do you think you're going, you bitch?" Jason barked at her. His nostrils flared. "I'm not done." Jason tried to move away from the desk; the handcuffs yanked him back. "You're supposed to stay until I'm done talking."

"No, you fuckwad. That wasn't the deal. The deal was you give us info," she waved the envelope in front of his face, "and you get to go to the prison of your choice. I never agreed to your whims." Dillon tilted her head glaring at him.

Jason ground his teeth as his jaw clenched. "You like being a bitch, don't you?"

She leaned in close to him. "It's something I live for." Dillon reached the door. She turned back to him. "Guards tend to forget about special directions for privileged prisoners. It's happened before. They let you out when the general population is out in the yard or the shower. Make sure you keep looking over your shoulder, Jason. Just because you got a cushy cell to yourself doesn't mean you're safe. Some big nasty man with a preference for farm boys can still get his hands on you." She walked out leaving Jason screaming at her.

The DA and the Director met her in the hallway. "Do you think that was the best way to handle him?" Director Fitz asked her.

"Listen, I told you how this was going to go down. That fucker in there can't back out of his deal." She handed the envelope to DA Peppers. She started down the hallway. She turned back to the men, "I wouldn't look at the contents of that envelope if you've just eaten."

CHAPTER EIGHTEEN

Joe leaned back against the seat and Damien's head rested against the steering wheel. Without lifting it, he glanced over at Joe. "You want me to drop you at your house, or you want to go back to the station? Since Dillon isn't home, I'm going to get this report done."

"I'll go to the station with you. My truck is there, and I have court in the morning. At eight." Joe's eyes remained shut.

"I forgot you had that. This is a preliminary hearing, right?"

"Yeah. I'm betting after this hearing the asshole will plead out." Joe stared out the window as Damien drove back to Central. "What did you think of Myra's little outburst?"

Damien chuckled. "I think Myra is in love with Father Ricin. Oh hell, I understand their frustrations. Here you have a priest, who wasn't happy. He asks for help from the bishop, who slaps him down. So, he continues with destructive behavior."

Joe cocked his head to the side. "You ever want to be a priest?"

Damien frowned. "Hell no. My mother would've loved for me to become a priest. Hell, I'd be canonized by my family if I chose to go to Seminary. Oh man, there is no way I could give up sex. No way. I don't care how wrong it is to have it before you're married."

Joe chuckled. "You got that right brother, I never understood why priests had to be celibate. I'd think not having sex would make you batshit crazy. I guess having a relationship would be a greater distraction from leading God's flock."

Damien ran his hand through his hair. "While you're at court tomorrow I'll speak with the captain and try to convince him to get us in to see the bishop." Damien paused. "How's this killer finding out about these priests?" Damien looked over at Joe. "I think it's got to be someone with access to the records of the priests. How they are getting the information, I have no fucking clue. If we could ever get in to see Bishop Cantor, we may get some kind of lead."

Damien pulled into Central's parking garage. Joe got out and went straight to his vehicle. Damien headed up to his office. Shift change had just occurred. Only Detective Jenkins sat at his desk. "Hey, Jenkins, why the hell are you still here?"

Jenkins shifted his gaze from the computer to his Lieutenant's face. "Hey, Lieutenant just finishing up this damn report. I sent Davidson on home. He's got a wife and kids. Only one of us needs to do the paperwork."

"Did you guys track down your witness?" Damien asked as he sat on the corner of Jenkin's desk.

"Sure did. He was in hiding at one of his sister's houses. I don't think I've ever seen someone involved in a crime so happy to see us."

Damien shook his head. "I don't understand."

"Seems our husband killed his wife and her father for the insurance. Idiot husband tells our witness, his buddy, if you help me out and be my alibi, I'll give you some of the money."

Jenkins took a drink of his soda. "While the husband is waiting for the insurance to pay out, he decides he didn't want to share his insurance money anymore. The minute the buddy sees us, he spills all the beans. Said he's safer with us, thinks the husband is out to get him. The DA put him in holding. He's deciding what charges to level against him and what not to for his testimony. The asshole husband is down at County Jail. We tracked him down at his girlfriend's house."

Damien tried not to laugh. Jenkins' New York accent was still very thick. "How long you been here in Chicago—what like five plus years?"

Jenkins frowned at his Lieutenant. "I think. Why?"

Damien smiled at him. "You think you would've lost that Brooklyn accent by now."

Jenkins leaned back laughing. "How the hell do you think I get laid so much? The chicks dig this accent."

Damien shook his head laughing. "Well, damn good job, even if you haven't mastered the English language yet." Damien studied the case board. "You aren't on call tonight, are you?"

"No, Lieutenant, just finishing up this paperwork." Jenkins typed again.

"Go on home, Jenkins. You can finish it up in the morning." Damien rose to go to his office.

"I'm almost done here. How's about you let me come in later in the morning?" Jenkins stared at Damien with one raised eyebrow.

Damien bobbed his head back and forth. "Sure. Be in by ten. Text Davidson let him know he can have it too."

"Hot damn. Thanks, Lieutenant." Jenkins went back to typing, whistling while he worked.

CHAPTER NINETEEN

Damien sat at his desk, intending to start his report. Instead, he pulled the photo of the dead priest from St. Constantine's and put it next to Father Mandahari on his murder board. Two priests. Two sinners. One a gambler and one a womanizer. Mandahari cleaned up his life, gave up gambling and devoted himself to the priesthood. Belgosa asked for a break, didn't get it and continued having sex with women. It didn't seem to matter to the killer that one priest had straightened up. The fact the priests had fallen from grace is what had doomed them.

Damien wrote Bishop in the center of the board and moved the pictures to either side. He researched the second verse left nailed to Belgosa's chest. This referenced leadership, which could be the leadership of the priest or the leadership of the Catholic Church.

Pulling his phone from his pocket, he needed to make one quick call. "McGrath."

"Hey gorgeous, are you coming home anytime soon?"

"I'm on my way now. I should be getting there around ten-thirty."

Damien heard the strain in her voice. "How did the visit go?" He asked.

"Umm—about that. We need to talk about it, but I don't want to get into it over the phone. We'll discuss it when I get home."

"Alright. When you get home then. Now you sure you aren't too tired to drive?"

"No, plus I want to sleep in my own bed with you. You've spoiled me. What am I going to do when I have to go out of town for an extended amount of time?"

"I'll buy you a teddy bear." A smile crept across Damien's face.

Dillon giggled on the other end. "Wow, won't that do wonders for my career? Traveling with a teddy bear. How'd your day go?" Dillon asked.

Damien sighed. "Another priest was killed this morning. The killer slit his throat then left him in a confessional. Stuffed a whole bunch of communion wafers down his throat. Oh, and get this, his pants were pulled down, and his hand gripped his *pene*. Can you guess what his sin was?"

Dillon laughed on the other end of the phone. "I shouldn't laugh—the picture that popped into my head was way too funny. Oh man, it's been a long day. I'm guessing sex addict?"

"Close enough. He had sex with several women of the parish. Didn't try to hide it either. I'll fill you in on all the details later. Oh, so listen—Camilla called me today. I told her you were moving in with me, although I haven't told her your name. I told her my girlfriend was moving in with me. Joe thinks she may be coming unhinged."

"Well don't tell her my name. I don't want the crazy bitch hunting me down. Do you think she's coming unhinged, or just jealous and regretful?"

"Beats the shit out of me. I believe she expected me to take her back by now, and I believe she's shithouse crazy. I don't believe she's violent or going to try to take one of us down. I do think she'll try to break us up. She'll try to put me, maybe even you, in a compromising situation."

"Hmm. So how do you want to handle her? I'll do whatever you feel is the right thing to do."

"I don't think we have to do anything. I just wanted you to be aware, and if she continues to call me, I can talk to Captain Mackey and see what he thinks is the best way to handle it." Damien sat silent for a moment. "To be honest, I think when she sees us together, she'll see it's over. I think in her head she thinks there's a chance. Maybe that's all it will take."

"I'm not sure about that Damien. For months now, she has tried to spend time with you. You don't have anything to worry about at least where I'm concerned. There's nothing your crazy ex can do to make me not trust you. Let's not worry about it. We can cross that bridge when we come to it. Although, right now she has no idea you're seeing a Federal Agent. She may think I'm a regular girl. This could play in our favor. We could use that against her."

Now it was Damien's turn to laugh. "Let my FBI girlfriend fight my battles with my crazy ex-girlfriend. Talk about a blow to my manhood."

"You know what I mean. Don't worry about Camilla."

Damien pinched the bridge of his nose. "Okay, I'm finishing up this report. Then I'm heading home. I'll see you when you get there. I love you."

"I know. Bye."

CHAPTER TWENTY

Mackenzie couldn't believe how easy it had been to take care of Father Belgosa. Entering her spacious living room, Mother's ashes beckoned to her from the mantle. Standing in front of her picture, Mack ran through the events of the morning.

"Mother, I've begun the purging of the Catholic Church, of those who are not performing God's will. Today I took care of Father Belgosa. He slept with women! He had no regard for breaking his vow to serve God in a pure and clean way." She shimmied and cackled. "I left him in the confessional. After all, he needed to confess for all that sex he had. The man couldn't keep it in his pants."

She placed her finger on her bottom lip. "I should go after the whores he slept with, too. Some of them were married. They didn't care about their vows of marriage." Her eyebrows wrinkled together. "No. It's not the time to take care of whores. Their time will come."

Mack skipped to the kitchen. Taking the jug of orange juice from the refrigerator, she took a long drink. "Mother, I also took care of Father Mandahari. He worshiped money, and gaining fortune took the place of his pastoral duties.

"I have several more priests who must be removed from the bosom of God. Especially Father Martin. He didn't help when he could. He had such an excellent opportunity to help you, and he didn't." Mackenzie frowned at Mother's picture. Her tone softened. "I know you cared for him. I know how attached you were to him, but he fooled you. I'm sorry Mother. I know it's hard to hear."

Mack spun around with her arms outstretched. Joyful giggles bubbled out. "Oh mother, this is working out better than I dreamt it would. I have a special place right under their noses. Sometimes I stay there at night. That's why I haven't been here all the time, Mother. You can understand though. My secret place keeps me close to Christ. These men are so stupid. They should never have been put in their positions. They don't deserve to lead a flock."

Mackenzie giggled. "And guess what? I read the emails of someone vital to the church. His private emails. This person has a few bad habits of his own. He acts like he is such a pious man. He is nothing more than a pompous fool. His time will come. He has been too busy doing things for his satisfaction and pleasure. He hides behind his status and position. He lies to the entire Church congregation. But I know his secret."

Mack spun several more times in the center of the living room. "My work with the Archdiocese has afforded me unlimited access to their files and their property. God has given me this position. He blessed me and this task. He has entrusted me with the job of purging the evil which has tried to gain a toehold in the Church. He will protect my journey, Mother. Soon, soon, I promise, your death will be avenged, and God's grace will be restored to His Church."

CHAPTER TWENTY-ONE

Damien walked in from his garage. Coach sat right in front of the door with a scowl on his face. Damien peered at the fat furball. "What's your problem? I have a job, you know. How else am I supposed to keep you in prime kibbles?" Damien reached down and scratched Coach's head. "C'mon, I'll give you one of those cans of tuna you live for."

As if Coach understood every word, he ran ahead of Damien and spun in circles as he waited for his kitty bowl to be filled.

Once fatso was satisfied, Damien grabbed a glass of whiskey and headed into his office. He placed the pictures of the Belgosa crime scene next to Mandahari's picture. He sat at his desk and put his feet up. Staring at the board, he studied everything he had so far. Damien had a decent idea of what the killer wanted; he wanted to run it by Dillon.

Damien felt there was a personal element to these murders. A specific connection to someone and it had everything to do with the Catholic Church. Even though he hadn't narrowed in on the person, he was sure it would lead to the bishop or end with him.

Damien re-read the verses left at the second crime scene by the killer. The first verse addressed the sin. But it was the second one that piqued Damien's interest—it addressed the leadership. Damien pulled out a Bible from his desk drawer. Opening to 1st Timothy, he found the verses the killer had combined to make his point.

The verses all referenced serving God. Those who are in a position of teacher or preacher have a greater responsibility to fulfill the word of God. Teachers must keep themselves in favor with God. If they sin, those sins will hinder the message from God to the flock. The leaders of the church are tasked with an even greater responsibility.

They must make sure those who teach are living God's scriptures, and not sinning. *How can you teach God's word if you are not living your life as Christ did?* The priests led the flock astray by their actions. The killer believed the Church had a responsibility to weed those priests out. Instead, the Church had allowed them to stay in a position of authority.

Damien placed his notes alongside the two scriptures on his murder board. All that time in Religious Education was paying off. He sat back and stared at the pictures on his board. Either of these priests could be replaced with another who had sinned. The sins were the binding factor. Not the priests. We all sin every day; these sins, however, interfered with the priest's ability to lead the flock.

He looked at his watch. Nine-thirty, it wasn't too late. He dialed a number.

"Father O'Connor."

"Father, it's Damien. Sorry for such a late call."

"Damien Kainetorri. You haven't been to Mass these last few Sundays, lad. Where have you been?"

Damien smiled. "I know Father; my job has had me out of town a few of those. The others—well, I need to come to confession for those. I promise I'll be at Mass. However, I'm calling for another reason."

"Your mother tells me you have a new lady in your life. She says she is the perfect lass for a daughter-in-law."

"Yes, I have a new girlfriend. I'll bring her with me to Mass so you can meet her. Listen, Father—I can't tell you anything, but I need your help."

"It has to do with these horrible murders, doesn't it?" Father O'Connor asked.

"Yes, it does. How hard would it be for someone to get information on priests? I mean personal stuff; like any problems they've had or trouble they might be in. Is that information pretty hard to come by for the average person?"

Father O'Connor sighed. "Priests aren't perfect, lad, as much as the Catholic Church would like everyone to think. We are fallible. There are those who get into trouble. Or put other priorities ahead of their duties as a leader of the Church. When one of us has a slip in our walk with Christ, Bishop Cantor keeps track of the incidents. He's the, for lack of a better word, Chief Bishop. He handles the discipline of the priests in the Diocese. If the offense warrants a slap on the wrist, nothing may come of it. If it is something which could cause a problem for the Church, then written reports are kept."

"Father, do you know if the reports are done by hand or kept on the computer? You've seen his office; you know how it works."

"Damien, have you called Cantor's office and asked them about this? I'm sure if they realized you think these priests are being targeted, they would surely assist you."

"Fat chance. I've already had my ass chewed because I've tried to get a meeting with Cantor. Two dead priests aren't enough to warrant a sit-down. Please tell me what you know. I won't let anyone know how I acquired the information or that I received it from you. I'm sure some-one is targeting priests because of information in those records."

"I'm not worried about what you tell anyone. I'm saddened Bishop Cantor hasn't put forth more effort to help. I'll tell you what I know."

Damien sat and listened as O'Connor explained the inner workings of the bishop's office. He needed to figure out a way to use this infor-mation to his advantage and protect O'Connor at the same time. "Father, I can't thank you enough for taking the time to speak with me. There is another reason I've called you. Please be careful. If you have a regular routine, please do something different. Don't be alone. At least not until we catch this guy. Don't take a meeting with anyone new, at least not alone. Please promise me."

A hearty laugh came over the phone. "Damien, you aren't implying I'm a filthy sinner with a nefarious habit that may get me killed, are you?"

"No. Unless this killer knows the way you cheat when you play chess. I don't want anything to happen to you. One day when I marry this girl of mine, I need you to do the ceremony. Please be safe. Promise me, Father?"

"Yes, my son. I promise. I will not be alone."

Damien hung up the phone. Father O'Connor had given him an ex-cellent understanding of how the bishop's office kept records on the priests. All of it kept on the computer, no paper trails. The killer had either mad tech skills or worked for the Diocese. O'Connor also ex-plained the power and authority Cantor had. He acted as the archbishop's assistant, taking care of most of the daily workings of the Diocese. Rumor had Cantor pegged as the next Archbishop. Damien needed to speak with Joe to figure out the best way to approach this.

The house alarm buzzed. Someone had activated the garage door sys-tem. In five minutes or less, the door should rise. If it didn't, Damien had an intruder. The garage door opened with a special control. Once pushed, you had three minutes to key in a four-digit code or the system locked down the house. Within two minutes the system made a sound, announcing the code had been entered. Dillon.

The door opened from the garage. Coach bombarded Dillon with his meows. Damien walked into the living room to find Dillon holding the cat in her arms. "Seriously, you treat him like an actual baby. Hugging him and cradling him. It's disgusting."

"He is my baby, my fat furry baby. If I ever leave you, I'm taking him with me. Plus, you're just jealous." She smiled at him. She kissed the cat and placed him on the floor. She put her arms around Damien's waist. "You, however, are my other baby. The one I like snuggling so much more." She kissed him. She could taste the whiskey on his tongue and wanted more.

She sank into his arms. The kiss deepened. She wanted to forget that interview with Jason. Wanted to block it out of her mind. She needed to erase those pictures of Beth. Dillon grabbed his hair as she ferociously kissed him. As his hands slid her jacket off her shoulders, Jason's memory slowly faded. Damien unbuttoned her shirt. He pulled it off her arms. She returned the favor, making quick work of his shirt. She had all the buttons undone and was tearing it off him when he broke the kiss. His blue eyes, now indigo, stared at her as if she were his prey. Her heart stammered in her chest.

Damien quickly knocked her feet out from under her and brought her to the ground. He pulled off her shoes and yanked her jeans down. Damien got one pant leg and her panties off at the same time. He shimmied out of his own pants. He unsnapped the front hook of her bra and pushed her legs apart. Damien checked, making sure she was ready. His fingers slid easily in and out of her.

Damien pushed into her, filling her. His breath hitched as he slid into her warm, velvety opening. She met each of his thrusts. Her legs wrapped around him as her hands grabbed his ass. Her muscles clenched around him. Damien's pulse echoed in his ears. Dillon begged for him to go faster. Harder. He raised up on his knees and pulled her hips into him. She arched her back as he thrust into her. She called his name and mumbled something he couldn't understand.

Warm liquid coated the length of him. His own climax burst from him. Dillon's muscles contracted around him, milking every ounce of fluid from him. Damien stayed buried within her for a few moments. Dillon's body glistened with a light sheen of moisture. Her arms rested at her sides.

Damien eased himself from her sheathing. The movement bordered on painful. She was so tight it was like extracting himself from a vice.

He lowered himself onto her and placed his head on her chest.

Dillon wrapped her arms around him. "You still have your pants on."

"Sorry. I couldn't get my shoes off. I had to leave them on." He laughed. "Damn, Dillon, what have you done to me?"

"Me? How's this my fault? All I did was kiss you. You decided to flip me on the floor and fuck my brains out. I think I feel them running out my ears."

"You did more than just kiss me. I couldn't help myself. This primal urge came over me, and I couldn't wait."

"Hmm. It's okay. I'll let it slide." She giggled as she pushed him off her. "You're heavy. Roll over."

"I don't think I can move."

She gave up trying to roll him off. Instead, she ran her fingers through his hair. She had needed this. Dillon closed her eyes, blocking the memory of those photos as best she could. They stayed like that a few moments longer. Damien pushed himself up onto his knees. He looked at her still flushed skin. He watched her breasts rise with each breath.

"Quit looking at me like that."

"Like what?"

"Like you want to eat me."

"I do." His eyes traveled the length of her body. "You're gorgeous like this. With your legs spread apart. Wet and ready, beckoning me to ravage you again."

Dillon rose on her elbows. "Pull my pant leg off so I can stand up. Please."

He frowned at her. He lifted her leg and pulled her pants off. He stood pulling his pants up. He held out his hand and pulled her off the floor. He smiled at her as he pushed her hair out of her face. "I'm glad you're home."

"Hmm, I bet." She walked naked into the kitchen and grabbed a beer from the fridge. She took several long gulps as Damien stood in the doorway staring at her. "You've got that look again."

"You're naked in *our* kitchen drinking a beer. I'm pretty sure I've died and gone to heaven."

"Are you done working or do you still have something you need to do?"

"Nope. No more work tonight."

She finished her beer. Placed the bottle in the sink and walked past Damien heading toward their bedroom. She peered over her shoulder at him. "Well, you coming or what? You're not going to make me shower alone, are you?"

"Nooo. I would never dream of letting you do such a thing. Did I tell you how glad I am you're home?" He followed her laughter into the bathroom.

CHAPTER TWENTY-TWO

December 1st
Thursday morning

Damien sat at his desk with his eyes closed. He shuffled the information in his brain around. As much as he loved his Catholic faith, he was becoming disillusioned by it. His conversation with Father O'Connor clarified that Bishop Cantor was aware the priests were being targeted when he had the ability to protect them.

Damien stared at the picture of the bishop's assistant, Anthony Marcum. This man and the bishop had the answers. Damien needed to figure out a way to get them to talk to him. Before he gave the captain his completed report, he needed to get Joe's take on a few things.

"Yo, Lieutenant." Joe entered Damien's office. "Hey, who's the new guy on your board?"

"Didn't you have court this morning?"

"I did; it got pushed out."

Damien nodded. "Close the door."

Joe's eyebrows wrinkled. "What's going on? You only shut that door when shit is about to fly around the room."

Damien stared at Joe's intense green eyes. "That guy is Cantor's assistant."

"Why is he on the board?"

"I spoke with someone last night. Got the low down on the way Cantor's office works. It stays between us. My informant explained that if a priest has a problem and that problem might cause trouble for the Church, then that problem is documented. Everything is kept on the computer."

Damien pointed to Marcum's picture. "The assistant set up the Diocese's whole computer system. My source informed me that in Marcum's prior life he had a job in finance, and had a reputation as somewhat of a computer whiz.

"All the parishes are linked. All personnel records are kept secure. Only this guy and Cantor have access to those records. Cantor handles the discipline of the priest. Now Captain Mackey had explained a little of this earlier to me. My informant made it clear that no one else would be privy to the information on the priests."

Joe's lips puckered as he nodded. "Do you think Marcum is involved?"

"I'm fairly certain this guy isn't our murderer. I can't see him doing this and bringing it back to the front door of the Church. Plus, I can't find any motive on his part. He has nothing to gain. From what my informant said, this guy was hired for his ability to clean up the Diocese and keep the scandals away.

"He's Cantor's right-hand man. You've got to go through him to get to Cantor." Damien placed his elbows on his desk. He lowered his voice. "My informant explained to me there are four priests with major issues. Issues which have been documented."

Joe's mouth hung open. "Son of a bitch. You're telling me we have at least two more priests that can wind up dead, maybe more?" Joe pulled at his hair as he ran his fingers through it. "That means the bishop knows two more priests are in danger and he isn't lifting a fucking finger to help. Are you going to use this to get into see the bishop?"

"I want to. I also want to protect my source. Here's the thing, the Diocese uses an IT person. We need to find out who that IT company is, or who the IT person is. I'll approach the subject with the captain. See if this information will help me at least get an appointment with the assistant. This whole thing is bullshit," Damien said.

He leaned back. He interlocked his fingers and placed his hands on his head. "Because this case involves the Catholic Church, we are being stonewalled. They don't want the Church blemished, so they just want to sweep this shit away. I can't force anyone to do a damn thing. I can't even get Captain Mackey to go to bat for me without something substantial."

Joe took a handful of jellybeans. "Article 57 says you don't have to divulge your source. If this goes to trial, it can be called into question, and you can be compelled to relay this information. Are you willing to go that far? I'm assuming this informant is more than a CI, and I'm sure I know who it is. With that said, are you willing to bring this out if you must, knowing it can hurt him in the end?"

"He isn't worried. He's disappointed in Cantor's office. He feels they should be more invested in the deaths of two priests. Good men, good priests despite their problems. If it comes down to it, my informant will stand up. Although I'd rather not put him in that position."

Joe glanced at the picture. "Now, question number two. Have you used your computer to find anything on this guy?"

A sly grin filled Damien's face. "I may have researched him, and I haven't found a single thing on the man. He could've cleaned his record, but I don't think so. If he was that good, I'm damn sure he wouldn't be working for the Catholic Church. I think he's smart, and I think he knows a lot of damaging secrets about this Diocese. I pulled up what information I could get on the Diocese. I found no mention of an IT company, but my source assures me they use one."

Joe leaned back in his chair. He dragged a hand over his face. "Bloody fucker." He grabbed another handful of jellybeans. "Here's my suggestion, now that I'm in this bloody bog with you. Give the assistant's name to ECD. Have them run an official check on him as well as everyone in the bishop's office. There is no reason you shouldn't have that done. There are dead priests, you need to run everyone associated with them to rule them out. Put that in the report. Leave Father O'Connor out of it altogether. Why did you call him anyway?"

"I knew he'd tell me the truth. More than that, I wanted to warn him. I don't want anything to happen to him."

"*Christ on a bike.* Let's get a list to ECD. Let's run the priests from the churches, the secretaries, and the maintenance. Let's throw in the assistant and direct office personnel associated with the bishop's office. You think we can throw in the bishop's name?"

"Are you fucking nuts? Our asses may have a few chunks taken out as it is. I think I can swing the running of the names, though. I'll take the heat. The captain said we couldn't interview anyone from the Diocese. He didn't say we couldn't run their names. Don't worry. Once the captain chews my ass, I'll chew yours. That's fair." Damien smiled as he drank the soda he brought in with him that morning.

"You just want a reason to put your mouth on my ass. I'll drop my pants so you can kiss it anytime." Joe made smoochie sounds as a knock rattled the door.

"Come on in," Damien yelled.

Joe rose, heading for the door, "I'll get right on those names, boss."

Damien frowned at the title. "Make sure ECD has all those we discussed. Put in a call to the lab and see if they have anything new to report."

Officer Ivanski stood in the doorway. "Hey Lieutenant, you have a Father Ricin here; he has a lady with him says he needs to speak with you."

Damien turned to Joe. "You need to stay for this. Bring them in." Damien motioned to Joe to slide the board cover over the pictures of the dead priest.

Father Ricin walked in with an attractive older woman. She was small in stature but lean with muscle. Her ebony black hair hung around her shoulders. Damien could see the beach through her Caribbean blue eyes.

Damien held out his hand. "Father Ricin, you didn't have to come here, I could've come to you. Please have a seat."

Father Ricin's faint smile seemed pained. "Margarete wanted to come in here. I contacted her late last night, and she wanted to come and speak with you. I'm here to offer moral support." The father glanced at Margarete. "Go ahead, tell him what you said to me. Tell them everything."

Margarete made the sign of the cross and mumbled what Damien thought was a blessing. She blew out a shaky breath and glanced between the two men. "I went to confession yesterday. I go every Wednesday morning. I like it because it's quiet, and you don't have to wait long. I got there about nine-thirty and noticed a young man sitting in the pew nearest to the confessionals. It seemed unusual. Most waited on the benches right near the confessional for their turn." She fidgeted with the purse she held in her lap.

Damien wanted her to relax. "Take your time Margarete. You're not in any trouble."

She smiled at him. "*Gracias.* There were two people ahead of me as I walked to the bench. One person went in leaving the other gentleman and myself. The gentleman sitting with me was older maybe in his sixties. He smiled at me, but we didn't speak.

"While I waited, I kept watching the young man in the pew. He seemed out of place or as if something wasn't right. I can't explain what bothered me about him, but something seemed off. Anyway, he sat there stone-faced. No looking around. Simply staring at the statue of the Blessed Mother.

"My turn for penance came up, and I went in to see Father Belgosa. When I exited the confessional, the young man had moved to the altar where you light a candle for someone who died. He knelt there for a few moments. Then as I left the area, I moved to a seat in a pew to pray. That's when the young man went into the confessional."

"Can you tell me about what time did you leave and notice the young man was still in the confessional?"

She tilted her head to the side as if she contemplated the question. "I guess it was right around ten-fifteen, definitely not past ten-thirty."

Damien spoke in a calming soothing tone. "Margarete, can you describe the young man to me? Let's start with basics. But before you start, I want you to close your eyes and take a few deep breaths. I know you're nervous, and I want to calm your nerves."

Margarete regarded Damien and Joe. "I'm sorry for my nervousness. When Father Ricin called me, I was so scared. The thought that I may have seen the man responsible for the death of Father Belgosa has me rattled. I spent the night worrying that he would find out who I was."

Damien noticed the slight tremble in her hands. "Margarete, you don't have anything to worry about. We don't even know if the man you saw is a suspect. As of right now, he is just the last person to see Father Belgosa alive. You don't have anything to fear. Now, close your eyes. Take a deep breath and think back to sitting in the pew and watching the young man. Describe the front of the church to me."

Margarete sat with her eyes closed. Her breathing slowed the more she relaxed. "The candles around the altar were lit. Several of the prayer votive on either side of the church were lit as well. They created a soft glow. The *flores* from Sunday's service still sat on the steps of the altar."

"Excellent. Now tell me what the young man was wearing."

Margarete's eyebrows crinkled together, then relaxed. She took several deep breaths. "I remember he seemed young, early twenties or mid-twenties. Not over thirty. His hair was a little long but not shaggy or dirty. It came to the top of his shoulders. He looked like he had a thin mustache, almost like he was trying to grow a goatee. He wore a thick winter coat. Heavier than the temperature called for. He wore basic blue jeans and tennis shoes. Nothing fancy about them." She opened her eyes and inhaled a deep breath of air.

"That was great, Margarete. Can you guess how tall he may have been? Did you notice anything about his walk when he stepped up to the confessional?" Damien asked.

She sighed. "He wasn't tall. I'm not tall, maybe five foot seven. He may have been my height or a little taller. The man was rail thin, though. That I noticed. The jacket seemed to engulf him." Margarete's eyes widened a little. "And he had small feet."

Damien glanced over at Joe. "Small feet?"

"*Si*," she said. "Now I realize that's what has bothered me. It struck me as odd."

Damien's head tilted to the side. "I don't understand, what do you mean by odd?"

"I'm sorry. I'm not explaining this *bueno*." Margarete glanced over at Father Ricin.

He reached took her hand in his. "It's okay, Margarete. Take your time. Tell the lieutenant everything you remember."

Margarete patted the priest's hand. "Nothing looked natural. I mentioned that something had bothered me about the man, but until now I was unsure of what it was. His feet were *poquito*, they just seemed too small. He was skinny, and the facial hair didn't look real. I had this fleeting thought like he was hiding. You know an umm—what do you call it?"

"A disguise?" Damien asked.

"*Si*. He looked like he tried to hide. He never looked at me, and he kept his head down or turned away. At the time, I thought he was embarrassed about being at confession. Sometimes it is hard to perform the Act of Penance. To go before the priest and bare your soul, and to have someone see you, can be intimidating." She turned and smiled at Father Ricin.

Damien relaxed in his chair. "Is there anything else you can remember?"

She shook her head. "No. I've nothing else. If I think of anything, I will come to you."

Damien rose and came around the front of his desk. He reached out to take her hand in his. "I can't thank you enough for coming in today. Tell me this before I let you go—have you seen this man before?"

"No, *señor*. I have not." A slight blush came to her cheeks, as she looked Damien in the eye.

"Thank you, Margarete and Father Ricin, for your help. I'm grateful to you both." Damien and Joe shook both their hands. Damien leaned out his door, "Officer Ivanski, take them down and see them out." Damien turned toward the two, "if you think of anything, please let me know." He handed both one of his cards and walked them to the elevator with Officer Ivanski.

When Damien returned to his office, Joe had slid the cover back to the side of the murder board. He'd written the description of the young man to last see Father Belgosa alive. "What did you think of that?" Damien asked as he sat at his desk.

"The description won't help us one bit. The guy used a disguise. The one thing I garner from it, he is small and thin. No wonder he uses the chloroform. What he lacks in strength he makes up for in planning," Joe said.

"Go give those names to ECD. I'm going up to the captain's office and see if I can get in to see him."

"You got it," Joe said.

CHAPTER TWENTY-THREE

Damien stepped into Captain Mackey's outer office. His receptionist, Catherine, guarded the captain's inner sanctum like a devil guard dog.

"Hello, Lieutenant Kaine. How may I help you?" Catherine didn't stop typing, she just cocked an eyebrow at him.

"Does Captain Mackey have a few moments?" Damien smiled, knowing it would have no effect.

"The captain is a busy man. You should've called first." She continued to type. "Just a moment." She picked up the phone. "Yes Sir, Lieutenant Kaine is here to see you. Yes, Captain." She turned toward Damien. "Go on in."

"Thank you, Catherine."

The captain sat behind his desk, a huge monstrosity he'd brought with him. The word around DC was he brought this desk with him everywhere. He'd acquired it in the Marines, and the battle scars on it showed its age. Captain Mackey didn't look up as he waved Damien in. "C'mon in Lieutenant, have a seat."

The captain's desk was one of the largest Damien had ever seen, and yet the captain still dwarfed it. Damien wasn't sure if he should say anything or wait for Captain Mackey to speak first. He sat and waited.

The captain studied Damien's tired face. Mackey understood this man took all his cases to heart, living and breathing them. He interlocked his fingers and rested his hands on his desk. "So, Lieutenant—what can I do for you?"

Damien stiffened. He had yet to figure out what to say. He could lie, but that would get him in trouble later. "Sir, I'd like to ask your permission to arrange an interview with Cantor's office. While I understand questioning the bishop may not be acceptable now, I would like the opportunity to interview his assistant, Mr. Marcum." Damien sat and waited to be questioned.

"Why?"

Fuck. Damien gripped the arms of his chair. "Sir, two priests were murdered. I have reason to believe more will die. I also have reason to believe the bishop's assistant could help us narrow in on a suspect."

"Why and how?"

Fuck me. "Oh hell, Captain, c'mon. If two people had been killed from a local business, we would be interviewing all the people who worked there, had business there, or who took a dump in the bathroom there. Why is this situation any damn different? Because some arrogant SOB feels he's above questioning by the police?" Damien tried hard to rein in his annoyance and frustration. He didn't need to be slapped back because of his attitude.

Captain Mackey scrutinized his Lieutenant. "You're not telling me everything."

Fuck, Fuck, Fuck. Damien hung his head. "Okay, I have a CI. He has knowledge of the inner workings of the bishop's office. He's informed me that when a priest has a problem, depending on how poorly it will reflect on the Church, the bishop decides what course of action is taken.

"If the problem will embarrass the Diocese or the Church, then the priest gets a permanent record in his file. This way the bishop has a way of showing he dealt with the problem and took advances toward making it go away. The assistant set up the current Archdiocese's computer system when he came on. He hired an IT person to handle the day-to-day concerns, but he and the bishop are the only ones with access to the files of these priests.

"My CI has informed me that four priests had files like these. He had no idea the identities of these priests until two were murdered. If we can get the names of the other two priests, we may be able to set up protection, or sting, or something that might save their lives. At the least, we should be able to interview the personnel who have access to these files or opportunity to gain access to these records." Damien sat still again, trying to bring his heart rate under control.

Captain Mackey knew Damien would come up with a way to force the office of the bishop to answer questions. "I assume you don't want to release the name of your CI until it becomes necessary? I mean I'm assuming this is a priest we're talking about?"

Damien nodded. "Yes, Sir. He has no problem with his identity coming out. However, I see no reason for Bishop Cantor to know about him. If this information comes into question, my CI is more than willing to come forward."

The captain crossed his arms over his chest. "Have you ever met the bishop's assistant?"

"No, Sir. I have not."

"Well, I have. I can tell you this, he has a stick so far up his ass I'm surprised he can walk. The few times I've had the pleasure of being in a meeting with the tight ass pecker head, I've wondered how much trouble I'd be in if I pulled said stick out of his ass and beat him with it. From some of the people I've had private conversations with, I'm damn sure I wouldn't be prosecuted. The guy is an asshole to the tenth degree."

Mackey dragged a hand down his face. "Damn it." He pushed his intercom button. "Catherine, call the office of Bishop Cantor, ask his fuckwad of an assistant when he'd have time to speak with Lieutenant Kaine and Detective Hagan regarding the matters of the dead priests. Catherine, if he squawks do that thing you do."

"Do you want me to involve the chief if need be?"

"No, leave that to me. I'll call him in a few and fill him in on the case. Give me fifteen minutes before you call the pecker head."

Damien's eyes widened as his mouth curved into a tentative smile.

The captain displayed a wide grin at his Lieutenant's reaction. "I bring her with me to every assignment. She is one of the few women I can speak my mind in front of. You know she was my civilian secretary in the Marines, and trust me when I say I believe my men were more scared of her than of me."

Damien shook his head. "No Sir, I had no idea she was with you in the military."

Mackey laughed. "She hates the little pecker head more than I do. Listen, Damien, I can sense your frustration. This case is eating at you. You cannot let this asshole sense that. He's an arrogant little gnome, and he will stick his pointy little hat up your ass if you let him. Do whatever you need to do to put yourself in a calm place before you go in to see him. Keep your questions non-threatening. Make him think he's doing you a favor. I'd almost say bring that beautiful, calm FBI Agent you seemed to have charmed along with you, but I'm sure he's a eunuch, so she would have no effect on him.

"Don't tell her I called her beautiful, she'll kick my ass," he smiled an evil grin at Damien. "How is that going by the way? Not that I care about your love life."

Damien chuckled. "She and I are doing fine. She's moving in with me, so I haven't pissed her off that bad yet."

"Hmm, interesting. I'll make sure the chief is aware of what's going on. You'll get to ask the workers questions, get their take on things, I'm gathering you think this is an inside job, or someone is feeding the information to someone."

"Yes Sir, that's what I think. We have a description of the person last seen with Father Belgosa before his death. I believe this person is using a disguise. Once we get to talk to some of the workers at the Archdiocese, we may be able to narrow in on someone there or associated with someone there. Thank you for your help." Damien rose and waited for dismissal.

Captain Mackey leaned back in his seat. "There's no telling how long it will take for his highness to grant you a sitting. As soon as Catherine gets a date and time, I'll have her call you. Now get the hell out of here and get your ass on the job."

CHAPTER TWENTY-FOUR

Damien strolled through the bullpen, heading to his office, "Joe, when you get a minute get in here." Damien sat at his desk. He had no idea when he would get a sit-down with the assistant, and he needed something on this damn case to break.

Joe stepped in. "How much of your ass do you have left?"

"Surprisingly, all of it." He reached into his jellybean jar and took out a handful of the colorful beans. He handed some to Joe. "The captain has had a few meetings with the bishop's assistant, and he can't stand him. The captain said he's an asshole with a God complex. Did you get anything new from the labs?"

Joe swallowed his mouthful of candy. "You know that medal, the Dymphna medal left at the first scene? Well, the ME found another one inside Father Belgosa. Once the ME removed the Hosts from his mouth and throat, he found it stuffed inside. There's no way to trace the Hosts. I spoke with Father Ricin, and he said none were missing from the rectory. If the killer didn't get them there, he had to bring them with him. I checked on how easy it is to purchase Hosts. You can buy a box of a thousand on the internet from different retailers. No telling how many other places you can buy them from. They aren't blessed, of course."

Damien frowned. "I don't think the killer cared if they were blessed. I want to know what the Dymphna medal represents."

Officer Katie Baker knocked on Damien's door. A young officer, just a few months out of the Academy, her youthful appearance and voice made her the perfect officer to use when he needed a young cop to make a suspect think he was getting away with something during an interview. "Yes, Officer Baker, what's up?"

"I'm working with Alvarez and Hall on the floater case, they're out searching the addresses for the family members, and I got a strange hit on one of the men from the boat. I wanted to involve ECD, but I wanted to let you know first." Officer Baker looked at her feet.

"What did you uncover?" Damien waved her in and pointed to the chair next to Joe.

"I'm not sure. I pulled up all the family's business blog pages. Each of the men contributed to it, and it linked back to the salvage business. I thought maybe I could find out some extra information to help the detectives narrow down where the families are hiding. Anyway, before the murders, the members of the family corresponded back and forth quite regularly. They commented on various family and business stuff. I got the feeling it was more for business than family, kind of like a promotional tool. The posts were made to look like a casual conversation, but it reads like a promotional tool."

Baker's eyes darted between Joe and Damien. "Umm—ever since they went into hiding, there've been condolences and that kind of thing, but I noticed a few weird entries on their website pages. It looks like gibberish. I think it's some sort of code." She handed a few pieces of paper to Damien. His fingers brushed against hers, and she prayed she didn't blush.

Damien studied the postings. "What kind of code is this?"

Baker shook her head. "I'm not sure. This is a snippet of a longer posting. The postings started not too long after the men disappeared. Once they were found dead, the postings became more abundant. You can see this conversation has a rhythm, even though it doesn't seem to make any sense. They use a lot of pictures and combined text that almost seem random. I believe something is going on. I think they are using this to communicate."

Damien handed the papers to Joe. "I know pig latin, that's it. My sister used to make me speak it all the time. I think you might be onto something. Do you know if they spoke a different language? Maybe they're combining it with English."

"No Sir, I don't. I wanted your permission before I proceeded to involve ECD. Travis is working on the rest of the stuff for Alvarez. I thought I would take it to him."

Damien stared at the attractive young officer. "Take everything to Travis in ECD and tell him your theory. Maybe you guys can come up with something."

Officer Baker stood to leave, she got to the door when Damien called her name. "Officer Baker, damn good catch. Damn good."

She beamed a smile at him lighting up her face. "Thank you, Lieutenant."

Damien stared at Joe. "Let's hope it leads to something. She may have found out how to track them down." He turned toward the board. He looked back at Joe. "What do you think about Baker?"

Joe gave him a shit-eating grin. "I think she has a crush on you."

Damien gaped at him. "I've never encouraged her. I don't flirt with her—ever."

Joe giggled at him. "*Relax the cacs*, man. I didn't say it was because of anything you did. You don't see it, but the rest of us do. When you're out there giving a briefing, or talking to us about a case, she has googly eyes when she stares at you."

"Googly eyes? What the hell does that mean?"

"Listen why are you freaking out? She's a kid. She's an overachiever, and she thrives on praise. You saw her face just now."

"Well, I don't want her googly eyes on me. She's young enough to be my little sister. That's just weird."

Joe roared back in laughter. "She is like twenty fucking two you know. She is of legal age to have sex."

"I don't want to talk about Baker and sex." Damien turned back to the board. "Did you get the names to ECD?"

"I sure did. Travis said they would have something for us by this afternoon if not by first thing in the morning. Where do you want to go?"

Damien checked the time. "I'm hungry. Let's go to the Diner Grill and get something. Then we're going over to Father Belgosa's room at the duplex. I know CSU has gone over it and taken his computer, ECD is working on that now. I want to go through his personal items. I want to get a feel for the guy from his stuff."

CHAPTER TWENTY-FIVE

Damien used the keys from Father Ricin and opened the door to Father Belgosa's quarters at the rectory. The two priests shared the duplex. It had a central area and kitchen. Each priest had their own private living space which included a small living room, bedroom, and a private bathroom.

Joe and Damien searched in silence at first. Rummaging through someone's life was hard enough, rummaging through a priest's personal belongings seemed almost sacrilegious.

Damien moved things around on a shelf. "It doesn't look to me like Father Belgosa entertained here. Having a roommate in such close quarters, I don't see it."

Joe stopped and surveyed the surroundings. "I haven't ever seen a priest's living quarters. It's almost—normal."

Damien gawked at Joe. "What does that even mean? 'Almost normal.' They are men, you know. It's not like they're some kind of aliens."

"Shi—miny crickets, they're not normal. Any man who voluntarily gives up sex is not normal. And lest I point out, Father Belgosa couldn't even honor that commitment. Which makes him—normal. I hope God understands this. I mean He should. He friggin' created us in His image, so I think He knows what we crave. I don't understand how He could punish Belgosa for being a man."

Damien stood with his mouth agape. In some warped way, Joe sounded almost philosophical. "Wow, have you been watching those late-night talk shows again?"

"No, you fool. I'm just saying." Joe moved to the desk area. Nothing. No hidden drawer or secret cubby hole.

Damien had moved into the bedroom. A nightstand sat next to the bed. He pulled out the top drawer, he shut it. Pulled it back out, then shut it again. "Hey, I got something," he yelled to Joe.

Joe walked into the bedroom. He observed Damien pulling the drawer in and out. "Okay dingleberry, it's a drawer. You pull out, you push in."

Damien scowled at him. "Shut the he—just shut up and come here." Damien pulled the drawer out. "Look," he pointed, "the drawer has a false top and back." He set the drawer on the bed. A box had been built into the drawer. If you pull the drawer out to get something you might not notice it was shorter than it should be. It took him a minute to figure out the compartment slid open.

Joe nodded. "Well, hot damn. Oh, crap." Joe made the sign of the cross for cursing. Joe watched as Damien removed the lid. A leather journal lay inside.

Damien removed the book. His stomach rolled as he thumbed through the pages. "Oh shit." He made the sign of the cross.

Joe stared at him. "What? What is it?"

Damien cleared his throat. His ears echoed the beat of his pounding heart. "It's a sex book. Belgosa describes each woman, and what they did when they were together. He wrote about each woman's home life, no names just descriptions. Oh, this isn't going to be good." Damien leaned into Joe placing his mouth near Joe's ear, "we need to make a copy of this. The minute the Church and Bishop Cantor finds out about this, they're going to take it. Let's get to my house. We'll copy it and then read it before we show it to the captain. I'm betting after he sees what's in here this whole fucking thing is going to blow up."

Damien bagged the book and tucked it in his waistband of his jeans under his jacket. He put the drawer back together and slid it back into place. They headed out and gave the keys back to Father Ricin. Once in the privacy of Damien's vehicle, he handed the book to Joe. "Start reading. Commit it to memory. As soon as we get to my house, I'll make copies and hide the jump drive."

Joe sat in silence as he read. "This reads like a how-to book. I had no idea a priest had such an imagination." Joe scanned through the pages. He felt his chest tighten. "Oh man—oh man, this isn't good. You know that interview you want with the bishop? I think you might get a private one on one sit-down."

Damien observed Joe. His face paled. Damien's fingers tapped his thigh. His pulse sped up. "What the fuck? Why?"

"Umm—it looks like Cantor may have participated in a sex party. This entry Belgosa made states he and the bishop attended the Catholic Conference of Priests and Bishops in Indiana last November."

Damien pulled into his garage. He parked and shut the door before he got out. "You're shitting me?"

"Do I look like I'm shitting you?"

"Let's get this copied. Then I'll call Mackey and request an immediate meeting with him, and you'll be going to that one."

"This is going to suck shitbags."

***

Back in the vehicle, Damien dragged his hand through his hair. "I'll give that jump drive to my brother Nicky. He can lock it up in the safe at Dad's house. This journal doesn't just complicate this case; it puts a whole new layer on what the killer may do. I mean, the killer knew Belgosa slept with women. I wonder if the killer also knows about the bishop. If so, this puts him square in the killer's crosshairs."

Joe continued reading. "Oh man, listen to this: *Tonight was awesome. There were two other priests and Bishop Cantor. The women we hired were professionals. They didn't know who we were. We hired them through an old friend of mine, he paid for them and gave them the address to the house. It was his house so if this ever gets out, he hired them for a party. He paid for the limo to pick us up. Nothing could be traced to our names.*

"*The five of us enjoyed more sex than a man has a right to. The evening started off with the women priming each other. Damn, I love watching women go down on each other. It's the most stimulating foreplay ever created. Once they had their fun and our dicks were hard, they made sure we were taken care of. We started off in the living room. Nothing like watching old Bishop Cantor pound a chick from behind. Who knew the man had it in him?*"

The acid in Joe's stomach churned at the sight of Damien's incredulous stare. "I feel so—icky. I mean, there is nothing even remotely titillating about this. What the hell's going on in the Catholic Church? Has Cantor lost his fucking mind?" Joe closed the book. "Damn I need a shower."

"I'm sure he had no idea Belgosa kept a diary of his sexual encounters. Does he name the other two priests?"

"Yeah, but he says they're from a parish in Indiana."

Damien pulled into Central's garage. He shut off the engine, and his chin rested against his body. For a moment, he forgot Joe sat in the car next to him. He prayed out loud, asking God for forgiveness for what he wanted to do to these men. He looked at Joe, who sat with a solemn look on his face. "Listen," Damien said. "I'm going to push to keep this out of the press. I don't want to deal with endless press conferences, and being asked about the bishop fucking a whore from behind."

"Oh man, not good. This is not good." Joe's head hung to his chest.

CHAPTER TWENTY-SIX

Catherine pushed them through the door. The captain sat behind his desk. He glanced up. His eyes narrowed, and he pursed his lips together. "Kaine did you not understand what I said earlier? You couldn't wait till the bishop's office called?"

Damien glanced at Joe, who looked everywhere but at him. "Captain, this has nothing to do with our earlier conversation, although I think it may propel Bishop Cantor to cooperate fully with this investigation."

Mackey glared at Damien. "Son, what the hell are you talking about?"

Damien and Joe sat in the two seats facing the captain's desk. Damien pulled the book from his waistband. "We went back to the rectory. We wanted to go through Belgosa's private quarters to see if we could find the names of the women he slept with, or maybe something pointing to a suspect. During our search, we found a hidden drawer and this book inside it."

Damien held the book out to the captain. "If you open up to the page I've marked. I think it will become evident what we have."

The captain snatched the book. He sat with his elbows on his desk, opened it to the marked page and read. His nose wrinkled, and he swallowed hard. "Mother fucking son of a bitch." He threw the book on his desk. "Who else knows about this?"

"Only us. Joe and I brought it here. To you. What do you want to do? What do you want us to do?"

Captain Mackey leaned back in his seat. He stroked his throat and grimaced. "Son of a bitch. What in fuck's name is going on at the Archdiocese? Do you think the archbishop is involved, or just Cantor?"

Damien shrugged. "I don't know. I really don't know."

Captain Mackey sat with his head in his hands. He pushed his intercom button. "Catherine, get the chief down here. Tell him I need him, and he needs to come alone and clear his day." Mackey glared at the two detectives. "Sit tight boys, you need to be here when I tell the chief."

Within a few minutes, Chief Rosenthal strolled into Mackey's office. He had a tall, lithe body, his dark hair highlighted by gray. Damien and

Joe both stood and offered the chief their seats. They remained standing.

"Mackey, you better have a damn good explanation as to what this summons is about. Clear my day and get down here? This better be good, or someone's head is going to roll down the corridor."

"Chief, I apologize for doing it this way, but having you come to me looks less suspicious."

"Less suspicious, what are you talking about?"

Mackey focused on Damien. "Lieutenant, explain to the chief how we got here."

"Yes, Sir." Damien took the seat next to the chief putting him at eye level. "Chief, I'm sure you're aware of the murders of two local priests. We have established the killer is targeting priests who have a sin or a vice of some sort—something keeping him from performing his duties as a priest—or at least it seems like that's what the killer is rationalizing.

"This afternoon we went to the most recent victim's living quarters. Turns out, he'd had numerous sexual affairs with women. We found a journal containing descriptions of the women he slept with. It also included explicit descriptions of the sexual acts."

The chief held up a hand stopping Damien. "Do I look like I give a shit fart if a priest is getting his wiener yanked on? Get to the point Lieutenant."

Damien reached for the journal. He handed it to the chief. "I think if you read the marked pages, you'll see why the captain has convened this meeting."

Chief Rosenthal grabbed the book. He turned to the marked pages. As he read all eyes were glued to him, each man trying to guess and gauge his reaction. His eyes narrowed. He looked up at the captain then turned to Damien. "Who else knows about this fucking book?"

"Just us. In this room," Damien said.

The chief hung his head. He stared at the cover of the book. "We can't bury this. However, we can give Cantor and Archbishop Jacobs a chance to get ahead of it." The chief pulled out his phone. He dialed a number. "Hey Robert, look I need you to clear your schedule now. And you're going to need to get Cantor into your office. I'll be there in about thirty minutes." The chief paused and pinched the bridge of his nose. "Listen, Robert, I'll be there in about thirty minutes, have the damn Bishop in your office. Send your other personnel home for the day."

Rosenthal hung up the phone. "Lieutenant, get that fancy vehicle of yours and pull up out front. The captain and I will be down in ten. Do not repeat a word of this to anyone."

"Yes, Chief." Both Damien and Joe exited leaving the two men alone in the office. Damien overheard the chief curse and ask for a shot of whiskey.

Joe texted Taylor. She had arrived that morning instead of Wednesday night and finished her meeting earlier than expected. "Looks like I might as well ride home with you. Taylor is helping Dillon move a few things to your place. I'll have Taylor take me to Central in the morning. Those two together scare me—there's no telling what they will get us involved in."

"Ha, you got that right. Oh hey, my dad is having his gala on December seventeenth. I'm assuming you want to bring Taylor. Will she be up that weekend?"

Joe gawked at him. "Of course, it's her I want to bring to the shindig. She is my main squeeze, just not my only squeeze. However, I'm not excited about wearing a monkey suit."

"Hey if I have to wear one you have to wear one."

"Where is it going to be? The Governor's mansion?"

"No, it's at the Waldorf. Dad says he's lining up a super cool band. One we won't want to miss. I haven't told Dillon; I'll tell her tonight, so don't mention it."

"Who's he inviting?" Joe asked with a smile.

"The entire squad, the captain, the chief, I told him to invite ECD. I know Cantor was going to be invited. I texted Dad letting him know what was up. He may or may not invite him now." Damien looked over past Joe out his window. "It's show time."

The chief and the captain climbed into the vehicle. Chief Rosenthal tapped Damien on the shoulder. "Don't use the lights and sirens. I don't want to draw any extra attention to us. Do you have the book, Lieutenant?"

"Yes, Chief. No one will see us walk in with it."

The chief squinted at Damien in the rearview. "I know what you want to ask me. Yes, I'm going to let the Archbishop and the bishop read the whole chapter concerning that damn orgy the bishop had. Under no

circumstances will they get to keep the book. If you have to arrest someone, so be it, but the book will leave with us. I'll lock it up in my safe.
We will not discuss it until the need arises. Hopefully, we can keep this
from leaking out into the media. If the Church," the chief made the sign
of the cross, "tries to screw us in any way, that book comes out and goes
into the general evidence. If it is needed, as it pertains to this fucking
case, it will be made readily available."

The ride to Archbishop Jacobs' residence remained uncomfortably
quiet.

CHAPTER TWENTY-SEVEN

The four men exited the SUV. Damien tucked the book into his waistband. As they stepped up to the front doors of the Archdiocese, Damien shivered. The temperature must have dropped ten degrees.

They entered the foyer of the massive building. Ornate and beautiful, with enough baroque thrown in for good measure. A statue of the Blessed Mother cradling the baby Jesus stood in the center of the floor. Directly behind her, raised high, hung a huge cross with Jesus on it.

Archbishop Jacobs came out and greeted them. Surprise and concern washed across his face. When the chief ordered Jacobs to be available, Damien was confident he didn't expect an entourage to show up.

Archbishop Jacobs glared at the chief. "Chief Rosenthal, I assume there is a reason you so rudely ordered me to be here with Bishop Cantor. I pray you've used your authority wisely."

Rosenthal's eyes narrowed in on Archbishop Jacobs. "Listen, Robert, I'm not here to make nice." He pointed at him, "you have a huge problem, and you and Cantor are going to have to deal with some things when we leave, but first you need to hear Lieutenant Kaine out." The chief looked at Damien. "Lieutenant, tell Cantor what you're going to need from him regarding the case you are working on. Save the rest till I say."

Damien nodded. "Archbishop Jacobs, Bishop Cantor—as you are aware, we're investigating the murders of two Diocese priests. I need to interview the people in the bishop's office, and I need the names of all employees—full-time or part-time and volunteers—with access or the ability to gain access to the personal records of the priests. I will also need a list of all priests who have been counseled concerning possible behavior that may have warranted a write up by you. I..."

Bishop Cantor held up his hand. "I don't think that will be happening. Archbishop, there is no way these men will be allowed access to any such information. I may concede to giving them interview privileges as well as an employee list. They have no right to know what priests may be dealing with in their personal spiritual walk." Bishop Cantor remained seated in front of the archbishop's desk. His legs were crossed, and he inspected his nails as he waited for everyone to be dismissed.

Damien stared at the pompous ass. Before he could say anything, the archbishop spoke up.

"Chief Rosenthal, you have no authority to ask for such records. I'm under no obligation to supply them to you, either. So, I'm sorry you've wasted your time and mine with this nonsense. I think it would be best if you leave this facility."

The chief glowered at his friend. "You and I go back a long way Robert. I knew you when you were a simple priest on the east side. Cantor, I haven't known you as long, but I know I don't like you.

"Robert, you are about to hear something I hope and pray you have no previous knowledge of. I'm hoping my judgment regarding the kind of man and friend you are has not been wrong all these years." Rosenthal nodded to Damien. "Lieutenant read that entire passage from the book. Before you do, explain where you got the journal."

Damien reached underneath his jacket. "This afternoon my partner and I searched Father Belgosa's private residence. We..."

"This is an outrage!" Bishop Cantor stood. His eyes were wide showing the whites. He jabbed a finger in Damien's face. "You had no right or authority to do such a thing. That is the privately-owned property of the Catholic Church."

Before the chief or Captain Mackey could respond, Damien took over the meeting. He stepped up toe to toe with Cantor and looked down at him. "Listen, Bishop Cantor, you can spout that crap all you want. The Catholic Church is subject to the laws of this state and country. You do not have free rein to pick and choose what you are subject to. As for us searching Belgosa's residence, we had every authority to do so. His murder gives us access to his life, his property, his personal space. It is ours to search and do with as we please since we are trying to find his killer—something I would think the Catholic Church would be more than willing and happy to do."

Damien stood stiffly. He raised an eyebrow at the bishop. "Now sit down or stand up but do not interrupt me again. We searched Belgosa's residence hoping to find something that would point to his killer. We came across a secret drawer, and this journal was inside." Damien took heed of the bishop. His face had turned ashen. The tendons stood out on his neck, and his pulse throbbed. "As you are aware, Father Belgosa had a sexual preference for women. He engaged in several illicit affairs with various women in and out of the parish. And he kept detailed accounts of his encounters.

"Last year, he attended a conference in Indiana. I believe you participated in the same conference, Bishop Cantor. What I'm about to read to you is a written account of events from that trip." Damien again noticed the bishop's expression. The poor man was sweating profusely. Damien read the details of the party Belgosa and friends had attended. The particulars were stomach turning. It described in full detail what the two men had done and how many times and ways they did it.

When Damien finished the reading, Bishop Cantor's head hung to his chest. The archbishop sat in stony silence. Both Mackey and Rosenthal kept their heads down. No one took delight in the dismantling of this man's life.

Chief Rosenthal cleared his throat. "I don't know what you were thinking Cantor, but you're a disgrace. Now, you will turn over all the requested material to Lieutenant Kaine. I will guarantee none of the unrelated priest personal information will be disclosed. That snot-nosed bastard of an assistant you have wiping your ass will cooperate, or I will haul his ass into lockup."

"On what grounds?" Archbishop Jacobs asked, crossing his arms over his chest.

"On the grounds, he is a snot-nosed prick. As to this book," Chief Rosenthal held up his finger. "No. Do not even ask for it. I will keep it locked up in my personal safe. If it is needed for any part of this case, it will be produced. I have no intention of leaking this to the media. Nor does the captain.

"As for these two detectives, they're the two most trustworthy men on my force, and you should be on your knees before God tonight, thanking Him it was them who found this book. Or else you would be scrambling your asses to cover up the biggest fuck up to hit the Church in the last few years."

Chief Rosenthal stood and stretched his neck. The chief nodded at Mackey and held out his hand to Damien and Joe to head out the door. Before he walked through it, he turned back to the archbishop. "Robert, you need to clean this house. Sweep it and sweep it good. That is not a threat. It is a warning. Clean it well, my friend."

***

As they rode back to Division Central, no one spoke. Damien pulled to the curb. He turned toward the chief and the captain, holding the journal toward the back. Both men stared at it. Neither one moved for several moments. The chief reached up and took it.

"This stays between us. No one will repeat anything from this little field trip we took today. Damien, tomorrow you and Joe head over to that smug ass Bishop Cantor's office and gather everything you need. Set up whatever interviews you need to and question everyone. If that pinprick of a dick assistant, gives you a hard time, Shoot him. I'll clear it as a clean kill. When you meet him, you'll understand why I'm willing to look the other way on excessive force."

The door opened, and the two men stepped out. The chief hesitated, "if they give you a hard time, text me, and I will fix it. Do not call me, just send me a text." He handed Damien a card. "I meant what I said about you two. The archbishop and his sex-starved lackey are damn lucky it was you two who found this book." The chief slammed the vehicle door.

Joe's head tilted to the side. "What just happened? Did we enter the fucking *Twilight Zone*?" Joe asked.

"Oh yeah, 'the I fucked up my life twilight zone.' I almost felt sorry for Bishop Cantor. Almost." Damien half way chuckled. "Did you see his face as I read the entry? He wanted to crawl out of his skin. Or spontaneously combust."

"Well, Chief Rosenthal hates Cantor. I do feel sorry for his friendship with the archbishop. I got the feeling their friendship goes back quite a way," Joe said.

"Don't worry about meeting at the station in the morning. I'll pick you up at home, and we'll head over to Bishop Cantor's office. We'll get all that information and start interviewing who we can."

Damien pulled into his semi-private drive. Taylor's truck was parked in front of the condo. Another reason he bought this place, the garage and driveway area. Each condo had a semi-circle drive in front of the building, and the garages were large enough to accommodate two full-size SUVs. As his garage door opened and Damien pulled in, Dillon's beautiful red sports car was parked on the right side. "What happened to Dillon's car?"

Joe looked up to see a hell of a scratch on the driver's side rear panel. "I guess someone parked too close."

Damien wasn't so sure. Something settled deep in his gut.

CHAPTER TWENTY-EIGHT

Damien and Joe walked in the house to classic rock and roll and laughter coming from the kitchen. Boxes and furniture filled the living room area. They weaved their way into the kitchen, and there sat Coach, on the table, dressed in a Confederate army uniform. They fed him pieces of pepperoni and cheese from their pizza.

Joe laughed as he made his way to Taylor. "Seriously, you two should not be left alone." He kissed Taylor then turned and kissed Dillon on the cheek.

"Hey, you have a woman. Quit kissing mine," Damien said. He took Dillon in his arms and pressed his lips to hers. When he removed his lips, he cocked his eyebrow at her. "Did you get pizza and Chinese food?"

Dillon nodded. "We couldn't decide, so we got both." She undressed Coach, while Taylor set up the food on the table.

"That poor cat. Not only does he have to put up with it when Mrs. C. watches him, now he is forced to play dress up with you and Taylor," Joe said. "Hey, what happened to your car, Dillon?" He loaded up a plate with pizza, moo goo gai pan, and eggrolls.

She frowned and shrugged. "I don't know. I came out of work this afternoon, and it had a scratch on it. I called my insurance; they'll be arranging for it to be fixed. I called security, and they had nothing on the video. My current spot isn't covered by the cameras. I requested another spot right next to the stairs, so if someone does it again, I can catch them. I think someone pulled too close and hit me with one of their mirrors."

Dillon glanced around the table. "Seriously, it's nothing flagitious, it's just a scratch. If it happens again, then we can assume it's a problem. Alright?"

Damien nodded since his mouth was full. They ate and laughed. "Oh hey, my father is having his Christmas Gala this year. It'll be at the Waldorf on December seventeenth. You and Taylor will need fancy dresses. Taylor, Joe can fill you in on the details. I'm assuming you can come up for that weekend?"

Taylor sheepishly glanced at Dillon who nodded. "I don't think it will be a problem, seeing as how I'm moving up here at the end of next week." Taylor took a bite of her noodles.

Joe choked on his egg roll. After a minute of coughing, he cleared his throat. "What? I mean, why? No, I'm glad you're moving up here but—I'm a little surprised. What about your job?"

Taylor sighed. "I should've waited until we were alone to spring this on you. I'm not trying to ambush you; I'm just so excited. Director Jones put my name in to be considered for the administrator job at the Chicago lab. I was interviewed a few weeks back, and they offered me the job two days ago. I had to come and finalize the contract. I start in two weeks, so I'm here looking for an apartment, and then I'll be moving up here." She smiled and held her hands up. "Surprise."

Joe's heart pounded in his chest. The beat echoed in his head. He kept his hands in his lap because he didn't think he could prevent them from shaking. "Wow. You can stay with me until you go back to Springfield. I can help you find an apartment." He smiled at her. "I'm glad you got that position. I know you've worked hard for something like this. I'm proud of you Taylor."

Taylor exhaled the breath she held. "Tell us about the party. I love wearing dresses," she said.

"I forgot to mention, Joe, I reserved two suites for us, so we don't have to worry about going home. We can meet there early that day."

Damien caught the look from Joe. "Don't worry, it's my treat. This way the girls can get ready there, and we can ride the elevator down. No driving needed."

Dillon looked almost fearful. "Umm, I don't know the first thing about shopping for a dress. I've never worn a dress."

Everyone at the table stared at her. Taylor broke the silence with a snort. "Are you serious? You've never worn a dress?"

"No. Why is that so hard to believe?"

Both Joe and Damien shook their heads. Taylor's eyes widened and sparkled with amusement. "This weekend we'll go dress shopping. I have the perfect place. The boutique is small, the dresses won't cost a fortune, and they're stunning."

Dillon groaned as she took a bite of her egg roll. "I don't see why I have to wear a dress. A pair of pants and a festive shirt should be enough." She continued to scowl as she ate.

***

They finished the meal, and Taylor and Joe left. After a few minutes of clean up, Damien stood at the edge of the living room. "I didn't realize you had all this stuff. What's in all these boxes?"

She smiled at him. "I got all my stuff out of storage before I transferred up here. I'll go through it and figure out what I want and what can go. I'll have it done pretty quick, I promise. Before my grandparents get here for Christmas."

Damien shook his head. "Hello? That's less than four weeks away. Look, at the back of the garage, I have a storage area. You can load the boxes up in there and pull one out at a time and go through it. We'll get them put in by this weekend." He pulled his phone from his pocket. He texted Mrs. C. letting her know he got her a room at the Waldorf for the night of the gala. He also told her she could bring a friend.

"Are you texting your girlfriend?" Dillon asked as she came up behind Damien and wrapped her arms around his waist.

"Yes, and quit distracting me." He stuck his phone back in his pocket and turned toward her. "I can't wait to see you in a dress. You're going to look fantastic." He nuzzled her. "My God you smell good." He kissed her neck. His hand traveled up her back under her shirt. His fingers tingled as he skimmed her warm skin.

Her lips met his. He lifted her and carried her up the stairs to the bedroom. She giggled as she held on with her legs and arms. "I can walk up, you know."

"Hmm, I like the feel of you in my arms." He dropped her on the bed. He unhooked his badge and gun and placed them on the nightstand.

"Give me your foot," Damien said.

Dillon raised an eyebrow at him; holding out her leg. He pulled off her boots then her jeans. She sat on the end of the bed and lifted her arms so he could pull her shirt off. She reached behind her back and unhooked her bra. Dillon scooted closer to where he stood at the foot of the bed. She undid his belt and unzipped his pants. She tugged at his jeans. When he sprang free from the constraints of the fabric, she took the length of him in her mouth.

Dillon looked up at him as she dragged her tongue up and down his length. He stared at her with smoldering eyes. The intensity of the dark blue made her quiver. Damien threaded his fingers through her hair as he guided her head up and down. The way he reacted to her touch made her feel like the most desired women in the world.

She heard Damien whisper her name. His hips moved faster as her hand glided up and down. Her tongue and mouth teased every inch of him. Both of his hands gripped her head. He groaned as the first of the salty liquid coated her tongue. He called out her name as his orgasm ripped through him. He exploded in her mouth. She swallowed every drop, sucking him dry.

Damien pulled himself from her mouth. She looked up at him, her lips swollen and pink. He pulled her up and held her in his arms. "My God Dillon, if I wasn't in love you a minute ago, I am now."

She chuckled. "You're so easy."

She stood before him in a pair of pink panties and nothing else. His eyes raked over her. "You are so incredibly beautiful. How did I get so lucky?"

"Fate." She slipped past him and entered the bathroom.

***

Curled up in bed after he made love to her, she relayed part of what happened in Springfield. "We got busy, and I forgot to tell you," she said.

He sat up and turned on the light. "How the hell could this happen? Your director didn't even tell you about it? Have you talked to him yet?"

"Slow down, Andretti. No—I haven't spoken to him yet. I needed to calm down before I had that conversation. I plan on speaking with him in the next day or so."

Dillon sighed. "I had the envelope, it had all the papers with notes on the locations of the girls. There was no reason for me to stay. But I knew if I left, he would be able to say he got to me. I couldn't let that happen. So, I sat and listened to him describe with great glee the killing of his parents. I finally couldn't stand it any longer. When I left, he was furious. I handed over the file to the DA and walked out."

Damien pulled her into his arms. "He wanted to fuck with you. You were the only woman to slap him down. He knew making you sit through that interview would bother you." He lifted her chin. "You have to promise me you won't keep this stuff in next time. You promise me?"

She looked at him. Guilt slammed into her. She hadn't told him about the pictures. She wasn't sure why. "I promise." She snuggled in next to him. "You know, when I speak to my Director, I may say something I shouldn't, and you'll have to support me because I'll have no job."

He kissed her. "No problem. I'll make sure you're barefoot and pregnant."

"Oh God. I'll find another job. Quickly. How was your day?"

Damien filled her in on the bishop deal. He didn't tell her about the copied book. The fewer people who knew about that, the better. It had nothing to do with not trusting her, and everything to do with this nagging feeling he had to protect her.

"Hey, I'm going to have my brother retrofit your car. He's going to put in bulletproof glass and paneling, as well as bullet-resistant tires. I've been thinking of doing it to your vehicle, and now with this scratch, I believe it'd be prudent."

She raised up on her elbow and looked at him. "You're apprehensive about this. Why?"

"I'm not sure. I feel like this is more than a mere door ding. Plus, we do this for all our vehicles. I did it for Joe's truck. Let me do this for you."

"Oh baby, you can do anything you want for me. Take it to him whenever you want. I can always bring home a vehicle from the Fed's motor pool. Is there any reason you think someone is targeting me?"

"No. I just don't believe in coincidences. I think we need to be proactive."

Dillon leaned in and kissed him. "I love that you worry about me. Besides my grandparents, I haven't had anyone else care for me like you do."

"I couldn't imagine my life without you. If someone ever wanted to hurt me, all they would have to do is hurt you. That would destroy me."

"I still think you're making more out of this than is warranted. I mean, who could it be? I don't know anyone but you, Joe, Taylor, and people at Division Central. It can't be any of them."

Damien sighed. "I don't have any idea who it could be. Camilla comes to mind. I don't think she has snapped like that, and I don't believe she knows who you are yet."

"I guess if we are going to hypothesize, if someone is attacking me, maybe it is because they have a thing for you."

Damien sat up against the headboard. "Why would someone attack you if they had a thing for me? Wouldn't they at least let me know they had a thing for me first? No one has even flirted with me. Camilla is the only woman I know who has a thing for me."

"Well, you and Joe have been in the news a lot lately. Maybe someone has fixated on you, and they've seen us together, and they're jealous of my relationship with you. We aren't hiding our relationship so someone following you could surmise I'm with you."

Damien grabbed his phone and started tapping out a text. He noticed Dillon frowning at him. "I'm telling Nicky to come get your car in the morning. He'll bring one for you to use." He turned on his side and pulled her to him.

Coach jumped up on the bed and snuggled next to Dillon. She wrapped her arm around his fat belly. "I am the luckiest woman."

"Why do you say that?"

"Not only did I get you as a boyfriend, I got the sweetest warmest cat ever." Dillon kissed the top of the cat's head. His purring roared louder.

"Quit kissing the damn cat," Damien mumbled.

"You're just jealous."

CHAPTER TWENTY-NINE

Joe and Taylor rode in silence to his apartment. Once inside, she couldn't take it anymore. "Listen, Joe, I don't have to stay here this time. I can find a hotel to stay at while I search for a place. My car is here. I had Dillon pick me up earlier."

Joe turned to look at her. "I don't want you to stay at a hotel. I'm not sure why you didn't tell me you'd even applied for the position."

Taylor sat on the arm of the sofa. "I know you don't want a serious relationship with me. I'm trying to be okay with that. When I got the chance to apply for this position, I didn't think about anything else but the job. After I had interviewed for it, we had that talk, and you made it clear to me you didn't want a relationship—at least not more than what we have. I didn't want you to think I was trying to force your hand. I'm not going to beg you to be my boyfriend or not see other women. Even with me living here, I still won't do that."

She stood up and went to him. "I'll be honest Joe. I'm in love with you. I want more than this. I don't know how long I can continue this way. The thought of you having sex with other women drives me crazy. I hate it." Taylor had hoped by confessing her love for him she would elicit a reaction.

Joe rubbed his face. He didn't want to discuss this now. Between Damien harassing him and Taylor pushing him, the coil in his stomach tightened. A conversation would have to occur soon. He just didn't know if he'd be able to do it. He sat on the arm of the sofa and pulled her between his legs. "I care a lot for you. I'm just not ready to commit. It doesn't have anything to do with sleeping with other women. It's not you that I can't commit to, it's any woman."

Taylor was about to give in and follow him to the bedroom. But she couldn't. She'd had enough. She wouldn't wait for the scraps of love and affection he threw her way. If he wanted her, he would have to come to her. Taylor pulled away from him. "Well, I'm glad to hear it isn't just me." She started to gather her things.

Joe tilted his head to the side. "Umm—I thought you were staying here. Did I miss something?"

She stopped short of the door turning toward him. "Yeah Joe, you missed something. For someone as smart as you, you sure are acting like a dumbass. I can't—I can't do this anymore. I've already compromised so much of myself. I stood here and told you I loved you, and your response was you're not ready. When you are ready, you know how to reach me. I do love you Joe, more than I have loved any other man in my life. But I won't wait forever for you to choose me."

Joe stood at the door as he watched her load her stuff into her truck. The immediate sense of loss he had surprised him. "Wait, Taylor—stay. Please." He went to the passenger side of her truck. "Please stay, baby?"

"I'll be at the Ritz. I might as well splurge." She wiped a few tears from her cheeks.

"Please Taylor, I don't want you to go. Just stay."

"Bye, Joe." Taylor pulled away from the curb. She could see him standing in the middle of the street as she drove away.

CHAPTER THIRTY

December 2nd
Friday morning

Dillon rolled over as Damien reached for his phone. "No, don't answer it," she moaned.

"I wish. Kaine." Damien sat up. "Hello?" He glanced at the screen. Nothing. "Well, no one was there." He pulled Dillon into him. He loved the way she smelled—vanilla with a hint of citrus. "We have about an hour before we have to get out of bed."

"Hmm, well I'm awake now. I don't think I can go back to sleep." She wrapped her arm around his waist and melted into him.

He pushed her onto her back. "Well, I think I have an idea." He kissed his way down her torso.

She giggled softly as he kissed her stomach. "You have some of the best ideas."

Ninety minutes later they shuffled around the kitchen. Dillon made a quick breakfast while Damien fed the fatso cat.

Coach mewed at the sound of the can of tuna opening.

"All right already. Give me a minute." Damien emptied the contents of the can into Coach's bowl. The cat growled as he ate. "Listen to him. He's growling. As if his fat ass caught and killed the damn fish."

Dillon laughed. "He has to establish dominance somehow." She ate her eggs while standing. "When is your brother coming?"

"Not sure. If he isn't here before we leave I will text him to go to your work."

After breakfast, they headed out to the garage. Before opening the door, Damien checked the scanner. Making sure no one waited outside was a habit he got into after he installed the security system. As the door opened, he kissed Dillon goodbye and got in his own vehicle. He pulled out first and pulled away from the house when something caught his eye at the front door. He stopped his car and honked for Dillon to do the same.

She got out of her vehicle and walked to him. "What gives?" Dillon followed his line of sight. A box sat on the porch. "What is that?"

Damien glanced at her then back at the box. "I have no idea."

They made their way to the package. "It sure is pretty. Did you buy me something?" Dillon asked him.

He turned to her with no trace of amusement on his face. "No. I didn't."

Damien pulled his phone out. "Captain, we have a problem." He relayed the events of the morning.

"I'll get McMillen from the Explosive Ordinance Disposal Unit. He can bring the smaller bomb scanner out there. Don't touch it. We will have it scanned before we open it. I'll also have CSU out there. Who knows what the fuck is in that box. After the showdown yesterday in the office of Archbishop Jacobs, we don't need to take any chances," Captain Mackey said.

"I'm calling Joe now. Dillon is on the phone with AD Reynolds. Send a few officers to block my drive? I don't want news crews here. Thanks, Captain." After calling Joe, he turned his attention back to the box. This wasn't a bomb. No fun in that. Whoever left this wanted a substantial reaction.

Damien phoned his brother Nicky. After informing him of what had happened, Nicky said he would be there with some specialized equipment. He turned back to Dillon. She stood next to him looking at the box. "What do you think?" He asked her.

"I think someone wants our attention. Do you see a note attached?"

"No. I bet there will be one inside. This isn't a bomb."

Dillon bit her bottom. "Nope. It isn't a bomb. Whoever is doing this wants there to be some foreplay before the main event. Where's Mrs. C?"

"She is out of town until next week sometime. Thank God for that. I don't want anything happening to her. I'll check the security system. See if it picked up anyone approaching the door." Damien turned at the sound of cars. Two cop cars blocked the driveway. He met the officers and instructed them to let Joe through when he showed up. Under no circumstances were they to let anyone in without verifying who they were.

Damien grabbed his field kit from the back of his SUV. Back on the porch, he put on a pair of gloves and inspected the area. He pulled out an ultraviolet penlight. He found nothing out of place.

Dillon leaned against the porch railing. "You think this is Camilla?"

He stared at her. "I know she might be a little determined that she and I are getting back together, but I can't see her doing this. She's more the type to show up naked at my door. I can have two of my detectives check out her whereabouts for this morning."

A truck came down the drive. It was stopped by the police. Joe got out of the passenger side and walked toward them.

"Who was that?" Damien asked.

Joe shook his head. "My buddy Mark. He lives next door."

Damien opened his mouth, but Joe cut him off. "Don't ask me. I don't feel like getting a lecture from you." Joe peered at the box on the porch. "So, which one of you has the lover?"

They both pointed at each other.

Joe laughed. "Well, I'm not surprised. You think it's Camilla?"

Damien sighed. He wanted to know what the hell was going on with his partner but that would have to wait. "We were just discussing her. I'll ask Davidson and Jenkins to check on her whereabouts this morning. I'm also going to have Nicky check my phone—about five-thirty this morning, I got a call. When I answered it, no one was there." Damien turned once again to the driveway. This time the CSU van and the small Bomb Tech van made their way toward them. They were followed by two other vehicles.

Joe turned and followed Damien's stare. "Well, looks like the gang's all here."

Captain Mackey got out of his car, with Chief Rosenthal. Damien's brother Nicky got out of his vehicle too. Nicky stayed back with the captain and the chief. Crime scene techs waited at their van while the bomb squad guys made their way up to the porch.

"Hey, Damien. Hmm, got a girlfriend on the side huh?" Lieutenant McMillen was dressed in EOD tactical gear. His partner donned a bomb suit. McMillen smiled at Dillon. "I don't have other girlfriends, Dillon. I'm a one-woman kind of man. You know, if you ever want to dump this guy."

"I'll keep that in mind," she said as she smiled at the ruggedly handsome man.

McMillen turned to Damien. "We're going to put this in an x-ray box.

If it's a bomb, we'll know, and we can detonate it. If it isn't, you can have a CST remove it and open it up. Everyone, step back."

For the next few minutes, everyone held their breath. The Bomb Tech picked up the package and placed it in the x-ray box. Lieutenant McMillen focused on Damien. "It's not a bomb."

A CST reached in and pulled the blue box out and placed it on the ground. Everyone descended on it. Chief Rosenthal and Captain Mackey stood next to Damien, Joe, and Dillon. Everyone else stayed back a few feet.

The CST removed the lid. Tissue paper lined the inside. Carefully he reached in and removed the paper. Damien, who stood closest to the box, peered in. "*Santa Madre di Dio.*" Damien made the sign of the cross.

Dillon gasped. "Tell me that isn't what I think it is."

"Shit," Chief Rosenthal said. "We have a problem."

"Damien," Mackey said, "you and Dillon need some extra eyes on you."

The CST spoke up. "There's a note attached." He reached into the box and lifted out a human heart. A T-pin stuck through a piece of paper and pierced the heart. He read the note.

Sun or Snow, rain or shine
You will be mine
Forever Forever
You will see
You will be mine for eternity

Damien stared at Dillon. She had a frown on her face. "Really, your secret boyfriend is a fucking psycho, Dillon."

She snorted. "My boyfriend? How do we know it isn't one of those many girls you used to bang?"

Captain Mackey glared at them. "I will smack both of you. This isn't the time for jokes. Somebody is after one or both of you."

Rosenthal paced. Another car drove up the driveway.

"Well now, the party is really getting started." She smiled at the man who stepped out of the vehicle. "Assistant Director Reynolds. How gracious of you to join us."

"Cut the crap, Dillon. Tell me what's in the box." He snarled at her.

"Why don't you come see for yourself. It seems either Damien or myself has a secret admirer."

AD Reynolds moved next to the CST. "Oh, holy Mother of God."

"Hey, that's what Damien said." She shook her head. "Listen, I know you guys are freaking out. Yes, it looks like we have a very sick admirer, but getting our panties in a bunch over it will not figure out who it is. We'll have the lab examine the heart. How the hell we'll be able to trace it I don't know. I mean unless we have someone missing a heart show up unexpectedly and we can match blood or DNA. I'm hoping this doesn't become a regular occurrence. I don't want body parts showing up on my doorstep every week." She turned and walked into her home.

Captain Mackey rubbed his face. "Damien, do you think this has anything to do with your current priest killer case?"

Damien shook his head as he glanced over at Joe, who shook his. "No. I think these are unrelated. Look, Nicky is inside going over our surveillance video. He's also tracing a call I received on my phone earlier this morning. My father wants satellite recon set up. Nicky is working on that surveillance now. No one will know this place is being watched. Right now, getting the killer of these priests is my number one priority. That and the damn floater case Hall and Alvarez are on."

Joe laid a hand on the captain's shoulder. "Listen, Captain, Damien and Dillon will have surveillance 24/7. We need to get over to Cantor's office and get that information."

The CST came up to the group. "We're taking the heart and heading to the lab. The ME is waiting for us. We've dusted the porch, and we have reference prints. As soon as we have anything we'll notify you," the tech said.

AD Reynolds had followed Dillon into the house, and now he headed out to his car. Damien nodded as he walked by.

Chief Rosenthal addressed Damien. "Get over to the Diocese. There's no reason not to continue the line we discussed yesterday. We won't have anything to go on until we get results back from the lab. I guarantee the FBI have their guys all over this. And we know Dillon can figure out the head of this stalker. Damien, use your dad's resources to make sure your asses are covered. As soon as the results come in, I want to know. I also want to be kept in the loop if you guys start narrowing in on someone in this damn priest killer case. Mackey, let's get the hell out of here. You can buy me a coffee."

Captain Mackey stood at his car. "I want to know everything you get from the Diocese." He patted Damien's cheek. "This afternoon, I want an oral report."

Joe and Damien walked toward the house. They stood on the porch. "This is fucking crazy. Do you or Dillon have any idea who might be after you?" Joe asked.

"No. None. We'll talk about it later today. Let's go in and then get over to the Diocese," Damien said.

Dillon sat on the sofa. Coach sprawled out next to her. Damien kissed her. "I need to speak with Nicky, don't leave yet." He kissed her again. "Joe, come with me."

They walked into the office to find Nicky typing fanatically on a funny looking satellite computer. "Hey, bro. Just have to be the center of attention huh?" He laughed.

"Hell yeah. Are you setting up satellite surveillance?"

"Yes. This way you won't need human eyes on you. This house will be watched 24/7. We can watch from the compound too. This way if we see movement, we can call you. I'll be setting motion-activated cameras on your roof. They'll give us a 360-degree view. You have Mrs. C.'s keys, right?"

"Yes, she has a friend watching her dog. I can give them to you. Do what you need, I'll let her know when she comes home what we did to her house." Damien walked over to his filing cabinet. He pulled out the jump drive. "Nicky, I need you to put this in the safe at the compound."

Nicky took the jump drive. "Do I want to know what's on this?"

"No. Don't tell anyone; not even Dad I gave it to you. The less who know that drive exists, the better."

"No problem, Damien. Listen, I've got some kind of interference on your home security. It's almost like the person was attempting to jam the signal."

"Well, that would explain why my system didn't alert me to someone being on my porch," Damien said.

"Unfortunately, all I can make out is a shadowy figure. I can't tell you if it's male or female. I'll see if I can clean it up. I cloned your phone's SIM card and put it in this phone. You won't have any interruptions. All your contacts, phone numbers, and data, everything is the same. This phone, however, will track all calls. If you get any other odd call, the minute you hang up hit *99. That will put a backtrace on the call. It will also alert us." He handed Damien a second phone. "I have done the same thing with Dillon's phone. Give this to her. Make sure she doesn't leave before I speak with her."

Nicky continued to mess around on the computer. Damien stood and looked around the office. "Joe, you ready to head out?"

"Yup let's get to the bishop's office." Joe headed for the door. "Damien, I'll be outside when you're ready."

"I'll be right out." Damien walked over to Dillon and pulled her up to him. He held her tight as she clung to him. "*La Mia bella donna.*" He took her face in his hands. "You doing okay?"

"I'm a little rattled. It's different when the crazy is after you or someone you love, but I'm okay. SAC Marks is setting up a preliminary team. They're going to comb through a few of my cases and track some of the people I helped put away." She sighed. "Damien, my gut is telling me there's something we're missing. This feels like a new threat."

"Hey, we'll take this one step at a time. My family is setting up cameras and satellite surveillance. We'll be covered—at least here at the house." Damien handed the phone to Dillon. "My brother cloned this phone for you. He'll explain how it works. These phones have tracking systems on them, even if the phone is shut off, it will still work. Built-in batteries."

She pouted. "Now I won't be able to meet up with my boyfriend."

"Ha ha. Funny." He gave her a passionate kiss. "Joe and I are heading to the bishop's office. I'll check in on you. Nicky is taking your car and leaving his. Oh, one thing about these phones, everything is recorded, voice and text."

Dillon's eyes flashed with amusement. "Oh boy. Wait till I text you later. You should never have told me that." She started toward the office, glancing over her shoulder. "Damien, I love you more than I thought I could ever love someone." She winked at him.

CHAPTER THIRTY-ONE

Damien parked in front of Bishop Cantor's office. As they entered the building, a rat faced looking bean pole of a man ran up to them. Damien glanced over at Joe.

"You must be Lieutenant Kaine and Detective Joe Hagan." Marcum sneered at them as he checked his watch. "I expected you earlier this morning. I don't have all day to sit and wait on you two."

"We had an emergency this morning, but we're here now." Damien towered over the little man. "Mr. Marcum, we're going to need a list of all employees, full and part-time, as well as all volunteers who work in this office. The next thing we're going to need is the list of priests who have been written up for certain behavioral issues. I..."

Anthony Marcum rolled his eyes as he waved his hand dismissively in Damien's face. "I have that for you. The employee list that is. I have included this office and the Archbishop's. The archbishop has his own staff and personnel."

He handed a folder to Damien. "He has seven full-time employees. Three office staff, a house manager, a housekeeper, a chef, and one driver. Bishop Cantor has five full-time employees. Myself, one other office staff, house manager, a maid, and one driver. His chef is part-time. The maintenance man is full-time, but he covers the entire estate.

"I have included schedules and any meetings we have had in the last two weeks, along with who attended each meeting. We have three part-time employees. Two maintenance assistants and one gardener assistant, the archbishop's chef has a part-time assistant as well. The security is also listed. They are responsible for locking down the facility and the gates to the property and registering visitors.

"Everyone else on the list is a volunteer which includes our IT person and the florist. The IT person only comes in if I need assistance. Twice a week the florist delivers arrangements to both the offices and the residences. All contact information is included." Marcum glowered at Damien. "I will not give you the list of the priests. That is none of your business." He crossed his arms and deliberately raised an eyebrow.

Damien took one step closer to the man with the pointy nose and a sweeping forehead. Marcum's bright blue eyes darted between Damien and Joe. "You have five minutes to give me what I asked for." Damien checked his watch.

Marcum shifted from foot to foot. "I think you misunderstood. I'm not giving it to you. I've already spoken with Bishop Cantor and Archbishop Jacobs this morning. There's nothing you can do." Anthony Marcum stuck his nose up as he hissed at Damien.

Damien pulled his phone out. He texted the chief. He returned his phone to his pocket then sat on the corner of the desk. Within two minutes, Marcum's phone rang.

"Marcum. Yes, Bishop." Marcum sneered at Damien. Within seconds that look changed. His brow wrinkled, and he glanced between the two detectives. "Yes, Sir they're standing right here. No, Sir. I told you I didn't think it was appropriate. But... no, I thought... okay. Yes, I will."

Damien noticed the pasty pale color of Marcum's face. "Marcum, you look a little gray. You feeling sick?" Damien nodded toward Joe. "I think there's a bug going around."

"Oh, it's a nasty bug too. You might want to have the doc look at you," Joe said.

Marcum sat behind the desk. His fingers trembled as he accessed the computer and within a few moments, a document printed out. He handed it to Damien. "I trust you will maintain confidentiality with this list?"

"Of course. Can you tell me about the girl who does your IT?" Damien placed the list of priests inside the folder Marcum initially gave him.

"A young lady named Caroline Fredrick. She works for a computer software company here in the city. She's a programmer. Quite successful too. Her mother volunteered here at the Diocese before she died. Caroline wanted to volunteer after her passing, and we needed an IT person."

"How long has she been helping you out?" Damien smiled at him.

"Let's see. She did some work for us before her mother passed but she became more of a fixture after her death. I think about two or three months. That sounds about right."

Damien's phone signaled an incoming call from Dispatch. "Excuse me." He stepped off to the side. "Lieutenant Kaine." Damien stepped farther away from the assistant. "Kaine and Hagan en route. ETA thirty minutes or less." Damien's face showed nothing. "Mr. Marcum, I'll contact you in the next few days to set up some interview times. Maybe you can gather everyone here, and we can get it done all at once. Right now, my partner and I must leave. Thank you for your help in this matter."

Damien nodded at Joe as he walked to the SUV. "Son of a bitch. Do you know how close I was to shooting that fucker? I didn't like his ass one bit. What a prick head. I thought he was going to pass out when he received that call."

Joe chuckled. "I want to know what the chief did or said when you texted him, and who he did or said it to. I'm gathering we are going to another dead priest?"

"Fuck. At St. Xavier. Look on the list of priests. Is there one from this church?"

Joe pulled out the list. "No. There are four total on the list. The remaining two are John Michaliska and David Patterson." Joe continued to scan the sheet of paper. Michaliska is sixty-two and has or has had a drinking problem, and Patterson is gay, seems he has a gay lover."

Damien shook his head. "Well, who the hell is dead at Xavier?" He pulled into the church's parking lot.

Joe let out a sharp breath. "I guess we're about to find out."

CHAPTER THIRTY-TWO

Kaine and Hagan made their way up the steps of St. Xavier. Damien recognized the young police officer who stood outside the church. His eyes were wide, and his chin and lips trembled. "Hey, Officer Shelby. You feeling okay?" A slight smile tugged at Damien's lips. He remembered the first couple of homicides he covered.

"Oh hey, Kaine. Hagan. It's revolting in there. The killer caught Father Martin by surprise right in the foyer of the church. He beat him to death." The officer inhaled through his teeth, tears welling in his eyes. "I knew him. We were friends. We went to school together. He was only thirty-five." Shelby wiped the tears from his cheek.

Damien reached out and touched the officer's shoulder. "Go home, Shelby. I'll clear it with your commander. Check in at the precinct. I'll call your boss, don't worry." Damien nodded to Joe who called Dispatch.

Joe hung up his phone and watched the young officer walk away. "His commander okayed it. A couple more officers are on their way to cover the entrance."

They walked into the church, and the smell of blood permeated the entryway. "Fucking Christ," Joe whispered as he made the sign of the cross. "Forgive me, Lord."

Damien's stomach revolted at the sight in front of him. CST Roger Newberry stood off to the side while Dr. Forsythe hunched over the body. The doctor glanced over his shoulder and smiled. "Kaine, Hagan. We should meet over beers instead of dead priests. I think I have had my quota for the week."

"Really? I figured you had nothing else better to do." Damien pulled on a pair of gloves and booties and made his way to the body.

Joe picked up the broken candle holder lying next to the body. "This required a lot of force to do this kind of damage to this torch holder. This thing weighs a ton." Joe bagged it.

"Oh man, not much left of his head, is there? Where did it go?" Damien asked the ME.

The ME stood up and walked a few feet to the right. "The attack started here." He pointed to the wall. "You can see the cast off in this area. With each blow, blood and brain matter spattered everywhere.

The poor guy stumbled and fell where he lies now. The killer continued to strike him about the head and the upper body." The doctor raised and lowered his arm mimicking the movements of the killer. He pointed to the back row of pews. "You can see how far skin and tissue flew. This was a frenzied attack."

"I'm looking at this, and I don't see a reference to a sin. This looks like a rage kill. There is no note, either," Damien said.

Joe walked around the front of the church. He checked the first few rows of pews.

Dr. Forsythe studied the scene. "You're right. Rage fueled this kill. Once I get him on the table, I'll be able to tell you if your killer used chloroform, but I'm leaning toward no. I'm not sure if the killer hid and waited or if he walked in and found him. I'm not the detective, but I'd say this one had a personal connection."

Damien watched as Roger and the other tech collected all the evidence. "Who found the body? Do you guys know?"

Roger stood up from collecting brain matter off the floor. "Sister Webster. She's in the back with Father Cattaloni. She's going to need medication, I'm sure of it. We were here for about twenty minutes before you guys showed up, and it took at least that long for the wailing to stop." Roger wiped his chin with the back of his gloved hand. "How are you and Dillon doing?"

Dr. Forsythe turned to Damien. "Dr. Marshall is examining the heart. He's running every test he can on the damn thing. The lab techs are running every test on the box, and paper, and that pleasant note."

"Ha. Our stalker knows how to rhyme. We're okay. We'd be better if we could figure out who the hell it is." Damien looked at Joe, who stood in the middle of the aisle. "What you got, Joe?"

"You need to come here and look at the wall from this vantage point."

All movement in the church stopped. Damien, Dr. Forsythe, and Roger walked to where Joe stood. They turned and looked where Joe pointed. On the wall facing the altar of the church, the killer had left a note. It was different than the usual ones he'd left. This time, the killer wrote the note in the priest's blood.

Jeremiah 23:2

"Well, there's our note," Damien said.

Joe smirked at Damien. "No wonder you're the lieutenant. You're a regular genius. Do you know this verse by heart?"

Damien mouthed FU to Joe. "No, but hey we're in a church, and guess what's in the pew—a Bible." Damien thumbed through one and found the verse. "'Therefore, this is what the Lord, the God of Israel, says to the shepherds who tend my people: "Because you have scattered my flock and driven them away and have not bestowed care on them, I will bestow punishment on you for the evil you have done," declares the Lord.'"

Joe stared at Damien. "What's this guy's sin?"

Damien studied the verse. "I don't think it's a sin like with the other priests. I believe this priest neglected his flock. He didn't care for them like he was supposed to, so he had to be punished."

"Crap. What does that even mean?" Joe asked.

Damien frowned. "At this point, I'm not sure. Let's go talk to the other priest here and the other workers. Once we get an insight into Martin, this might make more sense."

CHAPTER THIRTY-THREE

Damien and Joe stood outside the door to Cattaloni's office. They listened to the muffled cries and sobs from within. Joe knocked and opened the door. Three people turned toward them. Damien stepped in and held out his hand. "Father Cattaloni, I'm Lieutenant Kaine this is my partner Detective Hagan. We need to ask you and the others a few questions."

"Yes, Lieutenant, I've been expecting you. Please come in." He gestured to two chairs at the far end of the office. "This is Sister Webster. She discovered Father Martin. The gentleman sitting next to her is Fred Hurst. He's one of our deacons." Father Cattaloni sat in his chair with an exasperated sigh.

"Sister Webster," Damien leaned into her. "Can you tell me what happened this morning before you found Father Martin?"

The nun's lips trembled as she stared at her lap. "I open the church every morning. I unlock the rectory doors and the offices. I turn on lights, get the coffee going, and check the appointments for the day. Father Cattaloni most often comes down from his quarters within the hour. Father Martin always walked through the church. He liked to make sure the pews were neat, and the confessionals were ready." Sister Webster let out a muffled cry. "I'm sorry."

"It's okay, Sister. Please take your time," Damien said.

"I walked out into the church. Father Martin stood at the altar. I told him that his first appointment was at nine-thirty. He smiled at me and said he'd meet me in the office in about ten minutes. The front doors opened, and a young man walked in.

"I didn't recognize him. Father Martin turned and started to walk down the center aisle. I heard the young man speak, but I didn't pay attention to what he said. Father Martin said something and stepped off to the side. I turned and walked back toward the offices. I didn't see Father Martin again until I found him about thirty minutes later."

Damien shifted in his seat. "Sister Webster, can you tell me about the young man? Can you describe him to me? Any detail, even if you think it seems minor."

Sister closed her eyes. "The man seemed young. Mid-twenties

maybe. Skinny, or maybe his baggy clothes made me think that. He wore an oversized coat, and his hair was shaggy. Or longer than a young man should wear it."

Damien scribbled in his notebook. "Did he have any facial hair, a mustache or beard?"

"I'm not sure. He stood some distance away from me." She closed her eyes again. Her forehead wrinkled. "That could explain it."

"I'm sorry, explain what?" Damien asked confused.

Sister Webster smiled faintly. "Did I not say? I'm sorry. He seemed so skinny with the baggy clothes, I got the impression he had some financial problems. His face looked dirty, but a thin mustache and beard would explain why I thought that."

Joe smiled at the older woman. Her eyes were puffy and swollen, and Joe wondered if they hurt as bad as they looked. "Sister, did it sound to you as if Father Martin argued with the young man?"

"Oh my," she said putting her hand over her mouth. Her eyes widened. "I hadn't thought of this, but as I turned to go into the hallway, the young man said, *you didn't do your job.* At least I think that's what he said. I stopped, and I almost went to the atrium to see if there was a problem. Father Martin placed a hand on the young man's shoulder when he spoke to him. I couldn't hear what he said for sure. It sounded like, *I did the best I could. I didn't know.*" Sister Webster fidgeted with her hands.

Damien nodded. Something nagged at him. "Sister Webster, did the young man seem familiar to you? Or did you get the impression Father Martin knew him?"

"Well, when Father Martin laid his hand on his shoulder, it impressed me he was familiar with the young man or at least knew what he was referring to. He seemed as if he was trying to reassure him of something. That's why I turned to go into the offices." Sister Webster wept.

Damien looked at the deacon. "Were you here at all this morning or did you get here after the fact?"

The deacon frowned. "I showed up after the police arrived. I've stayed here in the office. The officers didn't want anyone entering the sanctuary."

"Father Cattaloni, what were Father Martin's primary responsibilities?"

Cattaloni's eyes held pain and pride. A faint smile crested his lips.

"Father Martin was so young; he had such compassion. He worked with the families whose loved ones have died. He had a special way of making the families feel cared for at their most difficult time. The loss of a loved one is so hard. Father Martin cared for every member of this parish. I often told him he couldn't take on their grief. He could love them and give them comfort, but their grief was not his burden to carry."

Joe raised an eyebrow. "Have any recent deaths bothered Father Martin more than usual?"

Cattaloni reclined in his desk chair. His lips pursed together. "Fred, would you take Sister Webster to the chapel and sit with her? I'd like to speak with the lieutenant and his partner in private."

Fred put his arm around the sister and led her from Cattaloni's office. "Yes Father," Fred replied. "Sister come with me. We'll light some candles for Father Martin and pray for his soul."

Before she left the room, Sister Webster turned toward the detectives. "If I thought for one minute that Father Martin was in any kind of danger, I would've made my presence known. Maybe that would've made the boy leave." She leaned against Fred as they walked away.

Father Cattaloni braced himself on his elbows. After a moment of silence, he spoke. "I didn't want to discuss private matters with them in the room. It just would be inappropriate to do so."

Damien nodded. "I appreciate your concern. Please tell me what you know."

Cattaloni sighed. "Father Martin had a unique calling. He often dealt with individuals who were deeply troubled. He'd recently begun working with three women. All three were widows. They wanted to form a woman's group, specifically geared toward older widowed women entering their golden years alone. The women felt the church played a huge role in providing comfort and care. They wanted to give these women a sense of purpose."

Father Cattaloni removed his handkerchief from his pocket. He blew his nose and wiped his eyes. "Forgive me. I've kept the tears at bay while the sister sat in here, but now I find I'm overcome with emotion."

Damien gave the father an understanding nod. "It is okay, Father. Take your time and gather your thoughts. We're in no hurry."

The older priest folded the fabric and placed it on his desk. "Father Martin helped set up the group. During the last several months they'd worked out a tentative plan. They set up volunteering opportunities, special service projects, monthly dinners. The four of them got along so well. I believe the women thought of Father Martin as their surrogate son. They doted on him and loved his company. He had that effect."

"Did something happen within this group?" Damien asked.

"Yes; I'm sorry. I'll shorten my story. A woman in the group died. Father Martin took it hard. He didn't elaborate as to why it bothered him so, but something about her death rattled him. He never met the woman's family. He mentioned to me the woman had a daughter. She didn't go to this church."

Joe shifted around. "Has anyone had a problem with Father Martin? Complaints about a job he didn't do or anything along those lines?"

"No. I never had any complaints about Father Martin. None. After the death of the woman—I'll have to look up her name in Father's office—he took a break from the group. The remaining two women decided they'd start the group after the first of the year. The lady's death hit him hard. I wish I'd pushed him to tell me more."

"This may seem like an uncomfortable question to answer, and I mean no disrespect in asking it. Can you tell me if Father Martin had any type of problem which may have required intervention? Or even counsel with Bishop Cantor?"

Father Cattaloni's nostrils flared. "I know about the other priests. I know they were killed in horrible ways, relating to problems they had. Personal demons can affect even the ones called to do God's work. Father Martin had none of those kinds of problems. He did not stray from his vows. He didn't have relations with men or women. He did not gamble, steal, cheat or lie."

"I mean no ill by asking the question. This helps us narrow in on why Father Martin was killed," Damien said.

"I understand, Lieutenant. It just infuriates me. Father Martin was a good man and a good priest." Cattaloni's head hung low.

"Father, could you get me the name of the woman from the group who died, as well as the other two women Father Martin worked with? They may be able to shed some light on why Father Martin was so bothered by her death." Damien stood and waited for the priest to follow.

"It may take me a little bit to go through his files. Can I call you this afternoon with the information?" He asked.

Damien noticed how tired the man looked. It seemed to Damien he had a fondness for the young priest that went past colleagues. "That would be okay. Here is my card. Call me as soon as you have the information. You'll have to close the church for a few days. We won't release the scene for clean up before Saturday." Damien handed the man another card. "Here are numbers to several crime scene clean-up crews. They'll be able to remove the biologicals."

"Thank you. As soon as you give us the word I'll call one of these crews," Cattaloni said.

CHAPTER THIRTY-FOUR

Panting, Mack ran through the front door, stripping off her bloody clothes on the way to the shower. She threw her wig in as she stepped under the shower head. Blood and tissue mixed with water ran down the drain. A few times Mack had to run her foot over the drain to move the accumulating bits of flesh to the side so water could escape.

Hanging the wig on the shower knob to dry, she exited the bathroom. "I'm late again. I missed the meeting a few days ago, but it couldn't be helped." She grabbed clothes from her closet and ran into the living room. She spoke in a loud and bubbly tone to her mother's picture. "Mom, I did it today. I've been watching Father Martin for several weeks now. And today was the day. That stupid old lady almost blew it. You should've seen Father Martin's face when he recognized me. He couldn't believe it."

She pulled her shirt over her head and tucked it into her pants. "He tried to tell me he didn't know. I didn't believe him, Mother. He had to know. You spent all that time with him. He knew. He just didn't care. He was right in the middle of telling me how much he cared for you when I smacked him in the head. Those torches are heavier than they look."

Mack giggled. "God's Holy Spirit gave me strength. Whack, whack, whack. It was something, Mother. I crushed his skull like it was made from papier-mâché." She mimicked her actions, raising her hand overhead as she brought it down on an imaginary head. "His expression after the first blow was priceless. The minute his brain registered what had happened, half of it flew onto the wall." Mack danced gleefully.

Mack brushed her hair at the small mirror on the wall. Her breathing slowed. "There are two more priests. They need to be disciplined. The one who should be doing this is too wrapped up in his own sinful life to pay attention. He thinks he's been so careful. He too is a stupid man, led by desires of greed and lust."

Mack shook her fists at the crucifix hanging on the wall. "You've allowed the wrong man to remain in charge. You're all knowing and yet You still allow him to have power. I can only assume it is for a specific reason."

Mack used a soft cloth to wipe the face of Jesus. Her voice was calm and flat. "I know You have put various people in positions to do what is needed. I am honored to have been chosen for this. I know Mother paved the way.

Her death had a purpose. You allowed it so I would see the truth of their ways. You allowed all of this so You can rebuild your Church."

CHAPTER THIRTY-FIVE

Damien and Joe sat in the SUV, both staring at the front of St. Xavier church. Heavy silence engulfed them. Joe leaned against his window while Damien's head rested against the back of the seat.

Boston's *More Than a Feeling* broke the silence as it rang out from Damien's phone. He answered without noticing the caller's name. "Kaine."

"Where the hell do you get off sending detectives to my place of work and questioning me?" Camilla screamed on the other end of the phone. "Do you know how fucking embarrassing it was?"

"Camilla, I don't give a shit how embarrassed you were."

"You could've called me, and I would've gladly told you where I was."

Damien ran a hand through his hair. "Is that all you wanted to say, Camilla?"

"No. I was able to prove I was nowhere near your house this morning. I was flying back on a red-eye flight from California."

"Great, Camilla. Is there anything else?" Damien asked. He was too exhausted to argue with her.

"No. I wanted to make sure you knew whatever it was that happened at your house, it didn't involve me."

"Fantastic." Damien hung up. He turned to look at Joe. "It wasn't Camilla at my house. Unless she paid someone. Which I'm sure they will check out. I guess I hoped it was her." Damien started the vehicle.

"Don't worry. We'll track down your stalker." Joe opened the file from the bishop's office. "Do you want to go to these other priests and speak with them? We could give them the description of the suspect, warn them, or whatever to maybe make them aware of the situation."

Damien nodded. "That sounds like a good idea. If nothing else, it may at least make it harder for the killer to get to them and buy us some time to figure out who the hell it is. Where should we start?" Damien stuck his phone in the hands-free cradle.

"Father Michaliska is at St. Bevels. It's closest to us." Joe thumbed through the list of personnel that Anthony Marcum gave them. "There are three full-time employees, two part-time, and three volunteers who may have access to the bishop's office area. There are more who work there, but these have direct access. Our Mr. Marcum is very thorough. His list of meetings and employees that attended them should help us rule out several people quite quickly."

"I'll have one of our uniformed officers verify the whereabouts of all those on the lists. Those who can't verify where they were, we bring to the station. Question them on our turf. Rattle them a bit." Damien pulled a piece of gum from his console. "I want to bring the rat-faced assistant in to question him. He will get no consideration."

Joe laughed. "You mean dipshidiot? I'm looking forward to that interview. The other priest is at St. Tabitha's. On the way to DC." Joe glanced at his watch. "Hey, you want to eat before this first priest or after? I'm getting hungry."

Damien was still laughing at Joe's new name for Marcum. "Umm— let's see Michaliska first, then get something on the way to St. Tabitha's. Sound good? Or will you starve to death?"

Joe feigned collapse. "I think I'll make it."

***

Damien led the way into the offices of St. Bevels. No one sat at the front desk. Joe and Damien made their way toward laughter and music came at the end of the hall.

"Hello? Anyone here?" Joe shrugged when Damien hit him on the arm. "What?"

"We know they're here," Damien said.

"Well, I don't want them to think we're skulking around. Plus, if they're doing something inappropriate, I don't want to see." Joe chuckled.

As they rounded a corner, an older priest came out. "Oh Lord," he said clutching his chest. "I wasn't expecting to run into anyone. What can I do for you young men?"

Damien held up his badge and ID, as did Joe. "We're looking for Father Michaliska. Is he available?"

"Well, you're looking at him. What can I do for a pair of Chicago's finest?" He smiled at them.

Damien glanced around. "Is there somewhere private we can speak? We have something delicate to discuss with you."

Michaliska raised his eyebrows at them. "Oh. I see. Follow me to my office." Michaliska leaned in the doorway of the room he came out of, "Martha, I'm not to be disturbed for a few minutes."

"Yes, Father." She smiled at all three men and went back to the office party.

Father Michaliska led them through a winding hallway, to his office. "Please have a seat. I have to admit I'm curious as to why you need to speak with me."

"Father Michaliska, are you aware of the murders of the priests?" Damien asked.

"Yes. It's awful. What do I have to do with those?"

"We're investigating those murders. We believe the person committing these crimes is targeting individual priests. We're working in conjunction with the bishop and the archbishop. The bishop has given us the names of four priests who have had issues."

Damien paused. Michaliska had to know where this was going. "Two of the priests on the list were killed. Your name is also on that list. We're not concerned with why; we're here to make sure you're aware you may be a target."

Father Michaliska's face turned ashen, and he gripped the arms of his chair. "Are you sure? I mean, could you be mistaken?" His eyes darted between Damien and Joe.

"No, Father. Our killer is targeting priests who seem to have had an issue in the past."

Father Michaliska swallowed rapidly. He bowed his head. "I'm ashamed of my problem. I've sought counsel, and I'm sober. I have been for eight months, ten days, and fifteen hours." Father Michaliska produced an AA chip from his pocket. "I'm proud of this. I plan on keeping it."

Damien gave him a sympathetic look. "You don't need to be ashamed. I have turned toward alcohol to help me through some rough spots. We're all human, even you guys. We're simply here to warn you. We have a description of the suspect. We believe this is a disguise, but he doesn't seem to change his look."

"Father," Joe said. "We want you to be hyper-aware of your surroundings and the people around you. Don't be alone if you can help it. If you hear confessions, have another priest present, or at a minimum have your maintenance man or your secretary around you.

"The subject in question dresses in an oversized coat. He is slim and of average height with shoulder-length hair, and may give you the impression he is on hard times. Several eyewitnesses have stated he has a goatee, beard, or both. If you notice this person, leave the area immediately."

Father Michaliska's eyes widened, and his breathing became more rapid.

"Father?" Joe waited until Michaliska made eye contact. "Did you hear what I said?"

"Yes. Yes, I did. I'm scared." He laughed nervously. "I'm terrified."

"A healthy dose of fear may help keep you alive." Joe handed the priest his card and one of Damien's. "Listen, if you have a regular routine, like every morning you sit in the rectory and pray, or you go to the chapel or sit in the garden; don't do that anymore. Vary your routine and make sure you're not alone."

"This killer is blaming priests for something. We're not sure what is driving his desire to kill priests, but he is targeting those who have had a problem. Please heed our warning," Damien said as he rose to leave.

Father Michaliska stood. "I will. I will heed all your warnings, and I will take extra precautions. Thank you for telling me." He walked both detectives to the door of his office. "I hope you catch him—and soon."

"We do too, Father. We do too." Damien said.

***

Damien glanced at his watch as he pulled into St. Tabitha's parking lot. He picked up his phone and texted Dillon. "I want to see if Dillon can meet us at Central and come up with a profile. Or at least an idea of what is leading this guy. The same guy killed Father Martin; just for a different reason. I'm not sure what that reason is." Damien sighed. "The events of this morning have jumbled my brain."

"Uh—yeah. That's understandable. When shit like this hits literally on your doorstep, everything else gets pushed to the back. Even priest killers," Joe said.

Damien's phone pinged. He looked at the screen and laughed.

"What's so funny?" Joe asked.

"Dillon knows these phones are being monitored. She sent me a dirty message." He smiled at Joe waving his phone. "I'm going to make her do this later. Anyway, she can meet us at four thirty. Let's go in and talk to Father Patterson."

***

In the office area, a young girl sat behind a desk. "Hi. How can I help you?" She smiled at both detectives.

Damien looked around. "Would it be possible for us to speak with Father Patterson, is he available?"

"Oh. Let me check. Can I at least tell him who you are?"

"Lieutenant Damien Kaine and Detective Joe Hagan." Damien offered her no more explanation.

"Father Patterson? Two detectives are here to speak with you. Yes, I will." She hung up the phone. "He'll be right out."

"Thank you." Joe nodded.

Within a few moments, a large man walked toward them. "You two are here to see me?"

"Father Patterson, I'm Lieutenant Kaine, this is my partner Detective Joe Hagan. Can we speak in private, please?"

"Yes, follow me." He led them to his office and closed the door behind them. "I'm confused. Why do you need to speak with me?"

Damien smiled at the man. He had a hound dog face that was oddly attractive. "Father Patterson, we're investigating the deaths of the priests. Are you aware of the case?"

"Yes. I have followed the news. Why?"

"We are working with the bishop's office. And we believe the killer is targeting priests. According to records, the bishop has spoken with you about, your relationship."

Patterson's eyes widened, and his face flushed with color. He gazed downward.

"Father Patterson, we don't care about what or why you've had a private conversation with the bishop. Please understand no one else knows about this outside Cantor's office and us. We're here because we believe you're a target. This killer is targeting particular priests."

Father Patterson smoothed down the front of his shirt. He tugged on his sleeves. "I don't know what to say."

"You don't need to say anything. We want you to listen. Please vary your routines. Don't be alone. Don't meet with anyone new without someone with you." Damien said.

Joe leaned forward explaining the disguise their suspect wore. "If you see someone acting suspicious or dressed like this, please leave the area."

Father Patterson nodded. "I will. I will."

Damien and Joe rose. "Here are our cards. If you think you see this person or need assistance, please call us. We can see ourselves out."

Father Patterson stood and shook both their hands. "Thank you for your kindness."

"You're welcome, Father," Damien said. He hated that he had to speak with someone about such a private matter. Hopefully, the few moments of embarrassment would keep Father Patterson alive.

CHAPTER THIRTY-SIX

Damien had Joe call the lab. He wanted updates on where all the evidence stood with the dead priest and on the heart left at his door. He phoned the captain and gave him a quick update. He informed him of the visits to the two remaining priests on the list and what they told them. He discussed the most recent killing. Although it veered off course from the other murders, Damien assured him the same killer had committed the latest crime. He looked at his watch and had enough time to call his brother Nicky.

"Hey Nicky, you got anything yet?"

"No, not yet. I'm working on it, give me some time. Dillon's vehicle upgrades should be done in a week or so."

"Alright. Thanks. Give Mama a hug for me." Damien's face brightened when Joe walked in followed by Dillon. "Hey, babe." He came around his desk to kiss her.

Joe frowned. "You never kiss me when I come in your office."

"And I never will. What did you learn from the lab, any updates?" Damien asked.

Dillon listened to Joe rattled off the lab's findings. "Martin, the priest killed this morning, had the same Dymphna medal stuffed in what was left of his head. They're going through the evidence in trace; they aren't finding much. They found one synthetic hair on the priest, bolstering our disguise theory."

Joe turned toward Dillon. "Do you want the update on your heart or do you want to go over the priest stuff first?"

Dillon's eyebrows furrowed together. "I'd prefer to hear the priest case first." She regarded Damien. "You think this last priest was killed by the same killer but for a different reason?"

"I do. The killer bludgeoned Father Martin. Rage fueled this murder. The other two priests died in very premeditated manners. One for gambling, one for sex. The verses left at the scenes point directly to the sins the priests committed.

"The verse left at this last scene doesn't point to a sin. It references someone not doing his job. Sister Webster, who spoke with Father Martin before he died, witnessed an exchange between Martin and our suspect, she thought he knew the young man. It looked to her as if they were having a conversation."

Damien ran a hand through his hair. "Sister Webster thought she heard him say something like, 'you didn't do your job.' To which the priest responded, 'I didn't know' Something like that anyway."

Dillon reached over and took the piece of paper from in front of Damien. She read the verse the killer wrote on the wall. "Let me see all the verses." She re-read each of those. She studied the pictures of all three dead priests.

Damien watched with amusement as she mumbled to herself. She took a piece of paper from his notepad and scribbled a few things. He loved watching her work.

She looked up to see their expressions. "Stop staring at me like that. You know I like to shift things around in my head."

"I didn't say anything," Damien said.

"Neither did I," responded Joe.

"Right. I know what you two are thinking." She sat back and stared into Damien's luscious blue eyes. Her pulse raced just looking at him. "I think you're right. He killed Martin for a different reason. The verse he left with him, part of it says, 'I will bestow punishment on you...' he's punishing all the priests, but this has a much more personal feel. Where the others had an air of detachment, this did not. You can see the previous deaths; they were put on display. The killer used their transgression to show how they let the Church down.

"Martin's transgression relates directly to the UNSUB. The killer believes all the priests have enormous sins that they let get in the way of doing their job. They have disgraced God and His teachings for giving in to their sins. This last one, Martin, he offended the killer, because he didn't do something he should have." Dillon cocked her head to the side. "Do you understand what I mean?"

Joe closed his eyes for a moment.

While Damien stared at her.

"Let me see if I can make it a little clearer." Dillon turned toward Joe. "I take Taylor out. I let her get drunk. I don't pay attention, and she starts making out with some guy. I'm not drinking. You're going to blame me. Even though I didn't force her to drink, I didn't introduce her to the guy or make her kiss him. She's incapacitated, I'm not. It's my fault."

"Oh. That makes sense," Joe said. "I get it now."

Damien nodded. "So, what you're saying is, something happened out of Martin's control, and he had nothing to do with it. The killer has no one else to blame and needs to blame someone for what happened, so it must be Martin's fault."

"Exactly." Dillon took a handful of jellybeans. "I know you got a list from the Archdiocese including the reprimanded priests—was Martin on that list?"

"No," Joe said.

She leaned her head to one side. "Hmm. Something started this guy on his killing spree. I think it will have everything to do with Father Martin. I think whatever event it was, it happened recently. Within the last six months, maximum. Whatever it was, the killer used the other priests to prepare him to kill Martin or to hide the real reason he wanted to kill Martin. Either way, your killer isn't done. He'll want to finish with the two remaining priests. Although this may have started with what Martin did or didn't do, he now feels it is his responsibility to rid the Church of those not doing God's work properly."

Dillon glanced at the pictures again. "He may stop with this list. However, if he finds out anything else about any other priests, he could very well kill them. Just because he started with names he got from the bishop's office, doesn't mean that's all he has." She winked at Damien. "Now tell me about our heart."

Joe shifted in his seat. "The lab found nothing on the box or the tissue paper. The heart itself—well that's a little weird. It's human, but it showed signs of being frozen. Stuffed way inside the center of the heart they found an arrow tip."

Damien looked at Dillon. "What is that referencing?"

"Arrow straight through the heart. This person is in love with one of us," she said.

"That can't be good," Damien said. "That level of emotion means they've been watching us for a long time. It could be either one of us." He opened his mouth to speak when Dillon's phone chirped at her.

"Hang on a minute." She pulled her cell from her pocket and looked at the display. "Crap," she said. "Director Sherman, what can I do for you?" She pinched the bridge of her nose. "Why?" She shook her head. "You're kidding, right? No, Sir. I think you're quite capable of doing your job. I don't have to agree with you to believe you're capable." She sighed.

"I think you're worrying about something we can't control. Well, at least you're giving me all the information this time and not blindsiding me. Yes, I'm referring to Jason. Did you see what was in the envelope?"

Dillon remembered where she was and stopped short of revealing more details. She sighed. "I know that wasn't your intention Sir. I'm sorry. You're right. Hmm. Yes, Sir. Yes, I'll be at the office." Dillon laughed. "No, I'll set it up in the conference room." She paused, watching Damien as she listened to her director. "If I thought I could get away with it I would. I have a feeling you and Damien would hunt my ass down." Her expression softened. "I know you do, Sir. I wouldn't want it any other way. I still don't have to like it. Two hours, yes Sir."

She hung up the phone. A slew of curse words erupted from her. When she finished her rant, Damien and Joe stared at her. "Crap, sometimes I hate my life. I need to set up a conference call this evening with Director Sherman, AD Reynolds and some other agents here and at Quantico. Since we don't know if the heart is directed at you or me, they want to have a conference with everyone and their damn dog to set up a task force." She stood.

Joe stepped around Dillon. "I'll go check on ECD."

When Joe left the room, Dillon shut the door to the office. She spun around to find Damien standing right in front of her. She wrapped her arms around his waist and buried her face in his chest.

"Hey, what's got you so rattled?" Damien held on to her.

She didn't let go. "I don't know. It's everything. I feel like I'm not in control of anything anymore. And something is going on with Sherman, but I don't know what it is." She wanted to talk to Damien about her relationship with Director Sherman, but she wasn't sure how to. Dillon was sure that Damien would think she was overreacting, but something had changed between her and her boss, and she wasn't sure what to do about it.

He pushed her away from him and held her at arm's length. "Whatever is going on with Sherman has nothing to do with you." He kissed her chastely, but even that simple act ignited his desire. He moved his hands under her shirt when she broke the embrace.

Dillon swatted at his hands. "Listen, you sex fiend; I don't have time for this. I have to get to the office. This is going to be a long evening." She kissed him again and headed out his office door. "I'll text later."

"You might want to watch what you text."

She waved as she left the VCU.

"Joe," Damien yelled as he watched her walk away.

"Yo." He came back into the office. "What do you need, oh wise one?"

"Ha ha. You got the folder from the bishop?"

"Yeah, let me get it off my desk." He turned to leave.

"Are you ready to go? I can drop you off at home since you rode in with me."

Joe checked the time. "Shit. It's already past shift. Let me grab the folder and my jacket. I'm ready to go if you are."

"I'm ready, let's go." Damien grabbed a few folders from his desk and closed his office locking the door.

Joe put on his jacket and held the folder out to Damien. "Here's everything ECD put together on the bishop's office personnel. You plan on working on it tonight?"

Damien shrugged. "I might as well. Dillon won't get home till late. I'm starting to have no life with this job. If I didn't have Dillon at night, I would have no fucking life. Man, I'm turning into a wuss."

"You said it." Joe laughed as Damien gave him the finger.

CHAPTER THIRTY-SEVEN

Damien pulled into his garage, shutting the big overhead door before exiting the vehicle. Inside, he found Coach laying on the sofa. He looked—depressed. "Can a cat even get depressed? Hey, buddy. You so sad you can't get off the sofa to say hello?"

The cat rolled over, baring his belly. Damien rubbed the tub of fur then headed to the kitchen. He rummaged through the fridge. Leftover pizza and Chinese sounded perfect. Coach meowed at his feet. "Ahh, so you aren't that sad, huh? Nothing could make you lose your appetite." Damien pulled out a can of tuna and filled the cat's bowl. Coach pounced on it like he hadn't eaten in years.

Damien sat at the table with his food and the cat. Although it tasted good, his appetite waned. Father Martin's death bothered him. Not having Dillon around to bounce his ideas off had everything rolling around his head. He finished eating, picked up the cat, and headed for the office. Coached purred in his arms. "You're so spoiled. I guess I am as well, huh?" He set Coach on the desk.

His phone pinged with a text from Dillon. He laughed as he read the screen. "*Hey, just touching base. We took a small break. Getting ready to start up again. We should've had sex on your desk. I would've been in a much better mood.*"

He responded with a simple "I love you." He wouldn't encourage her. She knew the phones were being monitored. Damien settled in his office and thumbed through the pages of information from ECD. Nothing pointed to a suspicious person.

As much as Damien hated to admit it, Marcum, the little weasel, was very thorough. His detailed list of all employees, scheduled meetings, and those who attended them helped Damien rule out several people immediately. Three office employees were working the morning of Belgosa's murder, and today's murder of Father Martin. That ruled them out for Mandahari's murder. The one thing Damien knew for sure was that the same person committed all three.

He would verify the maintenance man and the gardener's whereabouts, but their schedules put them at the Diocese when Father Martin had been killed, ruling them out. Marcum had alibis for the days and times in question, which also ruled out the bishop, unfortunately. Damien thought that would have been justice if he could pin both for these murders. The security personnel worked for a security agency. All their information checked out as well.

Damien started his own list. The driver, the chef, and the maid didn't keep regular schedules. They would all need to be checked out. The part-time employees needed to have their alibis checked. Damien looked at his watch and made a quick call.

"Anthony Marcum here."

Damien bristled at the sound of the man's voice. "Mr. Marcum, this is Lieutenant Kaine. I need to ask you something. Do you have a moment?"

Marcum hissed into the phone. "Yes. What do you need Lieutenant?"

"First, the permanent employees, how many of them have access to the computer system. Specifically, access to the files on the priests?"

"Well, that's easy to answer, myself and the bishop are the only ones with direct access to it."

"Is it on a cloud or server, or is it on one computer?" Damien asked.

"We keep that record on a server. That way I or the bishop can access it as needed. Having it on one computer would make it complicated and time-consuming."

Damien could almost see the man's snarl through the phone. "I'm assuming that part of the server is password protected."

"Yes of course it is. We aren't stupid. The password is changed every thirty days. I change it then give the new password to the bishop. I share it with the IT girl when it is needed, which hasn't been too often."

"Do you keep that password locked up? I'm trying to see how accessible that information is."

"I assure you, Lieutenant, I keep that password hidden. Only the bishop or I have access to it. Is there anything else I can do for you?"

"One other thing, have you had any hacks into your system?" Damien asked.

"I haven't been made aware of our computer systems having been compromised, but Caroline, our IT person, can tell you all that."

"Thank you. Someone from my office may call you tomorrow to verify some of the employee's alibis. Thank you again for your time."

Damien looked over his list. If Marcum kept that information to himself, then it must have been someone else who knew about the priests' transgressions. Damien considered this—it could have been someone who worked in the office or someone who hacked the system. Damien used his computer to get all the information he could on the bishop's employees. He could go a few layers deeper with no one from DC suspecting, but if he found anything, he'd have to figure a way to get the information legally. He needed to stop this killer, and because of that, he had no problems pushing the boundaries.

He ran the part-timers and the volunteers. Damien printed out all the information and set it aside. The chef and maid had nothing in their records to cause suspicion. The maintenance man and the driver had a few misdemeanors going back six years; nothing that warranted a closer look. The house managers for both the Archbishop and Bishop had impeccable records.

Immediately Damien ruled out the high school kids performing their confirmation volunteer duties. The list from Marcum shows they were in class during Martin's murder. He would verify the information, but he didn't see either of them doing this. The two seminarians warranted a deeper look. They had a little more access to the property than most, because of their duties as priests in training. Their alibis would decide how much of a deeper look they required.

He read through the printed sheets on the part-timers and volunteers' records, all came up clean. They all had regular jobs that would more than likely give them alibis and once verified, they would be taken off the list of suspects.

He pulled up the florist online. Her website was a wealth of information. She had posted pictures of her and her workers with floral arrangements that had been made for two prominent weddings. The dates of those weddings were held the same days as two of the murders. Damien would have an officer verify the florist's schedule, but it was looking like she would be cleared from the dwindling pool of suspects. "Fuck. I can't catch a damn break on this case." Damien set the papers aside.

The last person to check out was the IT person. Damien picked up the sheet from Marcum with her information on it. He scrolled through it. She worked for Quantum Electronics, a major computer programmer group in the Chicago area. He typed in her information into his computer. "Damn, this chick has mad skills." He looked at Coach in his lap.

"She could definitely get into the system with or without the password from Marcum," Damien muttered as he scratched the cat's head. Caroline had a clean record. Excellent financials. Nothing in her records indicated any kind of trouble. Her movements shouldn't be too hard to track down, so that would be another potential suspect off his list.

Damien rolled his chair over to the board and tacked up the latest batch of pictures. Three dead priests. Two for entirely different reasons than the one killed today. Damien looked at his watch again. Too late to call Father Cattaloni tonight. He couldn't see how the death of a woman a few months ago would have anything to do with this case, but something troubled him about it.

He mulled around the information he'd gathered. He made a few notes and a more complete list to give one of his uniformed officers tomorrow. A handful of people needed to be checked out. Most of this information could be collected by a few phone calls. "Damn, we got nothing," Damien said out loud as he tugged on the ends of his hair. Damien's phone rang as he closed his computer.

"Hey, Nicky. How's it going?" Damien leaned back in his seat.

"Yo *fratellino*," Nicky said. "Got a minute?"

"You got something for me?"

"Maybe. That phone call you received this morning, you didn't hear anything on the other end, any noise or distortion of any kind?"

Damien thought for a moment. "No. I answered the phone, didn't hear anything—wait, I noticed a click maybe two, then the phone went dead. Why is that important?"

"It might be. I think your caller wanted to pin down your location. When you answered the call, a tracer pinged where your phone was located. I think the person who left the package is the same person who called you."

"Have you been able to trace it back to the caller?"

"We are working on that. Whoever did this is doing a decent job of hiding their location. They made the packet bounce all over the city."

"If the present was intended for me, then doesn't that make me the target?" Damien adjusted Coach and lifted his feet onto the desk.

"Well, sort of. First, the scratches on Dillon's car weren't random. It spelled DIE. When we lifted the layer of paint off the car, the pattern became legible in the metal. Dillon told me she parked her car in the garage that day and didn't drive it. I pulled the camera footage from the garage. Her AD is good friends with Dad, he let us have all the film. Her car wasn't in direct view of the cameras. The angle of the closest camera picked up a snapshot of what appears to be a woman."

Damien sipped his whiskey. "What do you mean, appears to be a woman?"

"Part of the tape shows someone dressed in all-black, with a black hooded coat. The jacket looked fitted, like what a woman would wear. I've tried to enhance the image. I can't pull anything else off it. I'm running the other levels of the garage and the exits and entrances to see if I can find a woman dressed like that. Or anyone dressed like that. Something else we're doing is running all the cars that entered the garage and tracking down their owners. The thing is, this person could've walked into the garage."

"Is there a camera on the walk-in entrance?"

"No, but there are cameras at all the elevators, so maybe we'll get lucky. Have your detectives ruled out Camilla?"

"Yeah, they interviewed her today. She has proof she was on a flight at the time of the incident. You think they're after Dillon because of me?"

"I do. I believe you have an admirer, and they want Dillon out of the way. That's why you got the phone call this morning. They wanted to make sure you would be there. The present was meant for you."

"*Merda!*" Coach hissed as he leapt down from Damien's lap. "What are we going to do?"

"Dad wants to set up a conference with you, Dillon, and your bosses. Dad figured if you and Dillon were at risk, he would cash in some favors. He wants to go over what we have so far. We could do something tomorrow morning—I can set that up. Get Captain Mackey patched in at least on audio, so he won't have to go into the office on Saturday morning."

"That'll work. Let's do it early. I'll call Captain Mackey now."

"Okay, let's do this by nine a.m. I'll text you before we go live," Nicky said.

"Thanks, Nicky. Give Mama a kiss for me. Love ya, brother." Damien disconnected the call.

Damien dialed his Captain. "Hey, Captain Mackey, sorry for the late call."

The captain sighed on the other end. "I expected something. Go ahead, Damien tell me what you've got."

He told the captain about Nicky's findings and the morning conference call.

The captain cursed. "Is your brother sure about this person being after Dillon?"

Damien sighed. "Well, as of now the evidence points that way. Dillon's car had that message and the phone call I got this morning appeared to track me. My secret admirer wanted me to be home when she delivered the package."

"All right. I'll talk to you in the morning. Hell of a week. Floaters, dead priests, and secret admirers. Damn." The captain hung up.

CHAPTER THIRTY-EIGHT

Coach jumped back up on the desk, tired of being alone. He slinked over to Damien and nudged him with his fat head. Picking up the cat and setting him in his lap, Damien leaned back closing his eyes. The silence was soothing. Coach's loud purring pulled Damien out of his short respite. He opened his computer and logged into his dad's secure network. He pulled up the satellite link and within minutes had his house on his computer screen.

This software allowed the user to view the target on a continuous loop. Damien could zoom onto his house, all sides. The layout of the condo mimicked row houses but wider and longer. Two condos stood side by side, then a space on either side, giving a feeling of seclusion, since the houses weren't on top of each other. The location and the privacy of the property were major selling points for Damien. It gave the feeling of a home rather than an apartment.

Nothing on the screen looked out of place. He could see his lights on and 360 degrees around the entire property. He sighed as he watched another few moments. Damien double checked the locks. He made sure all the rooms were secure before heading toward the master bedroom upstairs.

Damien carried the cat with him as he went up the stairs. He turned on the upstairs TV screen and connected to his laptop downstairs. The surveillance feed illuminated the room. He put the cat on the bed, where Coach took his share out of the middle. Damien stripped and carried his phone into the bathroom.

When he bought this place, he remodeled the master bathroom first. A Jacuzzi tub large enough to hold several people sat off to the side of the room. The shower took up one length of the far wall, tricked out with enough shower heads to hit every part of his body, enclosed in glass with a bench running the length of the wall. He stood under the rain head flow of hundred-degree water and let the jets pulse over him as he tried to let the stress of the day flow down the drain, but his mind wouldn't shut off. The floater case bothered him. He was sure the families of each of these men were hiding somewhere. He wanted nothing more than to get to them before the Cartel did.

The murdered priests also had space in his head. He had no power to stop this killer. He prayed the warnings given to the two remaining priests would help keep them alive. Then Damien had their stalker, who wanted Dillon out of the way to get to him. He had to catch a break on something.

Damien shut off the water and stayed there for a few minutes. The steam swirled around him. Stepping out of the shower, his phone rang. "Hey babe," he said.

No answer. He looked at the display, no number listed. He almost hung up on the call, then remembered the trace. The longer he kept the line open, the better the chance for tracking the call. "What do you want?" Damien asked. Standing naked and dripping, he growled into the phone. "Answer me. What do you want?"

"You," said the voice on the other end. It sounded like it was disguised or muffled.

"Well, that's not going to happen. I don't even know who you are." Damien wasn't sure what to say. He didn't want to be antagonistic, but he was pissed.

"You think you love her. You haven't even known her as long as you've known me. How can you love her? I'm your one true love. You and I are meant to be together."

"How do you know how long I've known her?" Damien asked. "I don't know who you are. How do you know anything about me or her?"

"You know who I am. Soon you will realize I am the one for you, not her. I've been waiting for you, but I won't wait much longer. You've grown to attached to her. I thought after Camilla you had learned your lesson. I guess I may have to help you with your decision."

The line went dead. Damien hit *99 and called his brother Nicky. "Hey, I know it's late, but I got a call. I'm sure it is a girl although she's disguising her voice. I kept her on the phone for as long as I could. I wanted to let you know now."

Nicky sighed on the other end of the phone. "Damn, you interrupted me and my plans with my beautiful wife. Rotten timing, brother."

"Sorry. Look pull the recording, do your magic and brief me tomorrow on the conference call."

"Yeah, yeah. I can do that. Tell me the conversation anyway."

Damien ran through it for his brother.

"Damn, you sure attract the crazies don't you, little brother? First

Camilla, now this chick. Are we sure it isn't Camilla? Maybe she set up the delivery and now is making the calls."

"But this time our girl referenced Camilla. She knows more about me than I thought she did." Damien dragged his hand through his wet hair. "I'll have someone consider her more closely. Hell, Nicky, this sucks. I'm not worried about my safety. I'm concerned about this fucking lunatic going after Dillon. This chick talks as if she's watching me or at least has information on me. Man, it's like she's right there under my nose and I don't know who it could fucking be."

"Don't worry, we'll figure out who it is. Nothing is going to happen to Dillon. Try to get some sleep. Hopefully, I'll have some answers by the morning." The phone went dead.

Damien finished drying off and threw on some sweats. He headed back down to the office, wanting to find something that would point to his stalker. He had just turned on his computer when he heard the garage door. Damien stepped out to see Dillon putting her weapon and keys on the table next to the door. "Hey babe, you're home earlier than I thought you'd be."

She smiled at him. "Yeah, I'm so damn tired. I'm just glad this day is over." Dillon's brow wrinkled. "Why do you look like I should have a drink in my hand? Something happened, didn't it?"

"I have some news on our stalker. You want to hear it now or after you shower?"

"Give me the details now. Let me get a glass of wine. Tell it to me in the office."

Damien followed her. "Those weren't just random scratches on your car—someone gouged the word 'DIE' into the metal. Second, it's looking more and more like it's a woman and she is stalking me. Nicky went over the tapes from the garage and found someone dressed in all black, resembling a female. Whoever called me this morning, they wanted to track my whereabouts. The click I heard on the line, was a tracer. Nicky believes my admirer pinged my location." Damien sat silent for a minute.

Dillon took a long sip of wine. "Why do I get the feeling there's something else you are about to tell me?"

"Because you are the smartest most beautiful woman I know," Damien said.

"Right. Go ahead and spit it out."

"I got a call tonight. I thought it was you. I engaged her in conversation and managed to keep her on the line so Nicky could get a good trace on it. Only you, me, Joe, your boss, my boss and my family know about the trace on the phones. Not even anyone else in the unit."

"Well, at least we have that going for us. Your admirer had something else to say, what was it?"

"She—I'm assuming it's a girl—she said I didn't love you, that she was meant to be with me, and she was my one true love. She spoke as if she knew all about us. She also said I knew who she was, and soon I would realize I loved her and not you. I got the distinct impression she's very close, like she sees me regularly."

"Oh man. She's pissed about me and you, and when I'm out of the picture then you're going to fall madly in love with her. Wow! You sure know how to attract them." Dillon laughed. "Of course, what does that say about me?"

Damien stepped closer and took her face in his hands. "I will not let anything happen to you, I promise you. When we get your car back, it's going to be as safe as it can be. Nicky is installing a system to track any kind of tampering along with all the other safety features."

She set her glass down and wrapped her arms around him. Dillon held him like that for a few moments, inhaling the fresh scent of his shower gel. Leaning back, she looked up at him, "I didn't know AD Reynolds and your dad were such good friends. He's damn happy I'm dating you. He said your family uses some of the best equipment on the market. Also, said your dad has given them some of their Intel for special ops. Seems your family can get information the US Government can't. Go figure."

Damien chuckled. "You're lucky you're dating me."

Dillon giggled. "Of course, if I wasn't dating you I might not be in this mess in the first place. You realize that too, right?"

"Ah, that may be true, but you wouldn't be as happy."

Dillon's smile filled her face. "Well, that's for sure. And you are good for sex. That's why I'm with you anyway. The sex. All your money and privilege is icing on my cake."

"I feel so used."

CHAPTER THIRTY-NINE

December 3rd
Saturday Morning

Damien's phone pinged. He looked over at Dillon. "We go live in two minutes." He punched in a code on his computer. Within a few moments, the landline in the office rang. "Hey Nicky, let me pull in the captain while you're setting up." While Damien conferenced the captain in by audio, his dad's conference room at the compound came on the big screen on the wall of the office. The screen split, and the conference room in Quantico came up. Director Sherman sat at a long table.

"Hey Director," Dillon said.

"Good morning, Agent McGrath. I'm assuming we have some news on your stalker?"

"Yes, Sir. Damien's Dad figured this would be easier telling everyone at once. I know AD Reynolds had something he couldn't miss this morning. I will brief him later."

Nicky spoke. "Okay, Dillon's personal auto is being retrofitted as we speak. The phone she is carrying will keep track of her movements. It looks like we have Captain Mackey on audio so let's get started."

Damien's father spoke up. "Before we get into the details, I thought I might remind my son and Agent McGrath that everything they text or speak about is recorded," Giovanni said.

Dillon snickered. "C'mon, you guys should've never told me these phones do that. A girl has to get her jollies some way."

Director Sherman frowned. "Agent McGrath, try and remember this will be used in a training series for incoming agents."

She looked at her director via the telecom. "You're aware of what happens in those barracks right?"

Muffled laughter filtered through the speakers.

Nicky jumped back in. "With regards to the phone calls—the first call Damien received had a tracker on it. It pinged his location. The caller wanted to make sure he was at home when the package was delivered. Additionally, underneath what looked like random scratches on Dillon's car, we could clearly see the word 'DIE'".

Director Sherman interrupted. "I'm gathering the phone calls aren't going to help?"

"You are correct. Our girl is smart enough to block the tracking. The best I can tell you, the calls are originating within a fifteen-mile radius of Damien's home," Nicky said.

"What else have you gotten? I know the lab hasn't found anything definitive." Director Sherman asked.

"You're correct again. There was an arrowhead stuffed into the center of the heart, and the pin used to hold the note was like those used to keep insects on display. The note had been hand-written, but there was nothing distinctive about the paper or pen used. It did appear the heart had either been frozen or preserved. If we are lucky, maybe this person isn't killing people and leaving body parts on my doorstep," Damien said.

"Back to that second call. This time, Damien elicited a longer conversation from the caller. We isolated the voice. I've cleaned it up. There is still some distortion, but I think this is close to what the caller sounds like. Damien, Dillon, you two pay close attention and tell me if you recognize her." Nicky hit a few keys on his laptop, and a young voice came through.

"Were you trying to piss her off Damien?" Captain Mackey asked.

Damien looked at Dillon and shrugged. "Not at all. She seems to know a lot about me. It makes me think it's someone close. No matter what I would've said I was going to piss her off."

Dillon spoke up. "Damien engaged her as best he could. He's in a no-win situation. Nicky, what else do you have?"

"Not much. The caller seems to have some sophisticated equipment available, but I get the impression she isn't using it fully. That's why I was able to at least get the triangulation of the call's origination. I'm not sure I can get much more information from the phone calls. Who else knows about the surveillance we're doing, phone and home?" Nicky asked.

"Everyone on this call—Joe—and that's it. I haven't told anyone else, and I know none of these other people have either."

Nicky nodded. "That's good. Let's keep it that way. We don't want her finding out we are trying to track her calls and movement. As of now, she thinks we know nothing about her. I want to keep it that way."

Dillon looked at her director. "You want my opinion on who we're dealing with, Sir?"

Director Sherman smirked. "Do any of us really have a say? Go on."

"I know the FBI was leaning toward this being someone from my past. It's evident after that call it's not. Damien is correct. This person sees or speaks to him, if not daily, at least weekly. She knows enough about him to find out where he works and lives, but can't follow his everyday movements. She's close enough to know about us, but not everything."

She paused, "see, at the time of her first call or the delivery of the package, she didn't know I had moved into his house. We just decided that this past Monday. Hell, only Joe and Taylor knew of it. This tells me she isn't privy to Damien's everyday life. I think this person works in some kind of capacity with Damien or the VCU."

"Where, though? That's like the fifty-thousand-dollar question." Damien said

Captain Mackey's voice boomed through the speakers. "Could be the Lab, the Morgue, another department here in Central."

Dillon nodded toward Damien as she spoke. "I believe this person has known you for some time, Damien. I also believe it set her off when we started dating. Before me, you had broken up with Camilla, and you weren't dating one woman. Banging women yes, dating no. She didn't feel threatened because you weren't serious about those other women."

Captain Mackey tried not to laugh at Dillon's description of Damien's past proclivities. "The voice sounds young. How will that play into this when she realizes the full extent of your relationship?" Captain Mackey asked.

"I think she is young, and not just from her voice. I'd estimate she is in her early twenties. This, for her, is probably her first real relationship. Through her interactions with Damien, however slight they may have been, she developed a severe infatuation with him. In her mind, they were falling in love with each other. I believe when she does find out I've moved in with him, she will feel betrayed. She thinks he hasn't given in to his true feelings, and all these steps she's taking—the phone calls and the gift—are helping him realize his mistake in being with me."

"If that's the case, won't her finding out you moved in make her go after you even more?" Sherman asked Dillon.

Dillon laughed. "Of course it will. Once she finds out, she may very well direct her anger at Damien. She may lash out at him to get his attention. She may find something or someone he is fond of and hurt them. Family, pet, even Joe is at risk. Worst case, she could decide that if she can't have him, no one can."

Nicky spoke up. "I agree with Dillon. I think we should use their relationship. I have an idea that might push this girl's hand, and it won't look like Damien did it purposely."

"Tell us the plan," Captain Mackey said.

"We have the gala coming up the middle of this month, let's use it. Everyone is going to be there; we will make sure to do a write-up with a picture of Damien and Dillon. Make sure it tells how they met, and they are now living together, a whirlwind romance come together out of tragedy, something like that. We can use George Peters from the Chicago Herald. He'll get it in the social section."

Dillon's head hit her desk. "No, no I'm begging; please no cameras and pictures. It's godawful I have to wear a dress."

Everyone laughed at her. "Dillon, most women enjoy wearing a glamorous gown and being the center of attention," Director Sherman chuckled.

Dillon raised her head as she spoke. "You of all people, know I am not like most women."

"I think using the gala is a good idea. Then maybe my stalker will get flustered and make a mistake," Damien said.

There was a little more discussion before the conference ended. Dillon turned toward Damien. "Great. Now I get to go dress shopping."

CHAPTER FORTY

Dillon went to the kitchen to get some coffee. Since the video conference happened so early, they still had a couple of hours before Joe and Taylor showed up. Walking back in she found Damien with his feet up on his desk and his eyes closed. "Hey, have some coffee. It will help wake you up." She handed the cup to him. "Have you spoken to Joe about why Taylor didn't bring him over yesterday?"

Damien gave her an eagle eye. "Have you spoken with Taylor?"

She shook her head. "No. I figured she was working these last few days at the lab, getting things in order. If she needed to talk she would've called me. But I'm thinking something has happened."

Damien rested his elbows on his desk. "I tried to talk to Joe, but he didn't want to discuss it. I told you this would happen. He would fuck this up."

"Well, if Taylor is supposed to come get me in about an hour or two, and they aren't talking, don't you think you should call Joe and see what's up?" Just then her phone rang. "I think we're about to find something out." She answered, placing her coffee on the desk. "Hey Taylor, what's up? We still on?"

Damien watched as Dillon's eyes got wide.

"Okay, sure. I'll come pick you up. I'll leave in about an hour. Sounds good." Dillon picked up her coffee cup. "Taylor wants me to come get her. She's at the Ritz."

"Get the fuck out. Did she say why?"

"She said she would explain later, but I bet she's been there since they left here the other night."

Damien dragged a hand down his face. "Oh man. I guess I better call him."

The doorbell rang. Both he and Dillon bristled.

"It's just the damn door," Dillon said as she walked out of the office.

Before she opened it, she dropped down the little security screen to check. She pulled open the door as Damien came into the room. She turned toward him, "it's Joe." Dillon stepped aside. "Hey, Joe. Come on in."

Joe raised an eyebrow at her. "Taylor called you, didn't she?"

Dillon smirked. "Yeah, but she didn't tell me anything. Just wants me to pick her up." She turned toward Damien. "I'm going to run up and get cleaned up really quick then I'm heading out."

Damien squeezed Joe's shoulder. "Come on in the office. I need to go over our conference call we had about our stalker."

"A conference call?" Joe asked.

"It was with Captain Mackey, Director Sherman, and my brother and father." Damien proceeded to fill Joe in on everything. When he was done, Joe sat quietly. Damien was about to say something when Dillon walked in.

"Hey, I'm going to go ahead and get out of here. I'll call you later." Dillon gave him a kiss and left.

Damien poured two glasses of whiskey and handed one to Joe. "Alright, what the fuck did you do?"

Joe leaned back in Dillon's office chair. "I have no fucking clue."

"Bullshit, Joe. I bet I can guess."

Joe interlocked his hands on the top of his head. "Okay, fine. We got home after we left here the other night. She said she loved me. And I freaked out."

"What the hell, freaked out about what? Haven't you ever loved someone? It's not the worst thing in the world."

Joe closed his eyes. "I like it the way it is. Casual."

"So—you'd be okay with her fucking someone else? You expect me to believe that?"

"No. I wouldn't be okay with that. Shit, it would piss me the hell off." Joe placed his empty glass on the desk.

"Then why do you expect her to let you dip your stick where ever you want to?" Damien glared at his partner.

Joe growled. "I don't understand why you keep riding my ass about this damn relationship. We've been friends for as long as we've been partners. I love you like a brother. I'd put my life in harm's way for you. But I am so fucking tired of you grilling me about Taylor. Why is it so damn important to you?"

"I don't know, to be honest. I can see how much you care for her. I just don't understand why you're dragging your feet on this."

"You know, not everyone wants to be in a serious committed relationship." Joe sighed.

Damien could tell Joe was wrestling with something. "What's going on, Joe? Something is eating at you."

Joe closed his eyes. "I don't want to get into it. Just let it go."

"No, I won't. You need to tell me what the hell is going on."

"You are a fucking pain in my ass, you know that?" Joe stared at the murder board on the wall. "I don't want to talk about all the details." Joe's chest tightened. He said nothing for a few minutes. "I've already let Taylor get too close."

"I see the way you look at her."

Joe turned toward Damien. "I don't want to talk about this anymore. You need to drop it."

"Fine, you stupid fuck. I'll drop it. Damn you make me mad." Damien sighed.

"I seem to have that effect lately."

CHAPTER FORTY-ONE

Dillon sat on the lounger while Taylor tried on her third dress. She tried to get Taylor to tell her what had happened, but she didn't want to talk about it. She just wanted to get to the dress shop. Dillon looked down at what she wore, wishing Taylor had been too distressed to even go shopping. "I can't believe I let you talk me into this. I'm sitting in a dress shop wearing a fuzzy robe," Dillon mumbled to herself.

Maryanne came out with a selection. "Dillon, I think you'll like these. These colors will go well with your skin tone." She smiled at Dillon, chuckling at her expression. "You're the first woman I've had to force to try on my dresses."

Dillon snickered. "I'm sorry. I'm not a gracious customer, am I? I do appreciate the time you've set aside for Taylor and me. I couldn't imagine doing this with a room full of women."

Maryanne laughed at her. "You are more than welcome. Taylor, come out so we can see it."

Taylor walked out in a floor-length silver dress. Dillon thought if she had to wear it she would most definitely shoot herself, but it was perfect for Taylor. "Wow!" Dillon said. "You look incredible."

Taylor spun around in front of the mirror, the soft organza material floated around her as it cascaded to the floor in loose layers. "It's so shiny. I love it."

"The color looks great on you," Dillon said.

Taylor looked at herself in the mirror. The A-line dress had a beaded bodice with a sweetheart neckline, accentuating Taylor's slender neck and shoulders. The built-in bra pushed her boobs up for maximum effect. It tightened at her waist then flared out. "I love this dress. What about the shoes?"

Maryanne held silver slingback pumps. "There are shimmery silver specks that will reflect the light. I think these will go perfectly with it without being too much."

Taylor took the pair of shoes and put them on. "Oh, my gosh. I love them." Taylor spun around several times. "I'll take this." She gave Dillon the hawk eye. "It's your turn girl. Get in there and try the dresses on."

"Uggh," Dillon moaned.

By the time Dillon came out with the first dress, Taylor had already changed back into her own clothes. "Bout damn time. I was beginning to think you left out the back door." Taylor frowned at the dress.

"What?" Dillon scowled at her.

"I don't like the cut or the way it fits you," Taylor said.

"No. The cut is all wrong." Maryanne fiddled with the shoulders. "Go try the bronze one on."

Dillon stared at her. "You're kidding? That one looks like a neoprene sleeve. I can't wear something like that."

"Go try it on. The material is soft, but the fabric is made with a special lining, so it will form fit to your body but won't look tight." Maryanne pushed her into the dressing room.

A few minutes later Dillon sulked out. "This is ridiculous." She stood there with her hands on her hips, staring at Taylor, who stared back with her jaw wide open.

"Holy shit. If I had your body, I wouldn't wear a damn thing. But since we can't go to the party naked, that's the dress. You need to wear it." She moved toward Dillon. "Maryanne, before she looks at herself in the mirror let's get her in the shoes and do her hair. You have some jewelry, so she gets the full effect?"

"Oh, do I ever." She handed Taylor a golden pair of ankle strap shoes. The straps were lined with stones of bronze and gold that accented the dress.

"Here put your foot in these, and I'll secure them. Do not look in the mirror," Taylor said. "How do you like to wear your hair?"

Dillon looked like she had been asked to explain nuclear fission. "Why does that matter? It's just on my head." She sighed. "Down, I guess? I planned on wearing it down. Maybe with some loose curls. That way I don't have to do much to it."

"That style will go perfectly with these," Maryanne said, and she came up behind Dillon. "Put these in your ears, and I will clasp this around your neck."

Dillon groaned as she gave into the process. "I don't like wearing a lot of jewelry."

Maryanne and Taylor both laughed. "We know," they both said at the same time.

Dillon stood still. Feeling like she was on display as both women stared at her. "What?" Dillon asked.

Neither woman said a thing. They stood and gawked with their eyes wide. Finally, Maryanne spoke. "You look unbelievably gorgeous. I have wanted to sell this dress to the right woman, and you are it. The jewelry goes with your skin and hair. My God Dillon, you are beautiful."

Taylor whistled. "You are fine as hell, mama."

Dillon turned to face the mirror. She didn't recognize the woman she saw there. The bronze color of the dress pulled out the amber in her eyes, and the jewelry complemented the different tones of color in her hair. "Wow," she whispered.

"Do you like it?" Maryanne asked.

When Dillon turned toward them, they were both huddled together waiting for her response. "Umm—I guess so." She looked at her feet then back at the two women. "You think Damien will like it?"

Taylor snorted. "I think he just might strip it off you and do you right in front of everyone when he sees you. He'll love it."

"Okay then. I'll take the whole get up. That way I can be done shopping." Dillon removed the jewelry and shoes handed them to Maryanne. "I'll go get out of this. I'm starving let's go eat."

***

Dillon and Taylor sat in a little café down from the dress shop. They both ordered sandwiches and huge glasses of ice tea. At first, they sat in silence enjoying their food. Dillon peered at Taylor over the top of her glass. "What the hell is going on with you and Joe?"

Taylor sipped on her tea. "When we got back to his house, I told him I loved him and couldn't stand him having sex with other women. He said he just wasn't ready for a committed relationship and I said okay. Then I packed up my shit and went to the Ritz." Taylor shifted around in her chair. "Dillon, I've never let myself get this far into a relationship knowing the man wasn't committed to me."

Dillon's eyes narrowed. "Then why did you do it this time?"

Taylor shrugged. "I fell in love with the big stupid Irishman. I compromised every part of myself for him. But I just couldn't do it anymore." She wiped her cheeks with her napkin.

Dillon smiled at her. "Listen, I'm not going to tell you to dump Joe and move on. I understand how frustrating and heartbreaking it is. Before Damien, I was involved with a colleague. We'd been exclusive for the better part of a year."

Dillon sat back in her chair. "I hadn't ever let a man that far into my life. One afternoon, we both had the day off, I went to his house. I wanted to surprise him. I found him in bed with another woman." She squinted at Taylor. "Talk about restraint. My hand rested on the butt of my gun. I was so tempted to shoot them both. But I was able to walk away from the relationship because I didn't love him."

Dillon leaned across the table. "I know Joe is in love with you. He's running from it. Whatever he's been through has had a long-lasting impact on how he handles his relationships. If I were you—I'd give him a little more time. With you moving here, I'd be willing to bet the other women will slowly fade away."

Taylor dabbed a napkin in the corner of her eyes. "I hope you're right. I know I walked away, but I can't help thinking I'm an idiot. These last few days being here but not seeing him have been so damn hard. I have no idea how I'm going to live here and not see him."

Dillon tilted her head. "Why are you buying a dress if you aren't even sure you and Joe are going to this stupid party?"

Taylor raised an eyebrow. "Hey, my heart may be about to shatter, but there is no way in hell I'm missing this party. I don't have to go with Joe—I'll just go with you and Damien. I'm sure there will be a few men I can dance with."

Dillon laughed. "That's the Taylor I was looking for. Not this sappy crying chick." Dillon sighed, "thanks for doing this for me today. I don't like shopping or dresses, but this was—tolerable." Dillon sat quietly for a moment. "I don't have many friends. I consider you my friend, Taylor." She stared at her food. "I haven't had anyone to talk to, not like this anyway."

Taylor recognized how hard that was for Dillon to say. She reached over and grabbed Dillon's hand. "I'll always be your friend. You can talk to me about anything. You can trust me."

"I know," Dillon said.

***

Heading home to Damien's, Dillon took the long way, a meandering road through one of Chicago's more charming neighborhoods. She noticed a car had been following them since they left the restaurant. "Hey

Taylor, did you tell anyone where we were going today?"

Taylor's posture stiffened. "No one other than Joe. Why?"

"There's a car following us. It's been behind us for a while now."

"It is a neighborhood. Could be a local." Taylor angled in her seat to get a look at it. "It's too far away. I can't get a read on the license plate." Taylor reached into her bag and pulled out her Walther CCP nine-millimeter. It was in a small holster which she clipped to her waistband.

Dillon laughed. "Is that a pink gun?"

"Hell yeah. I had this gun built for me. Cost me a fortune."

Dillon continued laughing then stopped abruptly. "It looks like our follower is trying to get a little closer. She hit the Bluetooth on the steering wheel. "Call Damien," she said at the prompt.

"Hey babe, where are you guys?" Damien asked.

"We are on Old Mill Road. We got a tail on us. Just wanted to make sure Nicky doesn't have someone following us."

"No, he doesn't. What's the description of the car?"

"Hang on. Taylor is trying to position herself. I'm going to slow down a little."

"It's dark, maybe a dark blue? It looks like a newer SUV, but it's on the small side. Slow down a bit more, Dillon. Draw it a little closer to us."

Dillon slowed the car bringing their follower closer.

Taylor continued, "I think it's a Jeep. Like one of the new Renegades."

"Dillon, don't do anything stupid. We don't know what this crazy bitch has planned." Damien told Joe to call Nicky. "I'm going to get Nicky to track your phone, and pull you up on the satellite. He might be able to get a picture of the car."

Dillon looked at Taylor. She looked calm and alert. Not one hint of fear. "Taylor, you should have been in law enforcement. You aren't even breaking a sweat."

"I'm ready, baby. After this last week, I'm ready to kick someone's ass." Taylor put her seatbelt back on.

Both laughed. Dillon could almost see the driver in the rearview. "The driver is definitely a female."

"I think you're right," Taylor said angling to look behind her. "She has dark hair, boxy style. Like a Cleopatra cut. She's wearing dark sunglasses, but she looks young."

"Dillon," Damien said. "Nicky has you on satellite. Try and keep her close but don't engage."

The jeep sped up as Dillon came up on a curve. "Oh crap, hold on, Taylor," Dillon yelled.

Dillon turned the wheels toward the oncoming lane just before impact. The jeep hit Dillon's bumper. The momentum of the impact caused Dillon's car to spin several times. When it stopped, a huge eighteen-wheeler was barreling toward them.

Taylor screamed as the truck slammed into the front bumper of the car, sending it spinning once again. As the vehicle hit the edge of the embankment, the car rolled over twice before landing on its tires.

CHAPTER FORTY-TWO

Damien stared at Joe. A loud scream came from the line just before it went dead. "What the fuck hit them?" Joe asked.

Damien dialed Nicky from his phone as he and Joe ran to the garage. "Nicky, give me Dillon's location. Did you see what hit them?"

"An eighteen-wheeler. Dad is on the phone with the local police. They are en route now."

"We should be there in twenty minutes," Damien said. He peeled out of his garage and hit the lights and sirens on his SUV. He glanced over at Joe who sat stone-faced. "They're okay. They're going to be fine."

Damien and Joe rode in silence. A cop car was just ahead of them as they hit Old Mill Road, and they could see several sets of flashing lights. As they pulled up, they saw Nicky's totaled car. It looked as if it had been picked up by a giant claw then dropped back down. The roof and sides were crushed, two tires were flat, and the entire front axle was askew.

Joe and Damien jumped from his vehicle and ran past the roadblock. Several officers tried to stop them from entering the barricades. They flashed their badges and kept running. As they ran up to the ambulance, they heard arguing.

"What the hell is wrong with you? Do you even know what you are doing?"

"Miss."

"That's Agent McGrath, not Miss. Ouch, that fucking hurts."

"Listen, Agent, I'll give you a damn lollipop if you would just sit still." The medic cursed as he tried to apply something to a gash on Dillon's head.

Taylor jumped up and ran over to hug Joe. She burrowed her face in his chest. "Oh God, I'm glad to see you."

Joe grabbed her and checked her out. "Are you okay? Holy shit, we heard the screams then the line went dead." He ran his hands over her body, checking for broken bones. He wiped the blood from her face.

"Yes, I'm fine. The cuts on my face and neck happened when the glass shattered, it sprayed everywhere. The paramedic checked out the cuts. There is no glass in them, they just look horrendous. Thank goodness I won't need any stitches. Dillon got a nasty gash on her head. Nicky's car is awesome. It may look like hell on the outside, but Dillon said it had a reinforced frame. The traffic cops and paramedics said it was the one thing keeping us from any real damage." She smiled at him.

Joe grabbed her and squeezed. He held her tight in his arms. "I didn't know what to expect driving here. I was so afraid of what I would find." He slowed his breathing down trying to stop his heart from racing. He had only been this scared one other time in his life.

Damien stared at Dillon. The paramedic had used something to slow the flow of blood from the nasty gash on her forehead. "You think she'll need stitches?" He asked the medic.

"I wouldn't get any. It will leave a nasty scar. The edges are mangled. I'm using glue. It'll help keep the skin together but keep it soft. When used in conjunction with butterfly bandages it helps the healing, minimizing scarring." He looked from Dillon to Damien. "You're going to need to replace the butterfly bandages if they peel up." He snorted as he glanced at Damien. "Good luck with that. She's a horrible patient. Also, she's going to be sore."

He nodded to Taylor. "They both are. Right now, they're hyped up on adrenaline. Once they come down, they're going to need something." He smirked at Dillon. "I suggest you give her something to knock her out."

"Haha. Screw you. Are you done?" She growled at him.

He chuckled. "Yes, Agent McGrath, I'm done. Your car and your driving saved you. Not to mention the quick reflexes of the trucker." They all turned toward the man who stood next to his truck. "If he'd hit you head on instead of clipping you, you'd be dead."

Dillon and Damien walked over to the Taylor and Joe. They stood next to some packages at Taylor's feet. Dillon glared at the boxes and bags. "Please tell me the dresses are okay?"

This was the first time Taylor saw fear in Dillon's eyes. She laughed. "Yes. Everything in the trunk was all right. I got everything out before they put it up on the tow bed." She pointed to the truck.

Dillon sighed with relief. "Thank God. If I had to go through another round of shopping for a dress, I'd be shooting someone." She stared icily at the paramedic.

Taylor chuckled. "Damien, you need to go tell them where you want the car towed. He's waiting for you."

"Thanks, Taylor. I'll be right back," Damien said.

Dillon looked back to find Joe staring at her. "What? It wasn't my fault."

Joe grabbed her and kissed her. "Damn, I'm glad you two are okay."

"Joe, how many times do I have to tell you to quit kissing my woman?" Damien asked as he came back to them. "We can go. The cops have been in touch with Nicky. He gave them all he had on the car that hit you. He couldn't get a plate number. He has forwarded them the satellite images of the impact. The driver of the truck is shaken but okay. I told him how to get in touch with Nicky to work out any damages he may have sustained to his vehicle. We'll make sure it's covered."

Joe grabbed the bags and headed toward the vehicle. He and Taylor got in the back seat. He pulled her next to him and fastened her seat belt.

"Seriously, Joe, I can buckle my own seat belt," she said.

"Sorry," Joe said as he scooted away.

Taylor reached out and took his hand. "It's okay." She leaned into him laying her head on his shoulder.

Joe kissed the top of her head but didn't say anything.

Damien glanced over at Dillon. She had a nasty bruise on her forehead. "You feeling okay? You don't feel sick or anything, do you?"

She frowned at him. "No. I'm fine. I'm pissed as hell. I want to know who this chick is. She had to have either followed us, or she knew where we were going to be and she waited for us." Dillon glanced back at Taylor who leaned against Joe with her eyes closed.

"I know Taylor didn't tell anyone where we were going. I didn't tell anyone. I didn't even know where the hell we were going until Taylor and I left this morning." Dillon shifted in her seat. "How the hell did she know where we were?"

"I don't know. I'll talk to Nicky after he's gone over the images. Hopefully, he will have some information for us." He reached over and grabbed her hand. "I'm so glad you were in one of our cars." He kissed her knuckles and held her hand as he drove home.

CHAPTER FORTY-THREE

Damien and Joe returned from getting sandwiches and entered the condo to eighties music blaring from the house speakers. "Dillon? Taylor?" Joe called out. They put the sandwiches on the kitchen table. "Where the heck are they?"

Damien frowned. "I don't..."

"We're up here!" Dillon yelled from the master bedroom.

Damien raised his eyebrows at Joe. "Hmm... I wonder what they're doing?" He smiled a devilish grin at his friend.

"Oh man, I hope it's what I'm thinking." Joe laughed as he followed Damien up the stairs.

They followed the giggles to the bathroom. The Jacuzzi tub overflowed with bubbles. A half empty bottle of wine sat on the floor, and both girls held a glass in their hand.

"Hey guys," Taylor said. She squinted at the two men. "Get that thought out of your head. We're just sore, and Dillon suggested we come up here and soak a bit."

Dillon moved closer to Taylor. She said something in her ear. She looked at her, and they both giggled. "Although, being in a tub with a beautiful woman can lead to the fulfillment of some fantasies," Dillon said winking at the two men.

Damien and Joe's mouth hung wide open. Dillon giggled at their expressions. "Oh man. You guys are pervs. Go back downstairs, and we'll be down in a few minutes." Dillon continued to giggle as Damien and Joe left the bathroom, pouting.

"You guys are nothing but teases," Joe called out as he left the room.

Dillon grabbed two towels from the heated towel rack. "I have some sweats you can borrow. You don't want to put back on those jeans."

"Oh man, that sounds fantastic. I don't think my aching body could handle getting back into those."

Dillon stood and stared at Taylor. "OMG look at your hip."

Taylor looked down. "No wonder I'm so sore when I walk. I didn't even notice that." She spun Dillon around. "Oh man. Your whole left back side is bruised. You're going to be so sore come Sunday." She put on the sweats Dillon gave her. "I think I'll drive home on Monday. I don't think I'll be able to sit in a car for three hours tomorrow."

"I think that's a good idea. Damien can even call Director Jones for you."

"I'll call him this evening. Let him know what happened. He won't mind." Taylor gathered up her clothes.

Before they headed down the stairs, Dillon grabbed Taylor's arm. "I'm sorry about today. This crazy girl is after me, and if you hadn't been with me, you wouldn't have all these bruises or almost have died."

"Hey, I had a blast today, despite the car accident. This crazy chick isn't going to run me off. Who knows how many crazy ass women will be after me if I can ever get Joe off the market. You may one day be coming to my rescue. No, you're stuck with me, Dillon." Taylor hugged her. Then pulled back with a sneaky grin on her face. "Plus, you're the only girl I've ever taken a bath with. If I ever want to do it again, it would have to be with you."

"Ha. You'd better have gotten your jollies; I don't see this happening too often. I'm hoping the reason this even happened won't ever happen again." Dillon chuckled.

"What won't happen again?" Joe asked.

"Letting you guys interrupt our bath. Next time we're locking the door." Dillon smirked at them as she sat next to Damien. She leaned over and kissed him.

"You like taking a bath with Taylor more than me?" Damien asked. He winked at Taylor as he glanced back at Dillon.

"Now I know why men are so fascinated with boobs. They are a lot of fun," Dillon said.

Taylor snorted. "You guys look like someone took your favorite toy."

Joe growled at them. "You guys are so mean. Just mean." He leaned in to kiss Taylor but stopped. "Umm—did the soak in the tub help?"

"I think the bottle of wine helped more. I'm going to let the hotel know I am staying until Monday. Riding for three hours in a car tomorrow is more than I think I can handle." Taylor moaned as she ate her sandwich. "This is the most delicious bread I've ever had. I'm going to buy some to make my lunches for work."

Joe's lips pursed together. "Kaufman's is the deli. It's near the lab," he said tersely. "We'll go and get your stuff from the hotel. I'll sleep on the fucking couch, but I'm not letting you stay at a damn hotel by yourself."

Damien and Dillon glanced quickly at each other.

Taylor's eyes were wide, and all she could manage was a nod.

Dillon gave Coach a piece of meat from her sandwich. "Has Nicky called you yet?"

"No. I was going to call him after we ate," Damien said.

They continued to eat in silence.

Joe glanced at Taylor. "You ready to go get your things?"

She sighed as she gathered the dishes from the table. "Yeah. Sure."

"Don't worry about this, Taylor. You guys go ahead and head out," Damien said walking them to the door.

Taylor hugged them both. "I'll see you guys when I move up here."

"If I don't see you or hear from you before Monday, I'll see you at work. Remember I have court Monday morning." Joe waved as he and Taylor got in his truck and left.

Damien locked the door and set the security system. He took Dillon by the hand and led her to the office. "Let me call Nicky. Then you and I can take our own bubble bath."

"You're just jealous." She ran her hands through his hair. "I like taking a bath with you. Girls do nothing for me."

His eyes darkened. "I won't say it wasn't arousing, but I'm glad to hear you say that."

Dillon laughed as she poured two glasses of wine. She handed him his. "I need this. Wait till you see the bruises on my body. Remind me to bring this bottle up with us for our bath."

Damien sat at his computer. He pulled his phone from his pocket. "Hey brother, have anything yet?"

"Dad and I have been going over the satellite feeds. We have a few makes and models the car could be. Both license plates were obscured. After I get a list of possible vehicles, we can maybe start narrowing down on employees of DC."

"I can start to work on some kind of list. Narrow in on women I have encountered through work." Damien dragged his hand through his hair.

"Tell Dillon that Mama wants you guys to come to dinner tomorrow if you're up to it. Plus, I should have those results by then. We can use Lois to run the vehicles."

"Lois would make it easier. She's great at that kind of stuff. If we do it the right way, I can do a run from home and tell the captain I didn't want any of the results to be seen on the DC computer system."

"Dinner is at four, so you guys get here by two, and we can start a run on some names. Try to stay out of trouble until then," Nicky said.

"Thanks, brother. We'll be there. Love you." Damien hung up and looked at Dillon as he sat at his computer. She was spinning around in her office chair. "You better not spin so much you puke. I'm not cleaning it up."

"I never throw up. I have to be sick to do that, really sick. What did your brother Nicky say and who is Lois?"

"Are you jealous?" He laughed at her expression. "Lois is Dad's computer system. Nicky wants to run a cross-check of vehicles matching our stalker's with DMV records. If you feel up to it, we'll go over for dinner and get there a little early and start a run on some vehicle registrations."

Dillon winced as she reached for her glass of wine. "Ouch."

Damien stopped what he was doing. "Hey, we'll go over all this stuff tomorrow, everything can wait. Let's go get into the bath."

Dillon hobbled up the stairs. She started the bath for the second time and winced as she removed her clothes.

"Holy crap, Dillon. Is that the state of Texas on your hip? Your body is a fucking road map of bruises." He spun her around. Bruises were along her hips and thigh. He watched her struggle to pull her shirt off. "Baby you can't lift your arms over your head." He stepped up to her and helped her pull it off.

"When the car rolled, I gripped the steering wheel pretty damn tight. It still didn't keep me from flopping around in that damn thing." She winced as she tried to unclasp her bra.

"Turn around. Let me do that." Damien spun her around. Once undressed, he lifted her over the edge of the tub and eased her into the water.

Dillon watched him undress. Her mouth watered. "My God you are the sexiest man alive."

Damien stepped into the tub. "Ouchy. Are you trying to boil us alive? I won't look so sexy with third-degree burns." He eased himself down, slowly adjusting to the water. He positioned himself behind Dillon and pulled her back against him.

"Here," he said handing her a glass of wine. He wrapped his arms around her. Caressing her legs and stomach. His hands moved up her torso. He caressed her back and shoulders.

"Oooh," Dillon moaned. "That feels incredible. That whole area feels knotted and tight."

"It is." Damien massaged her shoulders he made his way along each arm. She finished her glass of wine and was almost asleep in his arms. "Hey, baby let me take you to bed." He stood up and wrapped a towel around his waist. Grabbing another towel, he wrapped her up and lifted her out of the tub carrying her to their bed.

"You're going to stay with me, right?" She mumbled as he laid her down under the covers.

"I'm not going anywhere." He moved to his side of the bed. Made sure his phone was on the charger and crawled in next to the woman he loved. She snuggled her butt up against him. He reached around her waist and held her tight in his arms. "Thank you, God, for not letting anything happen to her," he said in a hushed tone as she drifted off to sleep.

CHAPTER FORTY-FOUR

December 4th
Sunday morning

Mackenzie sat in the back of the little chapel. It held around a hundred people. Once a month, Archbishop Jacobs and Bishop Cantor held a special Mass. Most of the city's dignitaries came, and then they held a small reception at the archbishop's residence. She watched as those around her listened to Jacobs speaking from the altar. His rhetoric captured their attention. He spoke about sin and entering Heaven. He said we needed to give up our fleshly desires and seek God's spirit.

Mack smirked at the hypocrisy of that statement. Archbishop Jacobs explained it wasn't just our faith but our deeds that granted us invite into the Holy Kingdom of God. However, you couldn't do good works if you weren't seeking to be more Christ-like. Seek and follow God's guidance. Without question.

Mack smiled as she heard those words. Was that not what she was doing? Had she not listened to God and done His tasks without question? That's why He had blessed her. Had brought her here to this moment. Her moment of truth.

Jacobs finished his Homily. He waited while those around him prepared for communion. He went through the rite of Transubstantiation, the moment the Host and wine were transformed into the blood and body of Christ. Today, Mack would take great joy in communion. Receiving the blood and body of Christ helped prepare her soul for the journey ahead. She knelt as the Host and wine were blessed.

As the congregation readied themselves for the walk down the aisle to receive the blessing of Christ, Mackenzie had trouble controlling her excitement. Her pulse pounded in her ears. She had to work on slowing her breathing. She had many preparations that still needed to be done. This sacrifice had to be perfect.

Archbishop Jacobs moved to the front of the altar. Mackenzie scrutinized him. He had to know what was happening under his watch. Maybe the priests weren't to blame. Maybe they needed extra guidance. Mackenzie considered that perhaps in her zeal to carry out the Lord's work, she'd overstepped.

She shook her head. No, she didn't. There needed to be examples. When Christ rebuilt the Church, those He would allow to remain in a position of power would need a reminder of God's wrath. If you stray from carrying out God's work, you must pay the price.

Mackenzie smiled as she headed down the aisle. Archbishop Jacobs stood on one side, while Bishop Cantor stood on the other. She waited for her turn. As Mack neared the bishop, she bowed. Stepping forward, she opened her mouth, waiting for the bishop to place the Host on her tongue. She crossed her chest and stepped to the side to take a sip of the wine.

At the end of the Mass, Mackenzie remained for a few moments in her seat as the others left the chapel. Both Archbishop Jacobs and Bishop Cantor stayed in the entryway greeting the parishioners. The organist continued to play. Mackenzie sat with her eyes closed and let the haunting music surround her.

As the last of the churchgoers exited the chapel, Mackenzie made her way to the far side of the altar to a large storage room. She used her key and stepped inside. The location of her sanctum was her secret. She couldn't stay here tonight, but she wanted to spend time here. In the silence, close to God.

Mackenzie settled in. The next few hours afforded her the time to speak with God. She had to make sure she'd followed His directions. Soon, the Archbishop would have choices to make. He needed to decide if he was willing to move forward with God's new plan—or if he wanted to join the bishop in Hell.

CHAPTER FORTY-FIVE

Taylor rolled over to find Joe gone. After getting her stuff last night, they didn't speak much. But she made him sleep in his own bed. It had been so hard to lay next to him and not reach out and touch him. She felt the sheets, cold. Taylor winced as she moved her legs to the side of the bed. She sucked in air through her teeth as she stood and put on her robe. "Oh my gosh," she whispered. Panting, she made her way to the darkened living room.

The glow of early morning light peeked through the curtains. Joe sat on the sofa holding something in his hand. "Joe, are you alright?"

Joe raised his head from the picture that had captured his attention. "Yeah baby, I just couldn't sleep. Why don't you come sit next to me?" He moved over and patted the sofa.

Taylor curled up at the opposite end. "What are you doing out here in the dark?"

"I couldn't shut my brain off. I didn't want to bother you, so I came out here," Joe all but whispered.

She shifted herself and faced him. She put her legs over his lap and laid her head on the back of the sofa so she could look at him. "Something's bothering you. Is it about last night?"

He handed her the photo. "No. This is Lisa. That was taken while we were dating in college. On a visit during the summer before my senior year."

She smiled at the picture. "She's a beautiful girl." She handed it back to him. "Why are you showing me her photo?"

"You and she are a lot alike. She got along with everyone. She could find the good in any situation. Lisa and I had been dating for some time when I decided I was going to propose to her. Her father had helped me plan how I was going to do it."

Taylor bristled. She wasn't in the mood to hear about a woman Joe wanted to marry. She almost got up when he continued.

"They didn't realize she was sick. She developed some rare form a Leukemia. By the time they got a diagnosis, it was too late. Her Dad called me and told me she was ill. He said I needed to come; that she didn't have long. I spent three days with her before she passed away."

Taylor's heart sank. She scooted closer. She reached out and held his hand in hers.

"I finished up my senior year of school. I was numb to everything around me. I slept with as many girls as I could. I figured if I filled my head with lots of other women, I would push her memory so far down or out that I would forget about her."

Taylor rubbed his arm. "Oh Joe, I am so sorry. I had no idea."

"Only my family knows. I haven't even told Damien about this."

"Joe, when someone like Lisa comes into your life, you aren't supposed to forget her. You should hang on to those memories and enjoy them. You also shouldn't let those memories hold you in the past."

Joe sighed as he kissed her knuckles. "I'm beginning to understand that now. When we heard the accident yesterday over the Bluetooth, my heart slammed into my chest. I was transported back to that day I received the call from Lisa's family. Driving to you and Dillon, I had no idea what I would walk into. I didn't know if you were hurt or dead.

"I promised myself after Lisa died, I would never let myself get that close to another woman. Then you came along. I've tried to keep our relationship purely sex. I've tried to keep any feelings for you pushed to the side. After yesterday, I realize I just can't do it anymore. It's just too hard."

Taylor's pulse raced. She could feel the tears forming. She blinked trying to stop them from spilling over. "I understand, Joe." She took her feet from his lap and struggled to stand.

"Where are you going?" He asked, grabbing her arm.

"To get my things. I think it's time I head back to Springfield. You've made your point. I understand now I can't compete with the memory of a dead girl. She holds too much power over you."

Joe shook his head. "No. You have it backward."

"What do you mean? I don't understand. You said you can't do this anymore."

"No! That's not it. I will always remember Lisa and love her. She will always be a part of my past that I can now look back at and remember it with gratitude. Thankful for the time I spent with her and for what she taught me about myself and about what love is. But now it's time I let her go. I'm so sorry it took you almost being killed for me to realize how important you are to me, and how much I need you in my life. I don't want to lose you. I don't want any other woman in my bed but you."

Taylor sat on his lap and wrapped her arms around him. "I love you so much, Joe. I just can't imagine my life without you in it."

"Taylor, I'm so sorry I've hurt you over these last few months. I promise I'll never hurt you again. I love you, Taylor." He kissed her. He rose from the sofa and carried her back to bed. The tightness in his chest he had since the accident yesterday was gone.

CHAPTER FORTY-SIX

Damien's parent's house was outside Chicago's city limits. The estates in this area sat on ten plus acres. Manicured lawns with horses in the pastures lined the two-lane road. Dillon ogled the massive Christmas decorations that filled many of the lawns just waiting for nightfall. The drive back would capture the spirit of the holidays with the Christmas wonderland displays.

Damien reached over and took her hand in his. "You have been awfully quiet. Are you sure you're up to going? We can always turn around."

She turned from the window and smiled at him. "No. I love your family dinners. I'm just thinking about what Sherman said to me."

"What did he say? You didn't elaborate at the house."

"He asked me about everything, wanting to know all the details of the accident. It started off as an FBI Director debriefing an Agent, but somewhere during the call it changed." She adjusted herself a little. "Man, I hope those drugs kick in soon."

She winced again as she moved around. "Sherman said he and Laura have become quite fond of me. He said he knows he gives me more leeway than he gives most under his command." Dillon stared at her hands. "He continued saying he couldn't help the way he feels about me. He and Laura think of me as a daughter."

Dillon glanced out the window. "My grandparents are good to me. They've always treated me like their child. But for so long it's just been us three. I knew I had a special relationship with Director Sherman. When the Bureau promoted him to Deputy Director and AD Reynolds became my direct boss, that's when I first noticed his attitude toward me had shifted. I knew he and his wife were fond of me, but to hear him say it—well I guess I wasn't prepared for that."

Damien kissed her knuckles. "Knowing his feelings for you makes you more uncomfortable?"

She nodded. "It does. It's been bothering me for a while. I just didn't know how to discuss it. I told you I feel like I can't find my footing lately. I can't change who I am or how I do my job."

"He doesn't want you to. You confuse his feelings for you with his ability to be your boss. Don't. They are two separate things." Damien chuckled as he squeezed her hand. "He'll still kick your ass when he needs to. And, I bet if we put some truth serum in him, he would say you bug the living shit out of him."

"Ha. I bet you'd be right. I can't wait for them to come down for the gala. They're coming in late the Friday before. He said Laura was super excited about hanging out in the suite with us. I told her to go ahead and bring her clothes, and she could get dressed with us, which means you and Joe have to hang with Sherman while we get ready."

Damien pulled into the long drive of his parents' home. "I like Deputy Director Sherman. You hang with my family, I hang with yours."

***

Dillon followed Damien into the house, and the aroma of Italian food wafted around them. "Oh man it smells so good in here," Dillon said as she inhaled through her nose.

"I bet Mom has made enough for a small army." He wiggled his eyebrows at her. "I bet she sends us home with gobs of food."

"That's the best part of coming here for dinner." She held his hand as they walked through the large entryway to the kitchen.

"*Mama, siamo qui*," Damien yelled out.

"Oh, Damiano, *siamo in cucina*," Angelina Kainetorri yelled back.

Dillon giggled to herself. This had to be the loudest family she'd ever been around. As they entered the kitchen, Damien's entire family gathered around the large island. Several dishes of cold cuts, cheeses, and antipasto dishes filled the counter. Kids ran crazy with play swords and yelling in broken Italian and English.

Dillon stared in awe at Angelina. She was a beautiful woman. Her long, lithe figure made her appear taller than five-foot-eight. The woman always dressed impeccably. Today she wore a pair of black slacks and black two-inch heeled riding boots paired with a light blue angora sweater. Who knew a sweater could be considered an accessory item to a pair of eyes? Angelina's were a lighter blue than Damien's. They had the power to pierce your soul and know the truth of who you were.

Angelina grabbed Dillon and kissed both cheeks and hugged her. "*Mia dolce ragazza.* How are you feeling?"

"I'm doing much better Mrs. Kainetorri," Dillon said.

"No, you are not to call me Mrs. Kainetorri, that was *mia Madre's nome.* You are to call me Angelina. Come; sit. I know you are sore. I can see it in your eyes. The weariness of the soul is revealed through the eyes."

Dillon wasn't sure if Angelina was telling her she looked like shit or not. Either way, Angelina could tell you what an ugly duck you were, but her accent and the smile in her eyes would make you take it as a compliment. "I'm sore, but I'm feeling better. Another day and I'll be back to normal. It smells wonderful in here. Can I help with anything?"

Damien's sister Daniella came over and sat across from her with two full glasses of wine. "No. You're still a guest here. At least for today. Next time you're here, we will treat you like family."

Nicky's wife, Catherine, laughed. "Dillon, you want to stay a guest as long as you can. Once they consider you family, your life is over."

Giovanni Kainetorri came up behind Catherine and hugged her. "You know you wouldn't have it any other way, Cat. You can't live without us." He gave her a kiss on the cheek.

"True, Papa, true." She turned to Nicky. "I used to think you were the best thing I ever got out of life," she threw her arms around Angelina, "but now I know your *famiglia* is the best thing I ever got."

Dillon drank her wine and watched the interaction with silent envy. She wanted nothing more than to have a family like this. She noticed Daniella's look out of the corner of her eye. "What?"

"I like you. Have you met Camilla yet?" She asked.

"Daniella, *chiudi la bocca grande.* I can't believe you're bringing her up." Damien scowled at his sister.

Dillon chuckled. "I don't mind. No, I haven't met her yet. For a while, we thought she might be the stalker."

Daniella pursed her lips taut. "I wish she was."

Dillon sipped her wine. "I do too. She has a hard time understanding Damien isn't interested in her anymore. She calls him more than an ex-girlfriend should. I may just have to have a conversation with her some-time."

Daniella's eyes squinted. "You should. Oh, there are so many things I would like to do to her. However, after her, I was so afraid Damien would screw up our lives again. Then he brought you home." She beamed a broad smile at Dillon.

"Brought her home? What, was she a lost puppy?" Nicky asked.

Cat had moved to sit next to Dillon. "Ignore the men. What Daniella is trying to say is, if you and Damien break up, we are kicking his ass out of the family and keeping you. You are so much better than him anyway."

Damien came up behind Catherine and tickled her sides until she cried from laughing. "I will make you pee your pants, just keep it up Cat." Damien bent down and kissed Dillon's cheek. "Believe nothing they tell you. I'm going with Nicky to try to come up with a list of suspects."

She nodded, not wanting to follow him. The medicine had kicked in, and with half a glass of wine, she wasn't feeling too much discomfort. A little dark-haired boy with the same blue eyes as Damien and Nicky ran up to her. "*La mia ragazza.*" He kissed her cheek and ran off.

Dillon looked at the ladies. "Did he just call me his girlfriend?"

They all laughed.

"Oh yeah. You are all Nicholas Jr. has talked about. He loves your blonde hair." Catherine looked over her shoulder. Angelina and Giovanni were dancing to a Dean Martin song that played softly. Daniella had run after some two-year-old that had apparently stolen his sister's dolly.

Catherine leaned in close to Dillon. "I love my husband more than I can tell you, but I'm dying to know," she glanced around then leaned in closer, "is Damien as good in bed as I think he is? I mean if he is anything like Nicky, you must be very satisfied?"

Dillon choked on her wine. She couldn't stop the giggle that came out along with a cough. She leaned in next to Catherine, "why do you think I moved in with him? For the sex. My gosh, the man is talented." She wiggled her eyebrows at Cat.

They both died laughing as Damien and Nicky walked back into the room. "What are you two up to?" Nicky asked as he sat next to his wife.

Both women answered at the same time. "Nothing." They drank their wine and laughed again.

"I don't believe them," Damien said. He kissed Dillon on the tip of her nose. "I don't even want to know what you two are talking about." He winked at Catherine who turned a dark shade of red.

***

After dinner, the kids were excused and played in the game room while the adults stayed in the dining room. Giovanni sat at the head of the table. He reached over and grabbed his wife's hand and kissed it. *"Lo sono l'uomo più fortunato."*

All conversation stopped at the table when Giovanni addressed his family. "Daniella's husband is handling a case for us up in Washington, I wish he were here. Then I would have my entire *famiglia* here with me. I look around this table and realize how lucky I am to have the love of a good woman." He looked at Nicky and Damien. "The love of a good woman makes a man great. Your mother's love has made me the man I am today. Nicholli learned early to love with his heart and not his *occhio* or *pene*. It took Damien a little longer to figure that out."

Everyone laughed around the table. Dillon had a look on her face that made Damien smirk at her. He leaned in and whispered. "I loved with my eyes and dick, not my heart."

Dillon guffawed. "If that isn't the damn truth."

Giovanni roared back in laughter. "She's the perfect woman for you, my son." He leaned over and kissed his daughter Daniella. He lifted his wine glass, *"Alla famiglia, salutare."*

"Salutare." Everyone responded.

Damien looked at Dillon. "You are part of this family. You're the best part of me."

CHAPTER FORTY-SEVEN

December 5th
Monday Morning

Damien walked into a quiet and empty VCU at seven-thirty. Detective Baker's things sat on her desk. He glanced around and spotted her and Travis in ECD talking animatedly. A quick glance at the case board showed Harris and Cooper's case remained open. He made a mental note to check in on their progress after his meeting. At his desk, Damien sorted through the files he'd taken home.

He gathered everything he needed and headed toward the conference room. Detectives Hall and Alvarez ragged on each other. "Alright, kids. The captain will be joining us, try to pull yourselves together. Where are you guys at in the investigation?"

Alvarez opened her mouth to speak when the captain strolled into the conference room. "Morning Lieutenant, Detectives. Are we ready to start?"

Damien watched as Travis and Baker raced across the pen. "We are." Damien waited for Travis and Baker before continuing. "You two look like you got something."

Travis beamed a smile at him. "Oh, Lieutenant I think you're going to want to kiss us for this." He blew past with Baker in tow.

Damien noticed Baker blushed as she went by. "Let's hear what you two have."

Everyone took a seat at the table. All eyes focused on Travis and Officer Baker. Travis started it off. "Officer Baker needs to explain what she noticed on the victim's business blog pages. Baker." He nodded for her to take over.

Officer Baker ran through the unique code she believed the families used to communicate using their salvage blog. "It was incredibly intelligent. They used pictures and text to hide secret messages. I'm not technically savvy in figuring it out. Travis can explain it better than I can. I noticed as I searched through the messages left on various blog posts that a pattern emerged. There were a lot of photos with text. Way more than what had previously been placed on their pages."

"Let me get this straight. You noticed a pattern on their business blog, leading you to think they communicated using some sort of code? The families of the dead men, used this to communicate with each other?" Captain Mackey stared at Officer Baker.

She cleared her throat. "Umm—yes, Captain, that's what I'm saying." She nodded at Travis. "He can explain how they hid their messages and then we can tell you what we've learned."

Travis nodded at Baker. "This type of code is used quite a bit, except it is usually done in a more sophisticated manner than what our families used. What they did to communicate is none the less impressive."

He turned on a massive screen in the conference room. "Alright. Here are some of the pages in question. If you look closely, you will see random letters placed in the text. Random spacing patterns, and different pictures embedded in the text as well. At first glance, it looks as if someone is posting things about the salvage company or random family notes, answering questions posed by potential clients and posting a lot of pictures."

Travis clicked on something, and it magnified the page. "The families used a form of Steganography, hiding text within images or other texts. Upon first glance, most everyone would see just these pictures and text. They wouldn't see anything that stood out. They wouldn't give it a second look. The family members embedded everything within the HTML of the pages.

"Once you see the pattern, you can remove all the excess 'noise' or letters, spacing, pictures, etc. and you get this." Travis hit a few keys, and suddenly all the text fell away, exposing a whole other subtext.

Everyone in the room sat in silence as they read the note on the screen. Damien gaped at Detective Travis. "That's fucking amazing guys. They've been holding entire conversations within a conversation."

Hall looked at Travis, his eyes were wide and gleaming with excitement. "Please tell me they tell each other where they are?"

Travis and Baker both smiled. "Yes. We have the location on two of the families. We're still decrypting some of the text. We should have all of it done within a few more hours." Travis glanced at everyone in the room. "Two of the families are at a place in the Poconos, registered under fake names. My suggestion is to let us get the location of the other three families before you move on them. That way you can hit all of them at once and take them into protective custody at the same time."

Captain Mackey rubbed his face. "We're going to need a hell of a lot of assistance to pull something like that off. Once we share our intel with the FBI, they'll take this case over." He turned toward Damien. "We need to bring Lieutenant Diego from Vice up to speed. Where's Dillon today? She in town or did she have to jet off somewhere?"

Damien realized Captain Mackey was unaware of the accident over the weekend. He glanced around. He didn't want to discuss it here. "She's at her office today."

"Okay. Get this room cleared out. I'm going to call her director. We need to have a conference call and bring them all up to date. There may need to be things they have to do on their end before we can get the families out. I'll be back in thirty. Get it together."

Damien looked at Hall and Alvarez. "I am going to push to keep you two involved as much as I can. You two need to be prepared for the FBI and DEA to take over. Both agencies have been after the Metacruze Cartel for a long time."

Hall and Alvarez exchanged glances. "We knew that would happen. Just remember, it's Vice, us, Baker, and Travis who put this nice little package together for the Feds. I want to stay involved as much as possible," Hall said.

Alvarez cursed in Spanish. "Listen, right now I want to get the families to safety. They think they can outrun this Cartel. They can't. Let's get them covered, and we can go from there." She glared at Damien. "Do not take my complacency at this moment for total cooperation and support. We're the ones who made the fucking Feds look like heroes.

"This unit and Vice need to get some of the credit. And I mean as a whole, the units, Division Central. I don't need my name in lights, but I don't want those fuckers taking credit for our hard work. Baker and Travis are the ones who have found the families."

Damien smiled. "I can guarantee Dillon won't let that happen. Even though the Feds will take over, she will make sure the credit gets put where it's due." He phoned Lieutenant Diego and told him to get his men up to the conference room.

CHAPTER FORTY-EIGHT

Joe walked into VCU as the meeting ended. Damien nodded at him. "Hey, how'd your hearing go?"

"Pretty damn good, I think."

"Well, you are just in time for an audio conference call with Dillon, her Director, AD Reynolds and Captain Mackey. We need to go ahead and update them on this floater case. Things are going to start to move damn fast." Damien glanced around leaning into Joe. "Let's try and keep the accident under wraps if we can. Nicky is going to get me some names from DMV that match up to the car at the scene. I don't want everyone knowing until we have more information."

Joe nodded. "That's probably a good idea. Since we don't know exactly where this chick is getting all her information. You at least going to tell the captain?"

"First chance I get for a private conversation." Damien set up the line for the conference call. He texted Dillon as the captain came back in. "Hey, Captain. We will be ready to go in just a minute."

The captain took a seat at the table.

Lieutenant Diego walked in and nodded at everyone, taking a seat.

Damien spoke on the conference room phone. He pushed a few buttons and audio filled the room. "Dillon are you there?"

"Yes. AD Reynolds and Deputy Director Sherman are also on the line."

"Captain Mackey, Lieutenant Diego, myself and Joe are on this end. Captain Mackey, go ahead."

Captain Mackey leaned forward. "Well, gentlemen, we have a case unfolding that you guys need to help us with." The captain brought everyone up to speed on the floater case.

Director Sherman spoke first. "Well, son of a bitch. What were these guys thinking? The minute they came across everything they had to know what it was related to. Everyone in this state and the surrounding area knew what was on that ship. Those drugs alone are worth millions."

"We're going to have to call in the DEA. The families must know where the drugs are hidden. And I'm betting it is in plain sight." AD Reynolds said.

Dillon remained quiet while everyone discussed a few of the legal and jurisdictional problems this case presented. "Listen, if the families knew about the items the salvage company brought up, there has to be one person who knows where everything is. Here's my theory: They bring up the motherlode of hauls. Between them all, they decided what to do. I'm betting they didn't tell anyone else but one family member outside the five men. One member who could be trusted not to tell anyone.

"They devised this elaborate plan should anything happen to them. I'm betting they knew they were going to be killed, so they didn't say anything. Trying to protect the one person who knew everything. I'm willing to bet the drugs have been stashed somewhere near the salvage company or their homes."

Damn good theory, Damien thought. "I think that's a plausible scenario, and if we operate off that one, we may be able to track the goods. My detectives...." At that moment, Captain cleared his throat and interrupted him.

"Gentlemen, what's your plan of action? I realize that we don't have the resources to bring in the families all at once, that's the main reason we're coming to you. I also understand the nature of this case gives you the clearance you need to take it over." Mackey paused, "I'm going to be blunt with you. I'm not going to have my men work this case for you, hunt down this lead and then let you get all the glory for our hard work. My guys have put in some long hours on this for the sole purpose of saving these families. I don't want them shut out."

"James Mackey, when have I ever tried to screw you over?" Deputy Director Sherman asked.

Mackey laughed robustly. "Shit, Phillip, every time we hit the damn fairway."

"Listen, Mackey, I want to get these families to safety. In the end, I'll make sure your men get the credit because frankly, we wouldn't have this if you hadn't given us the intel. One of the reasons we put McGrath in as the liaison to DC was because of the work the men and women at that group does. Especially Vice and the VCU. We wanted a working relationship, a good working relationship.

"I know it hasn't always been like that with the FBI, but this group works differently. Now if I am relieved of this post, that may change. Keep your people working on it. When do you think you'll know the locations of the families?"

Mackey nodded at Damien. "Director I think my guys should have that by the end of the day, or earlier," Damien said.

Sherman sighed. "Alright. Let's do this. AD Reynolds and Dillon will coordinate with DEA on the drug intel. Lieutenant Diego, we will keep you and your Captain in the loop as well."

Lieutenant Diego nodded as he made some notes.

"As soon as we know where everyone is, we can send in teams to bring them to a safe house. Hell, it might be best to take them to Quantico until we work out what to do with them. I'll work on that here and have some answers later. If I'm not mistaken, we have an undercover embedded with the Cartel. We need to bring her out before we go any further. We should be able to pull her in the next few hours. As soon as the locations of the families are known, then we can move on them."

"I'll check with my guys on their locations. I'll text that to Dillon and AD Reynolds as soon as I have it. I'll have the two detectives run down some of the main players of the salvage company, we might be able to narrow down where they hid the drugs." Damien said.

"Once we have the families and the location of the drugs, DEA can move on those," Director Sherman said. "That's a plan I like. I want updates all the way around by four today. If you find the cargo, do not move on it until we get the families. As long as that stuff is out there, it may help keep them alive if anyone gets to them first. End transmission of secure comms."

Captain Mackey stood. "Lieutenant Diego, where are you two detectives?"

"They had an overnight bust. They were processing some of our new residents in holding," Lieutenant Diego said.

"Okay. I'll make sure to inform your Captain." Captain Mackey turned towards Damien. "Get me any information as soon as you have it. It's going to be cluster fuck in a few hours."

"I'm going to update my team. Keep me posted," Lieutenant Diego said as he excused himself from the room.

Damien nodded and waited for Diego to exit. "Hey listen, Captain, we didn't have time to tell you, but over the weekend our stalker ran Dillon and Taylor off the road. Had she not been in one of my father's vehicles they would have been killed." Damien said.

Captain Mackey's mouth hung open. "Shit. I'm assuming your family is working on hunting down as much information as they can?"

"Yeah, we have some leads that may help narrow in on someone. I should have something by the end of the day or by tomorrow at least."

"Keep me posted." Captain Mackey left the room.

***

Damien and Joe headed into the pen. "Harris, where are you and Cooper on the strangled woman from the hotel?" Damien asked.

Harris smiled broadly. "It wasn't a woman."

Damien's forehead wrinkled. "What do you mean it wasn't a woman?"

Cooper walked up carrying two cups of coffee. "Hey, Lieutenant."

Damien looked between Harris and Cooper. "I didn't get the memo. If she wasn't a woman what was she? A man in drag?"

Cooper laughed. "Not quite. Seems we all thought, due to her enhanced breasts, we were looking at a female. We found out she was a he, in transition. The upper half had been completed but not the lower half."

Harris sipped his coffee. "Our girl was a regular at a lot of the conferences held at our fine city's hotels. She was quite popular too. Until a couple of days ago when she picked up a guy from Indiana."

Cooper rested against the back of his seat. He glanced at Harris. "We were able to track the video surveillance the hotel had of the conference. That night in question they were having a formal dinner party. Our dead girl was last seen leaving the main event with our suspect. Evidently, he was looking for a quickie when he pulled her into the family bathroom. When he realized she wasn't one hundred percent female, he went a little crazy."

"We have him upstairs in Interrogation. Letting him chill a little," Harris said.

Damien nodded. "Does the lab have anything?"

Cooper pulled a file off his desk. "When we found our suspect on video leaving with the victim, hotel security entered his room. We got a search warrant for his belongings and sent some stuff to the lab for DNA. We're still waiting to get the results. We recovered the clothes he wore in the video, and the lab matched the toilet water from that bathroom to a few stains on his shirt. That bathroom has one toilet in it. It was easy to make the match. That at least puts him in the bathroom, and since we have him on tape leaving with the girl, it goes a long way."

Cooper sipped on his coffee. "This guy is married with a couple of kids. He was looking for quick sex. The disgusting part, when he realized she was a he, he raped her—him. There was no seminal fluid, he had the smarts to use a condom, that hasn't been recovered. The lab found a pubic hair on our victim, which they are checking against both. With what we took from his room, we should get a DNA match if that hair matches our guy. We're letting him stew for a few, and then we'll go in and hit him with the security tape and the water stains. We'll get him to confess. If not, we'll wait on the lab."

Damien smiled at his detectives. "Good work guys. Let me know if you get him to admit to it."

Harris nodded at Cooper. "Hey, Lieutenant, me and Coop want to help in any way we can with this stalker thing. Whatever you need."

Damien grinned at his detectives. "I appreciate that guys. I do." Damien was going to have to bring everyone up to speed about the accident, but he wanted more information about this woman before he brought everyone in on it. Damien patted Cooper's shoulder as he turned to leave. "If I need any extra help, I'll let you guys know."

Damien nodded toward Joe. "Hey gather your shit, we are going to the IT company."

"You got it," Joe said.

CHAPTER FORTY-NINE

Damien pulled out of DC's garage while Joe reviewed the file. "ECD ran all the checks on the employees of the Archdiocese. Everyone's alibis checked out. The IT girl hasn't been in the office. Her boss told them she was expected back today. I thought now was as good a time as any to go interview her," Damien said.

Joe's eyebrows pinched together. "This girl is a genius. She's two years out of school and pulls in a six-figure salary. A high six-figure salary. Wow!"

"Franks from ECD said she has some of the best credentials he's ever seen. She runs this company's IT. She designed some kind of IT protocol, currently in research and development, set to revolutionize the industry."

Damien glanced at Joe. "How was Taylor feeling after Saturday? Did she go back to Springfield?"

"She did. She was sore but doing a lot better. Matt is going to help her pack everything up. She'll be up here next week. How about Dillon? She doing okay?" Joe asked.

Damien nodded. "She's doing okay. She could use another day or so. At least she doesn't have to travel. How did the rest of your weekend go? After you took Taylor to your place?"

Joe stared at his partner. He didn't want to get into his college days, but Damien deserved an explanation. "I told Taylor something that happened to me in college. It was one of the reasons I've had a hard time with relationships. I told her I only wanted her. No other woman means anything to me. It had nothing to do with her. It was my past and my insecurities. We're okay now. I'm glad she's moving up here." Joe glanced out the window as they drove along Lakeshore Drive. "You were right. I'm in love with her. It just took a while for my head to catch up to my heart."

Damien smiled broadly. "Well, it's about fucking time."

Joe smirked at his partner. "Now you can leave me the hell alone about this shit. Although I am sure you will find something else to nag me about."

"Duh, of course. I am the lieutenant. That means I'm smarter than you."

"You are a genius. I can only dream about being as smart as you one day." Joe laughed at Damien's scowl.

Damien double parked in front of Quantum. He placed his on-duty DC tag in his window. The façade was glass with lights running in parallel lines along the scale of the building.

Joe's eyes followed the lights up the side of the building. "Fancy. I guess we're in the wrong business. I wonder if they're hiring?"

"What, and give up this glamorous lifestyle we live? What other job allows us to park wherever the hell we want?"

"True, how silly of me to even consider a career change."

***

The entryway was clean and sparse. Three identically dressed people, two females and one male, manned several workstations. All three sat with headsets, frantically typing on computer keyboards projected onto their desktop.

"Welcome to Quantum, how may I direct your visit today?" One of the triplets asked.

"We need to speak with Caroline Fredrick," Damien said.

The second female at the desk glanced at them. She smiled ruefully, pressed a few buttons and spoke into her headset. "Miss Fredrick, you have visitors in the lobby. Yes, we will. Thank you." The woman pointed to the elevators. "Take the elevator marked Corporate and go to the top floor. Reception will take you to Miss Fredrick's office."

Joe and Damien walked in silence. They both glanced over their shoulders. Joe leaned into Damien. "Are we sure they're even human? You know I saw one of those electronics specials where they talked about new types of robot assistants. Maybe those are test models."

Damien frowned at him. "Any other time I would think you've lost your mind, but now, I don't know, Joe. I just don't know."

Upon exiting the elevator, Damien and Joe were greeted by another woman. "May I ask for your credentials and why you are here for Miss Fredrick?"

Damien and Joe both produced their IDs. Damien smiled at her. "Here are our IDs. As to why we're here to see Miss Fredrick, that shall be stated to her."

She huffed and thrust her chest out. "I need to know the nature of your visit. Or you can arrange for an appointment. A scheduled appointment." She puckered her lips as she waited.

Joe sniggered, causing Damien to give him a sideways glance. "Listen, the only scheduled appointment you're going to get is the one down at Division Central when I haul your ass in for pissing me off. I suggest you lead us to Miss Fredrick's office, or I will lead you out in handcuffs."

The tight assed assistant sneered at them before turning on her heels and leading them down a hallway. Three offices occupied this area. The first one they came to had an attractive young lady behind a half-moon shaped desk. She wore a headset and typed on two keyboards, while she called out voice commands. When they entered her office, she paused her work. "Yes, Marta?"

"These two police officers would like to speak with you." Marta spun around and stomped from the room.

Caroline Fredrick was small and thin, rippled in rock solid muscle. Her height put her right at Joe's chest, about five foot seven. She stood up and extended her hand. "I get the impression you're more than police officers. What can I do for you?"

"I'm Lieutenant Kaine, and this is Detective Joe Hagan, we're with Division Central. We're here to ask you some questions about your work at the Archdiocese."

She sat and gestured toward two chairs. "Please have a seat. I'm not sure why you need to ask me about my work for Bishop Cantor."

Damien pulled out his notepad. "We're investigating the recent deaths of a few of the priests in this area. First, can you tell me about your job in Bishop Cantor's office? How did you get started there?" Damien asked.

"My mother volunteered quite a bit. After her death, I decided I needed to do the same. I chose to use my IT skills to help get the Archdiocese's computer system up to date," she said.

"Have there been any system compromises, anything making you think an unauthorized user had accessed the protected files on the server?"

She shook her head. "No. I'm the one who has full range of the system and all its data. Besides Anthony and the bishop, of course."

Joe smiled at her. "We're concerned about sensitive information that

may be related to these cases. Do you have any idea how password protected information could've been compromised?"

Caroline shifted her chair around. She squinted at the two men before her. "Listen, I'm not sure what all this is about. I'm given the
password if I need to get into the system and make updates, but I don't
have regular access to the network."

"But you are one of three that can access this information. Please understand we're trying to clarify a few things. Can you tell us how hard it
would be to hack into the Diocese's system? I imagine you set up the
security on their network?" Damien asked.

Caroline's nostrils flared. "Yes, I set up the network, the protocols,
and the security. I don't think it would be too easy for anyone to hack
in. You'd need a certain skill set to do it," Caroline crossed her arms over
her chest.

Damien raised an eyebrow at her. "A skill set you possess." He let the
statement sink in a moment. "Can you tell me where you were last Sunday night? As well as Wednesday morning between the hours of nine-
thirty and eleven-thirty, and Friday during ten-thirty to roughly one
p.m.?"

She shook her head. "Why? Am I suspect?"

Damien glanced at Joe. He cocked his eyebrow at him and smirked.
He turned back to Caroline. She squirmed in her seat and pulled on a
piece of her hair. "Miss Fredrick, you're not a suspect, per se. Due to the
nature of the crimes, we need to question all employees and volunteers
at the Archdiocese. Can you answer the question?"

She reached into her desk drawer, retrieving a leather-bound journal. Flipping through the pages, she looked at the dates. "Sunday I was
at home. My mother's passing keeps me close to home these days. As
for the other days, I was here working. Wednesday, we had a meeting,
and I was here in my office. The same for Friday."

Joe leaned in glimpsing her date book. He caught her looking at him.
"Nice handwriting. It's unusual." He smiled at her.

"Thank you. I think I got it from my dad. He used to write like this.
Do my answers satisfy your investigation?" She asked.

"Actually, I'll need the names of those colleagues in the meeting with
you on both days. Did anyone see you in the office on either day? If so,
I'll need to speak to that person as well. And if you could provide the

times you entered and left the building that would be great. You guys must have some way of keeping track of your arrival and departure from the building?" Damien said.

Caroline's face reddened, and she struggled to make eye contact with Damien. Her lips pursed together. "It'll take me some time to get the list of names together. Human Resources has my arrival and departure times. It will take some time to get it from them. Can I call you with all that information?" She rose from her desk. "I have nothing to do with your investigation. I don't like being accused of something I didn't do. Now, if you'll excuse me, I'm on a tight deadline for a project, and I need to get back to work."

Damien rose. "Sure. I need those names and times by this afternoon. The faster we can eliminate the staff, the sooner we can move on to other persons of interest." Damien turned back to Caroline as he reached the doorway, "Miss Fredrick, do you know a Father Martin?"

Caroline's posture stiffened. She clenched her jaw before she regained her composure. "No, that name doesn't sound familiar to me. Sorry, I can't be of more help," she said.

Joe held out his notebook to Caroline. "Could you write down the best security software for a laptop? I know I shouldn't bother you, but I read about your abilities in this area, I thought I would get the best information from the best qualified." Joe smiled one of his sexiest smiles at her.

Caroline's eyebrows wrinkled. She snatched the notebook from him. She scribbled on it as she spoke. "Thank you for the compliment. I've worked hard to learn my craft. It's delightful when someone outside the field recognizes it. This list should give you the best ones to use on any system."

"You've been a great help. Thank you. Please get me that information. We can see ourselves out," Damien said as they left her office.

Outside, Joe stared at the building. "I don't know about you, but that was the weirdest interview I've ever conducted. I felt like I stepped into a futuristic version of *Logan's Run*."

Damien smirked. "*Logan's Run?* Where the hell did you come up with that one?"

"Hello, did you pay attention to all the assistants? Uniformity, no individualism. That place is creepy. Not to mention our girl in there was *off her nutts.* She was a tad bit defensive."

"Now, that I agree with. Why did you ask her to write in your book?"

"When she pulled out her appointment book, I noticed the unusual handwriting. The notes that were left at the crime scenes were hand-written. I wanted to look at them side by side."

Damien pulled away from the curb. "Good catch. We can swing by the lab you can run it in and give it to Roger. They can see if there are any similarities to the other notes. Regarding her times in and out of the building, Human Resources wouldn't have given us any information without a warrant, but I'll say this; I don't believe her alibis. I think she's lying to us."

Joe nodded. "I got that. If she was here Tuesday and Wednesday, that keeps her from being our killer. However, her defensiveness to our questions puts her at the top of my list for getting the information about the priests. Maybe she just inadvertently told someone about the private information in the records."

Damien eased into traffic. "If I don't hear from her by tomorrow morning, I think I'll send an officer to pick her up and bring her back to DC. We can see how she likes our building."

Joe chuckled. "I'm positive she won't like it. Not shiny enough for her."

CHAPTER FIFTY

Walking back into the VCU it looked as if the inmates were running the asylum. "WTF? Is the President coming for a visit or what?" Joe asked as he watched the chaos unfold.

Damien watched as his motley crew hustled about. "Fuck if I know." He whistled. All movement stopped. Then started right back up again.

Detective Cooper came running over. "Lieutenant, we were about to call you, but we wanted to confirm the information first. I know Travis has information on the family members, and we think we've located the drugs. Vice is here, and Baker and Travis are pulling some satellite intel on the area in question."

Damien glanced around the room. "We're gone for a few hours, and all hell breaks loose. That's great Coop, where did they hide the drugs?"

Cooper turned toward ECD. Turning back to the Damien he smiled. "Give us ten minutes. Let me get Travis and the others into the conference room and we can better explain."

"Okay. I'll be in there in ten minutes. I need to notify Captain Mackey anyway. He wanted to know the moment we found the families and the drugs. Ten minutes. Where are Hall and Alvarez?"

"They're out with some of Diego's men en route to the site."

The conference room filled up. Damien stood in the doorway as his detectives, Vice, and several others worked in a choreographed routine of laying out all the data. Travis from ECD had grabbed another uniformed officer to help him, and Officer Baker worked on the satellite images. He noticed Joe wasn't in the room. He scanned the squad room; no sign of him.

Damien heard footsteps behind him in the corridor. "Hey, Captain. They're setting up to give us the data. Once we have the location, we're going to send a few undercover officers out that way to do a visual and sit on the site until we can retrieve the drugs. Once the load has been visually verified, then we can notify the DEA, and the FBI can then move on the families."

Captain Mackey stood at the door with his arms crossed. "Your men have found the locations of all the families?"

"Yes, Sir. Baker and Travis located the three remaining families about an hour ago. One is in the Hamptons, and two of the families are at a secluded resort in Sedona Arizona. They have the names they're using as cover. Did the Feds pull out their undercover?"

"Yes. As soon as our conference was over. Director Sherman figured after our update things were going to move rather fast. Instead of waiting then doing it, he went ahead and pulled her out."

Damien led the captain into the conference room. "Tell me what you guys have. Travis, I need a list of the families, the names they're using, and their exact locations to give to the captain. He's coordinating with the FBI on their pickup." Damien turned toward Captain Mackey, "have they decided where they'll take the families?"

Mackey sat at the head of the conference table. "To Quantico. That compound is secure, and the families can be debriefed and protected 24/7." Captain Mackey dragged his hand down his face as he leaned back in the chair. "These greedy bastard fishermen have no idea the danger they put their entire families in. Their whole lives are about to be turned upside down."

Damien sighed as he sat next to his Captain. "Travis, are you ready?"

"Just about, Lieutenant Kaine." He fiddled with his computer.

Lieutenant Diego walked into the conference room. "Hey Captain Mackey, Kaine. Using the preliminary information, I have several officers on their way so we can be ready to do a visual confirmation. My understanding is this area is sparse. Not a lot of foot or vehicle traffic."

Travis looked up at the room. "We're ready." Using a laser pointer, he motioned to a satellite image on the screen in the room. "After this morning, it didn't take us long to narrow in on the remaining families. They're getting a little sloppy in their comms, so it was a lot easier to track them down." He nodded to Officer Baker who handed a printout to Damien. "I don't think we have time to waste. If we could find them, so can the bad guys."

Captain read the list as he handed a card to Travis. "Here it is. Make that happen now. Deputy Director Sherman is waiting for the information. He can have teams out in the next hour, after locating the drugs."

Travis handed the card to Officer Baker who sent the information out via a second laptop. "Done," she said as she gave the card to Mackey.

Travis stood next to the image on the screen. "Here is where we believe the drugs are being stashed. This was genius on the part of the fisherman. This facility is a cold storage the salvage company uses when they need to store their fish. It has the capacity to handle live storage. The fish remain alive and fresh until just before their scheduled shipment.

"I know from the work logs of the salvage company they hadn't brought in a load of fish in the last few weeks. I tapped into the electricity usage of the facility and noticed an increase in the amount of power usage. These tanks make it ideal to hide the drugs. All they had to do was package the drugs and load in some fish on top—literally hide them in plain sight."

"How far from the salvage company is it?" asked Damien.

"Within a mile. This area is used for other industrial enterprises. This building that the salvage company uses has had some recent upgrades to their security. When I considered their holdings, I noticed some of their paperwork indicated this site, and it seemed like a logical place to start." Travis looked at Lieutenant Diego, "did you send your guys in like I said?"

Lieutenant Diego laughed. "They were glad they didn't have to dress up like bums this time." Diego turned to Captain Mackey. "He wanted us to go in as maintenance for the security system. It's the perfect cover. I sent in three to get close to the building, and there are another eight in the surrounding area."

The security team came into view on the live satellite feed. "There they are," Diego said. All heads turned toward the screen.

Captain Mackey focused on Diego. "How quickly can your guys get in and verify?"

Diego nodded toward Travis. "He got us the codes to get in the door. They should be texting me if they find the drugs."

Mackey pulled a card out of his pocket along with his cell and laid both on the table. "As soon as you know, I know. I have the DEA team leader for this area on standby. He'll have a team there to back your guys up and take the drugs into custody."

Diego and Kaine's phones both pinged at the same time.

"They've verified the drugs are on the premises," Diego said.

"Hall and Alvarez confirm as well. The rest of the team is surrounding the area," Damien said.

Captain Mackey picked up his phone. "Give me the address," he said to Travis. "Johnson, it's Mackey. Our guys got a fix on the drugs." Mackey read the address on the sheet of paper Travis handed him. "Let me know when your team has sealed the area. I've contacted Sherman, he should have his teams en route to pick up the families. I'll make sure you know when I know."

Captain Mackey looked around the conference room. Everyone had stopped what they were doing and waited. Captain Mackey walked to the large screen. Several officers glanced at Damien, who merely shrugged.

The captain turned toward everyone in the room. "Very few times in my military or police career have I been impressed. This is one of those times. You set aside your differences and worked together on a case where lives of woman and children literally hung in the balance. Damn good job." He zeroed in on Officer Baker. "You, if you hadn't found those weird entries, this would've taken longer to put together. Damn good work Officer Baker, Detective Travis. All of you, damn good job." Captain Mackey left the stunned and silent room.

Damien focused on Officer Baker. Her round eyes locked on his. For a quick moment, he saw something fleeting. He wasn't sure what it was, just something—odd. *Googly eyes.* He smiled at her, and she turned bright pink. "Good job, Baker. Everyone, wrap it up. Document every-thing. Lieutenant Diego, make sure your men write up everything, even when the DEA comes on the scene. I want everything in writing so that when those fuckers try to take credit—and you know they will—I don't want there to be any confusion as to who put this op together. Today we made the DEA and the Feds look like they have a clue how to do their jobs."

Lieutenant Diego laughed. "You got it, Kaine." He walked over to him. "Listen, I know your girl is a Fed, I hope we can count on her to make sure we aren't left out."

Damien took the lieutenant's extended hand and squeezed a little too hard. "You don't have to worry about Dillon. She's made sure her bosses know she takes her liaison job to heart. She's looking out for Division Central, the entire DC and all the units in it. That includes your sorry ass as well."

Diego smiled. "It'll be my sorry ass that takes her off your hands one day. Oh, by the way, thanks for the invite to the shindig in two weeks. I got a hot redhead I'm bringing with me."

"Don't thank me. My Dad invited the entire place. Even those on duty can show up. They just can't drink. Relay that to your guys."

Diego nodded as he headed out the door. "Hey Joe, you missed all the excitement," he said walking by.

Joe looked around at the few remaining detectives and officers in the room. "Damn, I missed it again?"

Damien scowled at him. "Where the hell have you been?"

"Talking with the DA. What happened here?"

"Well, the DEA is securing the drugs as we speak." Damien nodded as he headed toward his office. "The FBI should be rounding up the families. I was about to call Dillon and see if she had any updates. I want to call Father Cattaloni and see if he was able to get the names of those three women."

Damien's desk phone rang as he entered his office. "Kaine. Okay, send him on up." He squinted at Joe. "That was the front desk, Father Michaliska is downstairs. I wonder what he's doing here?"

Joe cocked an eyebrow at him. "Hmm, maybe he has some information on our guy."

"Well, we'll find out now, here he is." Damien walked toward his door. Father Michaliska had circles under his eyes, his skin pasty. "Father what can I do for you?" He gestured to a chair next to Joe. "You remember my partner, Detective Hagan."

"Yes, yes I do. Detective. I'm sorry to bother you Lieutenant Kaine, but I thought you should be told about something." The Father sat in the chair and held his hat in his lap. "Yesterday, in the evening—wait, let me back up. We keep the chapel open late. The rest of the church is locked down. The chapel has its own entrance. Anyway, we leave it open late for parishioners to come in and spend time in prayer. Well, I'm the one who locks the chapel at night. After your visit, I decided to close the chapel early. I didn't want to put anyone else at risk, and I didn't want to be alone in it."

Damien noticed he shook. "Take your time, Father. Can I get you something to drink?"

Father Michaliska let out a long shaky breath. "No son, thank you. I might throw it up."

"All right then. Take your time," said Damien.

Michaliska took several deep breaths. "After your visit, I was terrified. The thought of being on someone's hit list had me rattled. I confided in our maintenance man, and he agreed we should close the chapel early. So about seven he and I went through the church. He's decided to stay late with me for the next few days. He locked up the church while I was in the chapel.

"I'd locked the doors and was blowing out a few of the worship candles. I heard someone trying to open the door. At first, I thought I should open the door and let them know we would be closing early for the next several weeks. Then I remembered your warning. I peered out through the side window and saw the man you described—except something seemed wrong."

Both Damien and Joe leaned into the priest. They exchanged glances with each other.

"What do you mean something seemed wrong?" Joe asked.

Father Michaliska sighed. "I know your description said it was a skinny young man. He was dressed as you described, and he had a scruffy goatee. It wasn't real. The goatee looked fake." The priest squirmed around. "I know you two are the detectives, but I would swear on the Holy Mother, it was a woman. A petite woman."

Michaliska lifted his gaze to see Damien squinting at him. "I know you think I've spent too much time at the bottom of a bottle. I swear to you it was a woman. I yelled through the door, telling her the chapel was closed and said to come back tomorrow. The person looked around—somewhat surprised—and ran off." Michaliska shook his head. "I swear it was a woman."

Damien studied the father for a few moments. It made sense. "Father, not for one moment do I think you're making a mistake. I believe you. I want to thank you for coming in and telling us. With this incident, please keep up the extra security. Maybe you could take a short vacation."

The father smiled at Damien and Joe. "Yes, a trip to see my sister in upstate New York might be the best thing."

"Don't tell anyone about your trip, though. Tell everyone you're going somewhere else." Joe said as they all stood.

"Yes, yes I will." Father Michaliska shook both their hands and left.

Joe and Damien sat back down. "What do you make of that?" Joe asked.

"I'm not sure yet. Before today and the interview with Caroline Fredrick, I wouldn't have considered it. Couple that with Father Martin and the circumstances of his death, it had a way more personal feel. But whether Caroline did it or helped feed the information to someone I'm not sure. I need to run this by Dillon." Damien pulled his phone out.

"Hey, babe. What's up? Do you have any updates on the FBI and their round up of the families? Wait, I'm putting you on speaker. Go ahead. I'm sitting here with Joe."

"Hey, Agent," Joe said.

"Hey, Joe. As for the update, the teams have rounded up all the families. They're on their way to Quantico. I spoke with Agent Michaels who headed up one of the teams, he said it seemed as if the mothers were grateful for the help. Every member of the family in the Poconos was tired of hiding out.

"They didn't know what to do. It looks like the wife of the owner of the company has some papers which should explain what her husband and the other men got themselves into. They didn't mean for any of this to happen. It's a damn shame all around. I just got off the phone with Captain Mackey and Captain Shapiro of Vice.

"The DEA and the FBI will hold a press conference this evening at DC, along with Mackey, Shapiro and Chief Rosenthal. AD Reynolds and I will speak. Have your squad and Diego's team there to watch. I think it's going to take place at seven, that's what I have been told anyway."

"Great, as long as I don't have to speak," Joe said. He popped a handful of jellybeans into his mouth.

"Listen," Damien said, "there's another reason I called. Father Michaliska came in. He's one of the priests we warned about being in danger. Long story short, he got a glimpse of the suspect. He showed up at his church last night. He swears it was a woman at his doorstep."

"He's positive it was a woman?" She asked.

"He swore on the Holy Mother. Hear me out—if we separate Martin's death, is it a stretch to think he was the one person this killer wanted dead? The attack was so personal, so filled with rage and anger."

There was silence for a moment. "No, I don't think that's a stretch. It makes sense. Something he did or more than likely didn't do made the killer very upset. If you can figure out who he was close to, or someone with lots of interaction with Father Martin, you should be able to find your suspect.

"I will say this; I hadn't considered a woman just because of the nature of the crimes. Women don't usually kill in this manner. The beating of Father Martin isn't something a woman would usually carry out. This person is dangerous. And if she can't get to the priests on her list, she may go for someone else. Someone who will make up for the two left. Someone with standing and importance."

"I was leaning that way. I think I have an idea on that," Damien said.

"Okay, we'll talk more about it later. I'll see you at the news conference," Dillon said.

Damien checked the clock on the wall. "Crap, it's almost six now." He got up from his desk and went to the bullpen. Alvarez and Hall were telling everyone about the drugs. Travis and Baker and all of Vice were sitting and talking about the op. Lieutenant Diego caught sight of him and nodded.

"Hey, Kaine. Did you hear about the press conference?" Diego asked.

"Yeah, I was coming out to inform everyone. Hall, order up some pizza from the canteen, tell them to charge me."

Hoots rang out through the squad. "You got it, Lieutenant."

"Travis, rig the board to carry the press conference. We can all watch from in here."

"Not a problem at all Lieutenant." Travis tapped out commands on the whiteboard.

Damien called Captain Mackey. He asked Damien for specifics about the case. He wanted to be prepared for the questions from the news corps. For a few moments during the conversation, Damien thought the captain would tell him to be at the press conference. He hung up the phone and sighed. "Damn we squeaked by. We don't have to participate in the conference."

"Hot damn. That's something worth celebrating." Joe took another handful of the colorful beans.

"You owe me a bag of jellybeans. And not the cheap ones either. I want Starburst and the Jelly Belly ones."

Joe frowned. "You're so damn picky."

CHAPTER FIFTY-ONE

Everyone gathered around the board in VCU. Several other officers and detectives from other divisions were present as well. Damien figured his bill to the canteen would be several hundred dollars based on the display of empty soda cans and pizza boxes. Captain Mackey, Captain Shapiro, and Chief Rosenthal stood behind the podium set up out front of Division Central. AD Reynolds stood next to Dillon, and DEA Special Agent Johnson stood next to the chief.

Hall nodded to Damien. "Hey what did you do to Dillon? How did she get that nasty cut on her head?"

Damien glanced at Joe, then smiled at Hall. "My nephew got a little excited this weekend. Hit her with one of his toy trucks."

"Well even with that big ass bruise she's still too beautiful for your ass," Lieutenant Diego said laughing.

AD Reynolds spoke first. He outlined the case from the beginning. After running through certain facts of the case, he handed it over to the DEA Agent in charge. Damien didn't like him from the minute he stepped to the podium, he made the hairs on the back of Damien's neck stand up.

"Good evening. First, I want to explain our intel and how it gave our agents the ability to recover the drugs. This operation has helped us cripple the Metacruze Cartel." As the Agent continued to speak, the VCU became more and more unruly.

"Are you fucking kidding me?" Lieutenant Diego yelled. "This guy is making it look like his unit did all the work. He hasn't once acknowledged our work." Diego threw his empty can across the room.

"*Eso bastardo pésimo!*" Yelled Alvarez. "He knows he didn't have shit until we gave it to him."

Damien looked at Joe. His partner's jaw was clenched. "Look at Dillon. She's pissed."

Joe stared at the TV. "What do you think she's saying to AD Reynolds?"

Diego glanced over at Damien. "I don't know if even your girl can fix this, but look at our Captains. I think one of them may shoot the guy in the back."

Everyone murmured as they continued to watch the news conference. Finally, Agent McGrath stepped up to the podium. Damien noticed AD Reynolds glare at Captain Mackey and made an almost unnoticeable nod.

Dillon stood at the podium as questions rang out. She said nothing. She waited for them to be quiet. Within a few moments, the news reporters got the message and quieted down. "I'm Agent Dillon McGrath, the liaison between Division Central and the FBI. I'm also a profiler with the FBI. I need to correct my esteemed colleague Special Agent Johnson. I believe in his zeal to explain the role the DEA played in this operation he may have misrepresented his men and himself."

Dillon turned to glare at the DEA Agent. "Through the efforts of Vice and the VCU Detectives, Detective Travis and Officer Baker of Division Central, these men and women spent the better part of two weeks hunting down the intel which led to the safe return of five families and the confiscation of drugs with a street value of several million dollars."

The squad room cheered. "That's my girl!" Yelled Hall. "I knew she wouldn't leave us hanging."

Everyone high-fived each other. They watched the rest of the press conference unfold. The tension between Agent Johnson and Agent McGrath was evident even on the television feed. Within a few minutes of its conclusion, the panel from the press conference entered DC. There was a loud argument as both Dillon and Agent Johnson entered the pen area. All conversation stopped as everyone watched the interaction.

"Listen, McGrath, you had no right to embarrass me in that news conference. Who the hell do you think you are?" He spewed at her.

She spun around and faced him. "Who the hell do I think I am? Who the hell do you think you are? Where the hell do you get off trying to take credit for all the intel? Acting like your agency put this whole operation together? How many years have you been working on the Metacruze Cartel with no headway? And in two weeks this group of men and women gave your agency a fucking gift, and yet you stood up there at the news conference and tried to make yourself look like the damn hero."

About then Chief Rosenthal, Captain Mackey, Captain Shapiro and

AD Reynolds walked up behind them.

"This group got lucky. We're the ones who put in all the hard work. They're a small part of the operation."

Dillon moved a little closer to him. "You are completely delusional. This team gave the Feds and the DEA more information than we've gathered in months. Because of the work they did, the Cartel has suffered a severe blow, one that might shut them down. And I will not stand by and let you or me take the credit for something we didn't do."

He poked her in the chest. "Just because you're fucking the almighty Kaine and have access to his family doesn't make you anything special. It makes you a fucking whore."

All heads turned toward Damien. Joe grabbed his shoulder. His fingers dug in as he shook his head.

Agent Johnson's finger still rested on Dillon's chest as he spoke. She looked at his hand, in a quick and agile move she grabbed his finger, bent it awkwardly to the right, bending his hand backward at its joint and brought his arm up behind his back. The move put enormous pressure on his joint causing him instant pain. He struggled against Dillon's hold.

Dillon leaned into him. "I don't care what you want to call me, but if you ever lay another hand on me again, you will draw back a bloody fucking stump."

"Agent, that's enough. Let him go." AD Reynolds said. "Johnson, you were way over the line. I'll speak to you and your superior later."

Everyone remained quiet as Johnson rubbed his wrist. He turned to leave. Before exiting, he looked back at Dillon. "This isn't over." He stormed out.

Hall leaned into Damien. "Lieutenant, I'm so in love with your woman."

Everyone within earshot chuckled.

Dillon shot a side glance at Damien before addressing her superior. "I'm sorry for that, AD Reynolds. He had every right to be upset with the conference, but it was his stupidity that made him look like an ass, and he had no right to lay a hand on me."

"We'll discuss this later. Enjoy your time with these men and women. We'll have a debriefing tomorrow at the office via telecom with Deputy Director Sherman. Nine o'clock sharp Agent. Gentlemen." Reynolds nodded to everyone as he made his way out of the unit.

After a little more laughter and high fives, everyone not on-duty headed home. Dillon told Damien she would meet him at the house.

Damien grabbed his notes and files on the dead priests and noticed a fax on his desk. Father Cattaloni had sent names of the three women. Damien stuffed it in his file not wanting to deal with it now.

CHAPTER FIFTY-TWO

Damien parked in his garage, grabbed all his files, and headed into the house. He made his way to the kitchen and leaned against the doorway. Dillon had a large glass of wine and was dancing to the music as she stirred a pot on the stove. She stopped to feed a morsel to Coach, who sat on the counter before she continued stirring. Damien smiled as he stood there and watched her hips shake to the beat of a Rick Springfield song, completely oblivious to his presence.

She turned around. "Oh my," she said as she clutched her chest. She quickly recovered and smiled at him. "I wondered where you were." She stepped to him and put her arms around his neck. "I was beginning to think you'd run off with your secret admirer." She bit his bottom lip before she kissed him.

His chuckle swallowed by her kiss. "Yeah, I'm here to pick up a change of clothes." He grunted as she punched him in the stomach. "How are you feeling?"

"I'm doing better. Movement helps keep me from getting stiff. Set up some glasses with water. I'll pour you a glass of wine." Dillon pulled another wine glass from the cabinet, filled it, and then filled two bowls with leftover spaghetti she'd been reheating. "Hey grab the bread out of the oven and cut it up for me."

As Damien did that, she got a bowl of salad and a jar of dressing from the refrigerator.

"This looks great, Dillon."

"Well, it's your mother's cooking. Can't mess it up too much. Since it's so late, I didn't have time to make the chili I wanted to. I'll do that another day. I got a recipe from Taylor. She has promised to help me become a better cook."

Damien took a bite of the spaghetti. "Oh man, this is great. I didn't realize how hungry I was. I bought the guys pizza, but I didn't eat."

"Why does Italian food taste so much better a day later?" Dillon asked, putting a bite in her mouth.

"It's the gravy."

Dillon tilted her head. "Huh? We aren't eating gravy."

Damien chuckled. "If the sauce has meat in it, it's called gravy. No meat, it's called sauce, or just marinara. The juices soak into the pasta, and the flavors develop more."

Dillon's mouth hung open. "Do all Italian boys know this?"

"Yes. If you don't, you aren't really Italian."

They sat in silence for a few moments. Damien stopped eating and looked at her. "If Joe hadn't stopped me, you may have been visiting me in jail tonight. When that fucker called you a whore, I was ready to pound his sorry ass into the ground."

Dillon took a long sip of her wine. "He hates you and your family. He only called me a whore to get at you."

Damien's spoon stopped midway to his mouth. "What do you mean? I don't even know that guy. We've never had to deal with DEA before. Why the hell does he hate me?"

She swallowed a bite of food. "He knows who you are. Your family has a prominent standing with several government agencies, including the DEA. I know Johnson's supervisor has consulted your dad on a lot of cases. Johnson's investigation into the Cartel had stalled. He took this opportunity to make himself look better to his superiors."

"How do you know this? And more important, when did you know this?" Damien set his fork down.

"I knew about some of it when you guys briefed us about the case during the telecom conference. Director Sherman and AD Reynolds informed me we'd be dealing with him. They told me about his disdain for you and your family—you, especially."

"Is that why you did what you did during the news conference?" Annoyance laced Damien's tone.

Dillon raised an eyebrow at him. "Do not take that attitude with me. I can feel the tension rolling off you." She shifted in her chair. "When that asshole started to use the news conference to make you and your guys look like you had nothing to do with this op, it infuriated me. I leaned over to AD Reynolds and told him I wasn't going to allow him to do it. So I corrected it. Even if I weren't dating you, I would've done the same thing.

"Now, when he called me a whore, I couldn't have cared less. He did it to get a rise out of you. And had you taken the bait, he would have no doubt used that to mess with you and your family. To discredit you or to piss you off.

"However, when he put his hand on me, that was against me. He figured he could embarrass me by poking me in the chest, he tried to make me look like a weak woman. Implying that I got my standing by fucking my way to the top. So don't give me shit. I had every right to protect myself. I've had just about enough of fucking men telling me what to do when to do it, and how to do it."

Damien rubbed his temples. "I'm not giving you shit. I sure as hell have never told you what to do." Damien's lips pinched together. "I don't need you fighting my battles. If that asshole wants to come after me, fine. You don't need to run interference and protect me. I'm a grown man."

Dillon's eyes shot daggers at him. "Are you serious? You think I was sticking up for you? Trying to fight your battles? You're acting like an ass. I was just letting you know why I think he called me a whore. Solely to get a reaction out of you. And it seems to have worked. His name calling doesn't bother me. But he had no right to touch me. Here's a thought for you, I don't need you to come to my rescue. I did just fine on my own without you!"

They sat in silence, both too stubborn to give in. Damien pushed his food around. Lifting his gaze, he smiled at Dillon. "I'm sorry. I would've done the same thing if I was in the news conference."

Dillon didn't acknowledge his apology. "I received a call from Sherman earlier. AD Reynolds phoned him and gave him all the details."

Damien sat and waited for the rest. He watched her pick at her food. "And?"

She sipped her wine. "My actions during the news conference didn't sit well. Right after the conference, Sherman got a call from Johnson's boss. He bitched about my actions. Said I needed to be reined in. After speaking with AD Reynolds, my director had to call Johnson's boss back and fill him in on the facts. Then he told him about Johnson's behavior in the pen.

"Sherman is upset I put him in that position, but I explained I wasn't going to let people take credit for someone else's work. He said I may have been right, but I handled it the wrong way."

Damien noticed Dillon's posture stiffen. This wasn't about him. She rarely let things get to her. "Something else is going on Dillon. What is it?"

Dillon sat back in her chair. "I have done everything for this damn job. Until you came along, it was my entire life." She glared at Damien. "I had to sit in that interview with Jason and act like we were having a normal conversation. He started off asking me how I liked getting fucked. He wanted to watch my reaction to those photos of Beth. It took all I had not to let him see how much those damn pictures bothered me. Then listening to him explain in detail how he hated his mother and how at twelve fucking years old he killed her unborn child. He enjoyed telling me how he poisoned his mother five years later. Oh, and it wasn't a quick and easy death. No. The bastard used antifreeze and fucking rat poison. It had taken months before her body gave out. Reynolds saw the photos today. He couldn't even stomach them."

Damien tried to understand. But his anger began to boil. "What photos? You didn't say anything about photos. Just that he had papers with all the details. You didn't tell me any of this the other night. Why not?"

Dillon rubbed her forehead. "What are you talking about?"

"The other night, when you told me about the interview, you neglected to mention a few of the details. Why?"

She pushed back from the table. "I don't have to explain every little part of my job to you. I don't ask for daily accountings of what the hell you do all day."

Damien rose from the table. "Are you fucking kidding me? I'm not talking to Agent Dillon McGrath. I'm talking to Dillon. The woman I love. When are you going to trust me? When are you going to let me in all the way?"

"I can't believe you. You are the most egotistical man I know. Not everything has to revolve around you."

"I can't help you if you don't let me in. You've been carrying this fucking interview with Jason around for days now. It has festered, and it's eating you from the inside. You can't do that. You need to talk to me, Dillon. You need to realize I'm not the enemy. I'm here for you. I will always be here for you." Damien closed his eyes. "I know you aren't used to this. I know you've been on your own and you're used to dealing with things by yourself. But you have me now. You have my family and Joe. You even have Taylor. You have people who care about you. Don't shut me out."

Dillon sat with her head hanging. Her hair fell forward and obscured her face. She didn't say anything. Damien stood there frozen. Something else was going on. Something that had nothing to do with whatever the hell this argument was about. He moved to her and pulled her from the chair. He wrapped his arms around her and held her close. He felt her body shudder against him. "Dillon, baby. Talk to me. Something else is going on. What is it?"

Dillon held on tight to him. She knew she had let him in, but it was so hard. For so many years letting people in backfired. Just look at what her director was doing to her. "This is hard for me. I didn't keep it from you on purpose. You have your own case going on. The last thing I want to do is burden you."

"Oh, baby. You'll never be a burden." He lifted her chin. Her eyes were wet with tears. He rarely saw this level of emotion with her. "I know the Bureau is giving you a hard time but is there something else going on?"

"Not really. I guess just having all this shit piled on at once, just snuck up on me. I'll get over it." Dillon hugged him.

Damien pushed her back. He moved the hair from her face. "You're lying. Tell me the rest."

Dillon sighed. "It's Director Sherman. I feel like I am dealing with Jekyll and Hyde. One minute he treats me like I'm more than just a profiler or an Agent. I told you on Sunday how he and his wife have been there for me outside of work. I've been to their house and cried on his wife's shoulder. Then next minute I feel like he's throwing me to the wolves. Ever since I was put in this position as a liaison, I feel as if I'm in a tug of war. I don't know what the hell is expected of me. I told you I can't change who I am. I feel like I'm supposed to act a certain way because of this position."

"He's fond of you. Have you ever thought how hard this might be for him? He has no choice but to treat you like any other Agent. Actually, he has to appear to be harder on you than any other Agent. He can't be perceived as playing favorites. And yet I know he has a soft spot for you.

"Since you have taken this position, he has had to deal more with you. You guys are in a learning period. You need to separate the two. Dillon McGrath means something different than Agent McGrath. Give yourself time. Just know that I'm here always. Bitch at me. Scream at me. Just get it out. Alright? No more keeping this crap inside. No more lying about cases. I understand if you can't share something because it is an ongoing case, but everything else, I don't want you to hide it from me."

She glanced up at him. "I am really sorry. I'm sorry for what I said. I had no right to jump on you like that. You're right. The Jason interview has been eating at me. I have been so mad at Sherman for not telling me everything before I went down there. Then to have that bastard Johnson come at me, I had just had enough." She ran her hands through his hair and placed her lips on his. "I promise I will let you in more."

Damien kissed her. "That move you put on Johnson was sick. Remind me never to piss you off and let you within striking distance."

She held him tight for a moment more, then turned to clear the table. "I trained in Krav Maga while in college. I wanted to be prepared for everything the Academy threw my way." She placed the dishes in the sink then leaned back against the counter. "There was this enormous guy at the Academy. He thought his size meant he had an advantage. I was the only girl who volunteered to take him on in hand to hand. He laughed at me as I came up to the mat. He taunted me. The other guys smirked and made their little comments.

"This meathead came at me, and I took him down in one strike. I made sure not to use full force on him, but still, I sprained his wrist during the match. After that, no one wanted to be my hand-to-hand partner." She winked at him and walked toward the office.

"Like I said, next time you're mad at me I'll keep my distance." Damien picked up his files as he followed behind her. He sat at his desk, and she sat at hers, in the new chair he had ordered for her. It was identical to the one at the Forensic Lab in Springfield Il.

She grinned, pushing her cheeks up. "I love this chair. Thank you for getting it for me."

"During the Freestone case, I remember thinking I wasn't sure you even paid attention during any of the briefings. All you kept doing was spinning around in that damn chair."

She laid her head back and laughed. "You were so mad at me."

"I wasn't mad at you. I was so damn attracted to you I couldn't figure out what to do with myself."

Damien pulled out his notes and was thumbing through everything on the dead priests when he remembered the fax. He pulled out the papers and read through what Father Cattaloni had sent him. Mrs. Shelly Whitman and Mrs. Martia Conlin were the two women who wanted to start the woman's group. The third had died a few months ago. Damien scanned through the notes. She had committed suicide because of pain from a bone and joint disease. He read the notes searching for her name. When he found it, he couldn't believe it. "Damn. I knew something was off with that girl."

"What girl?" Dillon asked.

"We interviewed this woman—girl actually regarding the dead priests. She does the IT for the Archdiocese. Both Joe and I got the feeling she wasn't truthful with us regarding her whereabouts during the time of the murders. We've had no cause to bring her in—yet."

"I'd asked Father Cattaloni for the names of these three women who worked with Father Martin. He faxed me some notes today that he pulled from Martin's files. One of the ladies who worked with him, she committed suicide a few months back. The woman's name—Patricia Lou Fredrick. Our girl from the IT company—Caroline Fredrick."

Dillon stared at Damien. She spun around in her chair. After about three revolutions she stopped. "A mother's suicide could be the catalyst. Did Caroline go to the same church?"

"No. She didn't." Damien paused, as he paced. "This does explain the medal she left behind."

"It does. St. Dymphna represents those who suffer from mental illness. It's easier for a grieving daughter to believe her mother had to be mentally ill to kill herself. And that would explain why she wanted Father Martin dead. If she believed her mother was mentally ill, then she would blame Martin for not helping her." Dillon spun around in her chair.

Damien took a sip of his wine. "I have no proof. If I took my suspicions of her being the killer to Captain Mackey, he would laugh me out of his office and probably put me on Psychiatric leave."

"Tell me about her."

Damien sighed. "This chick is brilliant. She finished school two years ago, and she works for Quantum Electronics. She has a new IT protocol she developed. Apparently, when it gets out of R and D, it is going to set the networking world on its head."

"Even if you blow her alibis out of the water. No way you get a warrant of any kind to arrest her."

"I know that. The only small thing we have is a handwriting sample." Damien explained what Joe had done at the end of the interview with

Caroline. "It isn't much, but Roger said that there were definite similarities to the notes left at the crime scenes but not enough to get a warrant. If I can blow her alibis up, I might be able to use that and con her into thinking we have evidence."

"If this girl is as smart as you think she is, there is no way she'll fall for your ploy. She knows she didn't leave anything behind, evidence wise. You have nothing tying her to any of the crime scenes. How the hell are you going to prove it?" Dillon asked.

Damien moved to the whiteboard. He removed the pictures of the dead priest. "Alright, the evidence against her: nothing. No fingerprints, no hair. Nothing putting her at the scene. Circumstantial, tons." He started a list on the board.

1.   Mother committed suicide.
2.   Mother worked with one of the dead priests.
3.   Has access to the secure files on each of the priest.
4.   Can't account for her whereabouts during the murders.
5.   Defensive and hostile when questioned.
6.   Possible handwriting match.
7.   She's weird.

Dillon laughed at him. "The last one will seal the deal for you. Now all you have to do is catch her."

Damien paced around the office.

"What else is bothering you?" Dillon asked him.

"She tried to get into the chapel at Father Michaliska's church. We'd warned him about the suspect, and when she showed up, he was prepared. She's going to be pissed she couldn't get to him." He continued to pace. "If she can't get to the two remaining priests do you think she'll complete her mission?"

Dillon frowned. "I alluded to that earlier. It's a real possibility she's going to feel the need to finish the task she has started." Dillon moved to the files on Damien's desk and shuffled through the photos. She pulled all the ones with the Bible verses. She pinned them to the board. "Look at these verses. All of them reference God's work. His plan. His house. She's trying to clean up God's Church. I don't know much about the hierarchy of the Church, but who does most of the work? Who disciplines, fires, hires, enforces the rules? Would the Archbishop do that or would he have people in place to handle those?"

"The archbishop has the ultimate say, but he would delegate that to the bishop." Damien remembered Father Belgosa's journal. "Is it a stretch to think if she knew the bishop had committed his own transgressions that she would need to rectify it?"

"Without a doubt. I think she would be furious. The head of the very Church she is trying to purify is sinning. Add to it, he isn't disciplining the priests under his command. Oh yeah, she would need to correct that." She took a sip of her wine.

Damien tilted his head back. "Son of a bitch. The archbishop is on her short list, for sure. But the bishop is her end game. How the hell am I going to stop her?"

CHAPTER FIFTY-THREE

Monday evening

Mack growled as she stomped around her living room. "That stupid priest at St. Bevel. He had the doors locked early. Who does he think he is? He isn't allowed to close the church. That arrogant fool. It's God's house, not his."

She yanked on her hair. Small clumps ripped from her scalp. "It has to be those stupid detectives. They must have said something or done something to make Father Michaliska alter his pattern." She yelled out. "They're messing everything up!" She reached for a metal statue on a nearby shelf and chucked it across the room. It clattered and smashed against the tile floor.

Mackenzie's body trembled. Mother's picture stared at her. Judging her. "I'm doing all I can. It's not my fault, Mother. It's the stupid police. Those detectives. They're ruining my plans." She hit herself on the side of her temples as she screamed out. She glimpsed the crucifix hanging on the wall. She cocked her head to the side.

"You. You started me on this. You need to tell me what to do now!" Mack fell to her knees. She panted; her breath hissed through pursed lips. "I need Your direction. Show me what I need to do." She grabbed the rosary beads hanging from the crucifix.

Kneeling she chanted the Rosary. Rocking back and forth, Mack waited on the Lord. Praying the Hail Mary on each bead, Mack's mind cleared. By the time two decades had been completed, Mack knew what needed to be done. "Oh Father, I have been so blind."

Mackenzie rose. She moved slowly about her living room. "It's so clear now. I know what I have to do." Grabbing a bag, Mack put the supplies needed to carry out the rest of God's plan. This one wouldn't occur in just any church. This one needed to make a statement. It wouldn't be hard to put the plan in motion. Mack had the keys to the residence, but she couldn't just go in there and take him. Or could she?

Mack placed the bag by the door. Laughter bubbled up. "Oh, that's it. That's exactly what I'll do. It's time. I've waited long enough. The time has come, Mother." Mackenzie said to her mother's picture. "The Lord has *shown me what I need to do. The beginning of the Church's rebirth; the day the Lord took back His Church is upon us. When it is done, Mother, the Church will be cleaned, stripped and ready. The righteous will lead the flock, and God's Church will bathe in the Glory of His Light."*

CHAPTER FIFTY-FOUR

December 6th
Tuesday early evening

"I'll take you home after this. I can come get you in the morning," Damien said.

"No problem. I hope this works." Joe stared at the lake as they drove by it.

"No shit. I know her work has 24/7 reception workers because I called. I spent most of today arguing with the ADA. She shut me down on every warrant I asked for. I know this is our girl, but everyone else thinks I've lost my mind." Damien pulled up in front of Caroline's work.

He and Joe walked up to the reception desk. Evidently, after hours the office robots took a more relaxed approach. This evening, two young girls manned the desk dressed in jeans and matching polos.

"Hi, can we help you guys?" One of the girls asked licking her lips as she leaned across the desktop.

Joe smiled at her. "Hi. I'm trying to get some information. This is Lieutenant Kaine, and I'm Detective Hagan, we're trying to reach Caroline Fredrick. Do you know if she's around?"

The second girl at the desk looked around nineteen, Damien scooted down the counter to speak with her while Joe talked to the other one. "We were here during the week; it seems more laid back this evening."

The girl blushed as she spoke. "I usually start work in the early afternoon. I love working later in the day. The evenings and weekends here are a lot less hectic. Not as many people."

Damien leaned closer to her. "When we spoke with Caroline, she said she would have some information for us up here. Maybe you can help me. She was supposed to let me know what time she came in last Wednesday and Friday. She also said she would have some names for us. By chance did she leave anything for us?"

The young girl looked around. "No, I don't see anything left up here." She looked up and smiled at Damien. "I bet I could look it up for you. You said Wednesday and Friday of last week? Let me pull up those days." She typed commands on the virtual keyboard.

"When employees come in do they swipe a card or punch a clock?" Damien asked.

"They swipe that key card reader." She pointed to a little box at the edge of the counter. "Some workers have different times they come in, some work from home. If they work from home, they electronically key in. You don't have to work all your hours here; they just want you to put in at least forty a week."

"Nice perk, not having to come into work. Do you know if Caroline works from home a lot? By chance can you tell me if she was here yesterday and today?"

She glanced at her screen. "Yesterday she was here all day, but today she left at three pm." The young girl looked down the counter where her coworker still spoke to Joe. She glanced around. "I don't know how Mackenzie gets away with it, sometimes; I guess it has to do with the project she's working on."

Damien's brow furrowed. "You said, Mackenzie. Who's that?"

The young girl's eyebrows wrinkled. She stared absently at the handsome cop. "Oh—Caroline doesn't ever go by Caroline. She goes by Mackenzie. Mack most of the time. She hates Caroline."

Damien tilted his head. In his computer search, he found no middle name for Caroline. "Is Mackenzie her middle name?"

The girl shrugged her shoulders. "I don't think so. We only have her listed as Caroline Fredrick. I think I heard once it was her father's name, and a long time ago she started going by it. Anyway, she's *the* girl right now because of some high-tech thing she's developing. That and since her mother died, she's spent a lot of time away from the office." The young girl continued typing. "On Wednesday she wasn't here until one pm. I remember Mr. Marston was pissed. Mack missed a crucial meeting, they needed her to give an update on her project. There were some notable players in that meeting. On Friday, she didn't come in until close to one-thirty."

The young girl leaned into Damien. "Don't tell anyone I said this, I'm not supposed to give information out about our employees. But since you're the police, I'm more afraid of you than Mr. Marston."

"I won't tell anyone. Do you have a way to print that out for me? I would appreciate it." Damien winked at her.

The girl turned bright pink. She hit a few buttons on the keyboard and reached behind her for a piece of paper. "Umm—here you go." She handed him the paper and leaned closer. "If you ever want to go out, I'm always working up here most evenings and Saturdays. Just call me, I'm Shanna." She held out her hand.

Damien reached over the counter and shook her hand. "I'll keep that in mind, Shanna. Thank you for this information." He winked at her again and nodded toward Joe.

Joe grinned at the girl behind the counter. "I'd love to take you up on your offer, but I can't tonight, Jessica. I don't doubt it would be a memorable and entertaining evening. Thanks for all the information."

Once in Damien's vehicle, they both stared at each other. "If Dillon can use flirting to get what she needs I think it is entirely acceptable for us to do the same," Damien smirked as he started the car.

"It was done in the line of work. It's not like I would take the girl up on her offer. Although some guy is going to be happy, come tomorrow morning."

Damien laughed. "So besides inviting you to join her and her friend, what other information did you get?"

Joe pulled out a piece of paper. "Jessica gave me the low down on Miss Fredrick. She wasn't here either Wednesday or Friday like she said."

"I saw that from the time print out I got from the other girl," Damien said.

"Jessica also said even though she's a genius Caroline isn't fun to be around. She keeps herself cocooned in her office and is more comfortable with computers than people. She used to be easier to get along with. Jessica mentioned that after Caroline's mother had died, Caroline changed," Joe said. "It seems as if Caroline has become more judgmental. She looks down on everyone, and she has started to have a problem with the men she works with."

"Does anyone know how her mother died?" Damien asked.

"Caroline told everyone she was sick and died from complicated health issues."

"Not telling anyone how her mother died isn't a crime. It won't help us in our quest for a warrant. She did lie about being at work on Wednesday and Friday, and that still isn't enough to get a warrant for an arrest or to search her premises."

Damien slowed as he pulled onto Joe's street. "This woman is dangerous. Let's assume for a minute it's her, which I believe it is. She killed both Belgosa and Martin then went into work. Shanna didn't say she seemed upset or had any problems. She must have come in and gone about her day like nothing had occurred. I can't imagine beating someone to death, then showing up at work and acting like it was a typical day."

***

Damien got home before Dillon. She had a late evening meeting. He sat at his desk studying the information on Caroline Fredrick. He wanted to find something that would get him a warrant. He used his computer to research deeper on her but found nothing. There was nothing in her past that alluded to a mental break that would lead her to murder priests. Her father, Ralph Mackey Fredrick, died when she was a teenager. Her mother never remarried. They weren't hurting for money, but they weren't rich. By all accounts, Caroline Fredrick presented as a normal, well-adjusted woman. Damien yanked on his hair. "I'm going to be bald by the end of this damn case," he said just as his phone rang.

"Kaine." The other end was silent. "What do you want?" He growled.

"Da-mi-en. I love the way your name rolls off my tongue. It's perfect for you too."

"Thank you. I'll be sure to let my parents know you approve of it. Is that the reason you called me? To tell me you liked my name?"

The caller giggled on the other end. "Our children will be so perfect. We won't be able to live in your condo. It just won't do. It's too small. I have the perfect house in mind. I just have the small issue of the current owner, but that won't be a problem."

Goosebumps broke out on Damien's arm. His heartbeat thrashed in his ears. *Did she plan on killing someone for a house?* "Listen. You don't want to be in a rush for kids. After all, you want to spend time with your significant other before that happens. That's what I plan on doing with Dillon. We want to wait to have kids...." Before he could finish his sentence, a howl like scream came from the other end of the line.

"Don't talk to me about that whore. That's what she is. Even her own colleagues think so. She doesn't deserve you. You're mine. Mine, Damien, and I will have you all to myself. I will not share you anymore. I have given you enough time to dump the whore. Do you hear me?"

The line went dead. "Oh shit," Damien whispered.

Dillon stepped into the office. Damien stared at his phone. His shoulders sagged. "What is it, Damien? What's happened?"

"Our girl called again. She's really pissed now."

"Why? What did you two talk about?"

Damien's phone rang again. "Kaine."

"Little brother, you need a lesson in how to talk to the crazy chicks," Nicky said.

Damien punched a button on his phone. "I put you on speaker, Dillon is here with me. Did you hear the conversation?"

"Yes. She's going off the deep end. I get why you did what you did, but dude, wrong time to bring that up."

Dillon's eyebrows squished together. She tilted her head to one side. "Nicky, what did your brother say to piss her off?"

"He told her you and he planned on waiting to have kids, spend this time getting to know each other."

Dillon rolled her eyes at Damien. "Really, that's the topic you chose to talk about?"

"It wasn't my fault, it's batshit crazy stalker's fault. She talked about how perfect our kids were going to be and about this house she had her heart set on, only she had to take care of the current owner. But that's not the weirdest part. She called you a whore, and mentioned your colleagues even thought you were a whore."

"What does that have to do with anything?" Nicky asked.

"Holy crap," Dillon said.

"That's right," Damien responded.

"Guys, what's right?" Nicky asked.

"Yesterday at Division Central, Dillon had an incident with one of the DEA agents. He called her a whore."

"What guy called her a whore? He needs his ass...oh man, that means she was there, or she heard about it, through the DC grapevine. Listen, sit down with Dillon and go through everyone who was there yesterday. See if anyone remembers anyone asking specific questions about the news conference. I can't get a location pinned down on her. She's still bouncing the call all over the place. The radius is the same, she's within fifteen miles. I'm working on the list from the DMV, but I need a list from you of the women you've encountered or worked with. That would help narrow the list of vehicles. I'll call you later."

Nicky hung up. Damien looked at Dillon. "I know the DC grapevine works fast, but I think this means she's way closer than we thought."

"Let's put your computer to good use. Pull up all the female employees at DC. Then pull up a list of all the women in the peripheral offices; like the Morgue, the DA's office, any other area you have regular contact with."

Damien sat at his computer. "I'm going right up to the line, possibly over it, to access this information. Essentially I'm hacking into our systems at DC." He cocked his head at Dillon. "You want to stay or step out?"

She smirked at him. "I'm stupid when it comes to the computer. I have no idea what you're doing."

"Okay then." He typed on this computer. He went into a password protected area to access the databases of DC. "There are three hundred women employed at DC. This includes police officers, administrators, and canteen workers."

"Aren't you worried about DC knowing your hacking their computer system?" Dillon scribbled on a notepad.

Damien glanced up from his computer. "Wouldn't that make you an accomplice if you knew the answer?"

"Hmm, good point." She grinned at him. "Can you set up parameters?"

"Sure. What are you thinking?"

"Let's set up categories. Filter police, workers from the canteen and so on."

Damien typed in commands. Within minutes, the names separated into several columns. "All right. How about reducing this list by age? We know she's young, let's go with twenty-two to twenty-six."

Dillon nodded. "I think that's a good range. Also, narrow that down by marital status."

"I definitely don't think our girl is married. Those parameters alone have brought that down to seventy-eight women. Not all that manageable, but better than what it was."

Dillon scribbled on her notepad. "Alright, more than likely this girl is white. I believe that's a reasonable assumption. We can always change this later if we need to."

"I agree with you." He typed in another command. "That brings the list down to fifty-four. Better still."

Dillon paced. "What other areas do you spend a lot of time at?"

"Let's see. I have a lot of interaction with the Morgue, the Lab, that would be the Forensic Lab here in Chicago. It's where most of our samples go. The Morgue has a small on-site lab, but if they need more test done on evidence from bodies, they send it over to the central lab." Damien typed on his computer. "Using the same parameters, I've combined all the areas, all the offices I have contact with. The list is back up to ninety-five."

"Can you remove any divorced women?"

Damien frowned. "You don't think our girl could've been married before?"

"No, I don't. I think it's one reason she is so enamored with you. You're her first one true love, literally. She's never had this type of intense feeling for a man before. That's one reason she is so angry at you for dating me."

"Okay, if you say so." He typed away. "The list is now down to eighty-two. That's still a lot of women to investigate."

"We have to narrow that list. Use the fifteen-mile radius."

"How about if we make two lists. We will take those women who have a home address in the fifteen-mile radius. The second list will have everyone outside that radius." Damien finished typing. "Okay. Our list within the radius is now down to twenty. Much more manageable."

Dillon stood in the middle of the room. "What about interns? Are they on this list?"

Damien's forehead wrinkled. "No. This is the actual employees. I'm not sure I can even get that information." Damien smiled at the look on Dillon's face. Her lips puckered together, and her forehead wrinkled. "Let me explain. When an intern is hired at the lab, they work under a special account. Some are paid, some aren't, it depends on the position. They receive credentials, logins, and passwords, but all their access is limited. They're treated like employees, but none receive benefits." He grabbed his phone. "Hey Harris, are you at the VCU?"

"Yeah, why? You need something?" Harris asked.

"What's the scuttlebutt about what happened yesterday between Dillon and the DEA Agent? Specifically, what have you heard?"

"Man, everyone's talking about it. Me and Coop were up here last night for a few hours after the news conference, and everyone was buzzing about it. Several people saw Joe hold you back, but after what she did to Johnson, everyone laughed said she could be your bodyguard."

Damien smiled. "Funny, real funny. Have you spoken to anyone outside of DC, like someone from the Morgue or the DA's office?"

"Yeah, this morning I had to call the lab to see if there were any results on our case."

"Did anyone mention it you?"

"Debbie at the front desk asked me all about it. She heard about it from Stacy at the canteen. Debbie mentioned how everyone was talking about it."

Damien sighed. It made sense why the girl called him now. "I need a favor. Call Debbie, and ask her to tell you the names of all the interns at the Morgue. Make up any reason but don't tell her it has anything to do with me. Also, ask which ones are paid and which ones aren't. See if you can get any information on whether any of them are getting hired full-time."

"This has to do with your stalker, doesn't it?"

"It does. Have you heard anything about that? Has anyone mentioned it?"

"Everyone here at VCU knows, as well as the Morgue. After all, they're working on the evidence over there and at the lab. Outside those areas, I haven't heard anyone talking about it. I'll call Debbie now and call you right back."

"Thanks, Harris." Damien looked at Dillon. "Harris is checking on a few things. He's going to call me back."

"I would love to find out who this chick is. She is quickly becoming more and more unstable."

Five minutes later Van Halen's *Jump* rang out from his phone. "Kaine."

"It's Harris. I got the list. There are five on it. I'm going to email it to you now. One thing. There is one girl on the list, a Rachel Banks. She came on about nine or ten months ago. She's some kind of prodigy. Went to Harvard, and graduated at twenty-one. Debbie went on and on about her. The others on the list include two other women and two men."

"Are they paid?" Damien asked.

"All are paid and slated to get full-time jobs. Right now, they're in the intern status. As a job opens, they're moved into those slots. I hope this helps. I got a friend in the DA's office. She might be able to give me information on their interns."

"If you can get the information without raising any suspicions, do it. But I don't think our girl is going to be there. I don't think I have enough interaction with anyone from the DA's office. Thanks, buddy, if I need anything else, I'll call you."

Dillon stood in front of his desk. "What does he have for you?"

"There are five interns at the Morgue. One stood out to Harris. This young girl who's some kind of whiz—Rachel Banks." Damien pulled up the email from Harris. "Here's the list." He typed out commands. "I think it's fair to say the men are off the list."

Damien frowned at the computer screen. "The two other women are also married. That just leaves Rachel. The address she has on file is just outside our working radius. For now, I'll put her on the short list. I'll run her and pull all her information. I'm going to send this entire list to Nicky. He can use it to narrow down his DMV list. I'll also give this information to the captain, and to ECD and have them run a quick query on them. It's a lot of names, but that will add to my scheme."

He looked at Dillon. "I'm not telling anyone I've already done it." Damien pulled up something on his computer. "Great, Travis is working tonight. If I email Travis and the captain this information now and inform them about the phone call, it keeps the appearance of transparency. This way it's all above board. More or less." He grinned at Dillon.

"You are a reprobate, Mr. Kaine," she winked at him.

CHAPTER FIFTY-FIVE

December 7th
Wednesday 7:30 am

Anthony Marcum unlocked Bishop Cantor's office and turned on his computer. Caroline had scheduled regular maintenance on the computer system, and today he expected her first thing this morning. Marcum glanced through the bishop's appointment book. Although he didn't keep Archbishop Jacobs' appointments, he made a note when something may overlap with Bishop Cantor's schedule. Today Archbishop Jacobs had several appointments that would keep him away for most of the day.

Anthony expected Bishop Cantor at any moment. He had an early morning radio spot that had been on the bishop's schedule for several weeks. It would be done over the phone. However, some prep work had to be done. He glanced at his watch. "You're cutting it close, Bishop. Where the hell are you?"

Anthony continued to go over the schedules. Tons of things had to be accomplished "They just don't pay me enough for this crap," Anthony mumbled as he skimmed the meetings for the day. He looked at his watch again. "Where the hell is Caroline? I should just maintain the system myself. It isn't like I don't know how to run a network," Marcum said out loud. Although that added responsibility would ensure he had no free time.

Cleaning up after Bishop Cantor and all these other priests seemed as futile as trying to herd cats. Archbishop Jacobs had been blinded. Anthony was sure he had no clue about Bishop Cantor's proclivities. The bishop was as holy as a whore in church on Sunday morning.

Anthony glanced at the wall clock and at his watch. Same time. "Where the hell are you, Bishop Cantor?" Anthony's phone rang. "Marcum here."

"Mr. Marcum, this is Jeff Blake from WTLY radio, we're supposed to have a radio interview with the bishop, is he there?"

Oh great. Another mess I have to clean up. "No, Mr. Blake. I'm so sorry for the inconvenience, but Bishop Cantor has had an emergency that has forced this interview to be postponed. I just became aware of it, or I would've contacted you sooner."

Marcum could hear the hiss of the man's sigh on the other end of the phone. "Again, I apologize. I will have the show rescheduled at the bishop's earliest opportunity. Again, I am sorry." Anthony disconnected the call. No sense trying to give more explanation for something he had none to give.

Anthony called the residence. Cantor had a house manager who remained on the premises, always. No answer. That was odd. The house manager wore a Bluetooth earpiece so he could answer the calls from anywhere. "Something isn't right," Anthony mumbled.

He phoned upstairs to the archbishop's office secretary. The residences of both the bishop and the archbishop sat at opposite ends of the same palatial property, with offices centrally located in the middle.

"Thank you for calling the Archdiocese of Chicago, how may I help you?"

"Angela, it's Anthony Marcum. Has the Archbishop come into the office yet?"

"Oh hi, Anthony. No, I'm not expecting him until after ten-thirty this morning. He had a breakfast meeting with the heads of the Chicago Chamber of Commerce. They're planning a Christmas event this year."

"Okay. I just needed to make sure." Anthony hung up. He had to figure something had come up, and Bishop Cantor had neglected to tell him. He called Caroline's business to check on when she would come in to work on the network today. "Is Caroline Fredrick available?"

"No, I'm sorry, Mrs. Fredrick hasn't come in yet this morning. I can take a message for her?"

"No thank you." Anthony hung up. "Can no one do their fucking job this morning?" Anthony headed over to the bishop's residence. He took one of the many golf carts used to get around the estate. "I have way too much shit to do to worry about this kind of crap," Anthony hissed as he pulled up in front of the residence.

The building itself dated back over fifty years. It had been updated and remodeled. Anthony stood and marveled at the classic beauty. Large steps led to a porch lined with four majestic pillars. A grand entrance of ornate double wooden doors sat squarely in the middle. The carvings on them depicted the opening of the tomb after Jesus' death.

Anthony rang the bell; no one answered. He started to use his key, but the door was ajar. He pushed the door open and peered around before he entered. "Hello? Anyone home? Hmm, I guess no one wants to work today." Upon entering the residence, an odd scent hit him. His pulse pounded in his head. The hairs on the back of his neck stood on end. Something told him to turn and leave; curiosity pulled him in. He moved through the foyer.

Anthony slinked through the living area. "Hel-lo? Anyone here?" He peered into the kitchen. No one. He came back to the entryway. He started for the stairs, remembering the small coat room located off the foyer. More than a coat room. A double room in which the back half held the heart of the house. All the electronics were located there. Caroline was supposed to do some work on the bishop's home network system today as well.

"I refuse to do everyone's damn job for them," Anthony said, attempting to bolster his courage. He entered the coat room to the same odor from the front door, only stronger. He swallowed. A metallic taste coated his throat. He almost gagged on the stench. "What is that smell?"

He moved toward the half-open door that led to the electronics control area of the house. His hand trembled as he pushed it open; a pool of crimson red liquid spilled across the floor. He took one step in, and the sight made him stagger back. The house manager lay on the floor with a gaping wound in his stomach. His entrails spilled from his body. Anthony ran from the room, stumbled out onto the porch and threw up over the railing.

CHAPTER FIFTY-SIX

Damien sat in his office. Dillon had left that morning to go to Quantico. He was glad to have her away from the city, at least until they had a better handle on their stalker. Last night Nicky had emailed a list of vehicles and their owners that may have been involved in the accident. He crossed referenced the names Damien had sent him, essentially giving Damien a preliminary list of five instead of ninety. If none of these panned out, he would have to start over.

Damien's pulse raced as he glanced at one possible name of his stalker. Officer Katie Baker. He needed to tread lightly there. He was certain she was not involved in this. Or maybe he hoped she wasn't.

He glanced at the board. He planned to assign each of his detective teams a girl to investigate. Damien devised a plan for his men to help interview the women on the list. He and Joe would handle the intern from the lab. He sat back finishing his coffee before he headed up to the captain with his plan when Joe walked through his door.

"Hey, boss," Joe said.

To Damien's surprise, Joe poured a bag of Starburst jellybeans into his jar. Damien's eyebrows squinted together. "Are those poisoned?"

Joe laughed. "No, I just decided I should fill the jar at least every few months. Then I won't feel rotten for eating them. How's Dillon doing?"

Something seemed different about Joe. Damien eyeballed him. "She could've used another day, but she had to go to Quantico. They wanted her in on the interviews with the family members of the salvage company. They'd already pushed the interview back because of the accident. She should be back by Friday at the latest." He squinted at him.

Joe sat with a handful of jellybeans, picking out the flavors he liked best. He glanced up to find Damien staring at him. "What?"

"Is there anything you want to tell me?"

Joe laughed. "What are you fucking psychic now?"

"No. You just seem different."

A smile pushed Joe's cheeks up to his eyes. "I spoke with Taylor this morning. Have you ever had phone sex?"

A goofy grin filled Damien's face. "I'm not answering that." Damien's phone rang. "Kaine."

"Dispatch. Lieutenant Kaine report to Bishop Cantor's residence. CSTs are en route. Multiple homicides have been reported."

"Kaine and Hagan ETA twenty-five minutes. Notify Captain Mackey." Damien pocketed his cell as he and Joe were running out the door.

In the SUV, Damien hit the lights and siren. "I'm not sure I want to know who's dead. I called Caroline's office this morning, she hadn't come in yet, and she didn't call in. I was about to have you and I go to her house and see if she was there."

"Oh man. I have a knot in my stomach. This isn't going to go well." Joe made the sign of the cross. "I don't like it, Damien. Something's not right."

Damien pulled through the gates of the Archdiocese. There were several police cars. Captain Mackey's name came up on his phone as he exited the vehicle. "Yes, Captain? Yeah, we just got here. Give me a few minutes to assess, and I'll call you back."

Damien and Joe stepped up to the front steps of the bishop's residence. Anthony Marcum sat with his head in his hands. "Mr. Marcum?"

Anthony looked up. "Lieutenant Kaine, I—I came here because Bishop Cantor hasn't come into the office yet. He had an early morning radio interview. I didn't think...I didn't touch anything. Once I found him, I ran outside and called the police."

Damien watched as Anthony Marcum breathed in through his nose and out his mouth. "Who's dead inside?"

"Umm—I don't know. I just found the bishop's manager." Marcum's body shuddered. "It's horrible."

"Listen, Mr. Marcum, don't leave, okay? We're going to need some information from you." Damien and Joe headed into the residence. An officer stood at the doorway. "Officer Tomias, where are the CSTs?" Damien asked.

"Two are in there, and two are in the maid's quarters off the kitchen. Evidence points to a struggle in the bishop's bedroom quarters. Another crew is up there. CST Newberry is through that doorway there. He's expecting you." The officer pointed to the electronics room.

As Damien and Joe entered, Roger Newberry stood over the dead manager. He turned toward the detectives. "Hey, guys. Listen, from what I can see, your killer came in through the front door, no sign of forced entry. Surprised the manager in here, and ripped open his stomach. He then went to the maid's quarters, off the kitchen. The killer slit her throat while she slept in her bed. Upstairs a struggle took place. I found some blood on the bedroom floor. No sign of the bishop, though. I have a team going through it to see if we can get any prints. As of yet, I'm not finding any."

There was so much blood on the floor, the smell coated the back of Damien's throat with a heavy metal taste. He swallowed several times. "You haven't found any notes anywhere?"

"No. Nothing yet. I've called one of your ECD guys. We need someone to go through this security."

Travis from ECD walked through the door and stopped dead in his tracks. "Oh, fuck me. That's disgusting." Travis gazed open-mouthed at the dead manager.

"Travis, get anything you can off the surveillance. See..." Damien's phone rang. "Kaine."

"Kaine, it's Mackey. Shit is hitting the fan. The secretary for the archbishop just contacted the chief. She says the archbishop didn't show up to a meeting this morning. She hasn't gone to the residence yet. She's too scared. Take one of the CSTs with you and get over there. Chief and I are on our way."

"Yes Sir, Captain." Damien stuck his phone in his pocket. "Roger, you need to come with Joe and I. We need to get over to the archbishop's residence. Could be another crime scene."

Roger grabbed a field kit and followed Joe and Damien out the door. As Damien passed Marcum on the steps, he waved one of the police officers over. "Take Mr. Marcum over to his office. Make sure he doesn't call anyone."

"Yes Lieutenant," the officer responded.

Joe stared out the window as Damien drove down the drive that led to the archbishop's residence. "What the hell is going on?"

"Captain said the secretary for Jacobs called said the archbishop never showed up for a meeting this morning. She couldn't get any of the staff to answer the phone at the residence." Within minutes, Damien drove up to the grand house. Two grand pillars stood on either side of an enormous staircase. The steps were lined with blooming flowers in all colors of the rainbow. The red brick popped against the white accents. The two front doors had the Stations of the Cross etched in them.

As they moved to the doorway, they could see it was cracked open. Damien and Joe drew their weapons. "Roger, you carrying?" Damien asked.

"Always." Roger placed the field kit next to the door and pulled his weapon from underneath his overalls.

All three entered the residence. Off to the right of the door, lay the body of what appeared to be the archbishop's house manager, his head almost decapitated from the slice across his throat. They fanned out covering all the areas of the first floor. They found the maid dead in the hallway leading to her quarters. Damien led the way up the stairs. At the top of the landing, Roger went down a short hallway to the left while Joe and Damien headed toward the right. All rooms were clear.

As they came to the master bedroom, Damien pushed open the door. The bedcovers had been dragged off the bed. Tables and chairs had been overturned, and vases that held flowers were scattered on the floor in pieces.

"The house is clear. Roger, get some more CSTs here. Joe, you and I need to go question Marcum. Caroline has the bishop and the archbishop somewhere. I have no idea how much time they have left."

CHAPTER FIFTY-SEVEN

Anthony Marcum sat at his desk with his head down. As the detectives entered the room, he raised up. "What's going on? No one will tell me anything. Please?" His eyes darted between the two men.

"Mr. Marcum, it looks as if a struggle happened at both residences. We believe Caroline has abducted Cantor and Jacobs. You need to tell me everything you knew about their plans yesterday." Damien pulled over a chair and sat in front of Marcum.

Anthony dragged his hand down his face. "I—I don't know. I don't understand. Caroline? Why would Caroline do that?" Marcum rocked back and forth.

"Mr. Marcum. I need you to concentrate. Tell me this—what time are the gates closed and locked in the evening?"

"Umm—okay, okay I know that. Usually by five pm maybe five-thirty, unless there's something special at night." Marcum rubbed his eyes. "The gates were closed when I got here this morning. I had to call maintenance. I came in earlier than normal. I had to prepare for the radio show. They had to buzz the locks for me."

"Can you tell me what the bishop and the archbishop had going on yesterday?" Damien watched the trembling man. His face still pale. Damien sympathized with him. Seeing a dead body was disturbing enough. Seeing one gutted like a fish would give Anthony nightmares for weeks to come.

"Yesterday they both had meetings all day. I had an appointment, so I left around three pm. I believe both the bishop and Archbishop had no evening plans yesterday. If you check with security, they can tell you exactly when they arrived home."

Damien glanced at Joe, "call security."

Joe stepped out into the hallway. A few moments later he returned. "Security has them coming in around five-thirty. Both men checked in upon returning to their residences. Security also had Caroline coming onto the property at four pm."

Anthony's head snapped up. "Caroline shouldn't have been here yesterday; she was scheduled for this morning. I was mad when she and the bishop didn't show up. That's why I went to the residence in the first place."

Damien spoke calmly to Mr. Marcum. "Anthony, I need you to tell me about this property. What buildings are on the grounds?"

"Umm—let's see. Maintenance, security, gardening has a shed. There's a storage facility at the back of the property next to the chapel."

Damien's eyes widened. "What chapel?"

"The original Diocese chapel. It's where Mass was held eons before parish churches were built around the city."

Damien stood. "Mr. Marcum, we need to know where that chapel is. Can you show or tell us?"

Anthony's colored paled even more. A light sheen of sweat bubbled on his forehead. "Yes. Just follow the road to the right. It will end at the chapel."

Damien and Joe ran out the door. "That's got to be where she has them." He dialed the captain and explained what he had found out. He and the chief were fifteen minutes out. As Damien and Joe exited the building into the parking lot, Damien yelled for several officers. "Listen we think we have a hostage situation at the original chapel. It's located down this lane. I need you guys to follow us. Keep your sirens off." Damien and Joe sprinted to the SUV and sped down the lane.

The chapel came into sight. The stained-glass windows depicting various stories of the Bible gleamed in the sunlight. The dark brick and evergreen trees that surrounded the building made it look as if a Thomas Kinkade painting had come to life. Damien gathered everyone. "Joe, see if you can see anything through a window." Damien faced the officers. "Turn down your radios. I want as much surprise on our side as possible."

Joe came back to the group. "I can see the bishop and the archbishop at the front of the chapel. The bishop is tied to the Baptismal Font, and the archbishop is laying on the top step leading to the altar. I don't see Caroline anywhere."

Damien glanced around at the building. "It's just not a very big building. She must be somewhere inside; she wouldn't have just left them. She isn't finished with her task." He turned to four policemen, "You guys follow us in, sweep the back of the church. Quietly. Joe and I," he pointed to three more officers, "and you three will follow us. As we clear the front near the altar, you stay with the victims, do not attempt to move them."

Damien and Joe led the officers into the small chapel. Four peeled off and searched the back area, securing it and the entrance. Damien and Joe led the other three officers toward the front of the church. Lit candles on the altar and on the steps of the predella gave an eerie glow to the chapel.

The archbishop's wrists and ankles had been bound, and he lay in a bloody heap on the top step of the altar. On the opposite side of the altar stood the baptismal font. This font had a large front façade shaped like a cross. Caroline had tied the bishop there. He sagged against the restraints. His face was covered in blood, and a large amount of blood had seeped through his shirt. Damien wasn't sure he was even breathing. Two of the officers took posts on opposite sides of the altar, while a third officer swept the back of the altar area. Damien and Joe made their way to an alcove to the right of the atrium. A door was located at the back of the small jut out. They approached it with caution. Quietly Damien turned the knob and pushed the door wide. It appeared to be a storage room.

Joe tapped Damien on the shoulder and pointed to the back of the room. A soft light filtered through a small crack on the back wall. As they stepped closer, they heard soft chanting. Damien moved to the door, reaching out slowly, he turned the little knob and pushed the door open.

A small lamp illuminated the interior room. Every inch of the walls had been covered with crucifixes, rosary beads and torn pieces of paper with verses from the Bible scribbled on them. Caroline had her back to them. She knelt at a makeshift altar. Damien couldn't see her hands, but there was blood on the floor next to her.

Caroline remained in her trance-like state, muttering what Damien thought was an old Latin prayer. "Caroline," Damien said softly.

Caroline stopped chanting. Her head tilted to one side. "God?" She whispered.

"Caroline," Damien said louder, "I need you to stand and turn around slowly."

Caroline's back stiffened. A sound that started out as soft cry slowly rose into a howl as she stood and turned around. Damien saw the long-bladed knife in her hand.

"It's you!" She shrieked pointing the knife at him. "You're ruining everything."

With his weapon trained on her, Damien spoke in a calm tone. "Caroline, I need you to drop the knife."

Her face contorted into a feral snarl. "You! Get out! This is my space. This is where God talks to me. You aren't worthy of being in here. Get out! Get out, now!" She waved the knife around.

Joe stepped to the side just slightly. "Caroline, we need you to drop the knife. Just let it go, and we can talk."

Her head twisted unnaturally to the side. She pointed the knife at Joe. "I don't want to talk to you. God gave me this position. He wants me to clean His house. He intends to rid the Church of the filth and slime that has seeped into its cracks. Men like Cantor and Jacobs are like mold. It gets in and sticks to the walls and floors. It creeps from area to area, contaminating everything it touches. A simple cleaning solution takes the top layer off, but to get to the root of the mold, you have to tear down the walls and treat the foundation."

A couple of officers stepped up to the doorway. Joe motioned for them to get back and exit the area.

"Caroline, you need to put down the weapon. I don't want to shoot you. I think you need help. I know you're suffering from the loss of your mother, but this is not God's will. God forgives our sins. He allows us to try and make changes. He wants us to succeed in following His laws." Damien took a small step back, not wanting to be within striking distance of the blade.

"Do not speak as if you know God. You are a sinner, just like all men. You are led by your desires. Men think they can take the authority God gives them and do with it as they please."

"Please, Caroline. Let me help you. You've made your point. The Church needs to clean itself up. But it can't be accomplished by punishment. God will do it through His love and His Holy Spirit," Damien said.

"Don't talk to me about God's love. I know God's love and His Holy Spirit. It is that very Spirit that has directed my actions. He has given me a purpose. He showed me what He wanted me to do. He directed my path." She looked at the walls, "God spoke to me through His word. He gave me instructions, and you have messed everything up. Don't you understand? I must complete God's plan."

Damien's heart raced. His hand holding the weapon shook slightly. "Caroline, I need you to drop the knife. Please, Caroline."

Caroline brought the knife up over her head and took one step toward him letting out a horrific shriek. Damien had no choice. He pulled the trigger, shooting her once in the chest. She dropped the knife and fell to her knees. Damien kicked the knife away. Blood poured from the hole in her chest.

She looked down placing her hand over the open wound. She glanced up at Damien. "You've ruined everything." She slumped to the ground. Damien moved closer to her, checking for a pulse. He turned to Joe and shook his head.

Joe exited the small room. He pointed to several officers, "call the paramedics and get these men untied." He turned back to Damien. "You had to shoot her. She was coming toward you, ready to kill you." He placed a hand on Damien's shoulder.

At the sound of the gunshot, several officers including the captain and the chief ran down the center aisle of the church. Damien and Joe stood outside the little storage room.

Captain Mackey moved through the doorway and looked at the little sanctuary Caroline had built for herself. He spun around slowly; he had never seen anything like it.

Chief Rosenthal stepped up next to him. He glanced around the small room, rubbing the back of his neck. "Damn, this is all kinds of crazy." He saw the blade on the floor. He stared at Damien reaching out he grabbed his shoulder. "I know it's never easy to shoot someone, even when you have to. Take some time. The Post Incident Manager will speak with you at DC. This is a good shoot, Kaine, but you still have to go through the procedure."

Damien stepped back, nodding. "Yes Sir, Chief." He watched as a CST team came in with one of the medical examiner's staff.

Captain Mackey stood next to him. "Listen, there isn't much for you to do here. I had an officer get a recorded statement from Marcum and the secretary for Archbishop Jacobs. I want you and Joe to go back to Division Central. The chief and I are headed to the hospital. We'll get statements from the archbishop and the bishop. I have no idea how long it will be before they can even be interviewed. Stay at DC until I get back." The captain looked over at Joe. "Understand?"

Joe nodded. "Yes, Captain."

CHAPTER FIFTY-EIGHT

Joe and Damien sat in Damien's SUV in the parking garage of Division Central. Damien rested his head on his forearm as it draped the steering wheel. Joe sat with his eyes closed. Neither spoke.

Damien exhaled a long, loud breath. "Caroline was mentally ill. I think that's what bothers me most about shooting her. If she had just dropped the fucking knife."

"It was a good shoot, Damien."

"I don't know if she even understood what drove her to commit these crimes. I want to get over to her house and see if we can find any answers as to why she did what she did. As soon as the captain comes back, I say we go over." Damien rubbed his temples. A headache was just beginning.

"I don't think we'll ever get the answers we want. Before you had to shoot Caroline, you could hear the break with reality. Her rantings explained a lot. I think once her mother took her life, she completely cracked." Joe rubbed his forehead.

"She'll be remembered for the heinous crimes she committed; no one will remember or probably even know why. I get she's a crazy killer, and she blamed priests for things that she construed in her head." Damien paused, his head fell to his chest. "Although the cop in me knows and wants her to pay for the deaths of three innocent priests, the Catholic in me is disgusted with what I have learned about *my* Church and the leadership within it. The corruption that is so prevalent will stay hidden. The archbishop and the bishop will go on with their lives. That bothers me, and I just don't see anything changing."

***

The detectives of VCU sat at their desks doing paperwork. Joe told everyone about the shooting. As Damien entered his office, he closed the door. He needed a few minutes of quiet. He replayed the events at the chapel in his mind.

He sat, intending to rest his eyes for a few moments. That plan was interrupted when he noticed the folder on his desk. "Fuck." He said aloud. He needed to put the shooting out of his head for now. He still had a stalker after Dillon. He opened the file, refreshing his memory. He decided he would not tell anyone except Joe and the captain about Officer Baker being on the list. He opened his door heading into the pen. Every one of his detectives sat at their desks. "Did murder take a break today?"

Everyone stopped what they were doing. Hall pulled the lollipop from his mouth. "We all decided we wanted to do paperwork instead. And we missed each other." One of the other detectives threw a wad of paper at him.

"Listen I need all of you to come to the conference room for a few minutes. Damien led the way as his six detectives plus Joe followed him. Once inside he closed the door. "Alright, what I'm going to tell you stays between us. I don't want anyone outside this room to know." Damien sat in a chair. "I don't think any of you are aware of the things that happened this past weekend. Only the captain, Joe, and Dillon's bosses know.

"Over the weekend, Dillon and Taylor were run off the road by our stalker. Had Dillon not been in one of my father's cars, she and Taylor would have been severely hurt instead of walking away with bumps and bruises."

Several of his detectives murmured. Detective Hall raised an eyebrow at Damien. "Is that how she got the cut on her head?"

Damien nodded. "Yes. I'm sorry I couldn't tell you the truth the other day. There were just too many people in the room with us. We still aren't sure how she knew where Dillon was going to be."

Hall smiled nodding. "It's okay, Damien. I understand."

Detective Cooper spoke up. "Listen, Damien, whatever you need from us. We're here. Do you have any leads?"

Damien leaned on the table. "On Sunday, my brother and I went over the satellite images he was able to pull once he started tracking Dillon's car. The images don't provide us with a license plate number. However, Nicky crossed referenced several DMV records with a list of women I have had contact with, in a working capacity. I want each team to take a name. But I don't want you to go in and ask any questions that will lead them to think we're after them for the stalking. It may not be these women, but it's all we have to go off, for now."

He handed a piece of paper to each team of detectives. "I want you guys to question these women. Approach it from the angle their vehicle has been reported in a hit and run accident. Tell them you need to see the vehicle. Verify if any damage has occurred to the front right side. If no damage is present tell them, you appreciate their time. You get the idea. I just don't want them to know the real reason. Don't do this by phone. Go see them in person. I'd like for you to get this done by tomorrow afternoon at the latest."

Harris sat up. "Is that intern on the list?"

"Yeah, Joe and I are going to cover her. I want to meet her in person and see what kind of feel I get from her. Do you guys have any questions?"

Several detectives shook their heads. Damien stood up. "Let me know what you guys find out. If none of these women pan out, we have to start over."

The detectives filed out. Joe lingered behind. Damien closed the conference room door. "Listen I didn't tell them everything. I held something back that I am telling you and Captain Mackey, no one else. There was one other name on that list. Officer Katie Baker."

Joe's jaw dropped open. He pushed Damien's shoulder. "Get the fuck out. Are you serious?"

"Yes. She has the same make of car. Here's the thing, I just don't see it. She's been here since she graduated from the Academy. Dillon says I'm too close, that since she's one of my guys I don't want to see her as the possible stalker."

Joe rested against the edge of the table. "I'm with you. I don't think she's your stalker. She has a crush on you, but I can't see her going that bonkers over your ass. How do you want to handle her?"

Damien paced around. "I'm not sure. I thought maybe we could do a little undercover. I'll run it by the captain. I was going to use my system at home to see if I can track her movements. I'm hoping I can get enough answers to take her off the list. Then no one will ever know. What do you think?"

Joe ran his hand through his hair. "Oh man. On the one hand, I say that's a good idea. On the other, I say treat her like the others, except be upfront and honest about it. Tell her she's on the list, and you need to clear her."

"Damn it, that will make for a very uncomfortable working environment. Baker has potential, and she wants to be here. I don't want to mess that up with this kind of accusation. Shit. I just don't want to come at her with something like this. There must be another way," Damien said.

Joe got up from the table. "I got this. Give me a little bit, and I'll come up with a plan of approach with her. Do you want me to go to the captain's office with you when you fill him on this?"

"No. I'll do it. I'm going now to see if he's back. I want an update on the bishop and Archbishop Jacobs. Then I'm going to the PIM's office. Get that shit over with. Then we'll hit Caroline's place."

"Look don't worry about the PIM. This is something you must do because you were involved in a shooting, but it was clearly a good shoot. You may have to do some psych counseling, but that's standard." Joe opened the conference room door and headed out.

***

Joe made his way to his desk. He noticed Officer Baker on her phone in the hallway. She paced, speaking animatedly. He moved a little closer to see if he could hear her conversation.

"Listen, I pay you. Can't you do your job? If I knew what happened, I'd be able to tell you. I went into the store. I came out, and my car was bashed in. No. I was in there for twenty minutes, tops. Fine. It's at McBride's garage on Post Road. Yeah okay, I can't wait to hear from you." She hung up the phone. "Uggh, I hate insurance companies."

"Hey Baker, everything okay?" Joe asked.

"Yes. I had a little fender bender this weekend. My car is at a shop now, and I'm trying to get my insurance guy over there to see the damage."

"You weren't hurt, were you?" Joe asked as he smiled at her. He noticed she avoided eye contact and blushed.

"No. I wasn't even in the damn thing. I'd gone to a store and was inside for no more than twenty minutes. When I came out, it's all bashed in." Her phone rang. "Hey, that's my insurance guy." She walked off.

Joe slipped out and called McBride's garage.

CHAPTER FIFTY-NINE

Captain Mackey motioned for Damien to sit while he finished his phone call. "That was the hospital. Jacobs may be released as early as this evening. Caroline hadn't done much physical damage to him; a few lacerations and a deep cut on his arm. She was saving him for last. The archbishop said Caroline wanted him to choose between cleaning up God's house or continuing to allow sinners to lead the Church."

Captain Mackey placed his elbows on his desk. "How do people read the word of God and corrupt it so damn much? Jacobs said that Caroline believed God allowed her mother's death to happen so He could show her what He wanted her to do. She was fucked in the head. Pardon, that. But if she went to trial, she would've ended up in a padded cell. And to be honest, Damien, that just wouldn't be enough punishment."

Mackey studied Damien's weary face. The shooting was taking a toll on the young man. "I know that isn't the politically correct thing to say. But she killed a lot of innocent people in the name of God. I find that despicable. Now tell me why you're here."

Damien relaxed in his seat. "Concerning our stalker. I got the information I mentioned earlier from Nicky. By cross-referencing the DMV database, he narrowed the list down to five women. I've given three of them to my team. They're going to approach it as a reported hit and run accident." Damien looked down at his lap.

"Damien, what are you not telling me?" Captain Mackey asked.

"There is one other name on that list. Officer Katie Baker." Damien pinched the bridge of his nose. "I don't think she's capable of this. We've worked together for most of the last year, and I just can't see her doing this. Dillon says I'm too close to it. Joe is doing some undercover recon. If we find anything that puts her at the top of the list, we'll interview her." Damien bit the inside of his cheek. His stomach tensed. Until this point, he hadn't questioned his decisions regarding Officer Baker.

Captain Mackey leaned back. "I understand why you want to handle it this way. I think Dillon is correct, you're too close to this. However, with that said, I'll go along with this for now. If you uncover anything that remotely puts her at the top of the list, you'll need to question her. Where you do, that is up to you. I don't think you should bring her into

Interrogation. Unless the evidence becomes overwhelming. Understand?"

"Yes, Sir. How is Bishop Cantor?" Damien asked.

Mackey smirked. "I wouldn't say this in front of anyone else, but unfortunately, he'll survive. I don't mean that the way it sounds, but I dislike that man. With Caroline's death, there is no reason for that journal to come out in the press. Chief and I are still working on the particulars of how to handle that."

Captain Mackey rubbed his chin. "What pisses me off is nothing will change. I guarantee Cantor will stay in his position. Everyone will have sympathy for what he's been through, and no one will be the wiser to what a slimy bastard he is. And that is where I have a problem with my Catholic faith." Mackey saw the raw emotion on Damien's face. His young Lieutenant's pained stare said it all. "Do what you need to do today, get out of here early. Take some time for yourself. Understood?"

Damien nodded. "I will. Joe and I are heading over to Caroline's house. After that, we'll head home."

***

"How did the meeting with Mackey go?" Joe asked.

"Fine. He said if more came to light concerning Officer Baker, we'd need to formally question her." Damien leaned back with his eyes closed. He opened one eye at the sound of his office door shutting. "Something wrong, Joe?"

Joe sat and leaned toward the desk. He whispered, "I was in the hallway and overheard a conversation Baker had on her phone. She told her insurance her car was involved in an accident and what auto body shop it was at. I called them. Pretended to be an insurance adjuster but I needed a few questions answered before I showed up. Turns out the damage is on the right front fender. The damage to the car that hit Dillon should be extensive. The auto body guy said Baker's damage was slight. It looked to him like someone backed up into her. That may help relieve some of your fears about her involvement."

Damien sighed. "I like hearing that. I don't want it to be Baker. I like Katie. I think she has great potential. I'd hate for something like this to derail her career."

Joe leaned back in his seat. "I called the lab; spoke with Steve. I asked him what he thought of that intern, Rachel Banks. He said she was a little odd. He thought she did volunteer work at a mortuary, but he doesn't spend a lot of time talking to her. Steve said when she first came to work at the lab, he thought she was cute. Once in a blue moon, he would eat with her. She seemed to be a little possessive. She'd grill him on what he did the night before, who he had been with. He decided he didn't want any part of that and quit hanging out with her."

Damien pulled the girl's file from a stack on his desk. "The car is registered under her mother's name—Harper. I gave her name to Hall and Alverez not realizing who she was. They haven't been able to reach her. I ran Rachel's name through DMV records, and I couldn't find a car registered to her at all. I called the mother's place of employment, she's been on vacation and expected back at work tomorrow. That would give Rachel access to the car if the mother didn't take it with her."

Damien gathered all his files. "Listen, the captain said when we get done at Caroline's to call it a day. You want me to drive you home after we go there, you want me to bring you back here, or you want to drive yourself?"

Joe shook his head. "This feels like a test question. How about I ride with you, and you pick me up in the morning? Sound good?"

"Sounds like a plan." Damien pulled his phone out and called Dispatch requesting a CST tech meet them at Caroline's house. He wanted anything that would shed light on what happened to make Caroline Fredrick snap.

CHAPTER SIXTY

Damien dropped Joe off at his apartment. He'd picked up a sandwich on his way home. Coach sat like a statue, disapproval radiated from him as Damien entered his home. He bent over and picked up the fat feline. "I'm sorry, buddy. I know you missed me. I bet you miss Dillon more, huh?" Coach snuggled against his chin, his purring a sign of forgiveness for the neglect.

Damien carried him into the kitchen and put him in his chair at the table. A gleeful expression filled the cat's face as he waited for whatever food morsel he would be given. "You're like Pavlov's dog. You sit in that chair and you know food is coming. I can see the delight in your eyes." Coach followed Damien's every movement, meowing non-stop.

Damien gave Coach a few pieces of meat and cheese and a few pieces of bread. He wolfed it down staring at Damien, waiting for more. "Do not tell Dillon about this. She will never let me live this down." He and the cat ate in silence.

In his office, Damien read through the items taken from Caroline's house. Her mother had left a suicide note, and Caroline had placed the note along with her mother's ashes on the mantle as some kind of shrine.

It disturbed Damien. She perverted the word of God to fit her sick desires. Damien and Joe had found nothing that answered their questions. They surmised Caroline Fredrick had a break with reality, and her mother's death was the catalyst to send her over the edge. What made Damien even angrier was that nothing would change. The captain was correct. The Archdiocese would recognize the deaths of the priests and the courageousness of the bishop and the archbishop. Bishop Cantor would continue screwing women and getting away with it.

Damien's shoulders slumped. His actions from earlier in the day and the rising disillusion in his faith weighed on him. He again thought of Caroline. The pain associated with losing a parent, more so through suicide, was hard to take. Maybe even more difficult as a Catholic. Damien asked God to show His mercy to Caroline.

She was so young, and she had her whole life ahead of her. The image of her clutching her chest after he shot her replayed in his mind. The red blood poured through her fingers as she uttered her last words. Damien hung his head and wept.

The day was shitty and the night would be worse without Dillon. Damien glanced at his watch. It was after eight pm. He picked up his phone right as it rang. He glanced at the screen, no number.

"Kaine."

"Hey, baby."

This was one for the record books. Damien was almost glad it was Camilla. "Why do you call me?"

"You haven't been returning my calls. I didn't get an invitation to your father's gala this year."

"Did you really expect to?" Damien shook his head. *Of course, she did.*

"Well, I thought you would want to see me."

"Camilla. I've spoken with the captain. If you continue to call me, I will file a restraining order against you. I don't want you in my life. Do you understand me?"

She laughed. "Go ahead. You'll revoke it soon enough. You love me, Damien. You know you do."

"Camilla, this phone call is being recorded. I've explained to you that I am involved with someone. Someone I love and will marry. She has moved in with me, and you are not even a thought. You are however a nuisance. I'm going to say it again. If you continue to call me, I will file a restraining order against you. And if you show up at my father's gala you will be escorted from the premises. Goodbye, Camilla."

Damien had reached his limit. He wanted Camilla to leave him alone. He decided drastic measures were needed to make sure she did just that. Damien started to rise from his desk and head upstairs to shower when his phone rang again.

"What the fuck do you want now?" There was silence on the other end of the phone, then what sounded like two clicks. Next came the voice.

"How is the whore feeling? I was so disappointed the rollover didn't do more damage. I underestimated your stubbornness, Damien. I thought by now you would've left her."

Damien breathed slowly. He needed to calm himself and engage her the right way. He needed to get her to give him something to go on. "Why did you run her off the road? That isn't the best way to get my attention."

The sound on the other end was more of a cackle than a laugh. "I wanted you to realize that you're keeping her in danger by being with her. See, I decided if I can't have what I love, I will take away those things you love. And I know you love her. Or at least you think you do."

Damien's heart raced. He'd had enough of crazy women today. "What do you want me to do? I don't even know your name. How can I even get to know you if I don't know your name?"

"You don't need to know my name. You can call me lover. I don't like you spending time with her. I see that she spends a lot of time at your place. Why? Doesn't she have any sense of independence? I didn't think you wanted a woman who had to be glued to you all the time."

"Is that how you knew where she was going on Saturday? You've been watching my house?"

The voice on the other end giggled. "Maybe."

"Well, then you should've realized she lives here. That's why she spends all her time here."

A shrill shriek came through the phone line. "You bastard! You moved her in with you? How could you do that to me? All those times I helped you. All those times you came to me for information, and I gave it to you, even when I shouldn't have. How could you do this to me, Damien? I'm so hurt. If you don't change your mind and dump that stupid bitch, I'm going to make you hurt as much as I do."

The line went dead. Damien hit *99. Five minutes later his phone rang. He looked at his screen. "Hey, big brother. How's it going?"

"I heard the conversation. She's beyond pissed, Damien. Why did you tell her? I thought we were waiting until the gala?"

Damien rubbed the side of his head. The low throbbing pain from earlier now pulsed hard in his temples. "Look, she doesn't know Dillon is out of town. Maybe she'll make a move and think she's here. And we can catch her."

"Have you gotten anywhere on that list?" Nicky asked.

"I've given some of the names to my men. I should have something back by tomorrow. We had a blood bath at the Archdiocese today. Been sort of distracted."

"We heard about that. I'm sure you'll be asked about it a lot tomorrow at the press conference."

Damien stood. "What fucking press conference? I haven't been informed about any press conference." Damien paced his office.

Nicky laughed on the other end. "Dad got a call tonight from Archbishop Jacobs. He wanted to thank him for having such a wonderful and trustworthy son. He said something about he knew you will do the right thing during the press conference. Dad thought it was weird, but then..."

"Motherfucking son of a bitch." Damien hissed into the phone.

"Woah Damien, calm down. You've done these before."

"That's not it. That fucking bastard, Archbishop Jacobs used Dad to give me a message. I can't get into it now." Damien remembered the call was being recorded. "Listen, see what you can get from the latest phone call. I need to make sure you keep the recordings of all my phone calls. Okay?"

"Yeah sure."

"I'll call you tomorrow." Damien hung up and phoned the captain. "Hey, Captain Mackey sorry to call so late. We have a situation. Are you aware of a press conference tomorrow?"

"Damien, we aren't having a press conference until it is necessary. What are you talking about?"

Damien relayed what the archbishop had said to his dad. "He's putting something together. I guess he didn't think I would find out about it until just before it happened." The line was silent. "Captain, what do you want to do?"

"The chief is going to shit. He spent most of the day with Archbishop Jacobs. He never mentioned any of this. Damien, I know you understand the sensitive nature of that book. I also know you're smart enough to protect yourself. Jacobs has decided to take on the wrong group of men. He thinks with the death of Caroline that everything will go away. He was warning you, you got that right. We'll discuss this first thing in the morning."

Damien rubbed the back of his neck. The low throb in Damien's head was now a pounding pain at the base of his skull. He dragged himself to the master bedroom. He filled the tub and grabbed a glass of whiskey and called Dillon.

"Hey, how's it going?" She asked him. "I just got in from dinner."

"I had a shitty day." He told her everything. When he told her about the call with their stalker, Dillon remained quiet. "Dillon, you still there?"

"Yeah, I'm here. I should be there. Sometimes I hate my job. I'm so sorry about what happened at the chapel. I know you would rather have answers. Even if Caroline got the just punishment she deserved, those answers would've gone a long way. As for Camilla, I think it's time for me to pay her a visit at her office with a few men in tow. That will rattle her cage. Maybe I can scare the shit out of her. That would be fun. Now for the stalker, she's unhinged. Are you sure it isn't Baker?"

Damien relayed the conversation with Joe. He told her he and Joe would go to see Rachel Banks tomorrow after meeting with the captain in the morning. "I'm thinking after this call with her tonight, if it is Rachel, she should be quite upset. Maybe I'll be able to read her."

They talked for a little while longer. "We need to get our Christmas tree this week. Whatever night you come home we'll get it, and then this Sunday night we'll decorate it."

"Yes, that sounds great. I miss you. I love you, Damien Kainetorri."

"I love you too." After the call, Damien stayed in the tub another ten minutes. He crawled into his bed and pulled the hefty cat up next to him. "It's sad when I have to resort to sleeping with a fat furball." Coach snuggled up against him and snored.

CHAPTER SIXTY-ONE

December 8th
Thursday Morning

There was no press conference. Chief Rosenthal made sure Archbishop Jacobs understood if he put any of his men in front of the camera, the book would be read verbatim. He also told his friend he was saddened at his misjudgment of character. Damien and Joe were told by Captain Mackey and Chief Rosenthal that the press would be given a prepared statement concerning Caroline Fredrick. It would go down the way Damien figured it would. She was disturbed and used her grief to take the lives of innocent people.

"Damn, sometimes I wonder why the hell I stay in this miserable job," Damien said as they entered his office.

Joe plopped down in a chair. "Oh, man. I don't think this is going to go away that easy. Too many people know too many things. I'm just saying, be prepared."

Damien leaned forward on his elbows pulling at the ends of his hair. "I can't believe I'm saying this, but I think you're right."

Joe reached over and shut Damien's door. "Listen, about Baker—Jenkins unknowingly engaged her in a conversation about her weekend. She explained she left the store and spent the rest of the day and night with her boyfriend watching endless games of college football. She complained she needed a life, but she couldn't get enough of the sport." Joe popped a handful of jellybeans into his mouth.

Damien nodded. "I like the sound of that. I think that takes her off the list. I'll let the captain know." Damien closed his eyes again.

Joe ogled Damien. "What gives? Something else is on your mind. You were distracted in the captain's office earlier."

Damien frowned. He reached into his desk drawer. "I've called Rachel's mother, Shelly Harper. She was expected back last night, and she was supposed to come to work this morning. She hasn't shown up. Rachel hasn't come to work since last Friday. I think the two are connected. I think something has happened."

Joe's mouth hung open. "Are you just looking for shit to do? You know we have three new murder cases to close."

"Oh, shut the hell up and listen." He slid a piece of paper over to him. "I ran the mother on my computer last night. I don't give a shit what kind of trouble I get into. I need to stop this. Dillon is coming home tonight, and something has to fucking give. Anyway, look at her history. She's been married four times. She has a few domestics in her record. She always holds good jobs, but she moved around a lot. Rachel was in and out of five schools in one year.

"I'm thinking a young girl who's yanked around and has no steady male figure in her life would have no problem making up a relationship with someone when there was none. Also, during our last call, my stalker said something. It didn't register until about four this morning when I couldn't sleep."

Damien took a long drink of his diet soda. "She said 'I gave you information even when I shouldn't have. All those times I helped you.' I know what she's referring to. Do you remember a few cases we had back before the Jason Freestone case?"

Joe squinted at Damien. "No, what are you talking about?"

Damien grabbed a bunch of jellybeans. "We had like three cases that we needed the lab results before we could make a move on the suspects. We went to the lab, and Marsha got us the information."

Joe shook his head. "You've lost your mind if you think it's Marsha."

"No, I don't believe that it's Marsha. Just pay attention. Marsha got us the results. But do you remember a couple of times we had to get the file from her helper? Marsha always gave the file to her assistant to give to us. Marsha joked saying if she didn't hand us the info, she technically didn't give it to us."

"Okay, now I remember. How does this relate to your stalker?"

"I called Marsha this morning and asked her who her helper was back then. It was Rachel. Before she was hired as a paid intern. She used to work three days a week during her last year of college. She couldn't intern at the lab in a paid position until she had her degree. Marsha also reminded me that I have met Rachel before. She and I had a conversation a while back about this girl having a crush on me. But I never connected that girl being Rachel; until this morning."

Joe blinked rapidly. "Holy fucking shit. It's her. You know who the stalker is. Did you tell the captain?"

"Yes, I ran it by him early this morning. He gave me the green light to request a warrant. I'm waiting on one for the mother's house. But it's taking a while. The ADA is a little reluctant. The daughter doesn't live with the mother, but the car used in the crime matches the one owned by the mother. And the mother's house is located within the fifteen-mile radius that Nicky has determined the phone calls had been made from.

"However, she said we have no real connection to get a warrant for the mother's house. She said she might be able to swing a warrant for Rachel's place, but that would take some convincing, seeing as how we don't have any substantial evidence linking Rachel Banks to any of this."

Joe jumped up. "What are we going to do? Wait for a warrant? That could take days."

Damien stood up and put on his jacket. "No. I'm not waiting on a warrant. I'm going to the mother's house. You don't have to come. We will be violating all kinds of legal shit. Unless we find something when we get there. Say an open door or a broken window that would lead a police officer to think the homeowner has been hurt in some way."

Joe's brow wrinkled, and he grabbed Damien's shoulders, "I'm concerned that the mother may have had an accident. I think we need to get over and do a welfare checkup."

Damien patted him on the cheek. "I knew I kept you as my partner for a reason."

Joe laughed. "It's because you secretly lust after my ass. You know you do."

Damien roared with laughter. "Don't let my secret out."

CHAPTER SIXTY-TWO

Shelly Harper's house came into view as Damien pulled onto the street. Joe whistled. "This house is gorgeous."

Damien's gut rolled. "Oh hell. This is the house." Damien pulled his phone out but didn't make the call.

Joe stared at his partner. "Damien, you're not telling me everything. What the hell is going on?"

Damien turned toward Joe. "During one of the conversations our stalker made the comment that my condo was too small to live in, and she had the perfect house in mind. She just had to get rid of the current owner. This is the house. I know it. I just had no idea it was her own mother's house." He sighed. "I don't know what we're getting into."

He looked at his partner. "Listen, I should call the captain and go through the proper channels. This goes against all the rules. I understand if you want to hang back, you can say you tried to stop me. Joe, I know this is the girl, and this is the house. I'll call for backup, but I'm not waiting."

Joe squeezed his eyes shut. "I'd never let you walk in somewhere without me. We may be running that bar sooner than we think. If you're wrong, our asses will be fired."

Damien called in for back up. While they waited, Joe ran up to the front door. Damien watched as he fiddled with the doorknob. Within a few minutes, two police cars pulled up. Damien and Joe met them on the front lawn. "Listen, we don't know what we have here. This is a welfare call. But we have reason to believe harm may have come to the homeowner. The front door looks as if someone has broken in. Are you guys wearing your vests?"

All four officers nodded. Joe and Damien had theirs on over their shirts. "When we enter, three of you sweep the downstairs toward the back of the house. Use your flashlights if necessary, do not turn on any lights."

Damien and Joe lead the officers through the front door. Joe pushed the door open. Sunlight seeped through the large bay window, offering a soft glow of light. When the first floor had been cleared, Damien motioned toward the stairs. He could hear soft music coming from somewhere on the second floor.

Damien led the way up the large staircase. Joe flanked him on his right. At the top of the landing, they could see a door ajar. Nearing the open door, the distinct smell of decomposing flesh wafted from the room.

Damien motioned to an officer to sweep the room. Joe signaled the other officers to move and cover the doorway where the music filtered through. Moving closer to the closed bedroom door, they could hear singing.

Damien took a deep breath and reached for the doorknob. He turned it and pushed the door open. Rachel was painting the walls of the room. She didn't hear the men enter. Joe and an officer moved to the right of the room. Damien and another officer moved toward Rachel.

"Rachel, I need you to put your hands above your head," Damien said over the music.

Rachel turned at the sound of his voice. Her eyes wide and glowing as a smile filled her face. Rachel scanned the room, and her lips flattened out. "How could you bring these other people? The room isn't ready yet." She still held the paint roller in her hands. She tilted her head from side to side. She glanced at the police officer then Joe. Then she turned and smiled at Damien. "I knew you knew who I was. See I told you, you love me. It just took you a little bit to figure it out. Do you like the house? It's perfect, isn't it?"

Damien motioned for the officer to move into position. "It is a lovely house, Rachel. I need you to put the paint roller down. Can you do that? I think your mother needs help in the other room." All three men kept their guns trained on her.

"Oh, mother's fine. She's sleeping. She got a bump on the head. I laid her in the guest bedroom so I could work on our room. I wanted it to be masculine, but not cold. Do you like the color?" She bent down and placed the paint roller into the pan. "When I put on the second coat, it will be a beautiful gray." She stepped off to the side.

A large desk sat to the right of her. She stepped closer to it. "Rachel, I need you to turn around and place your hands behind your back. This is for your safety. I don't want to see anything happen to you," Damien said.

The uniformed officer moved closer to her. He still had his weapon pointed at her as he pulled his handcuffs out.

"Damien, are you going to have Joe be your best man at our wedding? I think he will look so handsome in a tuxedo." She turned toward Joe. "I know you two are best friends."

Joe stepped off to the side. Damien and the officer took another step closer to Rachel. The officer continued to inch toward her. "Hey there, Rachel. I'm going to put these on you. Could you turn around for me?" He placed his weapon in his holster. "I just want to make sure you're safe. Okay?"

Rachel's pleasant demeanor switched in an instant. Her face contorted as her voice rose. "You think I'm crazy, don't you? I know this isn't for my good. You just want to punish me for going after Dillon—that whore you call your girlfriend."

Damien scanned the area. He saw no weapons. She wore a simple pair of yoga pants and a shirt with no pockets. He didn't think she had any on her person. "Listen, Rachel, I just want to ensure your safety. This officer is going to put the handcuffs on you. Then you can ride in my car, and we can have a quiet talk. That's all I want to do, alright?"

She shifted her stance. "No, you don't. No! I know you want to hurt me. All the men in my life have hurt me. My mother was a stupid woman. She just had to have a man. She didn't love any of them. But I love you, Damien. I have from the moment I met you." She stepped closer to them.

"Stop! Rachel, let this officer put his handcuffs on you." Damien stepped to the right. He was now within a few feet of the officer.

Rachel stepped toward the officer holding out her arms. At first, it looked as if she was going to comply with the instructions when she turned around. The officer approached her and reached out to place one of the cuffs on her wrist. She spun back around and reached for his weapon, grabbing it from his holster.

Damien reacted. He pushed the officer out of the way, at the same time Rachel lifted the gun to shoot. The two officers that stood behind Damien reacted to the sound of the gun, and both shot Rachel. She dropped to the ground; the gun skittered across the floor. Damien looked over at Joe. He smiled at his partner. "Joe, are you all right?"

That was the last thing Damien had said before he hit the floor. Joe yelled for the officers to call for paramedics and ran to his friend's side. He grabbed him and rolled him from side to side trying to find an exit wound. At first, he saw nothing. "Hey, buddy." Joe smacked Damien's face. "Wake up. No sleeping on the job." Joe removed Damien's vest. He didn't look up from Damien as he barked out orders. "Someone call for an ambulance and someone grab me something to place over this wound." Blood seeped through Damien's shirt. Joe ripped it open. A gaping wound on the side of Damien's abdomen bled through Joe's fingers. He pushed the palm of his hand against the wound trying to stymy the flow of blood.

An officer came up with a handful of towels. Joe grabbed them pushing them against his friend's body. Blood soaked through the towels. "God, don't take him. It's not his time. Don't take him, please," Joe whispered.

***

Joe followed the ambulance in Damien's truck. He phoned Damien's family, then his own. He called Dillon. Her line went straight to voicemail. "Dillon, this is Joe. Damien was shot, we're on our way to General. I don't know when you'll get this but call as soon as you do." He called the captain.

Joe pulled behind the ambulance. A security guard came out. "You can't park here buddy. Move the vehicle."

Joe flashed his badge. "Fuck you," he yelled and ran in after Damien. He grabbed his hand. "You're gonna be okay. You hear me? Damien, you're going to be fine." Joe tried to follow the gurney through the doorway.

"Sir, you can't come into the OR. Someone will be out with an update." She pushed him back and through the doors.

Joe stood there with his best friend's blood on his hands and clothes. Captain Mackey and several of the VCU detectives came around the corner. Joe's shoulders rolled as the weight of the events slammed into him. "Captain." Joe's voice cracked. "They took him into surgery. I couldn't stop the blood. I couldn't stop it." The tears he'd kept at bay now spilled over.

Captain Mackey reached out and put an arm around Joe to steady him. "He's going to be okay, son. I need you to tell me what happened." He pulled back and gave Joe a moment. Several detectives turned away from the show of raw emotion.

Joe wiped his face smearing Damien's blood across his cheek. He took several deep breaths and proceeded to run down the events of the day.

"When the officer approached her, he holstered his weapon. He reached out to place the cuffs on her, and she spun, grabbing his gun from his holster and fired." Joe fell into a chair, his legs no longer able to support his weight. "Damien anticipated her movements and pushed the officer out of the way. Got shot in the process."

Damien's entire family ran through the doors. Joe jumped up and ran to Angelina Kainetorri. "I tried to stop the blood. There was so much of it." Joe said as she grabbed him and hugged him as if he were her own son.

"It's okay, Joe. Damien is going to be fine. I know this in my heart." Angelina led Joe to a chair. She glanced at her husband, and he and Nicky went to the captain to get the details of what happened.

Over the next hour, the waiting area filled with more cops from Central. Joe called Taylor. He needed to hear her voice. Joe's parents had shown up. Darcy Hagan sat between her son and Angelina. Joe's father Patrick sat on the other side of Giovanni. A nurse came through the doors several times with updates. Each time she said the surgeon would be out shortly to speak with them. Each time they waited for word Damien would be okay.

Joe's phone rang. His hand shook as he looked at the screen. "Hey, Dillon."

"Joe, what the hell is going on?" She asked.

"We were arresting Rachel, and she flipped out." Joe used his shirt to wipe his face.

"Have you gotten any updates yet? Can you tell me anything? Please."

"We're waiting for the surgeon. The nurse just came out and said it was taking longer than they thought because of the tissue damage, but he's stable."

"Shit. We are just now taking off. Call me the minute you hear from the surgeon. How's his family? Are they holding up okay?"

"Yeah. My family is here, all of Damien's and the whole fucking DC is here just about."

"How are you holding up Joe? Are you okay?" Dillon asked.

Joe rested his elbows on his knees. "No. I won't be okay until I know what's going on with Damien."

"He's strong, Joe; he's so strong. Damn, I hate this. The pilot is telling me to wrap it up. I'll call as soon as I land. Tell him I love him when you see him."

"I will. I know he loves you, Dillon. I'll call as soon as I know something." Joe hung his head.

Nicky reached out and put his arm around Joe. "Hey, Damien's a fighter. He'll be okay."

Joe leaned his head back against the wall. A calm silence settled over the waiting room while everyone waited for the surgeon. Minutes felt like hours, and hours seemed like days. Joe wasn't sure how much time had passed when the OR doors opened again. The surgeon walked out. He glanced at the room. "Well, I get the feeling this guy is well liked. Which of you are his family?"

Giovanni and Angelina walked to the man. "We are his parents, but everyone here is his family. Please tell us how our son is."

The surgeon smiled. "The bullet must have nicked the edge of the vest, which slowed down the velocity. That was a good thing. It didn't travel far into the body. The downside, the bullet tumbled around tearing up a lot of tissue and muscle. I wanted to take extra caution stitching that abdomen muscle up so that he wouldn't have any complications later as it healed. A couple of nights in the hospital to ward off any infection and he should be released. Recovery will be slow until that muscle heals."

The waiting room erupted in cheers. Giovanni hugged the surgeon and told him he and a guest were welcome at the gala the following Saturday. Angelina held onto her husband and wept, her fearless demeanor evaporating as a wave of relief swamped her.

CHAPTER SIXTY-THREE

Nine days later Joe, Deputy Director Sherman, and Damien waited on the first floor of Damien and Dillon's suite. Damien laughed at Joe and doubled over from the pain. "Stop, you stupid fuck. You're going to make me pop these damn stitches."

Sherman and Damien wiped the tears away as they drank their drinks. Sherman sat on the sofa and Damien sat next to him. "SAC Marks said Dillon yelled at the pilot the minute she got on the plane. Marks said the look she gave the pilot scared him. He didn't ever remember the flight taking that short amount of time."

Joe's voice lowered. "She came through those doors of your hospital room—you were out cold. She stopped and just stared at you. Whatever toughness she had on that plane was gone the minute she saw you. She's so in love with you, Damien.

"The nurses gave up trying to keep everyone out of your room. Your family brought enough food for them, so I don't think they minded." Joe placed his hand on Damien's shoulder. "I don't ever want to go through that again. Try not to get shot, Okay?"

Damien snorted. "Like it was my fault."

Joe laughed. "Oh, while you were out Dillon paid a visit to Camilla. She grabbed me and a few more of your detectives." Joe lifted his brow at Sherman. "You didn't hear this from me. We show up at Camilla's office. The lady behind the desk picked the wrong day to be a guard dog. She tried to tell Dillon she would have to make an appointment, that Camilla was in an important meeting. Dillon leaned over the counter. She explained to the girl if she wanted to continue to be able to use her hands, she needed to pick up that phone."

Joe laughed. "I know she broke every rule in the Fed's handbook, but this secretary almost peed herself. She could barely dial the number. So here comes Camilla; she recognizes a few of us, and at first, she thinks we're here on your behalf. Then it must have dawned on her who Dillon was. Dillon explained the FBI had phone recordings of her harassing Damien. She tells Camilla if she continued to harass you, State and Federal charges would be levied against her."

Damien turned to Director Sherman, "Camilla has been calling and harassing me to take her back. I'd already spoken with the captain. But I had no idea Dillon would go this far."

A boisterous laugh filled the room as the Director shook his head. "I'm not surprised she went this far. She has spoken to Laura about the best way to handle Camilla. Laura suggested she take a more proactive approach instead of just sitting on the sidelines letting you take care of it."

Joe smirked at them both. "Dillon whispered something in Camilla's ear. Camilla staggered back apologizing for her actions and said she understood now that Damien had moved on."

Joe glanced between Sherman and Damien, "in the elevator, Dillon told us she told Camilla if she continued to try and insert herself into your life, she would cut off her fingers and toes and feed them to her one by one. She would leave her one eye so she could see that she pissed off the wrong bitch."

Both Damien and Sherman's mouths hung open, and their eyes bulged. Joe doubled over in laughter. "We all had that same look on our faces. How can one woman be so damn gorgeous and scary at the same time? I'm telling you, you don't have to worry about Camilla anymore. She just might move out of state."

Sherman turned to see his wife and Taylor coming toward them. Both he and Damien rose from the sofa and walked toward the staircase. "You two look beautiful." Sherman moved to his wife brushing his lips against hers. "You look stunning."

His wife Laura leaned into him, "Wait until you see Dillon. She is beautiful, Phillip; just beautiful."

Director Sherman kissed her forehead as he handed her a glass of wine.

Joe stepped toward Taylor and grabbed her by the hand and spun her around. "Holy shit, woman. You look fabulous. The guys are going to be so jealous of me, and the women are going to hate you." He pulled Taylor to his chest. "I've never seen anyone more perfect."

Damien glanced back up the stairs. "Where's Dillon? Is she trying to escape?"

Taylor laughed. "No, she just keeps messing with the dress. She'll be down in a minute."

Laura smiled at Damien. "She thinks the dress reveals too much. She isn't used to seeing herself dressed up like this."

The conversation flowed as they sipped on their drinks. Damien glanced at his watch then up at the top of the stairs. His heart stopped for a few beats. The bronze fabric hugged her body. A mesh material ran down the sides, showing a thin strip of skin. She'd pulled her hair back, leaving soft tendrils of curls around her face, the rest cascading down her back in large barrel curls. Damien's chest constricted.

Director Sherman leaned into him. "Breathe, son."

Damien blew out the breath he held. Dillon glided down the stairs toward him. He glanced at Phillip and Laura. Smiles filled their faces as they watched Dillon descend the stairs. "She loves you, the two of you, you know that, right?"

Laura touched his arm. "She loves you more." She turned toward her husband and hugged him.

Dillon reached for Damien's outstretched hand as she stepped off the last stair. Her eyebrows wrinkled together. "You don't like it do you?" She looked down at the dress. "I told them this was the wrong dress for me."

He pulled her into his arms. He placed his cheek next to hers and inhaled her smell. "You are the most beautiful woman I've ever seen. The dress hugs your body perfectly. I've never wanted to rip off a piece of clothing as much as I do now."

She frowned at him. "Taylor said you would say that."

"Well, Taylor knows me too well." He stepped back and spun her around.

"Let's get going," Joe said. "There is a party waiting for us." He grabbed Taylor by the hand and led her out the door with the Shermans right behind them.

Before Dillon walked out into the hallway, Damien grabbed her and pulled her back to him. He caressed her cheek. "When I was coming out of surgery in recovery, one of the nurses asked me who Dillon was. She explained I kept calling out your name and thanking God for you."

Damien brushed his lips against hers. "The nurse commented you must be something pretty special." He kissed her soft lips again. "She has no idea how special you are to me."

Dillon's heart stammered under the stare of those gorgeous blue eyes. "When Joe called me and told me you were shot, I felt helpless. I had just come out of a meeting and checked my phone. I ran into Sherman's office, told him to get the plane ready and get my ass back to Chicago. The whole ride back, I begged God to save you. I reminded Him he already had my family; He couldn't have you too." One tear rolled down her cheek. "Then I threatened Him. I reminded him that he didn't want my pissed off ass in Heaven."

Damien laughed as he took her hand and led her down the hallway. "Oh Dillon, I'm confident God knows the trouble you would cause if He pissed you off."

"Well, he's a smart guy."

THE END

Other books by Victoria M. Patton
Damien Kaine Series
Innocence Taken
Confession of Sin
Fatal Dominion
Web of Malice
Blind Vengeance
Series bundle books 1-3

Derek Reed Thrillers
The Box

Short Stories
Deadfall

If you enjoyed this book, you would be doing me a great favor by reviewing it wherever you purchased it.

ABOUT THE AUTHOR

Victoria M. Patton is forced to share her home with a husband, two teenagers, three dogs, and a cat. If she isn't plotting her escape, she uses her Search and Rescue/Law Enforcement skills from the Coast Guard and her BS in Forensic Chemistry to figure out the best way to hide all the bodies and write amazing stories about the murders. If she has any free time, she drinks copious amounts of whiskey and binge watches Netflix. Check out her blog **www.whiskeyandwriting.com** where she tries to help new authors navigate the indie publishing world. Contact her at **victoria@victoriampatton.com**. She is on most social media outlets, type in her name, you'll find her.

Made in United States
Troutdale, OR
08/11/2023

11985345R00170